Murder Casts
a Shadow

Murder Casts a Shadow

A HAWAI'I MYSTERY

VICTORIA NALANI KNEUBUHL

A LATITUDE 20 BOOK

UNIVERSITY OF HAWAI'I PRESS
HONOLULU

13 12 11 10 09 08   6 5 4 3 2 1

Library of Congress Cataloging-in-Publication Data
Kneubuhl, Victoria N. (Victoria Nalani)
Murder casts a shadow : a Hawaii mystery / Victoria N.
Kneubuhl.
     p. cm.
ISBN 978-0-8248-3217-9 (pbk.: alk. paper)
1. Hawaii—Fiction.   I. Title.
PS3561.N418M88 2008
813'.54—dc22   2008005590

CONTENTS

PROLOGUE

FROM A BENCH in the garden, Mina Beckwith watched the clouds racing over the Koʻolau Mountains and the moon rising over Nuʻuanu Valley. She took a deep breath and turned her attention to the party inside. Stone arches framed a patio with sets of open french doors leading into the spacious and elegant parlor. From the garden, the arches created small moving vignettes of dancing couples, laughing groups, floating balloons, flying confetti, and moving figures in stylish and fanciful costumes. Beautiful as it looked, Mina couldn't bring herself to go back in. She'd kept her mask in place all night, avoiding recognition and interaction. It would take more than fancy dress, she thought, to disguise the same old crowd and the same old small talk. Her harlequin costume glittered as she looked up at the moon. Where was her sister, Nyla? And Todd, Nyla's husband, wasn't there either. They'd agreed to meet at ten o'clock, and here it was ten thirty. Tired of waiting, Mina decided to leave and see the New Year in at her own bungalow on the beach. She stood up and collided with a tall man dressed in a priest's cassock who seemed to have appeared out of nowhere. He wore a simple black mask that framed his eyes and was carrying a tumbler of brandy. A good part of it had just spilled on the front of his costume and the brandy smell filled the air.

"Well, forgive me father, for I seem to have sinned," Mina laughed.

"I'm glad someone has." The muffled voice behind the mask sounded British. "Didn't mean to intrude."

"No, no, I'm just leaving." Mina liked his voice. "Beautiful view from this bench. Happy New Year."

"And to you." He raised his glass.

Mina left through the garden gate. Her car, a 1934 Packard convertible coupe, was parked under the dark overhang of a tree, so when she got in the driver's seat and dropped the key, she was forced to bend down and grope around on the floor. A car pulled up near her, and then another. Car doors opened and closed. Then she heard voices she recognized, in rushed and animated conversation. Something made her stay down and hunched over in the dark, listening.

In the garden, the man who was dressed as a priest sat down on the bench, lit a cigar, and blew a smoke ring toward the moon. The explosions of firecrackers came at more frequent intervals as the New Year approached. He pulled out a flask from one of the cassock pockets and replenished his tumbler. Then, from the same vantage as his predecessor, he watched the same enchanting scenes in the house and up in the sky.

A few minutes later, he was joined by a man dressed as a sheik. "Ned, I've been looking all over for you. The party is in full swing and you're out here alone."

"Where the hell have you been, Todd?" Ned asked.

"I got held up at the station."

"Is the chief of detectives in big demand on New Year's Eve?"

"Nah, I just had to talk to someone. Took longer than I thought." The sheik sat down. "Have you seen Nyla?"

"I haven't seen your wife, old man. Perhaps she's deserted you. I keep telling her, she's way too good for you."

"Where's that brandy I gave you?" Todd held out a glass. "I can tell you've already gotten into it."

"Now I know why those priests wore these big robes." Ned fished around in the folds of the robe and produced the flask.

Todd raised the flask in a toast before he drank. "Here's to the New Year and the Twenty-first Amendment."

"There you two are." A woman came walking toward them dressed in the same costume as the harlequin who had just left. She linked her arm with Todd's.

"Was that you before, Nyla? Why didn't you say so?" Ned was confused.

"What?" Nyla's harlequin head tilted to one side.

"Before, out here, you bumped into me and said you were leaving."

"No, I've been asleep in Ginger's room."

"I'm sure I recognize the costume," said Ned.

"Rats! That was Mina! We rented the same costumes. She must have waited. She hates waiting. I bet she left. I dozed off, and now she's come and gone. I really wanted you to meet her, Ned."

"You mean you left me in the clutches of Ginger Raymond's mother and took a nap?" Ned complained. "I thought she would never shut up. She gave me detailed biographies of all, I mean all, of her ancestors, and then showed me every piece of her Lokelani china collection. Ghastly stuff!"

"Well, we're all together now." Nyla kissed Todd on the cheek.

Soon the party began to spill out into the garden and the hostess passed out sparklers. At midnight they lit the sparklers and toasted one another with French champagne as a ferocious explosion of firecrackers and skyrockets overwhelmed the city of Honolulu, warding off the demons for another year.

I

HAPPY NEW YEAR

ON THE MORNING of January 2, 1935, it was raining. Ned woke to the sound of water. From his half sleep, he realized it was water pouring from a drainpipe—the one off the roof, just outside his window.

A breeze came and went through the screen, lifting the thin white curtain. It swayed the garden bamboo into a rolling clatter, and made the morning feel clean and refreshing.

Ned sat up, yawned, and looked out the window. The house, up in Maunalani Heights, floated over a lake of clouds while somewhere below the city of Honolulu began another day. He thought he could smell carnations from the farms that stretched across the middle of the hill, separating the residential area at the summit from the rest of the city with a one-mile border of flowers. Maybe he imagined the fragrance. His imagination always seemed more alive in Hawai'i. He could relax. He wasn't the oddity that he was in London, or the oddity he felt he'd become in his birthplace, Āpia, Western Sāmoa. Honolulu was a mixture of all kinds of odd people and things. A part Sāmoan playwright and theatrical director, sometimes discreetly employed by a certain agency of the British government, was no more peculiar in Honolulu than the Chinese chief of police whose calligraphy and landscape paintings sold at high prices in the best galleries of San Francisco. Honolulu would be a place to live, mused Ned, floating in the ocean, between so many worlds. All it lacked was a professional, progressive theatrical community.

Ned found himself in Honolulu for two reasons. The first and less well known was his role as the chaperone of three important portraits being shipped from the British Museum to the Bishop Museum. It was a simple diplomatic request and a favor to the museum. It was much less complicated than other unofficial assignments he had been given, ones that required secrecy and employed his excellent skills of detection. Ned's public profile as a playwright of independent means suited his unofficial government employers. The second and much more publicized occasion for his visit was the production of his play, *A Long Way Home,* by the Honolulu Community Players. The Players had also asked him to direct the production, a job he had declined in the most polite way. Instead, he volunteered to consult with a local director. The theatre had chosen a young man, a recent graduate of Yale University said to have some real creative talent.

Ned looked out at the view and thought about how he had visited Hawai'i several times and never left the island of O'ahu. He decided that he would make an effort to see some of the other Hawaiian Islands on this trip. He wondered if it might give him time to plan a new work—something with echoes of symbolism and a mythological feeling, maybe something to do with rain and a house standing all alone on a high hill.

Ned's reverie was broken by the rude voice of his host, Todd Forrest, yelling. "Son of a bitch, Nyla, what the hell happened? There's no goddamn hot water!"

Next Ned heard Todd clumping down the stairs, an inaudible jumble of conversation between husband and wife, some stomping to the garage, clanking, banging, something that sounded like it might be kicking followed by general kitchen noises. Then Ned heard Todd bounding up the stairs toward him. Without knocking, Todd stuck his handsomely chiseled face into Ned's room.

"Hey, don't get in the shower for the next half hour, or you'll be in for a rude experience. Yesterday, the plumber turned the heater off and forgot to turn it back on."

"What's that? You're not going to have your man servant draw my bath?" Ned rolled over into a lazy pose.

"Sorry old man, it's his day off. You'll have to take a nasty American shower. Come down while the water heats up. Nyla's making coffee." Todd disappeared as fast as he had appeared.

A few minutes later, Ned stood downstairs looking out of the window at the magnificent view that stretched out before him. The morning rain clouds had vanished, and he could see the city below and the surrounding sea. Maunalani Heights lay behind Diamond Head, just above the Honolulu suburb of Kaimukī. The Forrests' home sat on the top of the hillside that rose from a broad base to an elevation of about a thousand feet. Behind the heights ran the ridges of the Koʻolau Mountains separating the leeward and the windward sides of the island. The house looked toward Diamond Head and the sea, with a sweeping view of Honolulu, Pearl Harbor, and beyond to the Ewa plain. The elevation kept the temperature at least seven degrees cooler than in the lowlands, and the frequent rain allowed for the cultivation of exquisite tropical gardens. Ned stared at the ocean to where it met the horizon. Today the line was subtle and diffuse, a change of color from the dark blue of the Pacific to the pale blue sky.

"You look so serious, Ned." Nyla's voice never felt intrusive. From a blend of her Hawaiian, Irish, and English ancestry she had inherited her father's pale green eyes and her mother's dark hair, which this morning was pinned up in a pretty twist. Her skin was smooth and golden brown. Although Nyla came from a very wealthy island family, Ned had always known her to be unassuming, warm, and kind to everyone she met. "What sort of wool are you gathering this early in the morning?"

"Old wool, the familiar kind. You know, the sort we always come back to." Ned answered.

"Well, right now, you have to come to the kitchen for one of Todd's fabulous breakfasts." Nyla took his arm and led him to the kitchen. "He'll have a fit if we don't eat right away."

Nyla seated him at a table set with flowers, cloth napkins, bowls of fruit, a stunning omelet in the center, and champagne. Todd raised his glass. "To the successful delivery of the Kalākaua portraits from the British Museum to the Bishop Museum."

"In their exquisite frames designed by the artist," Nyla added.

"May the ancestors reign forever in their homeland," Ned responded, as they touched glasses.

"Well, what do they look like? The portraits. Tell us." Nyla sipped her champagne.

"They're formal standing portraits, very nearly life size, quite impressive, really," Ned began. "The king is standing in his regalia, sword, and royal orders across his chest. His queen, Kapiʻolani, is dressed in an extraordinary gown that appears to be made with peacock feathers, and her sister is wearing some kind of pale yellow affair. The huge frames are really wonderful, each one a different flora motif. The king's is maile, I believe."

"How much do you think they're worth?" Nyla asked bluntly.

"The appraised value is about $25,000 each, the king maybe slightly higher. Any work by Jonathan Leeds is commanding a high price these days. At least that's what I was told when I left London."

"$25,000 is a small fortune," Todd remarked. "But who's got that kind of money during a depression?"

"My sister's been assigned to write an article about the portraits. I don't think she's very happy about it." Nyla said.

"How is it I've been here three times and never met your sister?" Ned asked.

"Consider yourself lucky." Todd laughed.

"Todd thinks Mina's a bit much," said Nyla, chewing on her parsley garnish.

"There's no denying she's got a large dose of the Beckwith brains," said Todd. "She's just unusual—for a woman, I mean. Of course, she had to go to college, but she refused to go to Mills with Nyla. No, instead, she insists on going to Ohio, to that Antioch College, where they taught her to think that a woman could be anything she liked in the world. It's that school that filled her full of nonsense."

"Mina works part-time for the newspaper," said Nyla. "She was also a correspondent during the Massie case for a San Francisco paper. She writes under the name M. Beckwith. The paper thinks no one will listen to her if they find out she's a woman."

"God forbid that no one should listen to her. She has ideas about everything," mumbled Todd.

"Ah, you see, Todd can't quite get over the fact that Mina, well, Mina is very interested in detection." Nyla was smiling.

"It's no job for a woman," Todd declared.

"I can recall a couple of times when she's provided you with some valuable information, dear." Nyla winked at Ned.

"So she's helped out, but providing information doesn't make a detective."

"You would like my sister." Nyla looked at Ned.

"You know me, Nyla, I'm not in the matrimonial market. I might be a big disappointment to your sister." Ned said it in a most sincere but honest way, hoping and praying Nyla didn't have ulterior plans for him during his stay. He was looking forward to a relaxing vacation.

"Matrimony," Todd snickered. "What was Mina's last comment on marriage? Twenty-four-hour service at no pay, no freedom, and no future. That's what she thinks about matrimony!"

"I wish it were otherwise," Nyla frowned, "but Mina has her own reasons for not being interested in marriage." She shot a pointed look at Todd, but then turned and smiled at Ned. "And despite what some detractors say, she's a great person to have for a friend."

"Nyla, I'm sure I'll be delighted to meet your sister," said Ned.

"Well, you would have in any case. She's doing the publicity for your show, and she's going to be your neighbor. Our bungalow you're going to stay in is just next to hers. It's our beach place, but yours for at least three months. And it's just on the other side of Diamond Head, close to the Aliʻi Theatre, where the play's going to be."

"When I asked for you to help me find a place to stay, I never intended that you should *give* me one. It would be easy for me to go to a hotel." Ned was surprised.

"N-o! We let all of our friends stay in the bungalow. It's a real island place, right on a beautiful beach," Nyla responded. "Besides, I want to be sure you'll be nice to me because Johnny Knight has cast me as the muse in your play."

"About twenty women auditioned for the part." Todd tried not to sound like he was bragging.

"That's great news. You're perfect for the role."

"I'll try to be," said Nyla. The phone rang in the hall, and she went to answer it.

"Don't say I didn't warn you, pal," Todd whispered. "You're on your own with Mina Beckwith."

"It's your office, Todd," Nyla reported. "They said it's important."

"Yeah? I bet some government official got a speeding ticket."

Todd rose and left the room with no particular urgency.

Nyla began to clear the plates from the table, and when Ned insisted on doing the dishes, Nyla smiled and handed him a pair of rubber gloves. He enjoyed feeling domestic. It was, in itself, a little bit of a vacation. He was soaping up his third plate when Todd came back and stood in the doorway. He crossed his arms, and an odd smile swept over his face.

"Well," he began, "it wasn't about a speeding ticket."

"What's up, chief?" Ned pulled another plate out of his sink full of bubbles.

"As you would say, one of the portraits has been pinched. Better take off the rubber gloves and leave the housework for later, dear. They're screaming for us up at the museum."

Ned heard a strange sound. He looked into the sink and noticed that he'd somehow pulled out the stopper. All the water was running out. "This is not the way," he sighed to himself, "the first day of a vacation ought to begin."

MINA'S APPOINTMENT

MINA BECKWITH didn't know if she should feel angry or not, but she felt angry anyway. She didn't want to become a society writer. She didn't want to do entertainment articles. She wanted to do real news stories. She wanted to cover things that mattered, and here she was, going up to the museum to do a story about some royal portraits. It's not that she wasn't happy the museum was getting them back. She understood the importance of the gift, and even appreciated it, but any rookie on the staff could write this kind of thing. Damn it, she thought, I bet I'm doing this because none of the men would. She grabbed her bag and raincoat, slipped on her shoes, and rushed out the bungalow door. As she walked out, she stopped for a moment. She took a deep breath, and looking out across the arbor to the beach and the ocean, she saw the waves breaking over the fringing reef. She took another deep breath and headed for her car.

Half an hour later, Mina's rain-dappled Packard slid into a parking stall, and the old stone museum loomed before her like a haunted castle. She recognized the car next to hers as belonging to Todd Forrest. Through the raindrops and clicking windshield wipers, she saw Todd come out of the big wooden entrance doors, examine the lock, talk to someone inside she couldn't see, reenter and close the door. Next, a uniformed officer came outside and began to block off the area. Something more interesting than the arrival of the portraits was unfolding. Mina figured that Abel Halpern, the museum director with whom she had an appointment, was most likely in the gallery taking part in the excitement. She decided to go to his office first. If he wasn't there, she could just tiptoe into the gallery through the staff entrance at the end of the hall and have a look at the scene without being observed. If discovered, she could truthfully claim that she was looking for Halpern.

Mina walked straight to the right side of the main building to an equally morose addition that bore the proud but restrained sign "Administration" above the arched doorway. It was just after eight, and the hall lights had yet to be turned on. There was a noticeable drop in temperature as she descended the stairs into the underground hallway of cut bluestone. The heels of her shoes on the polished concrete floor echoed off the walls as she made her way down the wide corridor to the basement offices. She stopped in front of a wooden door with a frosted glass inset. Emblazoned on a wooden sign across the center in gold letters was the word "Director." The thick, textured glass felt cold to the touch. All she could see were the vague outlines of things on the inside. She almost turned and went straight for the gallery door, but she stopped herself.

"Mr. Halpern?" She knocked on the door. "Mr. Halpern? It's Mina Beckwith."

She twisted the frigid brass doorknob and stepped into the office. It was dark except for the faded daylight of the rainy morning that managed to make its way through the small raised windows that just cleared ground level. The office was gray and colorless. She looked up at the artifacts on the walls and shelves, and thought that they had taken on the sameness of their surroundings, as if the vitality of their former lives had been sucked out of them in this academic prison. She turned, closing the door behind her. As she walked toward the stairs that led up to gallery, she felt something sticky on her left shoe. She stopped, took it off and examined it, and knew from the color what the something was and where it had come from.

She went back into Halpern's office and turned on the light. Blood, now dry, had come from under the desk and spread out over the floor. Behind the desk, she found Abel Halpern's body, his face turned up, and his right eye staring out as wide as a camera lens. His left eye was squeezed and crunched closed by the large encrusted gash on the left side of his head. His mouth gaped open on one side, and from it flowed a dark red streak shaped like an oversized teardrop. A wooden object that looked like an old war club lay next to him, festooned with small clumps of skin, little bits of hair, and more dried blood. She reached out and touched the cold body, and then went, turning out the light as she left.

In the shadows, no one saw her enter at the back of the large gallery. The room extended up three stories, with a staircase and exhibits placed all around the perimeter on each floor, so that the center vaulted up like a medieval cathedral. Suspended from the ceiling was the complete skeleton of a blue whale. On the ground floor, standing at various places in the hall were large carved images of Hawaiian deities. Feather capes and ancient artifacts from different times in Hawaiian history were all mixed up here, but it was the god images that always reached out to Mina first, and this morning she sensed their strong and watchful presence as she stood there on the brink of their sanctuary.

"Hell, they just carried it out the front door."

She recognized Todd's voice. Then, she heard another voice, softer, with a British accent, saying something about a lock, and although she couldn't quite make out his exact words, she'd heard enough to know that one of the portraits had been stolen. She stepped out into the light. "Todd, Todd," she called. "Over here."

"Mina, what are you doing here? This place is closed. We don't want reporters here now." Todd was striding toward her.

"No, you don't understand. Just come with me." She grabbed him by the arm and pulled him out of the room.

After seeing Abel Halpern's body and asking a few hurried questions in the hall, Todd parked Mina in the staff lounge, and in the authoritative tone he used when he got nervous, he ordered her to stay there. Mina was sitting on an old sofa, leaning against one of the arms with her legs stretched out, when Ned came into the room. He cocked his head to one side and looked at her with slight surprise.

"Nyla said younger sister. She didn't say twin."

"I am younger, by four minutes. She's still a bully, you know, always has to do everything first."

"Are you all right? That was an awfully gruesome sight first thing in the morning."

"I think I'm okay," Mina said. "Now that my heart has stopped pounding."

"Would you like a sip of brandy?" Ned offered. "Todd sent some in."

"Does he think the little lady might have hysterics?" Mina gave him a wry smile.

"It'll make him feel better. He's had to drink half of it himself already." Ned handed her a small flask with a glass top.

"Anything for the old brother-in-law." She raised the flask and took a swallow. "You must be that Ned Manusia person from London that Nyla's been jabbering about."

"She talks quite a bit about you too."

"Oh?" Mina took another sip of brandy.

"To tell you the truth," smiled Ned, "I think she's quite proud of you."

"To tell you the truth, I'm quite proud of her."

"Did you know the late Mr. Halpern very well?" Ned asked.

In a split second, Ned saw a look of wariness pass over her before she snapped back. "Is that part of the official police inquiry?"

"No." Ned was careful to be kind. "This is Todd's territory—official inquiries are his job. That was just an innocent question."

"No, I didn't know him very well at all." Mina relaxed. "I knew his daughter, Sheila, in high school. I heard her mother died too, a few years ago."

"It's always tough, losing a parent," said Ned.

"Yeah," she echoed.

A harassed-looking Todd Forrest barged into the room and fell into a chair. "Do you want to do this here or later at the station?" He looked at Mina.

"Here's just fine," she answered.

"You've already told me about finding the body, but why did you decide to do a story on the portraits?"

"I didn't. It was an assignment."

"Who set up the appointment?" Todd was making notes as she talked.

Ned just watched her.

"I don't know. I got a memo on my desk from my supervisor."

"So who else, besides you, knew about the appointment?"

"You mean from the paper?" Mina asked.

"Uh-huh." Todd was tapping his pencil on the arm of the chair.

"I don't know."

"How well did you know Mr. Halpern, Mina?"

"Not well. Just what I'd heard about him."

"What's that?"

"Oh, come on, Todd." Mina looked at him like he was being silly. "Same as you've heard. Same as Nyla's heard. He was unhappy. He drank a lot. He was unpopular, bad tempered, and he had a thing about the Japanese."

"I never heard about the Japanese," Todd said.

"He thought they were, you know, 'the yellow peril.' He was always writing or saying stupid things in public about the inscrutable Oriental mind, how it was foreign and cunning, how we could never trust it."

"He said things like that in public?" Todd seemed surprised.

"His last big clash was with Sam Takahashi."

"Sam?"

"Yeah. Sam and several other well-to-do businessmen from the Japanese community applied for membership in the Kama'aina Club and were all denied. There was some lame excuse like no new members were being accepted at the time, but, of course, they continued to accept haole members. There's been a lot of public name calling."

"I didn't know that."

"Sometimes the things you don't know surprise me, Todd."

"I wasn't raised on island intricacies like you were," Todd retorted. "I guess that's all for now. I know where to find you, of course." He stood to leave.

"No, wait a minute," Mina stood up too. "I want to ask *you* a few questions. Is it clear that the murder and the theft are connected?"

"I'll make an official statement *after* we review what we have here.

There could be things that we might not want made public, things that could hamper our investigation." Todd's vocal level had gone up a notch.

"Are you telling me not to write this story?"

"I'm telling you that if you just go off and write a story about this from your point of view, before we organize the facts, you could be jeopardizing our chances of solving the crime."

"I'll tell you what I'll do then," she said in a calm voice. "*Because* you're my brother-in-law, I'll go home and write my story, and I'll call you up and read it to you. If there's something you feel is harmful, you can tell me what it is and why we shouldn't print it, and we'll go from there. This is a big story. No reporter in my position would just sit around and wait for you to issue an official statement, for God's sake!"

The door opened, and one of Todd's assistants told Todd that the man from the coroner's office had arrived.

"You're pushing me into a corner, Mina." Todd was obviously irritated.

"Not any more than any other reporter would. I'd say you were lucky it was me. I can be reasonable, even sympathetic, if I'm not bullied."

"Look, I'm on the edge here," shouted Todd. "There's a dead man in there!"

"I know," answered Mina. "I found him."

Todd looked at her and then left the room.

"You handled that very well," said Ned as he stepped out of the background.

"I've had practice. He's part of the family," she said. "He's just doing his job."

"And you do yours, in a very effective way."

"Nyla didn't say you were perceptive." Mina couldn't help smiling as she stood to leave.

"Yes, and I have very good manners as well," said Ned as he gathered up Mina's things. "I'll walk you to your car."

They moved from the dark and confined museum offices out into the soft, cloudy light. Ned was amazed at how much she looked like her sister—the thick dark hair, the long-limbed body, the pretty pale green eyes, and the warm honey-colored skin. But there were differences. She was much more quick and direct than Nyla, and he sensed a certain tension in her disposition, as if she were about to break away and sprint toward a finish line.

As they passed the gallery entrance, they saw an elderly Japanese man examining the fragments of the lock from the large main double doors. He had the lock disassembled and spread out on a table and was looking at some of the pieces, turning them over with a pair of large tweezers. Ned and Mina stopped to watch. Some of them he picked up and smelled, turned them over, and smelled them again. The man lifted one toward Mina, turning it back and forth in front of her.

"Whoever did this wasn't fooling around," he said. "Had to have connections too. Hard to get here, you know, nitroglycerin!"

They moved on to Mina's car. Ned put her bag in the back seat and opened the door for her.

"You do have nice manners, Mr. Manusia," said Mina as she climbed into the driver's seat.

"I'm an interesting dinner companion as well," he answered, closing the car door.

"Call me," smiled Mina. "I love to eat."

"Where shall I call you?" Ned called out as she backed away.

"Ask Nyla!" Mina waved to him as she drove off.

What an extraordinary morning, Ned thought to himself, as he looked up at the museum facade and made his way back to the scene of what had now become two very serious crimes.

THE FUN BEGINS

THE NEXT DAY Todd sat behind his desk in the upstairs office of the Honolulu Police Station, on the corner of Merchant and Bethel streets. As the chief of detectives, he rated a roomy, now messy, office with glass windows that overlooked Merchant Street. He opened the folder containing the coroner's report. Ned lay stretched out on a sofa that sat near one of the large windows. He was staring up at the ceiling fan, watching the blades turn in endless circles.

"According to the coroner," Todd said, "he'd been dead for awhile —probably happened sometime around midnight on New Year's Eve."

"Sometime around," repeated Ned.

"He says sometime between 10:00 p.m. and midnight."

"Before midnight," mumbled Ned.

"What did you say?" asked Todd.

"Nothing. I was thinking about midnight. Sorry, go on."

"He doesn't say much else," said Todd, "except that it was so cold in that basement that . . . the body was . . . well, you know."

"Brace up, Todd, someday you'll get used to bodies. It's a regular part of your kind of work."

"Yeah," grimaced Todd. "I'm squeamish. I admit it."

"Anything else?"

"Well, nothing we don't already know. The victim died as a result of a blow to the head, and there were indications that the victim had consumed a large quantity of alcohol before death."

"I wonder what he was doing there on New Year's Eve?"

"I doubt if he was working late. Maybe he went to pick something up," answered Todd. "He could have been there when the thieves broke in. They could have been checking things out to make sure no one was around. They heard him rustling around in his office, and they went in and removed their problem."

"But wouldn't it have been easier just to wait until he went away?" Ned looked over at Todd.

"That's what I would have done." Todd began to tap a pencil on his desk.

"He could have been part of the theft," Ned said. "He could have come there. There could have been an argument. He could have gotten bashed on the head. Were there any signs of a struggle?"

"Nope."

"That makes it tricky."

"Then," said Todd, "there's always the outside possibility that the theft and the murder are two separate crimes. Someone comes to meet Halpern and kills him. Then later, the thieves come and steal the portrait."

"So." Ned sat up. "I guess so far we have three theories."

"Theory one," began Todd, "burglars discover man, man gets killed. Theory two, man is part of theft, and for reasons unknown gets killed by his cohorts. Theory three, man meets with someone, gets killed, killer leaves, thieves come and steal painting."

"I'm inclined to theory two or three," reported Ned. "It seems it should have been messier if it was theory one. And besides, I just, have this feeling—"

"It's one of your famous feelings, huh?" Todd smiled.

"I suppose it is."

"But remember, there are still the details of the theft itself," Todd remarked. "The door was blown open with a small amount of nitroglycerin. I'd guess there were at least two people involved in removing the portrait. The ground was a little damp, and there were a couple different shoe marks outside—vague, but enough to see that they belonged to different people. What do you think your instructions will be, from *your* office?"

"I've sent them a rather long cable. They'll wire back by this afternoon. I suppose they'll want me to assist in the recovery of the portrait while keeping a low profile. I know it's your territory, but I'm sure you can appreciate the diplomatic interest."

"I'll just say you're representing the interests of the British Museum in the recovery of the portrait, which would not be a lie."

Ned understood that this was Todd's way of establishing his own authority. It didn't worry him. He'd had quite a bit of experience getting what he wanted without stepping on other people's toes. But he could do that too, if he had to.

"Anything you say, guv. What's next?"

"You could come with me to have a chat with Mr. Christian Hollister," Todd replied.

"Is he a suspect?" asked Ned.

"He was one of Halpern's friends, and he just happens to be one of the richest men in town. He wants to know what's going on, so we'll humor him because he might be able to provide us with some information."

"Ah, I'm on my way to meeting the island elite." Ned smiled.

"He's also Mina's boss. One of the things he owns is the newspaper, the *Honolulu Star,* and he likes to run it himself."

The newspaper building was not far from the station. It was an impressive three-story complex, and Christian Hollister's office was located on the third floor, at the top of the wide staircase. Todd and Ned entered the silent reception area through tall wooden double doors. Behind the long reception counter sat a well-dressed and efficient-looking woman. After the obligatory questions, she led them to Hollister's office.

Christian Hollister was a man of order and taste. On the wall were a stunning volcano painting by the Frenchman Jules Tavernier and a scene of plantation workers by Joseph Strong. There was a set of framed drawings that Ned recognized as the original sketches of

Jacques Arago. The office was furnished with a combination of Asian and island furniture, and Christian Hollister himself sat behind a massive koa wood desk with ornate legs, carved in great detail, on an elevation that was just a little higher than the rest of the office floor. Hollister was handsome in the Yankee tradition—tall, fair, lean, but well built. His wire-rimmed glasses accentuated his bright blue eyes and Ivy League looks. Ned guessed he was in his early to middle forties by the shells of gray at his temples. Hollister moved toward them with an athletic grace.

"How are you, Todd?" He shook Todd's hand. Todd introduced Ned and explained his connection to the case.

"I'm happy to meet you, Ned," Hollister smiled. "I'll be seeing more of you. John Knight has cast me in your play. I'll be playing Armand."

"I'll look forward to working with you, Mr. Hollister," Ned replied.

"Please, call me Chris, and sit, sit down. Can my secretary get you something to drink? No? Then thank you, that will be all, Mrs. Lake, and please hold my calls."

They were all seated, not around Hollister's desk, but in an arranged corner with a sofa and two armchairs, set up to promote more intimate and casual exchanges. Ned accepted a cigarette.

"I'm shocked about Halpern. Terrible thing," Hollister began. "If there's anything I can do, of course, it goes without saying. I've already spoken with Sheila, his daughter. She called me. She said she thought I would know who should be told, among his friends and acquaintances. I suppose she doesn't feel quite up to informing people herself. But death does entail social responsibilities for the living."

"You've known Halpern for quite some time, then." Todd had adopted an almost casual attitude.

"We both went to Punahou School, although he's much older than I am. I got to know him when I got back from college. We belong to the same clubs. We have the same friends, and we shared an interest in philately. He was an aggressive collector."

"What's that?" asked Todd.

"They both collected stamps," offered Ned.

"Anyway, I'd like to know anything you could tell me about his death," Hollister said.

"To be honest, Chris," said Todd, "we don't know much more right now than what was printed in your paper this morning. Halpern was murdered and a valuable painting was stolen. So far, we have no real leads."

"Your reporter," interjected Ned, "Miss Beckwith, was the one who found the body."

"Mina was sent to do a story on the portraits. She didn't put that in her article. Of course, she wouldn't. It's not her style to capitalize on that kind of thing. Must have been a shock for her."

"She seems to have more than a little pluck." Ned smiled.

"You noticed that?" Hollister gave him a quick, intense look. "Mina, I should say Todd's sister-in-law, always does an admirable reporting job. For a woman, that is."

"I was hoping, Chris, you could give me an idea of what Halpern was like." Todd had taken out his notebook.

"You didn't know him?" Chris asked.

"I'd met him once or twice," Todd replied, "but I didn't know much about him."

Hollister leaned back in his chair. "Oh, he kept to himself, you know, a museum type. Sometimes he drank too much, like a lot of people in this town, maybe a little more since Ella, his wife, died. He had a large circle of acquaintances, old school friends, people like that, but he wasn't one that—he wasn't the kind that made close friends. He was always reserved."

"Do you know," asked Todd, "anybody he was involved with, any situation that might lead to this?"

"No, no I didn't—I don't, I mean." It was obvious that Hollister was thinking.

"No one he'd quarreled with, offended?"

"No."

"What about Sam Takahashi?"

"Oh that, so you heard about that. Look, it may seem serious, but no—Sam would never—that's ridiculous. It was just a—" Hollister paused for a moment. "It was, well, it was this racial thing. I admit, it wasn't very pretty. Halpern did have his opinions, and he was always announcing them in public, writing letters and giving talks."

"About what?" Todd prompted him.

"Oh, you know, about the Japanese, Asians in general, but it was the Japanese he was most worried about. He obsessed about Japanese military operations—their invasion of Manchuria. And then when they renounced the London Naval Treaty just before New Year's, that agitated him quite a bit."

"And this obsession affected what he thought about our Japanese community?"

"He didn't make any distinction between the Japanese in Japan and the local Japanese people. It didn't matter to him whether they were American citizens or not. He thought all Japanese were a danger to an American way of life here. He'd write things that—well, they were pretty heavy handed."

"And Takahashi took offense?"

"I'm sure everyone who is Japanese took offense, but what made Takahashi sore is what Abel did on the board of the Kamaʻāina Club. Sam and some other businessmen, American-born Japanese, wanted to join the club. And many of the board members were sympathetic to Asians joining, if they had money and a certain kind of status in the community. So these guys applied and the board took up the issue of their membership. Well, Abel had a fit. He began calling not only everyone on the board, but people in the general membership. He did everything he could to prevent them from joining. I think he may have even written some twisted letters to Sam and his pals. The board voted to deny their membership. Of course, they didn't say that race was the issue. They just wrote them all letters saying the board decided there would be no new memberships accepted at that time. Anyway, sometime last week, Sam was drinking at the Palm Garden Court and Abel comes in. I guess Sam was a little loaded. He mouthed off to Halpern. They exchanged a few words. I heard Sam took a swing at him."

"Did he say anything? Threaten him in any way?"

"I don't know. I'm just telling you what I heard. I wasn't there, but you could ask the staff. They could tell you."

"And I'm sure we will." Todd smiled at him. "Now, Halpern's wife is dead, but the daughter lives in the house?"

"Sheila," said Hollister. "She's divorced. Her husband ran out on her and left her with nothing. If she had a choice, I don't think she'd be staying there. There's a son too. I'm sure you'll meet him. He thinks he's an artist and lives down in Kaka'ako in some dive. No love lost there." Hollister made the last remark under his breath.

"I beg your pardon?" Todd was fishing.

"Look," said Hollister. "I'll be honest. I'm helping Sheila out because I was her father's old friend, but I'm not a friend of Sheila Halpern or her brother. And I don't want to say any more on the subject. It doesn't seem decent, I mean, Abel just dead and me telling you all these intimate details of his family life."

"I understand, but this is a murder investigation." Todd paused. "So, when was the last time you saw Halpern?"

"Well, on New Year's Eve. I stopped by to wish him a happy New Year and leave him a bottle of brandy. I think it was about eight or eight-thirty. I left about nine to pick up Lamby Langston. We went to dinner at the club."

"Was he agitated, upset, anything unusual? Did he say what his plans were for the evening?" Todd asked.

"No," Hollister answered, "he seemed the same as always to me. I didn't ask, but I guess I just assumed he was staying in because he didn't mention going out."

"You may have been the last person to see him alive," Todd said, "aside from his murderer."

"That's a sobering thought." Hollister glanced out the window. "As I said, if I can help in any way, please call me. I want to see this thing cleared up as soon as possible."

"We're in agreement there," said Todd. "Murder in Honolulu is a shock to everyone. We all want it solved, and we won't take up any more of your time. We do appreciate your help, Chris."

"Please let me know if there's anything else I can do," Hollister said.

"Mr. Hollister—Chris," Ned said, rising, "I'm sure you'll make a splendid Armand."

"I hope so," beamed Hollister. "He's a terrific character."

"Do you do much acting?" asked Ned.

"Whenever I have the time. It's a great challenge." Hollister's smile was charming.

"I'll look forward to seeing you at the rehearsal tomorrow." Ned shook Hollister's hand.

"It will be a pleasure," said Hollister, opening the door for them.

As they walked down the stairs from Hollister's office, Ned started to imagine him in the role of Armand. He had the charisma and the looks, although they'd have to get the make-up person to add a little weariness to that fresh face. And his voice. Ned wondered if he would have the vocal range to do Armand justice. After the first rehearsal in the theatre, it would be obvious.

"I can hear the old wheels turning, Ned."

"I hope he can act," mumbled Ned.

"Oh, Christ," said Todd. "I can see what's coming. This investigation is going to be in heavy competition with the production of your play. That's all you and Nyla and Mina will be talking about. She's in on it too, isn't she?"

"Don't whine, old man, it isn't attractive."

"This always happens when Nyla gets involved in a play. Our whole world starts to revolve around whether so and so can remember her lines, or the tantrum the leading man threw about his costume, or the bawling out the director gave everyone."

"You may have to hit the bottle."

"You're telling me, pal."

"'Pal,'" mused Ned. "Such a distinct American word. Well, can he act? Have you ever seen him in anything?"

"I don't know good acting from lousy, but he's never put me to sleep."

"That's an encouraging recommendation, Mr. Forrest."

"Nyla did say he liked to get the part, though."

"Oh?"

"Yeah, you know, he gets a little antsy if he thinks there's competition. Nyla said there was another guy on his staff, a good performer who was going to try out for the part in your play. She said Mina told her that Halpern sent him on assignment to the outer islands so there was no way he could audition."

"Ah, the cutthroat impulse," sighed Ned. "The sure sign of a splendid actor."

"Splendid," mimicked Todd. "I love the way you talk, pal. Shall we pay a call on the daughter?"

"Splendid," smiled Ned.

4

HOW GARDENS GROW

BOTH GATES TO the horseshoe-shaped driveway were closed, so Todd and Ned parked on the street and proceeded up the front walkway of Abel Halpern's Nuʻuanu Valley home on Dowsett Street. A tall lava rock wall separated the long lawn from the street. It was an old wall, now ornamented with lichens and small ferns growing out of pockets in the stone cervices. Midway between the closed gates, a pedestrian path led straight toward the house. It circled on both sides around a fountain placed in the middle of the yard, and then resumed a direct line to the porte cochere and the front door. The grass was trimmed, and the hedges fronting the wooden colonial exterior of the house were low and shaped in perfect rectangles. In precise symmetry, pots of blooming impatiens stood on either side of the front door. Two identical lantern cherry trees grew at each side of the house, placed in front of twin fences that cut off the side and back yards from view. The house itself was two stories, with immaculate white siding and dark green shutters. Little white lace curtains hung in the windows. The meticulous presentation made Ned feel uneasy.

Sheila Halpern unlocked the door and asked them to come in. They followed her as she floated through the living room toward the back of the house as if she were moving from one vague world to the next, until they came to a covered patio that looked out over the back of the property. In stark contrast to the front, the back yard was a virulent green jumble of plants and trees that had been left to shift for themselves for some time. Weeds grew waist high, and the tangled overgrowth concealed any signs of neighbors. Ned heard the sounds of a stream drifting through the foliage. Several kinds of birds chirped and sang.

"Please sit down." Sheila Halpern's voice was low and deep. "I'd apologize for the yard, but I've come to like it this way. All of this growth, it attracts so many birds. I might just let the front go the same way. Would you like a drink? I'm having one."

"No thank you." Todd was trying to be extra polite. "I haven't introduced myself, I'm—"

"I know who you are. You told me on the phone. You're a detective, Todd Forrest, and this is Edward Manusia, the playwright."

"Ned."

"Ned," she repeated. "And he's helping with the investigation. How about you, Mr. Manusia, would you like a drink?"

"Some of what you're having without the vodka would be lovely, thanks." Ned saw her smile at his accent.

"And you, detective," she said, rising and moving to the wet bar. "Aren't you married to Mina Beckwith?"

"No," said Todd. "It's Nyla. I'm married to her sister, Nyla."

"Oh, right, my mistake. I meant to say Nyla." Sheila's voice trailed off and she stared into the green thicket. Her movements were slow and almost lazy as she got Ned his drink. She then settled into her seat, drawing her legs up and tucking them to the side. "Mina is the one I remember. She was always so nice to me in school. No one else was."

Ned looked at Sheila Halpern as she sat in the oversized rattan chair hunched up like a child. She took a long sip of her drink before she put it down on the glass table beside her. A profusion of reddish blonde hair spilled down over her shoulders framing her large green eyes and a pale, powdered face. Under the makeup, Ned was sure he could see slight traces of bruising. She looked dazed, a little drunk, and on edge.

"I guess you could say I'm not myself," Sheila said staring into the garden.

"I'm sorry we have to do this," Todd said honestly, "but it's important to move fast in these kinds of investigations."

"Murder," she replied, "you mean a murder investigation? He was murdered wasn't he? Bashed on the head or something?"

"Yes, that's right," said Todd.

"And who would have thought the old man had any blood in him at all?" Sheila let out a small nervous laugh.

"Do you know," Todd moved forward to the edge of his seat, "anyone who would do such a thing?"

"No," said Sheila in a voice laced with contempt.

"So you don't think your father had any enemies?" Todd asked.

"I didn't say that," said Sheila. "My father could be an SOB. He was tyrannical, opinionated, self-centered, unfeeling, and, when he wanted to be, one of the meanest people you'd ever meet. He was cruel to my mother. He made her feel alone, unwanted, and worthless. He belittled Andrew, my brother, into being cynical and belligerent. He drove me out of the house and into a disastrous marriage to a dishonest and abusive man."

"But you lived here afterwards, after your divorce," Todd commented.

"Hadn't any choice. My husband liked to gamble and borrow. When he skipped out, I was lucky to still own my clothes."

"And how long ago was that?" Todd asked.

"Last year." Sheila took another long sip of her drink. "My father and I just ignored each other. That became our version of getting along. I know he hated me being here, but he didn't dare turn me out. Like the front lawn, you see, everything had to look right to the general public. He always maintained his public image."

"On New Year's Eve, did you see him?" Todd had taken out his small notebook.

"I think I heard his car about five in the afternoon. Then he stayed home for a while, and Chris, Chris Hollister, came over about nine. He stayed for about half an hour. My father left a little after Chris did."

"Chris Hollister? Do you know why he came here?" Todd was writing.

"I'd guess it was about stamps. My father was obsessed with them. They were always doing something with stamps. I don't know, maybe he came to say Happy New Year. He had a bottle with a ribbon when I let him in. They went into my father's study at the other end of the house. I can't hear anything from my room."

"Hollister left, and then your father left sometime after nine thirty. Do you know where he went?"

"No."

"And you were here all night?"

"All night, by myself."

"By yourself on New Year's Eve?"

"I didn't feel like going out. I fell asleep just after midnight. I got up the next morning, and some friends picked me up and we drove out to the country to see the winter surf. I got home very late. I was tired and went straight to bed. I didn't even notice whether his car was there or not."

"No one else was here on New Year's Eve?" Todd kept writing.

"Kikue, the maid. She left at about two in the afternoon. She had New Year's Day off."

"Now," Todd paused for a moment. "Now I need to ask you these questions, Miss Halpern. I'm not suggesting or inferring anything, but they are questions I have to ask. Would you say you father was a wealthy man?"

"My father," she began, "was wealthy because my mother made him wealthy. She had all the money. She had tuberculosis, and three years ago when she died, he had it all fixed so that it went straight to him. She told me all about it when things got bad, when she knew she was dying. She kept apologizing about not leaving me anything. I tried to tell her that it didn't matter, that I loved her, but she just kept on saying how sorry she was. She kept saying he made her do it his way. He made her do everything his way." Sheila was suppressing the emotion in her voice. "This was her house, you know, her family house."

"And now?" asked Todd.

"Now it's mine. Now it belongs to me and Andrew. I already checked." She paused and then her voice returned full of anger. "I suppose right now you're thinking that maybe I killed him. I didn't, but don't think I never wanted to." There was pronounced silence, and then she burst into tears.

"Is there anyone we can call for you, Miss Halpern?" Ned used a calm voice. "I think maybe you shouldn't be alone."

"No, I'll be all right." She wiped her eyes. "It's just that, everything's made me remember too much."

"Are you sure," Ned persisted, "that there is nothing we can do for you?"

"Well, you can forget all of this at rehearsal tomorrow night."

"You're?" Ned looked at her.

"Anna," she said. "I'm playing Anna. And I'm really looking forward to it. I need to pretend I'm someone else."

"I understand, and I know you'll be wonderful," Ned assured her. "I'm sorry we've had to ask you these things, just now."

"If there's anything else you remember, anything else you think I might like to know—" Todd stood up.

"Right," she said on cue. "I'll call."

"Don't bother showing us out," said Todd as he handed her his card. "We can manage."

As he left the room, Ned looked back at Sheila Halpern. She was standing, watching them leave. The patio framed her against the overgrown yard. Her whole being seemed compressed and dwarfed by the rapacious green background, as if the hungry landscape behind her were about to reach out and pull her away into its twisted interior.

ANGER AND THE ARTS

"**L**ET'S GO TALK to the brother next." Todd started up the car and pulled away from the curb. "I'll bet he's a nut case too."

"There's something else going on with that woman." Ned frowned. "Did you see the bruises underneath all that makeup?"

"I saw them." Todd sounded disgusted. "I wonder what that's about?"

"If I had known her better, I would have asked. Poor girl looks like she's living in a pressure cooker. But," he reflected, "sometimes that's useful for an actor. They have an outlet for some powerful energy."

"Oh God, what did I tell you? We're already seeing life through the veil of the play."

"You should try and relax, Todd," Ned chuckled. "You know the theatre is great therapy for some people."

"Oh, splendid!" Todd winked at him. "I can't wait for my first big break."

"Remember, dear, in Shakespeare's theatre the men played all the women's roles."

After lunch, they were driving over the unpaved side streets of the Kaka'ako district. It was an urban neighborhood of industrial activity and lower working-class housing. Some of the wooden houses, though worn, looked well kept. Many of the small yards were being used to grow vegetables and fruit trees. Ned was able to identify avocado, mango, lychee, papaya, and lime trees, and he was sure he saw more than one yard with a chicken coop. They passed a stray dog sitting on the corner, licking its side.

"Honolulu seems to be weathering the depression better than the States," Ned commented as he watched the dog amble away down a narrow alley.

"Yeah," said Todd. "I think we're at about 8 percent unemployment, nowhere near the 20-plus rate on the mainland."

"I saw some of the breadlines in New York. It's quite sad to see so many hungry people."

"The sugar industry may have had to tighten its belt, but it's still holding up our economy." Todd pulled the car over, turned off the engine, and looked out the window.

They got out of the car in front of a dilapidated one-story building. It was hard to tell if it was built to be a warehouse, or a dwelling, or both. There was a miserable-looking mango tree to the right of the front gate. The tiny strip of yard was littered with leaves, and some brown raggedy shrubs were clinging to life near the building's entrance. A couple of dented garbage cans rounded out the picture. Todd knocked on the peeling painted door. No one came to answer, so Todd knocked with more insistence and the door finally opened. A Eurasian woman stood there with something like a bedspread tied around herself. She had dark hair that fell forward, shading her face, and her fingernails were long, well kept, and painted a bright red. They stood out in stark contrast to her olive skin. She looked groggy and tired, and she spoke in an irritated voice. "What do you want?"

"We want to see Andrew Halpern." Todd showed his identification. "Is he here?"

The woman turned away, leaving the door open. She walked around a corner, yelled to someone, came back, and pointed one of her bright red nails. "That way," she said in an irritated voice, and then walked away down the hall in the opposite direction.

They headed where they were told to go, and the hall opened up into a huge room with a high ceiling. It was a work area scattered with metal, junk, stained canvas cloths, tools, and cans of industrial-looking liquids. The floor was greasy and stained. Beams of afternoon light from high windows captured the upwelling of dust, and Ned noticed several peculiar chemical smells. At the far end, large sliding doors opened from this space into a sandy driveway and a small yard with a patchy grass lawn. A few haggard banana trees stood in a clump beside a weathered picnic table and some old chairs. Ned spotted an outdoor shower and a barbecue.

In multi-stained denims and a torn ragged T-shirt, Andrew Halpern stood next to a large metal sculpture with spikes of varying heights and radial shapes welded on in different places. He appeared to be rubbing it with something that turned the metal verdigris. Other pieces of his work were scattered around him. None of them were realistic, but Ned thought they emanated a kind of raw power and reminded him of Vikings, barbarians, and all unwelcome invaders. Andrew was little like his work. Tall, thin, almost effeminate, he had the same red hair as his sister, and the same startling green eyes. His hair needed washing, and it looked like he hadn't shaved for a few days. He stopped what he was doing, set down the rag, and put his hands on his hips. "Do you want something?"

"I'm Todd Forrest, a detective from the Honolulu Police Department." Todd flashed his identification again. "I'm investigating your father's murder, and I need to ask you a few questions."

"As you can see, detective, I'm consumed by grief so I don't know if I'll be of any help."

"Well," said Todd, "either we can do this here today or you can come down to the station with a police escort for questioning."

"In that case, why don't you gentlemen step into my parlor?" Andrew pointed to the picnic table. "Want a beer?"

"No thanks," said Todd. "We're working."

"So was I," said Andrew. He grabbed a beer from an icebox, and the three of them sat on the old chairs under the shade of the banana leaves.

"This is Mr. Edward Manusia. He has an interest in the case. A painting was stolen at the same time your father was killed, a portrait Ned escorted from the British Museum. The museum wants to know what happened."

"I saw your picture in the theatre office. You're that playwright, aren't you?" Andrew looked Ned over.

"Guilty as charged," Ned answered, smiling.

"I'm doing the light design for the play," Andrew said. "My sister gets me these little jobs."

Ned saw a look of exasperation flash over Todd's face. There was an awkward moment of silence.

"Well," said Andrew. "Aren't you going to ask me anything?"

"Do you know anyone who would have a reason to kill your father?" Todd began.

"Hundreds of people might have a reason to kill my father. I'd say a good portion of the Oriental population in town had a good reason to kill my father." Andrew looked disgusted.

"Because of what he wrote?" Todd continued.

"Wrote, said, thought, did."

"Do you know a man named Sam Takahashi?" Todd was careful.

"Maybe, the name sounds familiar."

"So do you know if he had any quarrel with your father?"

"No, I don't," Andrew pouted.

"How about you? Did you get along with your father?" Todd was brusque.

"My father was a bastard, and I'm glad he's dead."

"And where were you on New Year's Eve between 10:30 and 1:00 p.m.?"

"I was right here, alone, working."

"So you spent New Year's Eve alone?" Todd asked.

"Parties are stupid."

"I understand," Todd went on, "that you know you and your sister will inherit quite a bit from your father."

"Does it look like I'm interested in money?" Andrew almost laughed.

"I don't know what you're interested in, Mr. Halpern. Can anyone confirm that you were here on New Year's Eve when you say you were?"

"My sister called me, just before midnight."

"Your sister." Todd tried to control his irritation.

"Look, if you want to accuse me of murder go ahead, but you'll never be able to prove anything because I was right here."

"When was the last time you saw your father, Mr. Halpern?" Todd looked at him.

"I saw him on New Year's Eve. I went over to the house around lunchtime, and we had a few words. Nothing unusual—we always had a few words." Andrew looked straight at Todd.

"What was it about?" Todd looked away and into the studio.

"I don't remember," Andrew answered. "I try to forget about him as soon as he's out of my sight, and, like I said, I'm happy I'll never have to see him again."

"On that note," said Todd, "I think we'll be going."

As Ned was leaving with Todd, he turned back to Andrew Halpern. "Your work has great energy as well as originality. I hope to see more of it some day."

Andrew took a last sip from his bottle of beer. Then he just stood there staring at the two of them as they walked away.

6

THE WATCHERS

IT WAS MIDAFTERNOON, around three o'clock, when Ned took a cab from the police station up to the museum for one more look at the crime scene. By the time he got there, it had started to rain again. The museum gallery was empty, except for the woman at the entrance desk and a young couple who looked like tourists.

Ned couldn't help but be affected by the heavy nineteenth-century design of the building. It reminded him of a penitentiary or an asylum. The style of exhibition within the bluestone walls reflected the European and American passion for "collecting." On the first level, ancient Hawaiian gods hewn from stone or wood stood silent and staring. Their large carved features seemed to be reaching out, as if they were trying to say something. Ned felt them touching him in a way that was both all too familiar and always unfathomable. He looked into the standing glass cases that lined the walls. They were filled with various antiquities—a carved bowl decorated with inserts of teeth, a large gourd believed to have held the winds, a staff with an exquisite wooden image of Lono, the god of the harvest and fertility, on its standing end. Lono, who also appeared as the lusty, shape-shifting pig god, Kamapua'a. What a marvelous world these things came from, Ned thought.

He was so lost in admiration of the artifacts that he didn't notice he had come to the wall at the end of the glass cases where the portraits hung. The two remaining portraits were still in their places, and a Hawaiian coat of arms had taken up the empty space where the king's portrait should have been. To the right of the coat of arms was the portrait of Queen Kapiʻolani. She was a handsome woman in her stunning nineteenth-century gown made of peacock feathers. She stood, poised, holding a folded fan. Her face was turned forward so that her intense eyes appeared to follow the viewer no matter where one stood. Her sister's portrait hung to the left. She was a younger woman, attractive in her own right, but without the stature and intensity of the queen. The younger sister's gaze was also synchronized to the viewer's, but it had a pleading quality as opposed to the purposeful look of her older sister. Both women reminded Ned of his grandmother in Āpia. His grandmother, Tavaʻesina, was a chief's daughter and possessed that haughty self-confidence so characteristic of the upper-class Polynesian women. Ned felt the eyes from the portraits locked on his.

Such a violent crime, he thought—not like being shot, or poisoned, or stabbed. Even if the man was a terrible person, it was still a brutal way to die, battered on the head with one of the artifacts in his own collection. The sight of Halpern's body flashed through his mind, and a wave of coldness passed through him. He sensed his feet as heavy objects glued to the floor. As he stood there staring, he lost his equilibrium. The whole room began to sway and shift. He felt things draining away as if someone had pulled the plug and his life force was leaving him. He thought he was seeing the wall open up where the coat of arms hung, and then he felt himself propelled down a long dark tunnel, flying on and on. He had the sensation of being pulled on and stretched farther and farther out. His stomach sickened. At any moment he knew he might loose consciousness and fall away into oblivion. Then, he felt a hand, warm and strong, reach out and grip his upper arm.

"Are you all right?" It was Mina Beckwith's voice. "You look . . . you look like a ghost."

"Good lord," mumbled Ned. "I feel like one. I think I'd better sit down."

"Are you ill?" Mina led him to a wooden bench in the center of the room.

"I was just standing there, looking around at the things in here, looking at the portraits, and thinking about the murder."

"Are you well enough to walk outside?" Mina asked sotto voce.

"I think so."

"Let's get out of this room." She glanced back at the portraits as she took his arm and led him away.

They walked out into the small courtyard behind the museum. There were several outdoor tables and a counter that sold refreshments. The small space was well planted with ferns and tropical flowers. It made Ned feel safe and contained. Mina left for a few minutes and came back with a tray of tea and some biscuits.

"I think you need this," she said as she sat down and poured the tea. "They make wonderful biscuits."

"I guess now I've made a truly great impression on you."

"Well, you have, Mr. Manusia," she said seriously. "I've never met an educated man who managed to remain so sensitive to things like that."

"Like what?"

"You know exactly what I'm talking about." She smiled.

"Oh," Ned replied, "you mean the strong but unexplained reactions of a person like myself of Polynesian ancestry to the concentrated presence of many ancient artifacts believed by our common ancestors to retain and carry immense spiritual power even today?"

"I couldn't have given a better lecture about it myself." She took a bite of one of the biscuits and watched him.

"Very well, I've said it. Now can we talk about something else?"

"Just so long as we acknowledge it."

"Oh, I do," he said. "I did, didn't I?"

"Okay." She tried to sound lighthearted. "Because you were so eloquent, I'll forget about it for now. Here, try this pohā jam on a biscuit. It's made from my favorite island berries."

The hot tea, the warm biscuits, and the presence of Mina Beckwith made Ned feel more like himself. They talked about trivial things for a few moments—the weather, Ned's trip, and his play. A tall, serious-looking woman wearing glasses walked up to their table.

"Hello, Martha, how are you?" Mina greeted her.

"I'm managing as well as I can after this horrible business," she replied. "I heard you found the body."

"I did," Mina answered. "Martha, this is Ned Manusia, the playwright. Ned, this is Martha Klein. She works in anthropology here at the museum."

"How do you do?" Ned stood up and shook her hand.

"Ah, you brought the portraits back, is that correct?"

"Just a small favor for the British Museum," he replied.

"So you must be very concerned about the theft. Are you helping with the investigation?"

"In an unofficial capacity," he said, noticing the directness in her eyes.

"I hope it turns up—it would be a terrible loss. Well, I just wanted to say hello. I'm off to an emergency meeting with the board of directors, but of course I'll see you at the theatre. I've volunteered to be the house manager for this production, so it was nice to meet you. Good-bye Mina." Martha Klein walked away with a purposeful stride.

"Did you know I'm involved in the play too?" Mina asked. "I'm doing the publicity and the program copy. Johnny Knight is our cousin, and he asked me." She reached for a second biscuit.

"It seems like everyone I meet is part of my drama."

"Very small island," she said, laughing. "Full of coincidences."

"What is it brings you to the museum this afternoon, Mina?"

"Want to talk shop? Talk about you know what?"

"Is that why you're here?"

"I came here," said Mina, "because I wanted some little details."

"And?" Ned knew there was more.

"And I had a little look around Halpern's office myself. I talked to some of the staff too."

"And did you discover anything?" He was careful not to seem patronizing.

"Maybe," Mina looked straight at him. "If I did, I'm not sure I'd tell you. You might go running to Todd, and then I'd never hear the end of it."

"What if I promised not to?" He poured another cup of tea.

"You'd have to promise more than that."

"Would I?"

"You'd have to promise," she said, "that we could be kind of like partners."

"Partners?"

"You know, partners, like you tell me what you know, and I tell you what I know, and we help each other out."

"Sounds intriguing, and I do have responsibilities to people at home, but my hands are tied. It's Todd's investigation."

"Listen, I'll let you make the decision about when and what to tell who—if we find anything substantial, I mean." Mina leaned forward and spoke with enthusiasm and interest. "We'd have to figure it out as we went along. You'd have to leave me out of the official picture, of course. I'd be your silent partner."

"Why do you want to do this?" Ned sat up a little straighter.

"Because I found his body," she said. "Because I know I'm good at solving things, and I think I would make a good detective. Because I'd like to try out my skills. But there's no way in hell the world will hand me an opportunity, so I have to make one for myself."

"You're a different kind of person, aren't you?"

"I guess I am," she said.

"Well, I'll do it for a while. I mean, I'll try it out. But if it gets dangerous or untenable, then I reserve the right to withdraw."

"That's very fair," said Mina. "I didn't think you'd agree to anything like this in a million years."

"It intrigues me," Ned said, "and I want a little more freedom to pursue my own way of doing things. Not that I don't have confidence in Todd. It's just a feeling I have about this case—that it would be better to take my own road. I'm sure, as a reporter, there's quite a bit you know about this town."

"I do," she said, taking another biscuit. "There's just one more thing. In the course of our partnership you have to promise to respect my privacy and person."

"You mean will I promise to be platonic?" he smiled.

"Yes."

"Of course, I've found that personal involvement between colleagues while conducting an investigation *or* staging a play is not a good idea. It can make quite a mess. Besides that, you're Nyla's sister, and she would kill me unless I were looking for a wife, which I'm not."

"Do you really mean that?"

"I do," Ned said. He had no idea why he was agreeing to the whole arrangement, but at this moment it seemed like what he should be doing.

"Fine." She laughed. "Do you like Chinese food? I'll pick you up tonight and we can go and eat, and I'll tell you what I know. Do you want that last biscuit?"

"Please," said Ned. "I wouldn't dream of standing between you and that biscuit."

7

COCKTAIL HOUR

NYLA FORREST GATHERED up her husband's shirts and took them downstairs. Tomorrow was the day the laundryman came to make his regular pickup. She sat down on the living room sofa with the clothes piled next to her and began to check the pockets. She and Todd had been married for five years now. They'd known each other for a year before their wedding. Six years, she thought, should be long enough to know someone. Nyla looked out of the large picture window at the fading afternoon light. Yes, she said to herself, I should know him by now.

"Now who's woolgathering?" Without making a sound, Ned had come in through the back door.

"Ned, how did you get here? I didn't hear Todd's car."

"I came back in a cab. I didn't mean to disturb you."

"No, I was just thinking about . . ." Her voice trailed off.

"About what?"

"I was thinking about Todd and how our lives have so much more to do with me than with him. We live in my hometown. We see my family all the time. So many of our friends were my friends first."

"You wouldn't want to live in *his* hometown. Somehow I can't see you in Chicago."

"He's always seemed to like living here. But if this were a mystery or an investigation, then he would have all the clues about me, and I would have almost none about him."

"Are you thinking," he said, "there's more you need to know about your husband?"

"I don't know what I'm thinking," she laughed. "What's to know about Todd? His heart is right on his sleeve."

"I think he could surprise you if he wanted to, Nyla."

"You know, Ned," she said, "I don't really like to be surprised."

There was a short, awkward silence between them. Nyla stood up with her bundle of shirts and started toward the back entry hall.

"Could you bring my costume for me?" She asked Ned. "It's just on the chair at the bottom of the stairs. I want everything in one place for the laundryman."

Ned jumped to his feet. "Hey Nyla, it looks like you shed a few sequins here," he said pointing to a little bare spot as he placed the glittering harlequin costume beside the shirts.

"Oh, well. I hope they don't charge me for it," she sighed.

"I'll be going out for dinner tonight," Ned said as they returned to the living room.

"We're going to a party. Why don't you come, and we can drop you there later," she offered.

"Well," he smiled, "I'm going out with your sister, and she's picking me up, just a friendly dinner. She told me she's doing the publicity for the play, so I thought we'd chat before the rehearsal tomorrow. We're stopping by the theatre first to meet with Johnny Knight."

"You're going to be the envy of about a dozen men in Honolulu if they find out about this 'friendly' dinner."

"I imagine Mina's quite a popular person."

"Popular? Men are fascinated by my sister's brains and her independence, but she almost never goes out, and, believe me, she has more than one persistent admirer. Chris Hollister, for instance. I can see he's a little sweet on her. I bet he would kill to have dinner with her."

"Kill?"

"Not such a good choice of words under the circumstances. Say, while you're on this casual dinner date, ask Mina what she's doing tomorrow afternoon. Maybe she could meet me at the bungalow and help straighten up. You didn't forget about the move tomorrow?"

"I guess I have, after everything that's happened."

"I've arranged for you to borrow my brother's car so you'll have your own transportation. He's away on vacation in Europe. We can pick it up tomorrow too."

"You're going to trust me to drive on the wrong side of the road?"

"Ned, you could never be on the wrong side of the road."

"Are you sure?"

"As sure as I am of anything," she chuckled. "Why don't you make us a drink?"

While Ned was getting the drinks, he heard Todd's car pull into the garage, and by the time Todd walked through the door, Ned had three cool gin and tonics prepared on a tray with little twists of lime. He brought them into the living room on a tray.

"Gee, Nyla," Todd said as Ned served the drinks. "Why can't you serve me a nice drink on a tray like this when I come home every night?"

"It's a good thing you're moving out tomorrow, Ned. You're a bad example." She took a sip of her drink and leaned back. "So what were the two gumshoes up to today?"

"Let's see," said Ned. "We met a charming young chap. A sculptor, Andrew Halpern."

"Oh, he's a charmer all right," laughed Nyla.

"You know, Nyla," said Ned. "I don't think your husband shares our enthusiasm for the fellow."

"I tell you," Todd growled, "it would have been pure delight to sock that punk in the jaw."

"I see what you mean," she said to Ned.

"And that crap he calls sculpture," Todd went on. "What is that? I mean, I think his stuff looks like a bunch of old scrap iron from a junk pile all stuck together."

"I see you're no friend of modern art," Ned smiled.

"And Ned here," grinned Todd, "is saying things like, oh, how original, oh, how energetic."

"I didn't say it like that."

"I've seen some of his stuff." Nyla swished her drink around. "It is original and energetic."

"You guys are nuts," groaned Todd. "If that's art, I'm Sherlock Holmes."

"Now mind you," continued Nyla, "I'm not saying that Andrew himself doesn't remind me of something that just came out of a junk pile."

"Shame on both of you," Ned shook his head. "No respect for the working class."

"I might have some respect for him if he *was* from the working class, but he's not. He's from a wealthy family. I'm sure he's had an education and opportunities handed to him with a smile. And what does he do? He pisses them away."

"Well," remarked Nyla, "if you had a father like Abel Halpern, you might have turned out all jumbled up too."

"Using your father as an excuse for messing up your life doesn't cut it with me." Todd's voice had a harsh edge on it. Nyla and Ned looked at him.

"Looks like you could use another drink, Detective Forrest," Ned suggested, attempting to lighten things up.

"Oh, I'll get them this time." Nyla was already on her feet. "You rationed the gin like we were still under Prohibition, Ned."

"So how did the afternoon go?" Ned asked.

"Interesting, very interesting," Todd said. "I went over to the Palm Garden Court and had a little chat with some of the staff about Takahashi's squabble with Abel Halpern. Takahashi not only argued with him and threw a few blows, but he also threatened to kill him in front of twenty or thirty witnesses."

"Sounds like he has a bit of a temper."

"You know, according to the staff, he doesn't. He comes in there quite often and is always quiet and polite, never causes trouble, and the staff likes him because he's a real good tipper."

"Hmm," Ned reflected, "a quiet but explosive personality."

"I'm thinking the same thing. It worries me when the quiet and polite types go over the edge. They can be real dangerous. I'm questioning him in the morning and counting on you being there."

"Hey, guess what?" Nyla returned with the drinks. "Ned's going out to dinner with Mina."

"Talk about dangerous," Todd laughed. "How'd you get hog-tied into that one?"

"Hog-tied," repeated Ned. "Another quaint American expression."

"They're going to talk about the play," retorted Nyla. "And I don't think the way you always talk about my sister is so funny."

"Yes, dear," said Todd.

"In about one minute, you're going to get a shirt full of ice cubes," Nyla threatened.

"And don't mind me, I thrive on domestic disputes," Ned winked.

"Don't say anymore, dear," Todd warned. "You could end up as a character in one of his plays."

"No," Nyla said as she sank into the chair. "I think you're a much more interesting character, Todd, or at least more of a character."

WHAT GIRLS KNOW

T HAT NIGHT MINA and Ned sat together in a second-floor Chinatown restaurant waiting for Mina's friend, Cecily Chang. Cecily
sold antiques and fireworks, and Mina was counting on her to help
find out about the nitroglycerin. Ned had insisted that Mina do the
ordering.

"You won't accuse me later of being bossy, will you?" Mina looked
at him over the menu.

"Never," smiled Ned, "in fact, I'm quite used to being bullied
about by women. I rather enjoy it."

Mina laughed, shook her head, and then went back to scanning
the menu. She ordered the house chow mein, roast duck, stuffed
tofu, deep-fried oysters, shrimp in ginger and onion sauce, cold ginger chicken, crisp won tons, and rice. Ned thought it was quite a bit
of food for three people, but Mina assured him that none of it would
go to waste. A waitress in black pants and a red silk blouse served
them some tea. The restaurant was noisy, and the clack and clatter of
pots and pans, as well as searing noises and loud voices, trumpeted
into the dining room each time a waiter or waitress went through the
swinging kitchen doors.

"Your sister said you covered the Massie Case for a mainland
newspaper." Ned sipped his hot tea with care.

"That was an exercise I'll never forget." Mina looked away. "It was pretty ugly. People from the mainland think they can come here and treat island people like we just came out of the caves."

"I think there were quite a few nasty things written about Hawai'i in the American press."

"Now that was the worst thing about the case, the sickening racial prejudice that was directed at the islands. It popped right into everyone's face here, and I think it made a lot of us realize that people outside of Hawai'i, on the U.S. mainland, really view us as some kind of foreign colony." Mina poured herself another cup of tea. "I should tell you what I found out at the museum before Cecily gets here." She seemed eager to change the subject.

"Do tell," said Ned as he sipped his tea.

"Well, there is a regular night watchman, but a phony memo was left in his box a few days before giving him the night off. Also, the librarian, Mrs. Kelly, said Halpern was spending tons of time in the archives researching something. She didn't know what because he insisted on going straight into the collections himself and wouldn't let the staff help him. It seems like they all hated him. No one I talked to had a nice thing say about him. Oh yeah, and there *was* nitroglycerin used in the break in."

"And how did you know that was a sure thing? You don't have access to Todd's reports."

"I know that locksmith who was working on the door. That's Shige, and he's my friend."

The waitress brought a bowl of crisp won tons, and right away Mina set to work mixing hot mustard and shoyu together in the condiment dish. Ned was looking at the large dragon painted on the wall whose tail curved and curled over the arched doorway, framing people waiting to be seated in its sinuous curves. As Ned sipped his tea and studied the dragon, a young woman appeared in the doorway. She looked both faintly Chinese and Polynesian. She was dressed in a pretty dark blue skirt and a lacy collared white blouse. On her head, sitting at a jaunty angle over her jet-black, bobbed hair, was a blue French beret with a red pompom. She looked around, spotted Mina and headed over to their table. Mina stood up to hug her and introduced Ned. They sat down, and Mina poured Cecily some tea.

"I'm sure your father gave you that hat," Mina laughed.

"Oh God," Cecily snatched it off. "He insisted I wear it."

"Cecily's father is a Francophile," Mina reported.

"Vive la France." Cecily waved her beret. "The household slogan. Dad's gotten even worse about what he cooks now—baguettes, omelets, soufflés, coq au vin, cassoulet, all these rich sauces. It's driving mom and me crazy. You don't know how happy I am to be eating Chinese food."

"You're not joking about his interest in France, then?" Ned was fascinated.

"Joking? He's been taking these French lessons from a tutor for over a year, and now he's started to speak to us in French. We have no idea what he's talking about half the time, and he thinks it's so funny."

The food began to arrive at the table, and Ned figured out quickly, by watching the two women eat, that Mina had not overordered. Both of them had hearty appetites. In between the plate passing and exclamations of delight, Ned learned that Cecily's mother was Hawaiian and had begun a business with her father, Wing Chang, just after their marriage. Mr. Chang was never very interested in the antique business, and soon Mrs. Chang was handling it by herself. She enjoyed running the business and had made quite a success of it. Mr. Chang kept the home front, which was just above the store, and wrote poetry and short stories. His work was often published in better literary magazines. When Cecily, their only child, graduated from high school, she refused to go to college and instead went right to work for her mother while taking business classes at night. It was Cecily, Ned discovered, who persuaded her mother to venture into selling fireworks. It had proven very profitable, and now Cecily was an expert on all kinds of explosives. She and her mother were considering becoming the Honolulu representatives for a company that made dynamite.

"But dynamite," Cecily reported, as she helped herself to another won ton, "is nowhere near as impressive an explosive as nitroglycerin, and totally unnecessary for breaking into a gallery. Your burglar must have wanted to make a statement."

"How do you think, Cecily, one would get such a thing here?" Ned asked.

"It would be difficult," Cecily answered. "Either with special permits and everything, or illegally. I'd put my money on the latter since it was used in a crime. And I'll tell you something else, too. I've heard that Halpern was involved in some fishy antiques operation."

"What? How do you know?" Mina's interest was aroused.

"On and off over the last couple of years, I've heard rumors. Chinatown is full of gossip, and some of it turns out to be true. Anyway, the rumor is, this valuable stuff, possibly stolen, from all over Asia, arrives from Japan on the sly, without duty being paid or going through customs. Most of it supposedly gets sold to mainland buyers. You know, we're an American port. If goods originate here, there's no duty, no customs."

"I'm sure, being in the museum business, Halpern knew his artifacts and antiques," Ned commented.

"Someone else was in on it too, most likely someone who had contacts in Japan. At least that's part of the rumor." Cecily was surveying what was left on the table.

"Do you know any more?" Mina asked.

"Some," smiled Cecily. Her dark eyes sparkled. "Are either of you going to eat that last oyster?"

Mina and Ned shook their heads.

"All I know," continued Cecily, "is that they say these things come in on all different kinds of ships, sometimes tankers, sometimes freighters. It's unloaded offshore, at night, probably onto local fishing boats or something. You know, I'm guessing it must be stuff like porcelain, jade, ivory, smaller items, but who knows? The next thing that happens is it gets stored somewhere until it goes to the States, and because we're a territory, there's no red tape. Pieces could even be sold here too. There's lots of collectors who don't care how things get to be on the market. And like Ned says, because Halpern's in the museum business, he must have quite a few contacts on the mainland. Didn't he used to work in Chicago?"

"I think so," said Mina in a muffled voice. She'd just started to eat the last won ton.

"I'll ask around about the nitro," volunteered Cecily. "See what I can dig up and call you."

"We would really appreciate it, Ceci," Mina said.

"I have a feeling, you should be careful, too." Ned looked at her. "Someone has been killed, and if the wrong person thought you were too curious—"

"Oh, don't worry," Cecily waved her hand. "I know everyone in Chinatown. We're a tight community. I know how to be careful. Say Mina? Do you have some change? I need to make a phone call."

"Anyone I know?" Mina winked.

"No," frowned Cecily, "and I don't want my father to know about him either. He isn't Chinese or French. Can you imagine how excited Dad would be if I found someone who was both?"

Mina reached into her purse and brought out a little flower made of leather that unfolded to reveal a number of coins. Cecily took one, and Ned commented on the clever coin purse. Mina showed him how it unfolded and closed up again when you put pressure on the folds. Ned unfolded it once and looked at the coins. He couldn't help but notice several large, bright sequins mixed in with the money. He lifted one out.

"You won't be able to buy much with these, will you?" He looked at Mina.

"Oh, those fell off my costume," Mina said. "I was going to sew them back on, but I got lazy."

Cecily came back to the table and looked at the empty plates. "Let's go have some dessert at that coffee shop down the street. Wouldn't you love a piece of pecan pie?"

Ned thought the last thing he would like to eat just now would be pecan pie, but he found himself walking the few blocks to a small café near the waterfront. Ned watched and drank coffee as Cecily and Mina devoured big pieces of pie smothered in ice cream. He couldn't understand why they both weren't fat. Cecily's mysterious friend appeared, and she introduced him as Tom. Well dressed and polite, he whisked Cecily out the door and into a waiting automobile. Mina ate the last bite of pie, wiped her mouth with her napkin and sat back in her chair.

"Are you quite full now, Miss Beckwith?" Ned laughed.

"I know. I look like a terrible glutton who deserves to weigh a million pounds, but if I don't keep eating I turn into an absolute twig."

"Some people would say that was not fair."

"It was food that began my friendship with Cecily in the fourth grade. We both went to Punahou. Anyway, we discovered we were the same about food. If we didn't eat twice as much as other kids, we just faded away."

"Is Nyla the same?"

"No. I mean, she never gets fat, but she doesn't have to eat a lot. She's not a loser like me." She laughed at her own joke. "Hey, how would you like a look at the cottage you're moving into tomorrow? I have some things to return to Nyla. We could swing by there before I drop you off."

"I would love a preview of my new abode."

As they drove along Ala Moana Boulevard toward Waikīkī, Ned noticed a vast expanse of trees and grass on the seaside of the roadway.

"That's our new seventy-six-acre Moana Park, with a great beach, built with Roosevelt's New Deal work funds," Mina said. "The president dedicated it himself last summer."

"I'm impressed with how large it is."

"I wonder if it will ever catch on." She sounded skeptical. "I wonder if people in the city will ever use it."

Mina turned on Kalākaua Avenue and headed toward Waikīkī. Ned gazed out the window, searching for familiar landmarks that he remembered from his previous visits to the islands. Mina became lost in her own thoughts, and they both rode along, comfortable in the silence. Ned recognized the pink Royal Hawaiian Hotel, with its expansive front gardens and coconut trees that were said to be the remnants of one of the oldest coconut groves in the islands. The Moana Hotel, now a favorite haunt of the glamorous set, stood tall and white as men in crisp uniforms at the porte cochere opened the doors of expensive automobiles. They passed by Kapiʻolani Park and began to round Diamond Head. A low white coral wall bordered the road on the right and soon Ned saw the lighthouse that shone above the cliffs just outside the car window. The sound of the surf and the salt smell of the sea permeated the air. The vista opened up and for a few minutes Ned could see the Pacific spreading out before him and the moon reflecting a path of light over the water. Just past the light-house, the paved road continued around the crater, but Mina turned onto a small one-lane side street, and then down a driveway toward the sea. A tall hedge in the front of the property concealed the yard from the street. In the dark, Ned could make out a long grassy lawn and a garage and parking area. She stopped the car, and they walked along a path leading to a wide hau tree arbor. On either side of the arbor were two identical wooden bungalows. The houses were sheltered by tall, hipped roofs, and surrounded with generous verandas. Pretty white pillars supported the eaves of the roof, and large windows promised that the houses could make the most of any breeze. A low hedge of naupaka separated the houses from the beach and the ocean.

"My grandmother, my mother's mother, gave this land to my mother the day we were born." Mina looked up at the night sky. "She said it was for Nyla and me. It had been in her family for a long time, and we were her first grandchildren."

"Were these houses here?" Ned asked.

"No, my father built them much later. We used to come here when we were kids and sleep in a tent. It was so much fun. The name of this place is Ka'alāwai. After the overthrow of the Hawaiian monarchy, when the loyal subjects of the queen decided to stage a rebellion, they landed their arms on this beach. My grandmother remembers being here."

"In other words, Mina," Ned smiled, "you're living in rebel territory."

"That's right," she laughed. "And you will too. Come on, I'll show you your new home. Todd and Nyla don't use this place much."

Ned followed Mina into the house. As she turned on a light, he made a mental note that the switch was on the left. To the right was a large room that spanned half of the house and included a kitchen, partitioned off by a low counter, a dining area, and a living room. The high ceiling created a feeling of space, and french doors could be opened to extend the living area onto the veranda. To the left there was a wall and a central hallway that led to three airy rooms and a bathroom. Each bedroom also had doors that could open onto the veranda. Warm-colored lauhala mats covered the floors, and in the living room the comfortable rattan furniture created a peaceful, tropical atmosphere.

"Everything's here," said Mina as she opened and closed the kitchen cabinets so Ned could catch a glimpse of their contents. "All you need to do is unpack your clothes and make a stop at the grocery store. If you can cook, that is."

"I can cook a little," Ned answered as he surveyed the stove. "Can you?"

"A little," she said with no hesitation. "Would you like to see my house? I have to pick up Nyla's clothes."

Mina's house was laid out in a mirror image of Nyla's, but it was decorated in a much more personal way. Interesting paintings, predominately island landscapes, hung on the walls. A spectacular scene of a volcanic eruption at night captured Ned's attention. The same kind of rattan furniture filled the living room but was accented with colorful throw cushions. Perhaps the nicest thing, he thought, was the profusion of green plants, placed in an effortless way around the room. He was looking at a group of framed photos on a corner shelf when Mina disappeared into one of the bedrooms. He recognized one of Nyla and Mina with people whom he assumed were their maternal grandparents, as the elderly couple were Polynesian, and he thought about his own grandmother and grandfather in Āpia whom he planned to visit after his stay in Hawaii. There was another picture of Todd and Nyla on their wedding day, and next to that was a small oval of an distinctive, handsome young man on a horse. Even from the photograph, his smile radiated a bright energy that caught Ned's attention. Mina entered the room with several dresses on hangers.

"Looking at the rogues gallery, I see," she observed.

"I like old photos," he said, "Is this your brother? This dashing young man on the horse? Nyla's told me about your family's ranch."

"Yes, my father comes from a ranch on the big island, but that dashing young man was my husband."

Ned couldn't disguise his surprise. There was an awkward moment of silence. "I didn't know," he said as if he'd just intruded.

"He's dead," Mina said with no emotion. "He died in a car accident a few months after we were married."

"I'm sorry. It must have been terrible for you. I had no idea."

"Of course you wouldn't. Nobody talks about it, and I changed my name back to Beckwith. I wanted to forget."

"I understand," he said. There was another awkward moment of silence in which Ned felt the subject was much more painful and complicated than she was able to say. "So," he said, "I guess you and your sister don't differ too much on your tastes in fashion."

"What?" Mina looked at him. "Oh, the clothes. Right. It's one of the advantages of having an identical twin. Your wardrobe can be twice as big."

Mina drove Ned back up to Maunalani Heights, and halfway up the hill it began to drizzle. "You know," she said. "I bet Halpern was in on stealing the portrait and things went wrong."

"It's possible," Ned agreed, "but there's not enough evidence to say for sure."

"Not yet."

"Tomorrow, we're questioning Sam Takahashi," Ned said.

"Did you know he's a talented architect?"

"I didn't."

"I find it hard to believe he could do something like that," Mina sighed, "but I guess you can never tell what's in a man's heart."

"What's in a man's heart?"

"I mean," said Mina, "what he's capable of."

Mina pulled into the driveway and asked Ned to take in Nyla's clothes. She said she was tired and wanted to go straight home. When Ned walked into the kitchen, Todd was pouring a nightcap.

"Hmm," mused Todd, "Mina take you shopping for a new look?"

"You're just envious, Detective Forrest," Ned replied, "Because you'll never have my figure."

9

QUESTIONS

NED SAT ON the sofa in Todd's office stirring a cup of coffee when Sam Takahashi entered the room. Todd would be doing the questioning, and Ned thought it best to be unobtrusive. Sam was tall and lean, and Ned couldn't help but notice that Sam's blazer and shirt were impeccably tailored. His slacks showed not one wrinkle, and his hair was perfectly cut and groomed.

"I'm sure you know why we want to talk to you about Halpern's murder." Todd sat behind his desk.

"I'm sure I do." Sam Takahashi sat across from him.

"This is Ned Manusia who's representing the British Museum. He'll just be observing. The museum is very concerned about the recovery of the portrait. Have you read about the portrait?"

"I have," said Sam. "Do you mind if I smoke during this conversation?"

"Please," Todd responded as he pushed a round glass ashtray toward Sam.

Sam Takahashi reached into his jacket pocket and took out an engraved silver cigarette case. His long, tapered fingers opened the case and took out a cigarette. He lit it with a matching silver lighter.

"I heard you and Halpern had a quarrel a few days before he was murdered."

"We did."

"I heard you threatened to kill him." Todd's voice got a little quieter.

"I was angry," Sam shrugged. "I lost my temper. It was something I said in the heat of the moment, and after I'd had a few drinks."

"I guess you didn't like the man." Todd looked straight at Sam.

"That man did everything he could to hold back people in the Japanese community and to whip up uncalled-for fear and suspicion against us. My grandparents came here in 1885. They were some of the first Japanese immigrants to Hawai'i. They had to struggle to make a life here, and my parents had to work hard too. I'm an American citizen, just like you. I work. I pay taxes. I contribute to the community, and I'm not a second-class citizen or person because I'm Japanese." Sam held his tension in check.

"I know about the Kama'āina Club business." Todd leaned forward.

"It wasn't just that he was prejudiced. He was a born bully. He wasn't happy unless he was shoving other people around."

"A bully?" Todd's eyebrows rose.

"He liked to prey on the weak." There was the slightest tremor in his voice. "On people he thought were weaker than he was."

"But you weren't one of those people."

"Look," Sam said as he crushed out his cigarette, "I think I've answered your question about not liking the man."

"All right," said Todd. "Where were you on New Year's Eve between about ten and say one-thirty or two?"

"I went for a drive."

"On New Year's Eve?"

"I wanted to be alone. I drove from Honolulu around to Waimānalo and then over to Kailua. I walked on the beach."

"Was anyone with you?"

"No, I was by myself."

"I guess you realize," Todd turned in his chair, "that you have no alibi, no witnesses to confirm what you were doing at the time of Abel Halpern's murder."

"I don't need an alibi or witnesses." Sam was calm and serious. "Because I had nothing to do with his murder."

Todd started to ask Sam other questions, like where he worked and lived, little details about his life. Ned tried to pay attention, but his mind kept wandering back to the night before. He saw Mina standing in her house by the photos. He tried to recapture the brief moment, and the way she looked as she told him about her husband and his death. As if examining a photo of his own, he searched his memory and tried to re-create how she appeared in that instant. There was something so remote and distant in her look—as if she were standing in an open doorway at the end of a long hall, and at any moment, she could turn, walk off, and disappear. He wanted to know how she felt, but saw that any attempt to try to unmask her real feelings on the subject would be expertly repelled. Todd's voice cut into his thoughts.

"I need to tell you, Sam," Todd said, shaking his head, "it looks bad—you having a fight and threatening to kill him."

"I know how it *looks*," retorted Sam, who was now showing his nervousness, "but I had nothing to do with his death, and you don't have any *real* evidence to the contrary, do you?"

"No," smiled Todd, "I don't. But I have to question anyone who might have had a reason to kill Abel Halpern. Thank you for cooperating."

"So we're finished then?"

"That's right." Todd still sat smiling in his chair.

Sam stood up and turned to Ned. "I finally get to meet you, Mr. Manusia, although not under the best circumstances."

"Please, call me Ned."

"I'll be seeing you again at the rehearsal tonight," Sam went on. "I designed the set for the play."

"Oh yes," Ned remembered. "Johnny Knight did mention that an architect had volunteered to design the set." Over Sam's shoulder, Ned could see Todd shaking his head.

"Well, I hope you like it. I tried to capture a certain timelessness." Sam sounded sincere. "I admire the play so much."

"Well, thank you. I'll be looking forward to seeing the design this evening." Even though he could be a murderer, Ned felt a certain affinity for the man.

Nyla sat with Mina on the veranda of Mina's bungalow. They were sipping iced tea and waiting for Ned to arrive. Nyla had arranged to meet Ned at the bungalows and then take him to pick up her brother's car. Ned had packed up his things and put them in Nyla's car before he and Todd left that morning, and she had brought them down to the bungalow and unpacked them. She had even ordered a grocery delivery for Ned. After it arrived, she put everything away.

"Don't you think it's interesting that you like to take care of people, and I like to see people take care of themselves? Well, in most instances that's what I like." Mina put her feet up on an old wooden outdoor table.

"Do you think I overdid it with ordering the groceries? Is that what you're trying to say?" Nyla looked at her over her sunglasses.

"No, I was just thinking that it would have never even crossed my mind to do that."

"Maybe we have two separate but equal roles in life. You torment them, and I baby them. Men, I mean."

"I never torment men, unless they ask for it."

"Are you going to torment Ned?" Nyla was lying on a steamer chair and still looking at her sister over her glasses.

"No, he's too much fun. I like him, as a friend, sister dear."

"Friendship has been known to blossom into romance, you know."

"Nyla, for the thousandth time, I don't want any romance in my life right now. I know that's a big disappointment to you, but that's how it is."

"Is Christian Hollister still asking you out?"

"Nyla, shut up about men, or I'll poison your next glass of iced tea."

"You want another glass?" Nyla sat up. "I do, let me get you one."

Mina watched her sister go into the house and then she turned and looked out toward the breaking waves. By the time Nyla returned a few minutes later with two fresh glasses of tea, Mina's face had clouded over.

"Oh dear," said Nyla, "you're thinking too hard again."

Mina looked at her sister. "You know, Nyla, our family comes first with me."

"What?" Nyla looked at her. "What does that mean?"

"It means if anything were wrong, I would close ranks with you."

"With me?" Nyla tilted her head to the side.

"If anything was up, I mean, if you were in some kind of jam, you know you could always count on me."

"Don't be silly, Mina. I'm not in any kind of jam."

Mina fell silent and turned again to survey the ocean. It irritated her when Nyla hid things from her. She always knew, but now that they were grown up, there were boundaries of privacy. Mina remembered that when they were very young, talking to Nyla was like talking to some part of herself, as if she and Nyla were two branches of a single tree, connected by an invisible trunk. As time went on they grew in opposite directions, but sometimes the residue of that early connection surfaced in feelings, ideas, dreams, and certain unmistakable cues that only they understood.

"Well oh well, our birthday's almost here, Mina, another year older." Nyla said it in a singsong voice.

"Oh God," groaned Mina as she turned toward Nyla and arched her eyebrows, "pretty soon we'll be two old hags blowing out candles with no teeth."

They looked at each other, and convulsed with laughter. They didn't hear Ned wander in. He had dismissed his cab at the top of the driveway and walked down.

"Did I miss something?" He smiled at the two of them, but they just kept laughing.

"My sister," Nyla finally said to Ned, "has a truly degraded imagination." Nyla stood up. "Come on, Ned, let's go get my brother's car for you. It's a wonderful '32 Ford Victoria sedan, much more of a lady than Mina."

DRAMAS UNFOLD

A CRIMSON SKY was fading into night as Ned arrived at the theatre. He was returning for the evening rehearsal. Earlier, after picking up the car with Nyla, he'd met with the director, Johnny Knight, at a café where he'd made it clear that he didn't want to take a big role in directing the play but would be available if Johnny needed help. Ned explained that he would come to the first few rehearsals, see the process get off the ground and then leave Johnny to do the job without any interference. He had noticed a marked look of relief on Johnny's face after announcing his intentions. Ned had seen playwrights become a pain for the director by trying to exercise control over every little aspect of the production, but as long as things looked like they were off to a solid start, he preferred to step out of the way. Johnny Knight was young, just out of college, but he was capable and passionate about his work. The cast of characters that Knight had assembled, and their various connections to the murder, was an astounding coincidence. Or was it? This play itself was all about a convergence of fate, and over and over again fate seemed to cast its hand into people's lives in the most unexpected ways.

The Ali'i Theatre was situated on a hill in the Honolulu suburb of Kaimukī, above the fire station. The hill was the high remnant of a volcanic vent, and commanded a panoramic view of the city and Waikīkī. As Ned crossed the parking area behind the theatre, he noticed a Hawaiian man, dressed in a chauffeur's uniform, smoking a cigarette and leaning against an expensive automobile.

"Good evening," Ned stopped to speak to him.

"Good evening, sir," the man nodded.

"Beautiful sunset, isn't it?" Ned smiled.

"Very nice," the man responded. "Always nice around this time of the year on this side of the island, because the sun sets right off Waikīkī."

"You must be Mr. Hollister's driver," Ned guessed.

"Kimo Kalewa." He extended his hand.

"Ned Manusia." They shook hands.

"Yep. Five years I been driving for him. You must be the writer fellow from England. He was telling me all about you. How you were born in Sāmoa."

"It's my accent, isn't it?"

"Not many people around here talk like you. Cigarette?" Kimo proffered a pack of Lucky Strikes.

"No thanks," Ned waved his hand. "This automobile is a real beauty, isn't she?"

"A 1930 Graham-Paige four-door sedan. You should see her on the open road. I tell you! Like driving on a cloud. Mr. Hollister has an Auburn Boat Tail Speedster too, 1933. That's the one he likes to drive himself."

"Good man, Chris Hollister." Ned hoped for information.

"He's the nicest man I ever worked for. He never makes you feel like, like you're his servant. You know, last year, when my son needed an operation on his bad leg, Mr. Hollister fixed everything up for us at the Shriner's Hospital. Very nice man."

Ned couldn't help but feel a little disappointed. After hearing the tone of voice Hollister had used while praising Mina, Ned was somehow hoping that Hollister with all his money and good looks would turn out to be a cad. "Well, it was nice meeting you. I guess I better get back to work."

"Aloha," Kimo answered, touching the brim of his cap.

As Ned walked up to the backstage entrance, an Asian woman was struggling to open the door. Ned assumed that she would be doing some cleaning, as she held a mop, a broom, and a bucket full of various bottles. He came to her rescue and held the door open for her.

"Oh, thank you," she mumbled without looking up at him.

"My pleasure," he returned.

Inside, the theater was a hive of activity. The stage crew was taking down lights and putting away the remnants of the set from the last production. The new cast was milling around, and several women with armloads of costumes were headed for the dressing rooms.

Johnny Knight began to call the cast and crew together on the stage. His brown eyes were lit with excitement. When everyone was assembled, Martha Klein, the vice president of the theatre's board of directors, gave a welcoming speech on behalf of the board. Next, Johnny Knight also gave a genuine welcome, said a bit about the creative artistry of the play, and emphasized his confidence in the cast. He introduced Ned and asked each of the cast and crewmembers to say a little bit about themselves. He then passed out the roster of names.

CAST:

Armand	Christian Hollister
Anna	Sheila Halpern
Daniel	Jerry McVay
Charles	James Russell
Charmion	Kīnaʻu Kelly
The Muse	Nyla Forrest

CREW:

Set Design	Samuel Takahashi
Set Construction	Eric Hamada, Jay Stevens, Steve Woo, Kalani Kelly
Lighting Design	Andrew Halpern
Board Operators	J. P. Burns, Dukie Tanaka
Costumes	Bridget McCandless
Sound	Brian Lee

The next hour was spent taking care of business. The cast went to the men's and women's dressing rooms to be measured for costumes and to try some things on for size. Ned and Johnny went over the set design with Sam, while Andrew Halpern lurked around them, listening, but remaining aloof while waiting for his turn to discuss the lighting plot. Mina was sitting in the first row of the audience going over some notes when she was told she had a phone call. There were several extensions throughout the theatre, and she decided to walk up to the lobby where it was quiet. When she picked up the receiver, all she could hear was some static and clicking noises. "Hello? Is some one there?"

"My God, Mina!" A faint voice replied at the other end.

"Who is this? I can hardly hear you?"

"It's me! Cecily." Her voice became a little more audible. "I'm calling from a pay phone with a lousy connection. You won't believe what I just found out about the nitro! Can you come over tonight?"

"We won't be through until about nine." Mina was almost shouting.

"Come to the shop. I'll get Dad to make some dessert. So long as you don't mind crêpes."

"Are you kidding?"

"Mina, you just won't believe it. Listen, I have to go, my cab's here. I just had to call."

"Okay, bye, Ceci."

Mina hung up the phone and went into the women's lounge just off the lobby. She nearly collided with the Asian cleaning woman, who was just leaving the lounge with her broom, mop, and bucket. Mina smiled at her, and the woman nodded but averted her eyes and rushed quickly into the auditorium. There were still about forty-five minutes until the cast was to reassemble and read the first act, and Mina thought she would rest for just a few minutes. The spacious lounge was quiet and empty. It was decorated with velvety flowered wallpaper and a thick red carpet. A long counter with mirrors occupied one wall, and on the opposite side sat two large sofas and a couple of easy chairs. Mina lay down on one of the comfortable sofas. She closed her eyes and began to drift off. She couldn't tell if five or fifteen minutes had passed in this half sleep, but she woke up to the sound of voices just outside the lounge door.

"Be quiet." It was a woman's voice. "Someone will hear you."

"He was hitting you, wasn't he?" the man said.

"Lower your voice," the woman pleaded.

"Goddamn it! Why did you let him do that?"

"Please stop it. It's over now."

"Why didn't you do something? Why do you have to be so god-damn weak?"

"I don't know. I don't know." The woman burst into sobs.

There was a pause, a short silence, and then Mina heard another man.

"What have you been saying to her? Why don't you leave her alone?"

"You're the one who should leave damn well alone, mister." The first voice was full of menace.

"Shut up both of you," said the woman. "Just shut up and leave me alone."

The lounge door flew open, and Sheila Halpern burst in. She threw herself into one of the lounge chairs without noticing Mina, and started sobbing.

"Are you all right Sheila?" Mina's voice made Sheila start.

"I didn't see you there." Sheila tried to control herself.

"Can I do something for you?" Mina asked.

"No, I'll be fine," mumbled Sheila. "I just need a few minutes alone."

"Of course, you do." Mina couldn't help but see that under Sheila's running makeup there were bruises. Mina got up and quietly left. The lobby stood hollow and empty, and she went back into the theatre.

The cast read through the first act, and Mina took some notes for publicity. With Hollister in the cast, she was sure the paper would run a big story just before the opening. They finished the read-through, and Johnny let the cast go home with the warning that future rehearsals would be much longer. Ned met for about half an hour with Johnny, and by nine o'clock Mina and Ned were on their way to Chinatown to meet Cecily. Mina told Ned about the argument she'd overheard.

"And that's not all," Mina continued. "Sheila's makeup was smeared because she was crying. I'm sure I saw bruises on her face. I think she has a black eye, maybe two."

"I saw that when we interviewed her. I hate men who hit women," Ned said with disgust.

Mina pulled the car up to the sidewalk in front of the Changs' store on Nuʻuanu Street. The shop itself was deep, and a faint light shone from the interior. Mina led Ned down the side alley to the back door. Red brick walls lined the alley, and the ground felt as if it had rained in the last few hours. Mina was about to knock on the door when she noticed that it was ajar.

"This is unusual," she remarked. "It's always locked."

Mina and Ned stepped in to a large storeroom with piled boxes and old furniture, some of it broken, some in good condition, but all arranged in an orderly fashion.

"I don't like the way this room feels," Ned said as he tried to get his bearings.

To the right was a staircase that led to a door to the upper floor. Across the room on the left was another door that led to the office and the shop.

"Cecily, we're here," Mina called, but there was no answer. "That's funny," Mina said as she moved toward the shop door. She was about to open it, but Ned put his hand on her shoulder.

"Wait a minute," he whispered. "I'm having a very bad feeling about this."

"Oh God, Cecily," Mina cried out, and in an instant she was through the door, and running to the office. There was no one there, but a burning cigarette, Cecily's brand, was in the ashtray. Its ash was almost whole. Mina turned and saw that Ned had gone into the shop. He was kneeling beside a body on the floor. It was Cecily, and she looked lifeless.

Mina gasped. "Is she?"

"She's still breathing, but it looks like she has a head injury. Call an ambulance."

Mina ran into the office, called, and then dashed upstairs to get Mr. and Mrs. Chang. A flurry of activity followed with blankets, an ambulance that arrived quickly, and the police. It was apparent that the front door of the store had been jimmied by an expert. The attacker had entered, struck, and let himself out into the alley minutes before Ned and Mina's arrival. The police were convinced that a burglar had walked in on Cecily. Cecily's mother rode to the hospital with her daughter in the ambulance. Mr. Chang and Mina followed in the car, and Ned was instructed to stay at the Chang residence until the police left, and to wait for Mina upstairs.

"It's lucky you two were invited for dessert," the officer in charge said. "I guess you got here just in time."

"If only we'd arrived sooner," said Ned, "perhaps this could have been prevented."

"Haven't I seen you before?"

"You may have. I'm a friend of Detective Forrest."

"Oh right," said the officer. "You're the guy from England with the portraits. You must have a great impression of our little city by now—theft, murder, attacks in the night."

"Is it quite common in this part of town?" Ned asked.

"Robbery isn't uncommon, but assault, that's much less common, and this section of Chinatown is usually pretty quiet. All the action takes place closer to the river. Doesn't look like there was much of a struggle, though. She must have surprised him, he panicked and clobbered her, realized he'd done something serious, and ran. Anyway, that's how it looks to me."

"It does look that way," nodded Ned.

After the police left, Ned went upstairs to the Changs' living quarters. On the first level above the shop was a large living room that overlooked the street, a dining room, and a spacious kitchen. The decor stood out in bright contrast to the dark antique shop beneath. There was no trace of Asia. Instead, it was bright and looked rural European. There were soft creamy walls, barn-wood flooring, a kind of half-timber interior motif, and solid country furniture. A farmhouse table provided a centerpiece for the kitchen, where gleaming copper pots and pans were suspended above an impressive stovetop. Ned surmised that the second staircase he found led upstairs to the bedrooms.

He sat in one of the comfortable chairs in the living room and mused about how much had happened in the last few weeks. He thought again about Mina and the way she had looked just before she rushed in to look for Cecily. He didn't want to think about the attack tonight, so he forced himself to reflect on the rehearsal. Chris

Hollister's reading was exceptional, and his voice was much more powerful than Ned had expected. It had been one of the best readings of the character he'd ever heard in amateur or professional circles. Nyla was very strong too. She could have a successful career as a professional actress if she chose. Sam Takahashi's design was striking, although Johnny confided in Ned that he wasn't sure of the technical crew's ability to build such an artistic set. He wondered if these gifted people got frustrated or bored in Honolulu, where their talents might be underappreciated, or worse, unnoticed. A wave of exhaustion swept over him. His eyes closed, and he faded into sleep like a thinning cloud. He dreamt about Mina and Nyla arguing over an article of clothing. Nyla was angry with Mina because a dress she had loaned her now had irises all over it instead of roses. Nyla was furiously demanding to know where Mina had hidden the roses. She turned to Ned to find out, but Ned said he didn't know because he was busy looking for some lost sequins. Nyla aggressively grabbed him by the arm and began to shake him.

"Ned, we're back." A soft voice had drifted into his dream. He opened his eyes to see Mina standing there, looking pale and tired.

"How is she?" he asked, still not quite awake.

"She's in a coma, and they can't say what will happen. Her mother is staying with her. Uncle Wing is making coffee in the kitchen. Listen, Ned, I think we have to tell him what Cecily was doing. I owe it to him. If I hadn't—"

"You couldn't have known someone would attack her." Ned put his hand on Mina's wrist. "I asked her to be very careful, don't you remember?"

"Yes, but I should have realized," said Mina. "I should have seen the danger."

"Don't blame yourself for not being clairvoyant. It's fruitless, and it wastes time."

They went into the kitchen and sat down at the long wooden table. Wing Chang placed steaming cups of coffee in front of them and plates of crêpes suzette. "No sense in wasting good food," he said as he sat down to eat with them.

"Thank you, Mr. Chang," Ned said.

"Please, call me Uncle Wing, like Mina does."

The three of them ate their dessert and drank the strong, rich coffee. Mina regained some of her color. After they finished, Uncle Wing cleared the plates, poured everyone a second cup, and sat back down.

"So Mina," Uncle Wing said, "what were you girls up to? Ever since you were kids, I could always tell when you two were up to something."

"I'm so sorry, Uncle Wing—" Mina couldn't continue.

"Listen," said Uncle Wing, "Cecily is a fighter, and she'll be right back with us. Now I want to know what was going on."

Relieved, Mina explained about Halpern's murder, the portrait, and the nitroglycerin. Uncle Wing listened and nodded. She also told him what Cecily had said about Halpern's smuggling antiques. Wing Chang showed no surprise.

"I just didn't know it would be so dangerous for her," said Mina.

"Someone," Uncle Wing began, "must have told something important to Cecily. I wonder who that unlucky person was. I wouldn't be surprised if there's another attack quite soon in Chinatown. Whoever is behind all of this is ruthless."

"And quick," added Ned.

"That's right," Mina reflected. "Cecily just called me early this evening. You know we had a bad connection, and there was quite a bit of interference on the phone."

"It would have been easy for someone at the theatre to listen in on your phone call," Ned said.

"I'll begin to ask questions around Chinatown," said Uncle Wing, "in a very discreet way, of course. I want this person punished."

"I think someone should be with Cecily at all times." Mina was so tired that she was staring at the table as she said it.

"I'll make sure she's well protected." Wing Chang looked at Mina. "You need to go home and get some sleep, both of you."

"I'll just go upstairs and rinse my face off before the drive home." Mina excused herself.

After she left the room, Ned said, "I suppose you're wondering why we didn't tell the police about this."

"In any other situation, I would," Chang said gravely. "But listen, there's something I want to tell you quickly. At your own discretion, you may share it with Mina. Her brother-in-law, Forrest, the detective, he knew about Halpern's illegal activities."

"Are you sure?" Ned was shell-shocked.

"I would never repeat something like that to you if I weren't sure. The Beckwiths are like family to my wife, and to me. Forrest was looking the other way. Maybe you should find out why."

They heard Mina's footsteps on the stairway and stopped talking. She asked Uncle Wing to call her as soon as there was any news about Cecily. Ned volunteered to drive home, and as soon as they were under way, Mina fell asleep leaning against the door. Ned looked at her sleeping face, and rolled down his window, letting the cool night air rush over him.

THE VALLEY OF SHADOWS

THE NEXT MORNING, at eleven o'clock, Ned and Todd were back at the Halpern residence in Nuʻuanu Valley, interviewing the housekeeper. Kikue Tsuruda stood about five feet four inches. She wore her hair pulled back in a tight bun. Ned guessed her to be between thirty-five and forty. She had circles under her eyes, and she looked a little pale and fragile. They sat at a table in an alcove off the immaculate tiled kitchen. The clear windows and crisp flowered curtains framed the untamed foliage of the back yard. In a spotless white uniform, Kikue sat with her hands folded on her lap, looking down at the table. Todd was thumbing through his little notebook, and Ned gazed out the window. All three of them felt a little uncomfortable with the physical closeness of the alcove, but no one suggested moving.

"Now, Mrs.—is it Miss or Mrs. Tsuruda?" Todd looked up from his notebook.

"Mrs., but I am a widow." She spoke the words with care.

"You understand about Mr. Halpern, your former employer, how he was killed, murdered?"

"Yes."

"So you understand why we're here?" Todd was doing his best to be low-key.

"To ask question."

"Yes, now, how long have you worked here?" Todd asked. Ned sat very still, doing his best to be unobtrusive.

"Three years. I come here after Mrs. Halpern die."

"I'm going to ask you to try to remember what happened here on New Year's Eve. Can you do that? Starting with when you got here in the morning."

"I come at seven. Make breakfast for Mr. Halpern. He leave at eight. At noon he come home for lunch. Leave at one thirty. I leave early at two because next day, holiday. Most days I leave at four. Please, you excuse me. I come right back."

"Yes, of course." Todd looked a little surprised.

Kikue stood up and left the room.

"What do you think is the problem?" Todd looked at Ned.

"She seems nervous," said Ned, "but I think she looks a bit ill too."

"Can you believe this yard?" Todd was looking out the window. "This family is disturbed."

Kikue returned. She asked Todd and Ned if they would like something to drink. They declined, but she helped herself to a glass of ginger ale before she sat down.

"Let's see," Todd again looked over his notes. "I'd like to ask you about the daughter, Sheila."

"Sheila?" Kikue seemed surprised.

"Yes, where was she?"

"Sheila stay in room. Come out to eat, go back to room. She always like that. Keep to herself."

"She didn't speak, maybe argue with her father?"

"She doesn't even see him. I never see them together that day."

"Did anyone else come here that day?"

Kikue hesitated.

"Mrs. Tsuruda?" Todd looked up at her.

"Son come at twelve thirty."

"Andrew Halpern?"

"Yes."

"And?"

After a brief silence she said, "He talk to sister. Then he talk to father. Fight. They always argue."

"Did you hear what they said? What they argued about?"

"I don't like to say. Andrew not really a bad boy. I think he only like to act bad and scare people. He always talk like that."

"What did they say?" Todd asked again.

"I don't want to say." Kikue shook her head.

"Mrs. Tsuruda," Todd said, "if you don't answer my questions here, I'll have to take you to the police station to be questioned."

"Okay, okay," she replied. "Only I don't like to talk about the family. I only hear loud part because I'm cleaning living room. They're in study. I hear Mr. Halpern yell, 'None of your goddamn business,' and then quiet for some time. Then I hear son yell, 'Don't do that or I . . . I kill you.' Then he slam door and leave house. But they always fight like that. Doesn't mean anything."

Todd paused for a moment, and asked for a glass of water. Kikue jumped to her feet as if relieved to get away from the table and the scrutiny of the two men. She returned with the water and just stood there, a few feet away from the table.

"Please sit down, Mrs. Tsuruda," said Todd. "I have just a few more questions to ask."

Kikue sat.

"Now, did you notice anything out of the ordinary going on with Mr. Halpern? Anything strange?"

Kikue began to have a very uneasy look on her face, as if a dark thought had just come to mind. "Phone calls," she said and turned to look at Todd with a frown.

"What were they?"

"Phone rings. I answer. Hang up. Happen over and over. If Mr. Halpern is home, phone ring, I answer, hang up. He tell me don't answer. He answer phone. But I can't hear what he say."

"How long had this been going on?"

"Two weeks, maybe."

"Any unusual visitors during that time?"

"No, same people always here, Sheila, Andrew, Mr. Hollister, they always talk about stamps. Mr. Hollister very nice man. Oh, was one other man came one day but he's . . ."

"He's what, Mrs. Tsuruda?"

"I think that time he's only delivery man because he has package.

He ask for Mr. Halpern. Mr. Halpern very upset with him. Tell him no just come here. Always call to arrange things. The man just say okay and laugh. He said it in a sassy way. Mr. Halpern turn around and walk inside."

"What did he look like?" Ned interjected.

"Oh, he's a tall local man, but he's very fair. Only you can tell he's local by the way he talks. He acts rough, but he has that kind of face, baby face, and he had a mark on his neck." She pointed to the left side of her neck. "Here, looks like a big heart, but it's a birthmark, I think."

"Do you know what was delivered?"

"No, small package."

"Now tell me, Mrs. Tsuruda," Todd continued, "how did Sheila and Mr. Halpern get along?"

Kikue's body stiffened. "I don't know. They never talk much so I don't know."

"But what was their relationship like? How did he treat her?"

"I don't know. I know nothing about that."

"How did you feel about Mr. Halpern?" Ned interjected.

"I need job and he pays me. I have nothing after my husband die."

"Will you continue to work here?" Ned asked.

"I don't know, maybe soon I leave. I don't know."

"Mrs. Tsuruda, have I seen you somewhere before?" Ned looked at her.

"Sometimes I clean theater at night. Lobby, restrooms, office, easy job, good pay. Sheila get job for me. I see you there with Mr. Knight."

"Jesus H—" Todd stopped himself.

Ned suppressed a smile, and remembered Mrs. Tsuruda as the woman he'd seen the night before at the backstage door.

"Well, thank you very much for your time, Mrs. Tsuruda. I think that will be all for today. If we have any more questions, we'll contact you." Todd stood up.

A surprised but relieved Mrs. Tsuruda showed them to the door.

"I think she looked peaky," remarked Ned as they walked to the car.

"I'll say," Todd agreed. "She's probably sick from having to work in that nuthouse."

"Nuthouse." Ned grinned as he repeated the word to himself.

"Yeah, nuthouse. Now, let's get out of here before we get a bit peaky too."

They got in the car and decided, because they were so close, they would take a little sightseeing detour to the Nu'uanu Pali lookout. The old two-lane road wove its way through a canopy of trees whose branches grew over one another like pairs of folded hands. Flowering vines hung in cascades from some of the trees, and as the road climbed slowly but steadily, the air became cool and fresh. For Ned, it was a welcome relief from the claustrophobic atmosphere of the Halpern residence. At one point the forest gave way to the open vista of a large reservoir, and the steep green valley walls rose up on either side like giant sentinels frozen forever in time. They bore the familiar feature of so many Hawaiian valleys—a succession of deep vertical grooves that looked as if they had been scratched or gouged out by the hand of a god. A light drizzle floated through the air. They rounded a turn, and Todd pointed out the famous "upside-down" falls. Water came pouring down only to be blown skyward by the strong winds that buffeted the upper valley. As they got closer to the Pali, Ned noticed that the treetops grew in twisted and bent shapes from their constant exposure to the heavy winds. They parked the car and ventured out. The wind intensified as they moved toward the lookout point. The Pali (or "cliff") was actually a pass in the Ko'olau Mountain range that divided the island of O'ahu's windward and leeward sides. From the leeward, or Nu'uanu Valley side, the assent to the pass was gradual, but at the pass, the mountains dropped away abruptly in sheer cliffs. In ancient times, a trail, steep and treacherous, served as the only way through these mountains, but now a narrow road snaked along the cliffs in hairpin turns, allowing automobile travel to the small town of Kailua on the windward side. Still, the gale force winds that often whipped up the cliffs sometimes forced the closing of the road.

At the lookout, Ned peered down over the wall at the dizzying abyss below. Mist funneled up in spirals, and he became transfixed by the movement. Clouds often enshrouded the Pali, and today was no exception. He could catch glimpses of trees, and rocks that looked like cold faces on the cliffs below as the thick gray curtains of mist opened and closed. The cold air was damp with moisture. Ned looked over at Todd, who seemed to be lost in his own thoughts. He watched Todd, remembering what Uncle Wing had disclosed last night. Could it be possible that Todd was untrustworthy, possibly even involved in something dark and criminal? Todd always acted the part of the typical copper, but coppers were always so close to the corroded side of life and sometimes it rubbed off. Ned tried to shake off the ominous feeling that seemed to saturate the landscape. He remembered it was here that the warrior Kamehameha had driven his opponents back and pushed many of them over the precipice in a bloody battle that won the chief this island. Someone had once told Ned that the land below held the unhappy spirits of the fallen warriors, and everyone made sure to stay away from that place after nightfall. Today, the wind sounded like distant screams, reminding Ned that he was no stranger to death or murder. He wondered, as he often did, if he had really chosen this path, or if it had chosen him in some strange and mutual attraction that had taken firm hold on him. And now it had come to something upsetting and distasteful. His own friend, standing there with him, was under his suspicion. The clouds began to break, and Ned looked up to see patches of blue flashing through the mist. In what seemed like a second, the whole vista opened up for miles, and he could see the green land rolling down to the shoreline, the turquoise sea stretching into deep blue, and the clear line of the horizon. Just as swiftly, the clouds moved back in and once again shrouded the scene in gray. As if both were obeying a signal, the two men turned and walked back to the car. They drove down into the valley in silence. Ned was still entranced by the spectacular scenery. Todd was the first to speak.

"Terrible about Mina's friend, Cecily."

"Terrible," repeated Ned.

"You and Mina found her, huh?"

"She'd invited us for dessert. We'd eaten dinner with her the night before. She seemed like a very nice person."

"Why were you eating dinner with her? Was Mina trying to fix you up?"

"I'm sure she wasn't." Ned paused. "You don't suppose there's any remote chance that there could be a connection between her attack and the murder, do you?" He tried to sound offhanded and casual.

"No way in hell," Todd said. "Chinatown has some rough customers crawling around its back streets, gamblers in debt, hop heads, smugglers, and your garden variety down and outs. I'd put my money on one of them. Why would you think there was a connection?"

Ned thought he heard a hint of suspicion in Todd's voice, but he wasn't sure.

"It was just a random thought." Ned looked away, out the car window, knowing that for better or worse he'd planted a seed in Todd's mind. Now there was a tiny chance Todd would wonder if Ned knew about his connection with Halpern in Chinatown.

"I could use something more than thoughts now," Todd sighed. "I'm getting pressure from above to come up with something solid, and all I have so far is sand. This wouldn't be happening if Halpern was a nobody. The country club set takes care of its own in this town."

"Not much to go on, is there?"

"Jesus," complained Todd. "I even checked out Hollister. Now there's a long shot."

"And?" Ned smiled. "Was he lying around as usual with that silver spoon in his mouth?"

"Now that's the pot calling the kettle black." Todd put on one of his wry smiles. "His alibi is pathetically predictable. He was dining at the Kama'aina Club with Lamby Langston."

"Lamby?"

"Yes, and she *does* have the brain of a sheep *and* the looks of a movie star. Miss Candace Furtado, their personal waitress that evening, says she served them in their private dining room until well after midnight."

"I wonder if he pulled the wool over her eyes?"

"Oh God," groaned Todd. "Get the man some lunch."

12

A SHIFTING TIDE

THE NEXT DAY, Mina was up early. She called the hospital and was relieved to learn that Cecily had regained consciousness. The morning looked bright and sunny so she put on a swimsuit, made a cup of coffee, and went outside to her veranda. She was looking at the ocean, trying to decide if she really wanted to swim, when from across the arbor Ned called out to invite her for breakfast. He informed her she had about twenty minutes, and she decided that a swim was just what she needed. The tide was high, but the water was fairly calm. She swam with lazy strokes and rolled over to float on her back, staring at the sky. She worried that what she and Ned were doing was wrong and dangerous. Right from the beginning she'd had her own reasons for doing this, and the attack on Cecily compounded those reasons. Someone is a murderer, she thought, someone is violent and could harm, even kill again, if they weren't stopped. And who would be the next victim? And then there was Ned and the twinges of guilt she felt about not telling him everything. She hadn't expected him to be so different and likeable. She knew already that he was someone she would not want to toy with or deceive, but could she trust him with everything she knew?

Ned paced along the veranda, watching Mina in the water. Even in faded khaki trousers and a plain white T-shirt, he couldn't shed his innate grace. He saw Mina's form move further and further away.

He thought about everything that had happened in the last few days, how things felt more dangerous and risky. How much further would she go in looking for the truth if she knew about Todd? How could or should he tell her? His thoughts were broken by the insistent ringing of the telephone.

The sound of the breaking waves caught Mina's attention. She noticed now that she had drifted quite a ways offshore and was very close to the outer edge of the reef. Treading water, she watched the breakers and listened to the sound of them folding and dissolving in white foam. Then she realized she was getting hungry, and with sure and strong strokes she swam toward the beach.

Bundled up in a terry cloth robe, with her hair still damp, Mina sat at the round table on Ned's veranda. Before her was a pitcher of orange juice, a pot of tea, two bowls of fresh fruit with nuts and raisins, butter and a basket of warm scones.

"I have to tell you," Mina said. "Cecily is now conscious. I'm going to stop by the hospital today."

"That's a great relief," said Ned as he poured the tea. "There's some news on our mystery front too."

"What is it?" Mina asked.

"If you don't mind, could we wait until we finish eating? I'd like to not think about it for a while."

"My mother was like that." Mina stirred the sugar in her tea.

"Like what?"

"Wouldn't let people talk about business over meals. She died five years ago. Complications from pneumonia."

"I remember Nyla telling me about it. I'm sorry."

"My dad took it pretty hard. He decided to move back to the Big Island and run the family ranch again, something he's always wanted do. He took my grandma there with him, my mother's mother. She loves it there."

"How old is she?"

"About seventy-five, I think, but she looks about ten years younger, and she's as sharp as a tack. She has some great stories to tell. You know, she was very close to the royal family during the time of the overthrow."

"My grandfather's around that age now as well. After my father died, my mother and I left Sāmoa and went to live with him in England."

"How did your mother and father meet?"

"My mother was a determined travel writer, you know, following in the footsteps of Isabella Bird. She ended up in Sāmoa and met my father."

"What happened to your father?"

"There was a terrible storm. An inter-island boat full of people was trying to land in Āpia harbor. He was the harbor pilot. He went to try to help and was swept out to sea."

"How terrible," she said. "How old were you?"

"It was 1911, so I must have been seven. A year later, I was in England. You know, it wasn't until I was much older, until I went off to Oxford, that I realized I'd been brought up in an extremely eccentric environment."

"Eccentric?"

"It would take me hours to explain it to you."

"Tell me something. Tell me two eccentric things."

"Two things, right." Ned thought for a moment. "Well, I never went to school until I started at Oxford. I had tutors, all kinds of tutors of every nationality. One of them was an Indian man, Mr. Gopal. He was engaged to teach me yoga. I'm very good at standing on my head."

"And the second thing?"

"Once a month, on a Friday, my grandfather had the housekeeper let some of the staff have a holiday, and we—the family, that is—did their work for them that day. It was supposed to get us accustomed to labor and to keep us appreciative of what others did for us."

"Is that where you learned to make scones?"

"What a clever girl you are, Mina."

"Those two things sound pretty good to me, even if they were unusual."

"To tell you the truth, I think I was very fortunate to grow up with a potty family in the Lake District who absolutely doted on me."

"Nothing luckier," Mina agreed as she helped herself to another scone. "So will you be lord watcha-ma-call-it some day?"

"Lord watch-a-ma-call-it? I love the sound of it." Ned laughed.

"Must have been great going to Oxford. I guess that's where you studied playwriting."

"I came to America to do that. I took up literature at Oxford, but then I went to Harvard. I wanted to be part of George Baker's Workshop 47. He's since moved it on to Yale. I thought the most exciting theatre was coming from America. I know Todd said you went to Antioch College."

"Did he say it with the usual smirk on his face?" Mina asked, smiling.

"I think you make him very nervous."

"I don't make you nervous, do I?"

"No, but my family has always insisted that women be educated and allowed to have careers if they'd like to."

"All this and how much Sāmoan?"

"I'm a quarter. My father was half Sāmoan."

"I see, so that makes you a two-bit Sāmoan." Mina laughed at her own joke.

"You know, Mina, if I ever need a bit of confidence, I'll be sure and come to you."

"So how come your last name is Manusia?"

"It's a name I was given after my father drowned." Ned's voice changed color. "My grandmother gave it to me. She said it came to her in a dream. I guess the meaning has to do with my father's death."

"Which is?"

"Surfacing, as if a boat were submerged and it came up again. Manusia."

"So being the son, you are your father surviving?"

"Something to that effect. My mother asked me to always keep it. My father's real name was Baker." Ned paused. "How about your name, Mina, where does it come from?"

"Promise not to laugh or tell anyone?"

"I won't tell anyone, but I can't promise about the laughing."

"My real name is Wilhelmina. Can you imagine naming your daughter Wilhelmina?"

"It's not so bad. Wonderful name for a battleship."

Mina stared at him for a moment and shook her head smiling. "I suppose I deserved that after the two-bit Sāmoan crack."

"Much worse, Mina, you deserve much worse."

Mina had finished with the juice, the bowl of fruit, and two scones. She stood up, shook the crumbs from her napkin onto the grass, sat back down and poured another cup of tea. She then placed the napkin on her lap. "Okay," she sighed. "I can't stand it anymore. Please tell me the news."

"Well, Wilhelmina," said Ned as he leaned back in his chair, "the portrait has turned up. The report is that the canvas appears unharmed, but the frame and the backboard are nowhere to be found. Some children playing in a park discovered it. They decided to take the wonderful picture home to mum. Mum recognized it and called the police. The police have looked it over and are returning it to the museum this morning. I'll be going up soon."

"I should go up there too for a follow-up story. So someone just dumped the portrait?"

"It's puzzling, isn't it?" Ned reflected. "Why would someone just steal it and then throw it away?"

"If it was just to confuse a motive for murder, why not destroy it?" Mina wondered.

"It seems more and more likely that the motive for the murder was something different from the motive for the theft."

"But," Mina reminded him, "it's still very probable that the murder is connected to the theft in some way."

"Still," he said, "why take the painting in the first place?"

Mina rose to her feet, looking out at the ocean. She knew its habits and moods in this one spot well, and she could see that the tide had reached its peak and was now beginning to recede. "Let's just forget the murder for a moment. Let's think now. You go to the museum. At some risk you steal something of value, in this case, a portrait. You take it somewhere, strip it out of its frame." Mina stopped and sat back down, then said, "What was the painting like? I never got to see it."

"It was big. I'd say at least six feet tall and maybe four feet wide. The king is standing there in formal dress. He's wearing a sword."

"And the rest," she asked, "the frame and everything?"

"The canvas is stretched over wooden bars, then placed inside the frame itself. It's a big frame, a good five inches wide and a couple of inches thick. Then, there's a backing, a wooden board over the back that holds and protects the back of the canvas. That's a bit unusual, I think. The whole piece is very heavy, very ornate, and very large."

"Big enough to hide something in?" Mina asked.

"Yes, it's possible the frame could have concealed something, and the backing board could have had a false center."

"That's the trouble," Mina threw up her hands, "anything's possible until we know more."

"Maybe today, we'll find out more." Ned stood up and started to clear the table.

"Here, let me help you." Mina went to gather some of the dishes together.

"Oh, don't bother about it," Ned said.

"You know Nyla always says that," chuckled Mina.

"Does she?"

"Yeah," said Mina, "and its true meaning is always 'I made this great meal and you damn well better help me clean up.'"

"Ah," sighed Ned walking toward the kitchen balancing plates and glasses. "I knew someday I'd meet a woman who understood me."

SECRETS PAST AND PRESENT

NED ARRIVED AT the museum at about ten thirty. Todd was already in the gallery speaking to Martha Klein. Martha was wearing a well-tailored blue suit, and with her hair folded in a neat chignon she could have easily been mistaken for a buyer in a high-fashion clothing store. She looked over her glasses at Ned as he approached.

"Ned, have you met Martha Klein?" Todd asked.

"Yes," he said. "Good morning, Miss Klein."

"Martha was just appointed acting director of the museum yesterday," Todd reported.

"Congratulations," Ned said.

"Well, I'm just waiting for our restoration expert to arrive," Martha said. "I'm sure you'll want to report to your museum on the condition of the portrait."

"Of course. They'll be relieved just to hear that it's been recovered."

Mina arrived, walked up to the group, and greeted everyone. "Todd, I need to ask you for a statement about the recovery of the portrait. Is this a good time?" A disgruntled Todd followed her into the museum courtyard.

"If you would like to come with me," Martha said to Ned, "we have the painting laid out in one of our workrooms." She turned, and as Ned walked behind her he was caught off guard by the exotic scent of her perfume. It smelled a bit like orchids and spices. They went through a back door and down a narrow flight of stairs to the basement. Off a long hallway, they entered a workroom. In the middle of the room stood a large table. The portrait was laid out on the table, and a man, whose most striking features were the absence of a single hair on his head, a large white mustache, and sparkling blue eyes, was examining the canvas. He wore thin white cotton gloves that were made for handling artifacts, and like a detective looking for clues, he held a magnifying glass.

"Oh Alfred, you've arrived and begun," Martha smiled. "This is Mr. Edward Manusia. He accompanied the portraits here for the British Museum. Mr. Manusia, this is Mr. Alfred Gisolfi, our island art conservation and restoration expert."

"You will both be happy to hear," said Gisolfi, "that I've found no great damage. The portrait is soiled, of course, but nothing we can't clean. I would say, Martha, you are more than lucky."

"That's good news," Martha replied. She turned to Ned. "The frame, you understand, is missing. It was the original frame and quite valuable itself. As you know, each of the three frames has a different stylized motif. The king's is a pattern of the maile vine. Since there are photographs, we can have a reproduction made."

"Better the frame than the painting," commented Ned.

"Come now, Martha," Gisolfi summoned her. "Help me turn this over so I can have a look at the back."

Martha put on a pair of the white gloves. She and Gisolfi turned the canvas over. Ned noticed some writing on the back.

"What is that?" He asked, moving closer to look at it. "It's in Hawaiian, isn't it?"

"That's the famous verse," answered Martha.

Ned looked confused.

"Ah, you don't know the history of the portraits, do you, Mr. Manusia?" There was a cheerful mockery in her tone.

"To tell you the truth, Miss Klein, when I agreed to accompany these paintings, I thought it would be a simple task. I never dreamed one of them would be stolen or that there would be a murder. Ordinarily, I wouldn't be that interested in their history, but now, I would be grateful for anything you could tell me."

Martha removed her white gloves, all the while looking at Ned. He got the impression she was making a decision about him. She glanced over at Gisolfi, who looked up, flashed her a quick smile, and went back to his work. Martha motioned to Ned to sit down on a nearby wooden bench. She sat next to him and spoke while Gisolfi continued his careful examination.

"In 1890, the English artist Jonathan Leeds was asked by the king to paint three portraits: one of himself, another of his queen, Kapi'olani, and a third of the queen's sister, Po'omaikalani. The portraits were completed in the fall. Mr. Leeds was also commissioned to design the frames that were being carved in San Francisco. When the king made his trip to San Francisco, Leeds was part of the entourage. They arrived on December 4, 1890. Leeds carried the portraits—rolled, of course—in order to see them in their frames and to have the king's final approval. Leeds wanted to make sure everything was made to his own exacting specifications. His finicky and unpredictable nature was legendary. Now, what happened between Mr. Leeds and the king in San Francisco is anyone's guess. The king took ill there and died. After the king died, Mr. Leeds claimed he had never been paid for the portraits, packed them up with the custom frames, and returned to England in somewhat of a hurry. He told the Hawaiian officials that he wished to keep his paintings, and since there was no paperwork to be found, and because after the king's death there was a period of general confusion in San Francisco, no one opposed him. He just left. Leeds died five years later and left all of his work to the British Museum. When the museum finally received the portraits, they were still rolled, and the frames appeared never to have been assembled. It was at the museum that this writing was first discovered and cataloged. It's no secret. It has been translated, of course, but no one knows who wrote it, what it means, or its kaona."

"Kaona?" Ned gave her a quizzical look.

"The kaona of something is its hidden meaning. Hawaiian songs and chants—they're full of these double entendres and symbolic meanings, usually cloaked in metaphor and similes employing natural phenomena."

"Often drenched in sexuality," Gisolfi commented, grinning at Ned.

"Would you mind if I copied this down?" Ned asked.

"Not at all. It's been published in various articles over the years. Almost any description of the portraits includes this little verse, and any researcher would have access to it." Martha Klein took off her glasses and held them up as if searching for a speck of dust on the lens. "Do you think this might be some kind of clue to something?"

"I don't think so," Ned said casually. "I'm a writer, and I often want to jot things down." Ned quickly copied the Hawaiian verse.

Luuluu ke akua
I kalani ui hele loa
He loa ke ala kai mehameha
Nana a hewa ka maka
I na mea huna i ka lipolipo
Pali ku makani o Kalakaua

"Do you know what it means?" Ned asked Martha.

"Roughly it says: the gods are sorrowful because of the passing of the chief, the path to the sea is long and lonely, the secrets are lost or disappear in the dark eyes, Kalākaua is a windblown cliff." Martha looked at Ned. "It can be translated many different ways, of course. That was very literal and simplified."

"Even so, it's quite haunting," said Ned.

"Well, Martha," Gisolfi said, having concluded his inspection, "I see no real damage here. I will simply clean and remount the canvas. If you will excuse me now, I'm going to have my coffee. It was a pleasure meeting you, Mr. Manusia." He smiled and left the room.

"Maybe you could tell me, Miss Klein. I've heard that Mr. Halpern worked for a while on the mainland somewhere."

"That's correct," she said. "He worked at the Field Museum in Chicago as a young man."

"Do you know when he was there?"

"I don't, but you could look it up in our archives. Would you like me to walk you there? I'll get the reference desk to help you."

"Yes, thanks," said Ned. "They're a few more questions I have, Miss Klein. They're a bit confidential."

"What do you want to know?" She asked in a brisk manner as they left the room and headed toward the archives.

"What did you think of Abel Halpern?"

"Personally or as a professional?"

"Both."

Martha paused for a moment, considering her answer. "As a professional, he was well connected in the community and because of that he was able to maintain his position here at the museum. I would not say he was a very good director for the institution, and academically, in his field, he was a nobody. He had not published anything of significance in years."

"And what was his academic field?" Ned asked.

"Art history," she grimaced, "with a specialty in Asian art. This museum specializes in Pacific history, and he was an odd choice to head it, but as you have probably discovered, in this town, whom you went to school with is everything."

"And as a person, did you like him?"

"As a person, and I know I am not alone in my judgment, he was not a very nice man."

"Sam Takahashi, do you know him? Apparently, he couldn't stand Halpern." Ned tried to sound confidential.

"Oh, I know," Martha responded. "And believe me the feeling was mutual. I've heard Halpern make the worst remarks about Sam. Is he a suspect?"

"So far, he's only been questioned. Just one more thing. Do you know if Todd Forrest had any dealings with Mr. Halpern?"

Martha Klein's eyes brightened. "They had a meeting two days before his death."

"I see," said Ned gravely. "Do you know what it was about?"

"No, but I just happened to walk by Halpern's office while they were meeting. I could hear their voices, and Detective Forrest sounded very upset."

"Miss Klein," Ned began, "I don't mean to alarm you, but for your own safety, I think it would be in your best interest if you kept that information to yourself for now. Does anyone else know about this?"

"One person."

"Who is that?"

"Mina Beckwith. She called me up yesterday. She asked me the same question, and I told her just what I've told you."

NEWS TRAVELS

MINA HAD JUST finished her conversation with Todd when she happened to see Alfred Gisolfi walk into the courtyard. She knew he must be there to evaluate the recovered portrait. Besides doing art restoration, Gisolfi worked as an art purchaser for the Honolulu branch of S&G Gump's, a company out of San Francisco. Gump's very exclusive shop was in Waikīkī and sold a spectrum of beautiful objects to wealthy residents and tourists. She watched as he bought himself a cup of coffee, sat down at one of the garden tables, and proceeded to light a pipe. She went over to his table and introduced herself. Gisolfi seemed more than happy to answer her questions about the portrait.

"How long do you think it will be before it's back on exhibit?" Mina asked him.

"That depends," he replied, "on what Martha—on what the new acting director—decides. The cleaning and mounting process of the portrait is a routine procedure, but reproducing the frame, that will be a long process. Of course, it can be placed in a temporary frame very easily."

"I wonder who stole the portrait?" Mina asked.

"I wonder too," he said. "What would the purpose be? It's not an art object that would have a wide market, and it's so easy to identify. I thought at first it might be the work of a greedy collector, but then to have it turn up in a rubbish bin! It makes no sense. I suppose it must be connected to the murder."

"I think so," she nodded.

"Do you know if the police have any suspects?"

"I'm not sure," she hesitated, "but I know they've called in Sam Takahashi for questioning, and I'd guess they've talked to Halpern's children. They always talk to people who benefit financially from something like this."

"It's a terrible thing," he said.

"Could I buy you another cup of coffee? I'm going to have one."

"That would be so kind of you, Miss Beckwith."

Over coffee, he asked Mina about her job and education.

"I went to Punahou High School and then I majored in English at Antioch College."

"Ah," said Gisolfi, "Martha Klein also went to Punahou High School."

"Yes," said Mina. "She was a few years ahead of me. She went on to Barnard, I think."

"You made a very unusual college choice." Gisolfi seemed amused.

"I didn't want to go where everyone else was going," answered Mina. "It's wonderful news about Martha's promotion. Do you think it will be permanent?"

"I'm sure of it. She is a qualified and capable person." There was distinct admiration in his voice. "Much more so than her predecessor, may he rest in peace."

"It must have been hard for her to work for Abel Halpern. I've heard he was difficult."

"You don't know," Gisolfi leaned forward and lowered his voice. "You can't imagine the indignities she's suffered through. Some of these local elites handle themselves and their positions in the most contemptible way. It's a shame there's no law against being tyrannical, rude, and insulting, isn't it?"

"If there were," remarked Mina, "we'd have to expand the O'ahu prison quite a bit."

He laughed and tapped his pipe out in the ashtray. "You've been most delightful, Miss Beckwith. It was a pleasure to meet you, but now I must get back to work."

"Thank you for your time," Mina smiled. As she watched him leave, she felt sure the rumor that she heard was true. Despite their age difference, Martha Klein was having an affair with Alfred Gisolfi.

Mina looked around for Ned or Martha, but couldn't find either of them. She decided to run by the hospital to check on Cecily and then go to the newspaper building and finish the story. She could call Martha later that afternoon.

Mina turned on to King Street and found herself slowing down behind a streetcar. The car was gliding along in its tracks with its balled arm singing through the overhead wire. Mina recalled the many Saturday afternoons of streetcar rides, when Grandma Hannah would arrive at their home on Kamehameha Avenue in Mānoa Valley and whisk her and her sister off for an outing. Mina's favorite ride was the one into Waikīkī. She and Nyla loved the long McCully trestle over the swampy water, even though the water often smelled funny. They loved to feed the ducks and used to take breadcrumbs that they flung out the open sides of the car when the conductor wasn't looking. The streetcar in front of her came clanging to a stop to pick up some passengers, and the conductor waved her past.

Mina's car rolled into the cool and quiet hospital grounds. Large monkeypod trees spread their branches over the parking lot. The hospital building stood silently with its thick ochre walls and terra-cotta tiled roof. Soft grass carpeted the lawns between the paved paths that led to the entrance. While walking toward the front doors, Mina heard the wail of a siren. She stopped and watched as an ambulance with its lights flashing pulled off the street and passed in front of her on its way to the emergency room entrance. Curious, she walked closer and stood on the shaded portico where she could observe without being noticed. Out of the ambulance came a woman on a stretcher. Then, to Mina's great surprise, Sheila Halpern got out of the ambulance and followed the stretcher into the emergency ward.

Mina walked at a swift pace around through the front doors, thankful at last for the summer her mother had forced her to volunteer at the hospital. Because of the endless errands, she knew how to get anywhere in the hospital quickly. In no time, she was peering through the small glass pane of a large swinging door that led from the hallway into the back of the emergency room. She could see the woman on the stretcher being moved onto a bed just to the right of the door. The hanging curtains around the bed were pulled to enclose the patient. Mina slipped in and moved to the vacant bed on the left, closing the hanging curtain. She sat, as still as she could, on the bed with her feet pulled up above the curtain line. Her heart was racing as she listened to the rush of activity taking place. She could hear several voices talking about the woman's condition and then someone questioning Sheila.

"Her name is Kikue Tsuruda. I think she's about thirty-seven or thirty-eight. I'm not quite sure. She works for us. She's our housekeeper." Sheila's voice was rising in pitch and intensity. "I came out of my room to go and get a stamp from the study, and I just found her there, passed out on the carpet. I wasn't sure—she was so cold. I thought she might be . . . I was afraid she might be . . . It was horrible."

A lower voice spoke, and Sheila answered.

"I have no idea. How should I know? I have no idea why she would want to kill herself."

Another voice broke in. It was loud and irritated. "This woman is pregnant. Why didn't you tell us she was pregnant?"

"How was I supposed to know that?" Sheila was now shrieking. "I didn't know that. How the hell was I supposed to know that?"

A woman's voice cut in; it was calm and steady. "Come out of here now. Come with me. You need to sit down, dear. You've had a nasty shock yourself."

Mina heard them usher Sheila away.

Some other voice said, "We found this bottle next to her."

"Chlordane," said the irritated voice. "You know, a Mickey Finn. Pump out her stomach. People are so stupid. She's going to miscarry too."

Mina peeked out from behind the curtain, made sure no one was looking, and darted out into the hall.

She then walked up to the third floor to see Cecily. A large man sat in the hall and stopped her before she could enter Cecily's private room. He called through the doorway, and Mrs. Chang appeared. "Oh Mina, my dear," she smiled and gave Mina a warm hug. "She's awake and impossible as ever. You girls visit while I run downstairs and get a bite to eat."

Mina entered the room and found Cecily sitting up in bed looking at a magazine. There were five bouquets of flowers spread around the room. "Well, you must have some secret admirers," Mina said as she walked in, sat on the bed, and kissed Cecily on the cheek.

"Oh, thank God you're here. I've only been awake for a few hours, and I'm already bored."

"Who's sending you all these flowers? Is it that Tom person?" Mina asked.

"I'm not telling for now. My mother is dying of curiosity too, but I won't tell her either."

"I am so sorry this happened. It's my fault for getting you involved." Mina stood and walked to the window.

"So what did I do?" Cecily asked. "My short-term memory is fuzzy, and the closer to the whack on my head, the less I remember."

Mina started with Abel Halpern's murder and reviewed everything that had happened, but for Cecily it was like listening to the plot of strange novel. She couldn't really connect herself to any of it. Mina tried to change the subject to other things, people they knew, the weather, but Cecily kept asking her questions about the events leading up to her attack, as if by hearing things and details she might be able to recapture her memory. Mrs. Chang returned, and Mina said she had to get back to work. Just as Mina was walking out the door, Cecily said, "Mina, when we went out to dinner, did we have some great shrimp in ginger and onion sauce?"

"Bingo," Mina said, and blew her a good-bye kiss.

Back at her desk in the newspaper building, Mina stared at the blank piece of paper in front of her. She had just finished a boring conversation on the telephone with Martha Klein. After a minute, she typed the date and tried to focus on the story about the recovered portrait, but the scene at the hospital kept intruding. A pregnant housekeeper trying to commit suicide: what could it mean? Mina redoubled her efforts to concentrate on the portrait story. She began to think and type. After two pages, she took it out, redrafted it, checked her grammar and spelling, and typed it over again. She started to read the final copy over once more.

"Hey, don't you ever quit?" A voice came from behind her, and she turned, surprised to see Chris Hollister leaning up against a newsroom desk. He almost never came into the newsroom.

"Look around you, Mina," he went on. "I bet you never even noticed that it's four thirty and almost everyone is gone."

"As a matter of fact, Mr. Holl—"

"Chris," he smiled. "Please, it's after hours."

"As a matter of fact, *Chris,* I didn't. I've got to get this story in tomorrow's paper. They found the portrait, you know."

"I didn't know that. Where?"

"In a park. It was dumped in the park. Lili'uokalani Gardens. Some kids found it in a trashcan and took it home. It wasn't even damaged."

"Hmm, how odd. What do the police make of it?"

"They're baffled," she said.

"And you? I know you must be thinking about it. Your wheels don't stop, do they?" He crossed his arms.

"I'm mystified too. I think it must be connected to Halpern's murder, but now," she sighed, "it's a little more complicated."

"Did you know Halpern disapproved of the monarchy? I mean the whole idea of it? He was always going on about how great the takeover was."

"No," Mina's interest perked. "I didn't know that."

"The way he talked you'd have thought it happened yesterday. His father was there when the king died. I bet you didn't know that either."

"In San Francisco?"

"Right in the next room, and his father's nephew, George Blain, was an ensign to Admiral Brown, the officer escorting the king. They were all there." Chris Hollister seemed pleased to be telling her something interesting that she didn't know. "But that's not what I wanted to tell you. I wanted to tell you that you're doing a great job here. I mean it. I wish there were five of you."

"Thank you," smiled Mina. "I want to do a good job." Mina wasn't sure, but she thought he might be flirting again.

"Are you going to rehearsal tonight?" he asked.

"I was planning to."

"Well, since you're almost finished, would you like to grab a bite to eat with me before we have to be at the theatre?"

She was quiet. He *was* flirting.

"We could just stop over at the club," he said, "whenever you're ready to go."

"That might be nice," she smiled. "I didn't realize I was getting hungry until you mentioned food. I think I forgot to eat lunch."

"Good. Let me walk that to the copy editor for you. It's late, and he might bark. You can get ready." Hollister walked over and took the story out of her hands, and before she could say anything he was halfway down the hall. She was about to go after him to tell him she hadn't finished reading it, when the phone rang.

"Newsroom," she said in an irritated voice.

"Mina?" It was Ned.

"Ned," Mina began, "I looked for you after my interview, but I couldn't find you."

"I was in the archives. Listen Mina, you and I need to have a little private chat."

"I know it." She felt her stomach sinking. "There's some things I should have told you."

There was silence at the other end.

"Look, I'm sorry, okay?" she said. "But when you find o̊ it why, it will all make sense to you—unless you know why all ready. We can talk after rehearsal."

"Fine. Look, there's something else." Ned sounded serious. "I'm at the police station."

"Is it about the maid?"

"The maid? No. This afternoon, Todd nicked Sam Takahashi for Halpern's murder."

"You're kidding."

"I wish I were. There was an anonymous tip about Sam's car at the museum on New Year's Eve. Todd got a search warrant, and they found a bloody shirt and some fragments of the frame in Sam's trunk."

"Sam's not that stupid."

"I don't think so either," agreed Ned. "But Todd won't hear anything else. He's sure he's got his man."

"A quick arrest always makes him look good. I guess I better get down there and get some kind of story. I may be late for the rehearsal."

"Just don't tell Todd I told you," Ned said.

At that moment, Chris Hollister returned to the room, and she looked at him. "I'll say that the editor sent me."

"Where am I sending you?" Hollister asked her as she hung up the phone.

"Sorry, I'll have to skip dinner. Something's happened."

"What is it?" He looked concerned.

"Sam Takahashi has just been arrested for the murder of Abel Halpern. I think I should try to get it in the morning edition." She started to gather up her things.

"I'll go with you," Hollister stated.

Without thinking, Mina gave him a sharp look.

"Don't worry," he immediately responded. "Of course it will be your story."

15

TIPSY TURVY

BY THE TIME Mina arrived at the theatre, it was almost eight. Her hair felt dirty. Her clothes were rumpled, and she was starving. She'd learned nothing more substantial about Sam's arrest than what Ned had revealed on the phone. Chris Hollister went to dinner on his own. She had gone back to the newsroom and pounded out a piece on the arrest for the morning paper. Just as she had finished, Nyla called and asked her to come to the theatre right away. As she made her way through the stage wings, she could see Johnny Knight working on a scene with some of the men. I couldn't take another day like this, she thought to herself.

Kīna'u Kelly came rushing up to her. "Nyla says to come straight away to the women's lounge," she said in a voice full of intrigue. "Our Sheila is soused."

"Oh Jesus," groaned Mina.

Kīna'u led the way to the lobby, marching like a foot soldier on a mission with her short mop of blond curls bouncing up and down. She was just twenty years old and adored both Nyla and Mina. Kīna'u pushed open the lounge door, and signaled Mina to enter first. Nyla was sitting on a chair while Sheila Halpern lay passed out on the couch. Kīna'u came in and twisted the lock on the lounge door so no one would enter. Then, with her arms crossed, she leaned against the door for added protection.

"At last, you're here!" Nyla was smoking a cigarette and waving it around in the air. She got up and paced around. "She gets here, blind drunk! This cab driver just shoves her out of the cab and makes *me* pay. Thank God no one saw her. I brought her in here. She threw up twice. Kīna'u got her a Coke, and then she passed out."

"I think she had a hard day." Mina flopped down on one of the chairs.

"And Mina," Nyla went on, "you wouldn't believe the stuff she was saying before her lights went out. She's been having an affair with Sam Takahashi! And don't you tell a soul, Kīna'u!"

"I swear, I won't." Kīna'u's eyes were like saucers.

"She said that?" Mina sat up.

"Yeah, she was going on and on about how he couldn't have done it. Have you heard about the arrest? It was on the radio. Where have you been?"

"Where do you think I've been? I had to write the story for the morning news," Mina said.

"Gee, Mina, you look terrible."

"Thanks a lot."

"So," Nyla asked, "do you think you could drive her home?"

"What?!" Mina bellowed.

"Well, charming Andrew isn't here. I'm in the next scene, and we can't put her in a cab like this."

"Oh, shit." Mina collapsed onto one of the chairs.

"Mina, don't swear. It's so vulgar." Nyla mashed out her cigarette.

"Shit, shit, shit," Mina chanted, and then fell silent, staring at the floor.

Kīna'u giggled to herself.

Scowling, Mina said, "Okay, but you owe me, Nyla. I want some coffee right away and fork over the candy bar I know you have in your purse. You and Kīna'u will have to get her into the car."

In record time, Mina consumed two cups of coffee, the candy bar, and a tuna sandwich that Kīna'u filched from her brother, Kalani. Then, Nyla and Kīna'u hauled Sheila out the front entrance, so no one would see her, while Mina drove her car around to meet them. They dumped Sheila unceremoniously into the back seat.

"And how am I supposed to get her into the house by myself?" Mina said out the open window of the car.

"Maybe she'll wake up," Nyla said.

"Just shut the door and let me get out of here," snapped Mina. "Tell Ned I can't meet with him tonight and that I'm going home to sleep." Then, she sped away from the curb in a huff. She threaded the car through less traveled streets, along the back side of Punchbowl and past Pauoa Valley. By the time the car turned on to Nuʻuanu Avenue, she felt a second surge of energy. The Halpern house was on fashionable Dowsett Street, and as she pulled into the driveway, she heard Sheila coming to in the back seat. Sheila was able to stand up, more or less, and Mina helped her through the house and into the kitchen. With Sheila's directions about where things were kept in the kitchen, Mina managed to brew a pot of coffee.

"Thanks Mina," said Sheila sheepishly. "I guess I made a fool of myself, *again*."

"No one saw you, except me, Nyla, and Kīnaʻu." Mina poured the coffee.

"That's bad enough. I know I'm an ass. I feel so stupid. Things happen and I just fall apart, I—" Sheila stopped herself when she realized she was about to make herself cry.

"I saw you at the hospital." Mina decided to take a chance.

"You did?" The surprise wrenched Sheila out of her self-absorption.

"Yeah, who was that lady?" Mina played dumb.

"That was our housekeeper." Sheila seemed eager to talk. "She tried to kill herself with poison right here in this house. They said I found her just in time. She'll be all right, but you know what? She's been a widow forever, but she was pregnant—three months, and now she's miscarried. I didn't even know."

"She must have had a boyfriend or something."

In an instant, Sheila's face was taut with anger. "No, it wasn't a boyfriend. It was that bastard. She said that he forced her! More than once! He forced her!"

"Who?" Mina had to know. "Who forced her?"

"My father!!!" Sheila screamed as she leaped out of the chair and then suddenly stopped herself and stood motionless. Mina walked over and gently sat her back down. After a few minutes, Sheila seemed to find herself again.

"Listen, Sheila," Mina said. "Did you know they arrested Sam Takahashi this afternoon for your father's murder?"

"He didn't do it." Sheila burst into tears. "I know he didn't."

"I know this is hard," Mina continued. "But I need to tell you that, tonight, when you were—I mean at the theatre, you said some things about Sam Takahashi to Nyla."

"Oh my lord, no," moaned Sheila. "Maybe I'm the one who should have taken poison."

"Don't say that," Mina scolded. "Now listen, Nyla will most likely tell Todd, her husband. You see how it might make things worse for Sam."

"But he . . ."

"He what?" asked Mina.

"Nothing. You know Sam's engaged to Elizabeth Katsuki, don't you?"

"No, I didn't know that."

"Well, he is," Sheila sighed. "He doesn't love her, of course. It's arranged, and he's bound to this family honor thing. That's why we sneak around, that and my father."

"Did Andrew know?" Mina asked.

"Leave Andrew out of it," Sheila frowned. "Please, he's suffered enough."

"Right now," Mina said, "it looks to me like you're the one whose suffered, and don't tell me those bruises under your makeup were from an accident."

"My father found out about Sam and me."

"And he did this to you?"

"That morning. New Year's Eve." Sheila's voice became very small.

"Who else knew?"

"Kikue was here. She promised not to tell but—"

"What's happened, Sheila?" A male voice jarred the intimate conversation. It was Andrew Halpern.

"Andrew, I didn't hear your car." Sheila sounded almost nervous.

"I parked out on the street," he answered.

"I got sick at rehearsal, and Mina brought me home," Sheila said.

"So now you're home," Andrew snapped.

"I suppose," said Mina without even looking at Andrew, "that this is your way of saying I should leave?"

"Andrew," Sheila broke in, "it was kind of Mina to take care of—"

"I'll take care of you now, Sheila." Andrew grimaced. "She's Forrest's sister-in-law for Christ's sake!"

"Sheila, will you be all right here?" Mina asked with concern.

"What is that supposed to mean?!" Andrew shouted.

"Shut your mouth, you childish bully!" Mina barked at him, and he backed away, stunned. She turned again to Sheila. "Sheila, if you are the least bit uncomfortable or afraid, you can get in my car, drive away with me, and I promise to help you in any way I can."

"Mina, that is the kindest thing anyone has said to me in ages." Sheila took Mina's hand and even managed a little smile. "But believe me, it's fine. I'm safe here. Thank you so much for helping me."

"You take care of yourself, and just call me if you need anything." Mina got up and left, resisting the overwhelming urge to stick her tongue out at Andrew.

On the drive home, Mina wanted to forget all the things that happened that day. She hummed to herself and tried to sing "Blue Moon," a new song she'd heard a few times. She couldn't remember the words so she switched to singing "Stormy Weather." By the time she was doing what she thought was a pretty sexy rendition of "Night and Day," her watch said 10:45, and she was pulling into the driveway at Ka'alāwai. Ned's house was dark, but she found a note pinned to her door. It read: "Mandatory Breakfast Meeting, 9:30, my place, N. M." As Mina slept that night, she dreamt she was having tea at a pretty table with cloth napkins and fresh flowers on the edge of a cliff. There were plates of honey-scented scones and pots of creamy butter.

TRUTH DOESN'T HURT

THE DAY OPENED with intermittent squalls moving in from the northeast. It was a chilly, gray day. Ned caught himself scowling as he removed a tray of scones from the oven. He didn't like it that she hadn't been completely honest with him. She hadn't exactly lied, but he still felt like he had been lied to. She'd concealed evidence from him. It aggravated him because he realized he'd done almost the same thing, by not telling her what Wing Chang knew about Todd. Trust, he thought, doesn't spring from the head full grown. Just then, Mina knocked on the door. He called out to her to come in. When she entered his kitchen, the sense of freshness she brought with her disarmed him. She was what his mother would have called a natural beauty. There was a kind of steadiness about her looks, something more enduring than the images of women that went in and out of fashion. She was wearing black slacks, a plain white blouse, and a cardigan sweater. Her dark hair was slightly damp (from a morning shower, he guessed) and was held off her face by two barrettes. He stopped himself and tried to put his feelings in check. She wasn't looking for romance, and neither, he reminded himself, was he.

Because of the weather, they were eating indoors. This morning the scones were accompanied by eggs and sausages. All through the meal, Mina felt a little uncomfortable, knowing she had some explaining and apologizing to do, but her appetite remained unaffected. After they finished eating, Mina got up to clear the table.

"Leave it," said Ned. "We can do them later."

Mina sat back down. They were both quiet for a moment, and then Mina said, "Okay, I've been bad. I've kept some things from you, but I guess you know what they are by now."

"I think I have a vague idea," Ned said, "but why don't you enlighten me? 'From the top' as you say here."

"From the top," Mina repeated as she let out a huge sigh, put her elbows on the table, cupping her face with both hands. "Well, first of all, I noticed my sister going strange on me. I don't know how to explain it, because to everyone else I'm sure she seems perfectly normal. But I can tell when something's not right with her. I can always tell."

"How long?"

"I'm not sure. I think about a month now, maybe more. I've asked her, given her openings, but nothing, no response. I know she's hiding something. I know she's scared, but she won't talk. And for her to not talk to me, well, it's like hiding something from yourself. I thought and thought and came to the conclusion that it must have something to do with Todd. You see if she was in trouble, I know she would trust me. She knows I'd do anything for her. So I figured it must be Todd because *she* would do anything to protect *him.* Anyway, it was hard to put it all together, and then came New Year's Eve."

"An eventful night," murmured Ned.

"I got to the party, and I couldn't find Nyla or Todd. I waited awhile and called Nyla at home. No one answered. I called Todd at work. They said he wasn't there. I got sick of the party and of waiting, so I decided to leave. Remember? I bumped into you on the way out. Anyway, I was parked in a dark spot, and I'd dropped my keys on the floor so I was bent down groping around looking for them. I heard two cars pull up and park, and then I heard two voices. It was Todd and Nyla. They were talking to each other in a nervous and sharp way. I couldn't hear what they were saying. I peeked out and saw Todd go back to his car and throw on his sheik costume. And then they went into the party."

"You couldn't hear *anything* they were saying?" Ned gave her a look of disbelief.

Mina hesitated. She looked at Ned as if she was deciding something.

"Look," said Ned. "I've been their friends for a long time. I care about them. I don't want to see them hurt any more than you do, but the truth is going to be the truth no matter what. Once we know what the truth is, then we can decide what to do. And if you aren't willing to tell me everything you know, what is the point of this little exercise?"

"I guess I'll just have to trust you," she said.

"I guess you will," he answered back.

"Nyla said, 'Are you sure no one saw us, are you sure?' And Todd told her to try to calm down and act like nothing had happened—that they could pull it off. He said he would find you and me and ask if we'd seen her. He told her wait a few minutes and then come looking for us. He said she could say she felt a little ill and was lying down in one of the bedrooms."

"That's exactly what she said," Ned remembered.

"Then, remember the day after the body was discovered? I ran into you in the gallery and you were—"

"I remember," he cut in.

Mina smiled. "Well, right before I saw you, I'd made an unofficial visit to Halpern's office."

"How did you get in?" Ned asked.

"A little hairpin in the lock."

"Mina, where did you learn such a thing?"

"From this boy in seventh grade. I think he's in prison now. But I got very good at it by practicing. I can pick almost any lock. Anyway, I found something."

"You found sequins from her costume, didn't you?" Ned watched her.

"How did *you* know *that?*"

"In the restaurant, with Cecily, when she needed a coin for the telephone. Don't you remember? They were there when you showed me how the coin purse worked."

"That was careless of me." Mina made a mental note of her error.

"It was a fluke. I had just seen Nyla's costume that evening with the missing sequins."

"I recognized it right away when I saw it. It was on the floor in the closet in Halpern's office." Mina paused. "Then I had that conversation with Martha and found out that Todd had an argument with Halpern just days before the murder. So, you can see how it looks to me. I think Todd was into something with Halpern, and maybe he was the one. Though I can't see Todd killing anyone unless they were having a fight. I've even thought maybe it was Nyla."

"Do you think your sister is capable of something like that?" Ned asked carefully.

"Not really," she said, "but I think we're all capable of killing a bad man, in self-defense of course, to protect ourselves, or the people we love, and Halpern was a very bad man." Mina then recounted what took place at the hospital, the things Sheila revealed the night before, and her standoff with Andrew Halpern. "And that's it," she concluded. "That's all I know. It looks bad for Todd and Nyla, doesn't it?"

"If," said Ned, "you knew they, or one of them, did it, what would you do?"

"I don't know," she answered. "I know I would want to protect Nyla. What would you do?"

"I don't know either." Ned looked out the window. "But there are a few things I should tell you too."

"Oh?"

"You're not the only one who kept secrets. I knew Nyla was lying about being asleep in one of the bedrooms because Mrs. Raymond hauled me all over the house, including the bedroom Nyla said she was sleeping in." Ned's brow darkened. "But the worst is what Cecily's father told me."

"He told *you* something and not *me?*" Mina looked hurt.

"He told me that Todd knew about Halpern importing and stashing illegal antiques, and that Todd was looking the other way."

"And now Todd's gone and arrested Sam."

"He did find some hard evidence," Ned pointed out.

"Doesn't it seem a little too easy to you, Ned? Anyone could have planted it there, including Todd. I could have picked the lock on his trunk myself."

"Right after he arrested Sam, he was adamant that the investigation was over. The portrait was safe, and he was convinced he had the killer. Case closed."

"He said that?" Mina didn't want to believe it.

"There was another not so subtle message for me in particular."

"Which was?"

"Which was—your concern and the British Museum's concern in this matter is over."

"Is it? I mean do you think we should back off?"

"If we continue," reasoned Ned, "we might find out that two people we care about committed a serious crime."

"Yes," said Mina, "but if it was Todd then he must have had a hand in the attack on Cecily too. Do you think he could do that? I know Nyla would never do that, and the thought of my sister married to—"

"Look Mina," Ned interjected, "you're imagining the worst. I don't think he could do that. There are several other people with motives and the opportunity to kill Halpern, including Sam Takahashi. My God! He's persecuted by Halpern's racism. He's having an affair with Halpern's daughter, and she's being whacked around by the bastard. And Sheila and Andrew, the two children who have every reason to despise their father and who benefit from his death, are classic suspects. They had ample opportunity. Now there's the housekeeper—"

"You know," she cut in, "if she hadn't miscarried, she would be ostracized for something that wasn't her fault. Her life would have been ruined. The suicide thing is bad enough, but it can be hushed up. It's much harder to hush up a pregnancy and a child if you don't have money. Still, how and why would she steal the portrait?"

"It's still possible that they're two separate crimes," he said.

"And that returns us to the idea that maybe something was hidden in the painting and that's the reason they destroyed the frame. But what could it possibly be?"

They sat together for a moment in silence, each thinking their own thoughts.

"I need to know who did this to Halpern and to Cecily," Mina said.

"I suppose I'd like to know that it wasn't Todd," he said. "But if it was, I guess I would like to know that too. But listen Mina, no more secrets, no more withholding information no matter how terrible it seems."

"That goes for you too."

"Maybe we should regroup," said Ned, "and take a bit of a step back. Things look clearer when you get a handle on the larger picture."

"Can you take a break from the play for a few days?"

"Johnny has the play off to a very good start. I've given him my ideas about it, and he's reviewed his plans with me. I think the best thing I could do is to just get out of his way for a while."

"I'm going to the Big Island next week, to the ranch. You know, you could come along. There's lots of room, and you could meet my father and my grandmother. Todd and Nyla have told them all about you. Do you know how to ride?"

"Do I ride?" Ned laughed. "In our family regime, riding every day was something like brushing your teeth. But won't our going there together give people ideas? It may make Todd suspicious too."

"I think I know a way to make it seem like it's Nyla's idea." Mina got up and started to clear the table. "We can try it at the party tonight."

"The party?" Ned gave her a blank look.

"I am so sorry. I was supposed to tell you days ago. Tonight is our birthday party at their house. We have one every year."

"Today is your birthday?"

"Today is *our* birthday, and I better get over there to help Nyla get everything ready."

"I suppose I ought to go out and shop for some presents," Ned said.

"That would be good," Mina laughed. "Because Nyla and I love birthday presents, especially ones we don't have to share."

HAPPY BIRTHDAYS

NYLA AND MINA had decorated the Maunalani house with an abundance of flowers and greenery. The staircase was wrapped in delicately scented vines of maile, and as Ned entered, their fragrance set off a chain of memories of his childhood in Sāmoa. Anthuriums and several varieties of flowering ginger were placed in large Chinese floor vases all round the room, with gardenias and lacy ferns gracing the smaller tables. By the time he arrived, the party was well under way. On a table full of presents in the living room, he placed two small lavender packages tied up with silver ribbons. Glasses tinkled to the hum of conversation and laughter, as a trio of Hawaiian women sang island songs in pleasing harmony. Todd waved to Ned as soon as he walked in, and Ned resolved to try to put aside all suspicions for the evening.

"I should have warned you," Todd grinned. "These sisters have a fixation about celebrating their mutual birthday."

"Do they do this every year?" Ned asked.

"Every year they invite about a hundred people. Every year they get these flowers and maile vines shipped in from the big island. Every year they hire a caterer to take care of the food. Nyla says it's in lieu of an annual Christmas party."

A young woman carrying a tray, dressed in a bright muʻumuʻu with a red hibiscus pinned in her hair, approached Ned and asked if she could get him a cocktail.

"Gin and tonic would be lovely, thanks," Ned smiled. On hearing his accent, the young woman gave him a dreamy look and walked away.

"Gee, maybe you could teach me to talk like that," Todd said as he watched her go.

"Sorry," winked Ned, "it's a trade secret."

"Let's go out to the garden," said Todd, "otherwise, we might be forced into dancing. And don't worry," he smiled, "your gin and tonic and Miss Bedroom Eyes will have no trouble finding you."

On the way to the garden, they passed through the dining room. The table was laid out buffet style with a wide choice of island delicacies. The colorful centerpiece bloomed with tropical fruit and flowers. There were several tables out in the garden set with pastel tablecloths and vases of gardenias. Todd chose one tucked in the corner. Ned's drink appeared in the hands of the infatuated waitress, and the two men sat back and surveyed the scene. Ned recognized a few faces from the theatre. Johnny Knight and Kīnaʻu Kelly, who wore a crown of tropical flowers over her profusion of curls, were engaged in an intense conversation, while her brother Kalani, with a substantial plate of food in front of him, seemed oblivious to everything else. Two women from the costume shop were sitting at a table with James and Jerry from the cast. Next to them, at a larger table, sat Christian Hollister, surrounded by a coterie of people. An extremely glamorous blonde, dressed in a way that screamed money, sat next to him, hanging onto his every word.

"I see Hollister has a fan club," Ned remarked.

"Yeah, and the blonde, Lamby Langston, is president." Todd laughed. "You know, it's interesting to me, someone born without a silver spoon in the mouth, to watch these people with money. There's two kinds in my book, the ones who it will never spoil and the ones who were spoiled from day one."

"I hope I fall in the first category," Ned said as he squeezed the lime into his drink.

"Don't ever change, buddy." Todd toasted him and downed what was left of his scotch.

"What did your father do, Todd. What line of work?" Ned asked.

"I'm adopted," said Todd. "My father was a cop."

"Adopted?" Ned was surprised.

"Yeah, who knows, my real father could have been an earl." Todd took a sip of his drink. "And what did your old man do?"

"If I had followed in my father's footsteps, I'd be a harbor pilot," Ned mused.

The pretty waitress appeared once again, this time with two plates of food that included sushi, shrimp tempura, and fresh sashimi. She took Todd's glass and went to replenish it. Ned and Todd continued to observe the party. Mina was circulating in the garden and greeting guests. She was wearing a simple silk Chinese dress in dark forest green, complimented by a pretty pair of silver hibiscus earrings. Her lei was made of three strands of plump white pīkake blossoms. As soon as Christian Hollister saw her approaching, he sprang to his feet, and with obvious admiration, kissed her on the cheek and wished her a very happy birthday. Lamby Langston declined to stand up, but she extended a languid hand to Mina.

"Now I wonder," snickered Todd, "if Miss Langston has any inkling of how she appears to others."

"Either she's so self-involved she doesn't notice, or she's not got a lot upstairs," Ned guessed.

"I'll vote for all of the above," said Todd as he started in on his shrimp tempura. "You should try having a conversation with her."

After everyone had eaten, a gong sounded and the party assembled in the sprawling living room. The waitresses passed around champagne, and Johnny Knight sat down at the piano. In a beautiful tenor voice Johnny Knight sang and played, while Nyla and Mina danced a hula for their guests. They moved in unison, mirror images of grace that captured the essence of the Pacific and what it meant to be of this particular place. As Ned watched, he felt touched to be part of this birthday tradition and to be taken with warmth into the lives of these people. He remembered how many things he'd missed when he and his mother moved to England, and how he now savored these island connections. It pained him to think of what he and Mina might discover, and, for a moment, he felt like Judas in the garden. The dance ended and the lights went out. Everyone sang "Happy Birthday" as a cake with glowing candles was carried in. Mina and Nyla blew out all the candles to cheers and hoots, and after the cake and more champagne were passed around, Johnny Knight played dance music. Todd and Ned perched themselves well up on the staircase, content as onlookers to smoke cigars and drink brandy while their waitress continued to spoil them with extra pieces of cake. Nyla and Johnny Knight had just finished singing a splendid rendition of an island song.

"Nyla has a lovely voice," Ned commented.

Todd was beaming with pride. "We've been married five years, and I still can't believe it. She could have had her pick of any of these rich guys here."

"Must be your handsome mug, detective."

"I tell you," said Todd, "I'd take a bullet for her. I swear it."

Ned watched the happy expression on his friend's face cloud over as Todd looked into his brandy tumbler and swirled the amber liquid around and around. Would you kill for her too, Ned thought, to protect her, or yourself and the life you'd made together in this beautiful place on the top of the hill overlooking the sea?

A little after midnight, the guests had all gone. Mina and Nyla sat on the carpet around a coffee table that was piled high with their presents. Todd and Ned (Todd had begged Ned not to leave him alone with the sisters in their birthday frenzy) lounged on the nearby furniture, still sipping brandy and blowing smoke rings. Mina and Nyla began to open their presents with all the enthusiasm of eight-year-olds. They were delighted with Ned's gifts. He had given each of them a beautiful pin from Gump's. Fashioned in the art nouveau style, the pins were an intricate filigree of silver morning glory vines with ivory flowers tinted a lavender-blue.

"In the language of flowers," Nyla informed Mina, "morning glories mean affection."

After the presents, the four of them lay around surrounded by discarded boxes, paper, and ribbons.

"I was thinking," Ned said in a lazy tone, "of taking a jaunt to one of the other islands."

"Sounds like a good idea," said Todd.

"The portrait is back, a suspect is arrested, and the play doesn't really need me for a while."

"Sounds like a *great* idea," yawned Nyla.

"I was thinking," Ned went on, "I might like to visit Hawai'i, the Big Island. I've heard there's quite a bit to see."

"Hey, Mina and I are going there," said Nyla. "Mina's going on Friday and I'll be there on Sunday. I've got a few days off rehearsal. You can come with me or go with her."

"Are you offering my services as a tour guide without consulting me?" Mina frowned.

"I have no real obligations this week." Ned sipped his brandy.

"Well, go with Mina," Nyla said, sitting up. "You can stay at the ranch. I'll call my father. They'll take good care of you, and you'll get to see all kinds of things most visitors would never be able to."

"You know that the airplane flight to Kona is a charter with some other people, and there might not be any room," Mina remarked with a yawn.

"I happen to know there are three empty places," Nyla stated.

"If you say so," Mina answered.

"Don't pay any attention to Mina. She'd be happy to show you around until I get there, wouldn't you, Mina?"

Mina, who was now stretched out on a sofa, did her very best to sound indifferent, mumbling as she turned on her side. "I guess it's okay, just so long as he behaves himself and doesn't cause any trouble."

LOOSE ENDS

EARLY ON FRIDAY morning, Mina put down the top to her car and loaded her suitcase in the back of her coupe. She was meeting Ned at noon for their charter flight to Kona, but this morning she was visiting someone special in Mānoa Valley who just might have some good information for her. The day was clear and still, a great day for flying if the weather held. She drove off, and as soon as she came over the rise near the University of Hawai'i at the mouth of the valley, she saw the clear green outline of the jagged mountains against the deep blue sky. Turning onto East Mānoa Road, she passed the little village with its stores and gas station and within minutes was knocking on the door of a well-kept cottage.

A profusion of plants surrounded the little house. It was a practical garden for the most part, full of fruit trees and vegetables. Patches of marigolds were placed at intervals in bright contrast to the green foliage. Mina remembered hearing somewhere that marigolds helped to ward off insects. She knocked on the door again. In a moment, a plump Japanese woman in an apron and a patterned navy blue dress greeted her. The woman's rich graying hair was neatly tucked up and held in place by a chopstick. She opened her arms to Mina and held her.

"Oh Mina, I'm so happy to see you," she said.

"Setsu-san, you look so good," Mina replied.

"Oh me! I'm getting so fat and lazy." She laughed. "Come, come let's go sit in the back. It's so nice in the morning."

They walked through the neat-as-a-pin parlor, through the kitchen, and out onto a small porch that looked over the rear garden. It was a large back yard enclosed by a high fence, covered in thick, blooming thunbergia vines. A small lily pond bordered the porch, complete with colorful gold fish and three water lily blooms. Several small white butterflies fluttered through the garden, while in one corner ricebirds hopped from branch to branch on a large mountain apple tree.

"This is so beautiful, Setsu-san." Mina's voice was full of admiration.

"Not one day goes by when I don't thank your mother for helping me." Setsu's voice carried traces of sadness and affection.

"She was so grateful to have you in her life."

"When I look back on it, it never seemed like work to me. But I know you and your sister were such rascals, always keeping me busy. Not like your brother—he was such a good baby. Somehow, I can't remember it like work." Setsu paused, "You wait, I'll get some tea."

Setsu had come to the Beckwith household just after the death of her husband. She had been their nursemaid from the time Mina and Nyla were barely six months old. After they had grown, she stayed on and nursed Mina's mother through her long and final illness. Mrs. Beckwith remembered Setsu in her will, providing her with enough to purchase this small cottage and live a secure and independent life.

Setsu returned with tea and a small plate of shortbread. She and Mina visited and talked about family and old times for over an hour.

"Uh-oh," said Mina, looking at her watch, "it's almost time for me to leave, and I didn't even ask you what I came here to ask you."

"What? What was that?" Setsu cocked her head to one side.

"It's very confidential."

"Are you snooping around again, Mina?" Setsu laughed.

"I'm not snooping," Mina answered. "I'm investigating."

"You always have to know everything. Even when you're little, you just jump from thing to thing, 'What's this? What's that? How come this? How come that?' So what is it now?"

"Do you know, or have you ever heard, anything about a woman named Kikue Tsuruda?" Mina asked.

"She's the one, works for that Nu'uanu family? The man just died?"

"That's the one."

"You know her?" Setsu asked.

"No, I'm looking into the man's, Mr. Halpern's, death. Not officially, but, you know . . ."

"Oh Mina," Setsu looked serious. "I know it's no good to tell you to be careful. I heard they arrested the Takahashi boy for the murder. Too bad for his mother. She's so proud of her son. He was engaged to that Katsuki girl, but I suppose now the family will break off the engagement. Too much shame, ah? Still, I don't think it was him. He's a nice boy."

"But do you know about her, the woman who works for the Halperns?"

"Well," Setsu began, "what I've heard is not very nice, and I'm just repeating it because it's you asking, Mina." Setsu sat and stared for a minute into the garden. "This woman, Kikue, she was like me, a picture bride from Japan. But she came to Hawai'i long after me, maybe 1917, 1918. I heard her family was famous for making furniture in Japan, but they began to have hard times. I don't know for sure. Bad luck she had. Her husband was no good. I was lucky. Yamasaki-san was good to me. Only bad thing he did was die too soon. But that Tsuruda man, he's really not nice, and she's a young country girl, only sixteen, maybe seventeen. Tsuruda likes drinking and gambling, and he has a mean streak in him. Plenty times he beat her. That's what everybody said. Anyway after about five years he gets sick and dies. He leaves a big gambling debt, and she has to work and pay it back, because if she doesn't, it's shame for her, see? So she works at the plantation, but then she starts making money from men too. Not every man who comes along, she just had her certain ones, bachelors all of them. Of course, once she starts that no one wants to marry her, but she doesn't care because she can pay all the money back, and pretty soon the debt is gone and she quits the plantation too. And she's smart about learning English. I don't know, maybe she had other jobs, but she always has these men, that's how she makes her money. Then a few years ago I heard she was working for this family in Nu'uanu. The man's wife died, and she went there. Everyone says she must be doing more than cleaning, but I don't know. Even though people say these things, she always looks respectable, and she always works hard."

"So she doesn't have any family. No children or anything?"

"People said she got hāpai sometimes, but she had ways of getting rid of it. Some women know ways of doing things like that." Setsu sighed. "You know Mina, we all had a hard life, coming over here that way. But she had it much worse than most of us—bad husband, beatings, big debts to pay by herself. I saw some women with lives not even half so bad just give up, go crazy, or take their own life. Too bad she turn out like that, but no wonder, yeah?"

Setsu shook her head, took a sip from her teacup, and placed it down on the table.

While Mina was talking to Setsu in Mānoa valley, Ned was visiting Uncle Wing in Chinatown.

"I want to call your attention to an article in yesterday's paper," Uncle Wing said as he placed a cheese soufflé and a basket of croissants on the kitchen table. He then picked up a folded newspaper and pointed. "Regardez, s'il vous plaît."

Ned read the headline:

MAN DIES IN RIVER STREET TRAGEDY

This morning the body of well-known Chinatown businessman, K. W. Zane, was found floating in Nu'uanu Stream. According to the ensuing investigation, Mr. Zane left the Riverside Bar last night at about 1 a.m. Reports stated that he had been drinking quite a bit, and more than one witness said Mr. Zane rebuffed offers of help and left the saloon on his own. It is assumed that on his way home, he fell into the stream and drowned. There were no witnesses, but according to his wife, Mr. Zane's usual route home takes him along a stretch of River Street where there are no guardrails near very deep portions of the stream. Mrs. Zane said her husband could not swim. Authorities are treating this as an accident, and unless any witnesses come forward to the contrary, there will be no further investigation. This is yet another example of how the neglect of civic improvements in our community has again resulted in tragedy. When will the territorial government realize that public safety should come first?

Ned put the paper down, and Uncle Wing served him a plate with a generous helping of cheese soufflé and another plate of fluffy croissants. He also poured him a strong cup of coffee.

"Please eat," said Uncle Chang, helping himself to the soufflé as well. "I wanted to tell you about Mr. Zane. He was known for his legitimate business of dry goods and tailoring, but also for his little black market. He specialized in weapons, you know—guns and things. He might have been able to find some nitroglycerin for someone if they paid enough. And now he's dead. Not only dead, but very conveniently dead, very neatly dead. There will be no further investigation."

"I imagine right now those words are music to someone's ears," remarked Ned.

"Sweet music," added Uncle Wing.

"A someone who knows how to tie up loose ends."

"I'm afraid so."

"How is Cecily?"

"She'll be coming home this afternoon, but she still has no recollection of the incident."

"Uncle Wing, this afternoon, Mina and I are going to the island of Hawai'i, to her father's ranch. We're hoping a little distance will give us some perspective."

"Just business?"

"Well, I've never been there. Of course, I'd like to do some sightseeing."

"With Mina?" Uncle Wing smiled.

"We've agreed that certain things are off limits," sighed Ned.

"Mina has always been good about handling the opposite sex."

"I had no idea she was a widow."

"Very tragic," Uncle Wing shook his head.

"I guess it was quite a blow."

"It was complicated for our Mina. People idealized the marriage, but to tell you the truth, I don't know if she was all that happy. That uncertainty made it worse when he died, of course. She took it like a champion—too well, I think. You know, when people don't express their grief, when they just try to pretend things didn't happen, it's not good."

Somehow, although Ned wanted to hear about these things, it made him feel depressed. "Nyla will join us on Sunday. If Cecily remembers anything important, you could send word or call us at the ranch."

"I will let you know if she does." Uncle Wing was emphatic. "How's the soufflé?"

"C'est bon."

PANIOLO COUNTRY

NED WAS WAITING at the John Rodgers Airfield, staring at the amphibious craft he was about to entrust his life to. The plane was an eight-passenger S-38 Sikorsky, and Mina had warned him that although they were taking off from an airfield, they would be making a water landing in Kailua, Kona. The other passengers were already giving their baggage to the copilot and starting to board by the time Mina arrived. Their suitcases were taken care of, and they boarded the plane by climbing up a kind of stepladder, and entered the cabin through a porthole-like door at the top of the fuselage. Inside was a tiny center aisle with wicker seats on either side for the passengers. Ned found a little packet on his seat containing chewing gum and cotton. Mina explained that the chewing gum was to equalize ear pressure and that smart passengers put cotton in their ears during takeoff on account of the noise. As they taxied down the field, the plane made a terrible sound, like tin being dragged over pebbles, but once they were in the air, the cacophony stopped and gave way to the loud, but not unpleasant hum of the engines.

After about three hours, they bounced into a water-landing off Kailua, Kona. Once on the dock, the first thing Ned noticed was the intensity of the afternoon sun, and he was relieved to slide into the back seat of the large sedan that Mina's father had sent to pick them up. Kepā, one of the ranch hands, was their driver. He wore a handsome cowboy hat, jeans with a silver buckle, and a pair of nicely polished leather boots. He greeted Mina with a warm hug and a lei of maile, and he shook Ned's hand as if they were already old friends. It was just a few minutes before the bags were retrieved, and they were on their way. Mina had warned Ned that the drive to the ranch would be long, but promised him that the scenery would be something special.

They sat watching the passing vistas as the road climbed away from the coast and into a cooler mountain elevation, passing many wooden cottages, flanked by circular water tanks and surrounded by coffee groves. Often someone sitting on the front porch or walking along the road would wave and offer a friendly smile. As they climbed higher, the coffee farms gave way to the forests, and after miles of tall trees and low-growing ferns the forest stopped and Kepā pulled the car onto a lookout perched on the shoulder of the road. They got out of the car to take in the panorama. The remains of an old lava flow lay just below them, and in the hard but sinuous black rocks, Ned almost thought he could see the shapes of living creatures looking back at him. In the distance they could see an older flow of lava, like long black fingers reaching out across the landscape toward the blue shoreline.

"Welcome to Madame Pele's island, Ned." Mina smiled as she looked out at the vista before them.

"It feels like her island, doesn't it?" Ned was enjoying the intensity of the landscape.

"It's a wise thing to remember," Mina said.

They continued, passing through forests and lava flows until they reached the pasturelands outside of Waimea. They stopped at a small park and ate the tea sandwiches that Mina's grandmother had sent along. The air was brisk and chilly enough for them to put on sweaters. Tall eucalyptus trees lined the road, and green hills rolled out to the backdrop of the tall citadel of Mauna Kea, whose summit was wreathed in snow.

"This doesn't look like a tropical island," remarked Ned as he bit into an egg sandwich.

"You're in paniolo country now, Ned." Mina had already started on her second sandwich.

"Maybe your friend would be interested in hunting some pipi

ʻāhiu while he's here." Kepā raised his eyebrows as he smiled at Mina.

"What's that?" Ned asked.

"It's wild cattle, and I don't think you want to accept. I need you in one piece." Mina looked serious.

"Wild cattle?" Ned looked confused.

"Yes, wild cattle." Mina put down her sandwich. "The first herds on the island were started from wild cattle. This British sea captain, Vancouver, gave cattle to the chiefs and told them if they left them alone there would be this great new source of meat. So the chiefs forbade anyone to kill the cattle, and they just let them run free. As time passed, they multiplied into thousands of cattle and became a real problem. They were wild and strange, and people had to dig big pits to keep them away from settled areas. A lot of them were rounded up and fenced in when the ranches started."

"But not all," Kepā said.

"When was this? The ranches getting started?" Ned asked.

"I think in the 1850s or the 1860s," Mina said. "They used to hunt the cattle before that, like wild game. Anyway, the ranches contained most of them, but there are still lots of wild ones roaming around in the uplands and unpastured places. And I'm telling you, Ned, they're wild, mean, and fearless. The paniolo mess around with them for sport."

"Sounds intriguing," said Ned.

"I'm warning you, for your own good, forget it," returned Mina.

"You could just have a look-see," Kepā chimed in.

"Ned," Mina was adamant. "There's nothing the paniolo on the ranch like better than to scare the pants off of unsuspecting male visitors by taking them to hunt for pipi ʻāhiu."

"Don't listen to her, Ned." Kepā shook his head. "It's not that dangerous."

"Well, maybe I'll think about it." Ned winked at Kepā.

"Oh God!" Mina rolled her eyes and reached for a cookie.

They drove north into the Kohala Mountains. The air got cold and damp, and by the time they reached the ranch house, everything was enshrouded in a still fog. Mina's father and grandmother greeted them as the car pulled up the long drive. The low white house was set up on a hill, but because of the heavy mist, it was hard for Ned to tell what the surrounding land looked like. There were quick introductions, a cup of hot tea, and then Ned was taken to his room. Grandma Hannah insisted that he and Mina get settled and rest after their long drive. Ned was excited and curious about the ranch and the house, but after he unpacked, he found himself wanting to lie down, just for a few minutes. There was a window seat that made a kind of day bed. A soft woolen blanket lay at one end. Ned made himself comfortable. He looked out at the mist, and a feeling of quiet and peace washed over him as he closed his eyes. The next thing he was conscious of was someone knocking on his door. It was dark outside, and he couldn't tell how much time had passed.

"Ned? Ned? Are you awake?" It was Mina's voice.

"Barely," he called back.

"We're having cocktails in a few minutes. I just wanted to let you know."

"I'll be right there."

GRANDMA HANNAH'S STORY

OVER COCKTAILS NED realized that Nyla's disposition was much like her father's. He was warm, welcoming, and cordial. Sure of himself, Charles Beckwith exuded charisma and self-confidence without snobbery, and it was very clear that he was proud of both of his daughters. His hair was a little gray and his face slightly weathered, but his youthful exuberance made it difficult to pinpoint his exact age. Ned knew, because Mina had told him, that Grandma Hannah was about seventy-five. Her luxuriant white hair framed her timeless face. She carried some extra weight, but her brown skin was smooth and hardly wrinkled, and her lively eyes suggested a sharp, observant personality.

"Well, Ned," said Charles as they went into dinner, "I'll do my best to save you from the clutches of Mina and Nyla while you're visiting."

"I came as a willing victim," smiled Ned.

"Kepā has already given him the pipi ʻāhiu routine," Mina reported.

"Mina, is that a note of disapproval I hear in your voice?" Her father quipped.

"I've warned him once, and now I wash my hands of it." She sat down at the table. "What's for dinner? I'm starved."

Charles Beckwith regaled Ned with stories about the ranch and the island. "Mina tells me you ride," Charles said with a note of approval.

"I do," said Ned, "but I'm not used to your luxurious cowboy saddles."

"Mina, take him out tomorrow and show him the ranch," Charles suggested.

"I thought we'd drive over to Hāwī and look around in the morning. We could go out riding after lunch." Mina looked at Ned.

"Sounds splendid," Ned rejoined.

After dinner Charles Beckwith excused himself, saying he had to look over some accounts before bed. Mina, Grandma Hannah, and Ned sat by the fire in the living room. Mina told Grandma Hannah about Ned's escorting the portraits to Hawai'i, the theft, and Halpern's murder.

"Such a sad time to remember, when the portraits were painted and the king died." Grandma Hannah's eyes were transfixed by the fire.

"You know, Grandma, we can't understand why anyone would want to steal the portrait and then throw it away."

"And that inscription on the back," Ned said.

"Ah, that verse!" Grandma turned to Ned.

"Do you know something about it?" Mina tried not to sound too eager. "The king's death and the verse. What it all means?"

"Such a long time ago," said Grandma. "So much happened."

"Will you tell us?" Mina asked. She knew there were some things her grandmother wouldn't talk about.

"It's a long story. Your friend might be bored." Grandma gave Ned a coy smile.

"Oh, no," Ned replied. "I would love to hear all about it."

"Well then, Mina," said Grandma, content to be the focus of attention, "you pour us more tea, and we'll all get comfortable. Maybe Ned would put another log on the fire. Oh, and get some of the throws, Mina dear. The night is getting colder."

Soon the three of them sat bundled up around the glowing fire and Grandma Hannah began. "I don't know if Mina told you, Ned, that I was very close to King Kalākaua's wife, Queen Kapi'olani. Our families were distantly related, and we had very strong ties, not just to Kapiʻolani, but to the king and the Hawaiian monarchy. The queen, of course, was much older than I was, but she took a great liking to me. She had certain young people she gathered around her. She admired fine needlework too, and so we shared a common interest because I had been doing fancy work since I was a child. We spent many afternoons sewing together, unless she had some appointment or engagement she had to go to. She was a wonderful woman. People have no idea, because she was quiet and kept herself in the background, but she was so kind. You'll hear people talk, but I know she loved the king and was a loyal and good wife, and he treated her with the utmost respect and admiration.

"It was well known, you know, by the 1880s that for many years a not so secret society existed in the kingdom, made up of foreign men who were bent on destroying the monarchy and annexing Hawaiʻi to the United States. The murdered man's father, Eben Halpern, was one of them, and your editor, Mina, Christian Hollister, his family belonged to it, and some people from other wealthy families. The group called themselves the Committee of Public Safety, and as the king turned more and more toward ways he thought would help the Hawaiian people, this committee became more and more active. The king received death threats. Of course, it could never be proved who was making them, but we all knew. His health began to fail, and in 1890 he took a trip to San Francisco to try to recuperate. He was met in San Francisco by U.S. Admiral Green and the admiral's ensign, George Blain. Blain just happened to be the nephew of Eben Halpern. Eben Halpern was there too, and Richard Hollister, Christian's grandfather."

"Chris Hollister never told me that." Mina frowned.

"All kinds of influential people liked to follow the king on these trips," Grandma Hannah continued. "Especially when he went to America, because he and everyone around him got so much attention in the press and there were so many formal meetings. I think too, these people wanted to keep an eye on what he was doing. Poor man, he lived his last days in a goldfish bowl. Anyway, there was a big entourage of people around him, some friends and some enemies. The portrait painter, he was there too, having the portraits framed.

The queen remained in Hawai'i. She'd taken a trip once to England for Queen Victoria's Jubilee, but after that she never traveled outside of the islands."

"While the king was visiting," continued Grandma Hannah, "his health began to fail, and he was attended by the U.S. Fleet surgeon, Dr. Moody. They said the king suffered from Bright's disease, which as you know, affects the kidneys. He became worse and died in the Palace Hotel on January 20th, 1891."

"Grandma," Mina interrupted, "is it true, do you think, what some Hawaiians say, that he was poisoned?"

"Well, Mina," Grandma cleared her throat, "that's an interesting part of the story I'll get to soon. The queen was consumed with grief when she heard the news. I'm sure you've seen pictures of his funeral. It's so sad to think about, when I remember the queen, how little she cared for the intrigues of politics, how much affection she had for her husband! Well, one afternoon about three or four weeks after the funeral, I was staying with her at her cottage in Waikīkī. I was married by then, and your mother was about five or six. Grandpa had gone to the Big Island on some business, and the queen asked us to come to her. Your mother had been swimming most of the morning and was having a nap. I remember the day so well. It was just after lunch. The queen and I were sewing, appliquéing a quilt with a pattern of breadfruit leaves. The sea was calm that day, and the waves were breaking a certain way on the beach. They made a gentle, quiet sound, like music in the background, drifting into the room. The maid came in to announce that Kahikina McNeil had arrived and wished to see the queen. Kahikina had been one of the king's most trusted advisers, and he was in San Francisco when the king died. The queen said he should be allowed in. When Kahikina came into the little parlor, he suggested that what he had to tell her was something I shouldn't hear. I rose to leave, but she stopped me.

'No, sit,' she said to me. 'She's a trusted friend, she won't repeat a word of what you say to anyone who shouldn't hear it.'

"It was then I noticed how drawn and tired Kahikina's face looked, as though he hadn't slept for a long time.

'It's such a delicate matter,' he began, 'I didn't want to upset you so soon after this tragedy.'

'If it's something of importance, just tell me,' the queen said.

"Kahikina was near tears. He mumbled something about it being his fault, and if he'd only acted on his suspicions. Then he just blurted it out.

'I have proof that they poisoned him.'

"He got up and paced around the room. We stopped our sewing and watched him.

'I have letters. I hid the letters. I stole them, you see. They may know everything. I'm not sure. I wrote it in the verse, and they'll never find them. But I can't stop this feeling that I could have prevented it. I would have if I had just—'

"He was interrupted at that point by the sound of a carriage coming down the drive. The queen sent me to see who it was. I came back and told her it looked like Eben Halpern and Richard Hollister. Kahikina looked as if he'd seen a ghost.

'I have to go,' he stammered. 'I shouldn't have come. They'll think you know.'

'Out the door,' whispered the queen, and she pointed to the door that led onto a back veranda that faced the beach. 'Go straight into the coconut grove. They won't see you.'

"Kahikina had time to get away, as the new arrivals had to go through the formality of being announced and admitted. When Halpern and Hollister came in, they inquired about the queen's well-being, and again offered their condolences and asked if there was any way they could be of service. The queen, in a formal and polite manner, offered them tea, made conversation, and answered their questions. As they were about to leave, Mr. Halpern casually inquired if she had seen Kahikina McNeil.

'Not since the funeral,' the queen replied with a serene smile.

"The next morning, we received the sad news that Kahikina McNeil had died in a house fire. In the newspaper, it was reported that he had been distraught and drinking quite a bit since the king's death. He lived alone, and his housekeeper stated that he had the bad habit of smoking in bed. She said that several times over the years his carelessness with cigarettes and matches had caused small fires. It was presumed that he was alone, drunk, and unable to save himself. The queen told me, in a very serious way, to forget about his visit and to never repeat a word of it. She said perhaps our lives depended on it. I stayed with her for about two weeks after the incident, and for several days I had the distinct sensation that we were being watched. There were noises at night and strange people walking by on the beach, but the queen never said a word. Whatever she thought or did about it, she never told me. Perhaps she never told anyone."

The three of them sat for a moment, staring into the glowing coals of the fire.

"Grandma," Mina began, "did you ever tell anyone?"

"Many, many years later. I told a few people," Grandma said. "I told your mother."

"I wrote it in the verse, and they'll never find them," repeated Ned. "That's what he said?"

"Word for word," Grandma answered. "I remember watching the king and queen pose for those portraits. They're beautiful, aren't they?"

"Exquisite pieces of work," said Ned.

"I'd like to see them again," Grandma sighed.

"I'll take you when you come to Honolulu," Mina said. "Do you want to come with us for a ride tomorrow? We're driving down to Hāwī."

"Oh, you don't want an old woman tagging along," Grandma shook her head.

"Not only do we want your company," said Ned, "we insist on it."

"In that case," smiled Grandma Hannah, "I'd better get some rest."

Goodnights were given all around, and Grandma Hannah was leaving the room when she stopped for a minute and turned back to them.

"You know who is fascinated with that verse? Hīnano Kahana, down at Hulihe'e Palace. It's a little hobby of his, Hawaiian riddles. He's worked out several meanings, you should go and talk to him."

OUT RIDING

THE NEXT DAY, the clouds cleared and the sun came out. Mina, Ned, and Grandma Hannah spent a pleasant morning driving to the North Kohala town of Hāwī. Before visiting the town, Mina drove down a dirt road that took them through the sugarcane fields to the impressive remains of a Hawaiian temple. Grandma Hannah refused to get out of the car to look at it, saying she didn't like the feeling of this particular heiau. They went next to Hāwī and then to the courthouse to see the statue of Kamehameha. It was almost identical to the one in Honolulu, and Grandma explained that it was, in fact, the original Kamehameha statue, lost at sea and then recovered. They next visited several scenic lookouts and then headed back home for lunch.

After lunch, Ned and Mina saddled up horses and rode out to see the ranch. Ned handled his sturdy appaloosa in an easy and natural way that impressed Mina. Her glossy palomino was spirited and quick to respond. They let the horses gallop over a wide, open pasture and then rode up a hill, and from that vantage Mina explained the layout of the ranch. Then, she suggested they follow one of the forest trails to her favorite waterfall. The horses became quiet and watchful as they left the pasturelands and entered the high forest. Birds called through vines and branches, and the afternoon sun filtered through the canopy in shafts of light.

The trail turned to follow a stream, and after a while they could hear the sound of the falls. It was not a spectacular waterfall. It rose about twenty-five or thirty feet, and the pool spanned about forty feet at its widest. But what it lacked in grandeur, it made up for in the luxuriant charm of the flora that surrounded it and the clear and brilliant quality of the water. Ferns and wild orchids surrounded the large smooth rocks that edged the pool. Long flowering vines hung from the trees, making the pond feel curtained and secluded. They tied up the horses, took off their shoes, and sat on the rocks, dangling their feet in the cold mountain water. There was a quiet, comfortable silence between them. After some time had passed, he turned to her.

"What do you think it all means, those things your grandmother told us? Do you think Abel Halpern wanted what that McNeil person hid?"

"I don't know." She furrowed her brow. "Maybe it's just a coincidence. At first I thought maybe Halpern just wanted to protect his family name, but that doesn't make sense. I mean if no one knew about it, why call attention to it? And then why would he end up getting murdered himself?"

"I just don't understand what anyone would hope to find, which leads me back to thinking that the theft was smoke and mirrors. Sheila and Andrew could have engineered the theft to distract from the murder and—" he stopped.

"Go ahead and say it." She threw a pebble in the water.

"So could Todd, but I'm not sure what his motive would be. Todd could have been taking money from Halpern, but still, it wouldn't be to Halpern's advantage to expose Todd for that. He'd just be exposing himself."

"I'll bet whoever did it planted that stuff in Sam Takahashi's car."

"It's still possible that Sam did it. He has a pretty strong motive."

"I doubt it." Mina threw another pebble in the water. "You know what I think we should do next?"

"I'm afraid to ask."

"I think we should search Abel Halpern's study. I'm sure he hid something in there that would shed some light on this whole thing. Oh, I know what you're thinking, that the police have already done it, but I know if something's there and they didn't find it, I could."

"You know we'd never get permission from Sheila or Andrew."

"I wasn't going to get permission," she said.

"That's illegal and dangerous."

"It would be easy. We just wait for a night when both Sheila and Andrew have to be at the theatre, and I'll do it while you keep them busy at rehearsal."

"And how were you planning to get in?"

"No one locks their doors in Hawai'i, and anyway, one of my basic talents is lock picking, remember?"

"I don't know, Mina."

"Look, we're hitting a dead end here, and I'm going to do it whether you help me or not."

"I bet you were a stubborn little girl."

"Especially when I knew I had a good idea," she said.

"I'm even more curious about that verse." He was making circles in the water with his feet. "I have a strong feeling that we should pursue its meaning. The other thing I think we need to do is nose around the museum a bit more. Talk to some of the other people who work there. People like secretaries and librarians, they see quite a bit without people noticing them."

"I'd say we should snoop around Kikue Tsuruda's house too, but I think that would be dangerous. She's a clever one." Mina lay back and stared up at the forest canopy.

"And no one's checked her for an alibi," he added.

"I wonder why she told Sheila that Halpern raped her? Did he, or was it just a bid for Sheila's sympathy?"

"Maybe she thought she could get Sheila to pay for her hospital bill." He threw another pebble in the pool and watched as it generated ripple after ripple. "And was she trying to kill herself or just hoping to cause a miscarriage?"

"Let's put her on our list," she said. "So now, we have Kikue Tsuruda to check out, the museum staff to get nosy with. And the visit to the Halpern residence."

"I'm not pleased with the last idea."

She just looked at him and shrugged. "I told you, I'm doing it. Let's ride. Further on there's a spectacular view."

The trail wound around, out of the forest and up the steep grassy incline of an old volcanic hill that had now been appropriated for grazing. From the top, they could see for miles, all the way down to the coast. Across the water, another island rose in the distance.

"What is that?" Ned asked.

"Maui, we're looking northwest."

"It looks so close."

"It is close, but the channel in between is very rough."

They rode back and he watched her in the late afternoon light. She rode a little ahead of him. He noticed the way the color of her skin took on a warm glow, as if it were holding the sun, and how her hair hung in disheveled dark curls around her shoulders. Her jeans were muddy and small brambles were stuck on her right sleeve.

"Nyla arrives tomorrow afternoon." She reined her horse in to ride beside Ned.

"I know."

"She's going to want to drag you all over the island."

"I won't mind. Your sister is very good company."

"I'm glad you won't mind. I want to spend some time with my grandmother. I think I'll take her down to Kona, and we can ask Hīnano Kahana about the verse. And I want to talk her into coming to Honolulu soon."

This was a heady mixture for Ned. Mina's closeness, the affection she had for her grandmother, the smell of the horses, the unbelievable beauty of the landscape as the hills and the pasture spread out before them, with the sea and the island in the distance. He felt connected to her through a significant heritage of island people and island landscapes. He could feel the twinge inside himself, the familiar ache, the one he always had when he wished the moment he was in could last forever.

22

BULLS AND BIRDS

EARLY THE NEXT morning, well before dawn, Charles Beckwith woke Ned. "Time to get ready," he said. "There's coffee in the kitchen."

After dinner the night before, Charles had taken Ned aside, out of Mina's earshot, and invited him to go on a wild cattle hunt this morning. Ned had accepted. The morning was cold. Ned hadn't expected this kind of terrain or weather in Hawai'i. He dressed quickly in his jeans, a T-shirt, a flannel shirt, and the quilted denim jacket that he had borrowed from Charles.

He drank his coffee as fast as he could in the kitchen and then went out with Charles to the stable where the paniolo had saddled up the horses. Lanterns cast a warm glow over the men and animals, and the familiar smell of hay and leather made Ned feel comfortable in an otherwise unfamiliar arena. He had been riding since he was a boy, but cowboys and ranches were a far cry from a gallop through the English countryside. Ned recognized Kepā, who introduced him to the other two paniolo, Kawika and Mākena. They welcomed Ned as they checked their gear one last time. Ned admired the tooled leather embellishments on their western saddles, and watched as each cowboy hung a leather lasso over his saddle horn and tied on coils of manila rope. Kepā slapped a weathered brown cowboy hat on Ned and said, "Okay boy, now you're ready for some swell fun.

You're riding 'Ehu. She's quick and smart, guaranteed to keep you out of trouble."

Ned recognized 'Ehu as the palomino Mina had ridden the day before. Once in the saddle, he sensed her awareness, as if she were already evaluating his abilities as a rider. Right away, Ned took her out of the stable and rode her around. Guiding her in a few small circles, he felt an instant response to his lead.

The five men rode out into the dark. There was no moon in the cloudless sky, and the stars stood out against the night, like an intricate fishnet holding up the heavens. In the crisp air, Ned could see his breath. After about a half an hour of riding up through the pastures, they stopped just before the forest line. There was at least an hour before dawn, and the paniolo made a small campfire. In no time, they passed out tin cups of coffee and hard crackers smothered in butter. Kawika went out to scout while the others waited. Charles explained to Ned that the herds of wild cattle often came down into the pasturelands at night, and then moved back into the forest to hide during the day. This morning, they were after a particular bull, the leader of a wild herd of about thirty or forty. The herd and the bull had been seen more than once in this area. "He's probably a good 1,600 pounds. The best-case scenario is we catch the renegade, get him back to the ranch, and castrate him. If he settles down, he'll make a damn useful ox."

"And if he doesn't settle down?" asked Ned.

"If he doesn't settle down, there's more meat for the hungry ranch people." Charles raised his tin cup in a mock toast. "Listen, Ned, when we go out, stick close to me, and be sure to stay uphill of any bulls you might encounter. If you're uphill and a bull charges, it's easier to dodge him, and if he hits you, it will be much less damaging than if he's barreling down hill. The weight and momentum are deadly."

"I'm going to make every effort to be an unobtrusive observer," Ned replied.

"If you got hurt on this excursion, I'd never hear the end of it from my daughters. Each of them on their own is bad enough, but when they join forces, well, a person might as well get paid protection."

Kawika returned and reported that the herd was just going into the forest about half a mile away. The campfire was put out, and everyone was in the saddle and ready to go in minutes. Pale morning light was beginning to wash away the night, and the first birdsongs were breaking the stillness. Ned could feel 'Ehu's excitement building as if she were looking forward to the events to come. When they reached their destination, the three paniolo rode into the forest. Charles signaled Ned to follow him, and the two of them waited on a rocky outcropping, a little distance away. It seemed to Ned that the minutes passed in slow motion as both he and Charles remained silent, alert, and watchful. Finally, in the distance, Ned heard the low dull voices of the bulls drifting toward them. It was an eerie sound, as if creatures from deep in the earth had broken out of their underground lair and were trying to speak for the first time in the open air.

"Next," said Charles, "the paniolo will surprise them, and drive them out into the open, down there, where we'll have a good uphill advantage. It will be easier to cut out the bull. The cows and heifers will scatter first, but watch out for the young bulls—they may take a shot at you before they head back for the forest."

Just as Charles was finished speaking, they heard the wild shouts and cries of the paniolo, and the thundering of hooves getting louder and louder. Suddenly the herd surged through the trees in a massive wave with the paniolo swooping down behind them. 'Ehu was dancing back and forth as the ground beneath shook and a deafening roar filled the air.

"Stay behind me," yelled Charles as he charged out to join the chase. 'Ehu, at the first urging, raced forward toward the fray. Yelling, whooping, and swinging their lassos, the paniolo scared and startled the herd into scattering. For a moment, Ned became disoriented as the half-maddened cattle started to run in all directions. The air was filled with the men's sharp cries and the whine of lassos, the bellowing of panicked cattle, and the pounding of hooves.

"Ned, behind you," Charles shouted. And Ned turned 'Ehu just in time to avoid the charge of a young bull. As the young bull was slowing to turn for another charge, Charles rode up and threw Ned a bullwhip. Ned's heart was pounding as the bull charged again. As if enjoying the challenge, 'Ehu faced the bull and then stepped aside like a matador, avoiding its horns, and Ned was able to turn, and give chase. He managed one sharp crack of the whip on the bull's hind that sent him fleeing into the forest.

As he turned back, Ned saw Kepā's lasso spin three or four times in the air above his head and then almost instantly a great brindled bull lay prostrate on the ground. With perfect timing, Kawika and Mākena each lassoed one of the bull's horns with a deft twist of the wrist while he was still stunned from the fall. The enraged bull got up, shook his horns and dashed from side to side. He charged blindly for his captors as the rest of the herd fled in fear to the forest. The exceptionally trained horses knew how to counter and steady themselves against the fierce wrenching of the beast. The paniolo added weight to the horses' efforts by swinging themselves over their saddles and hanging to the side on one stirrup. Kawika, Mākena, and their horses maneuvered the bull until he was snubbed up against a large tree. Kepā and Charles moved in and made sure the bull was securely tied to the tree.

There were whoops and exclamations of delight when the job was done. Kepā pulled out a flask of whiskey, and everyone had a victory sip. Charles told Ned that later in the day the equally dangerous and tricky job of bringing the bull into the ranch would take place. Then Ned accompanied Charles and the paniolo on the ranch's traditional ritual of picking maile, something they always did after a pipi ʻāhiu hunt. They all fashioned the fragrant vines into leis for themselves and their horses. They were delighted that Ned, who remembered doing this as a child in Sāmoa, knew how to strip the vines to release their perfume.

"Ned, make a nice thick maile lei and give to Mina." Kepā smiled a sly smile. "Wahines cannot resist a maile lei."

"Yeah, and don't forget the kiss," Mākena teased. "Wahines cannot resist a little kiss."

"Lay off, boys," laughed Charles. "Maybe Ned has a little kīhei pili back in England."

"Maybe," chimed Kawika, "but now he's met your daughter, and it's adios kealoha for the haole ladies."

"These guys only think about three things. Cattle, horses, and romance." Charles laughed and shook his head.

"You forgot food, boss," Kawika added. "We love food."

"See, Ned," said Kepā as he placed a lei of maile on his horse. "Good thing you never listen to Mina. This is swell fun, just like I told you."

"The swellest fun," Ned said as he sat astride ʻEhu, who seemed to nod her head in agreement.

The three paniolo headed back to the ranch. Charles wanted to check a fence line in one of the pastures and asked Ned if he would like to ride along. The sun was up, and the stillness of the morning had given way to a light breeze. Before them the hilly ranch lands rolled down toward the sea. Here and there, cattle grazed, and the occasional bird dipped in and out of view. They rode slowly and let the easy contentment that seemed to arise from the landscape settle over them.

"Have you known Mina very long?" Charles inquired.

"No," said Ned, trying to sound very casual. "I've only just met her. It's Todd and Nyla I've known for a long time. I met Todd some years ago when he was stationed in England. He was doing some training in the armed forces, military intelligence."

"I see. That was before he met Nyla."

"How long have you been up here on the ranch?"

"This was my father's ranch, and I used to manage it when I was younger. Just after the girls were born, Healani and I moved back to Honolulu, and I worked for my father's company, which I eventually inherited and sold. It was Len's death that brought me back. I don't know if Mina told you about her husband."

"Just that he died."

"Well," said Charles, "that's more than she usually tells people. They were up here on the ranch, and when he passed away I decided to come back. I'm glad I did."

"And Mina went back to Honolulu."

"It's too bad he didn't give her more of a role in the ranch, managing it, I mean. Mina's a girl who needs something more to do than run a house."

"I can see that," Ned smiled. "You've a smart and capable daughter."

"You say that with admiration, Ned. Most men think Mina needs her head examined, or to get married and have children."

"I think those men you're talking about should meet my mother," laughed Ned. "She'd set them straight."

Mina and Grandma Hannah left for Kona that morning before Ned and Charles returned. They sat in the back seat while Kawika drove. Grandma had insisted that one of the boys drive them so that Mina could enjoy the scenery. "Besides," she said, "it's a real treat for one of the boys to go down to Kona."

"So, Kawika," Mina leaned forward. "Did Ned survive your little hunt in one piece?"

"He's a swell rider, Mina," he answered with some enthusiasm. "One young bull charged him, and he went after it with the bull whip. Gave him one sharp crack on the 'ōkole."

"A sterling achievement," she said under her breath.

"What's that?" Kawika glanced at her in the rear-view mirror.

"Nothing."

"And he knows how to make maile leis too, how to strip the vine and everything," Kawika offered.

Mina settled back into her seat and looked out at the view.

"Ned seems very nice," Grandma Hannah commented.

"I guess he is," said Mina.

"What are you two doing anyway?" Grandma asked.

"What do you mean?" Mina wouldn't look at her.

"It's no good, Mina. I can see your wheels turning, so you might as well tell me."

"He's not my boyfriend or anything, if that's what you're thinking."

"I'm not talking about that," smiled Grandma. "I'm talking about this murder business."

Mina sighed, and on the way to Kona, in a voice quiet enough so that Kawika couldn't hear, she told her grandmother every last detail, including her suspicions about Nyla and Todd. Grandma listened with great interest, then patted Mina's hand and said, "Don't worry dear, everything will straighten out. Let's see what Hīnano can tell us about the verse."

Grandma Hannah fell into a meditative silence as she stared out at the passing landscape. Mina watched Grandma Hannah roll down the car window and let the wind blow the little wisps of her white hair that had come loose from her neatly pinned coif. Subtle changes of expression passed over her smooth brown face, and every once in a while she would glance down at her hands and then back out the window. Mina sighed, leaned back into the plush leather seat and fought the childhood urge to curl up, place her head in Grandma Hannah's lap, and close her eyes until they arrived safely at their destination.

It was late morning when they arrived in Kailua, Kona. The small town was nestled comfortably against the crescent shoreline. Its worn board and batten buildings were closed down this peaceful Sunday morning, and as if in compliance, the ocean lay smooth and calm, mirroring the still depth of the sky. As they stood before the black wrought-iron gate of Hulihe'e Palace, they heard the last strains of a Hawaiian hymn from the large stone church across the street.

Hulihe'e stood on the shore at Kailua surrounded by coconut trees and a well-kept lawn. It was an old gracious two-story building first built in 1838 by one of the islands' most prominent chiefs. During the years of the monarchy, all of the Hawaiian royalty had used Hulihe'e as a pleasant retreat. Now that the palace was nearly a hundred years old, a historical society had taken over its care, and turned it into a museum. Hīnano, one of Grandma Hannah's oldest and closest friends, had been hired as the caretaker.

Grandma Hannah waited until the hymn from the church finished before she began to chant a kāhea, calling out to her friend, announcing herself in the polite way of their ancestors, and asking approval for entry. Mina smiled to herself and wondered what the congregation must be thinking. She heard Hīnano's deep, resonant voice chanting back before she saw him. He came around the side of the building, and, still chanting, he walked toward them, pausing on the threshold of the palace stairs, where he finished his welcome. The sounds and feel of the chant lingered in the air, and as soon as they walked through the wooden gate, Mina became aware of a rustling breeze in the palm trees and the sound of little waves lapping on the shore. Inside, she felt the ocean air drifting through the open windows and the house as if everything were being swept clean by the sea. Hīnano and Grandma Hannah sat down at a round wooden table in the parlor and immediately started to chatter away in Hawaiian. Mina wandered to the shade of the back veranda. She found a rocking chair and sat contentedly enjoying the expansive view, while the two old friends visited. Finally, Grandma Hannah called Mina in. Hīnano had some papers with him.

"Mina, dear, Hannah tells me you're interested in the old riddle from the portrait." Hīnano had always had one of the most spellbinding voices Mina had ever heard.

"Yes, I'm interested in it. Grandma tells me it was written by a man named Kahikina McNeil."

"He was a close friend of my mother's," said Hīnano. "I remember him well. He was interested in hula and chant. Last night I looked at my old notes on the subject. You know, these words have been published in articles on the portraits. The riddle has always puzzled me. I don't know what it means, what the kaona is, the deep meaning, but I can tell you what it says."

"I'd be so grateful, uncle." Mina and Nyla had always called Hīnano uncle.

"One thing to remember is that this was written on the occasion of the king's death. This first line, *lu'ulu'u ke akua*," he began. "*Lu'ulu'u* is to be weighted down with grief, to be downcast. The line refers to the akua being sorrowful. And the next part *I ka lani u'i hele loa*. Now *u'i* usually refers to looks, being pretty or handsome in a young way, but it also means to be heroic, you know, vigorous. And, of course, *ka lani* refers to a chief and also to the heavens, and *hele loa* is passing. The chiefs were always associated with their divine genealogy, and I'm quite sure that this line refers to the death of the king. The gods would be sorrowful at the death of a high chief. Also, this could refer to the heroic way in which he cared for his people. The next line, *he loa ke ala kai mehameha,* says that the way or the path to the sea is long and lonely. This again might refer to the lonely way the king died, far away from his wife and his country. The next two lines are very interesting. *Nānā a hewa ka maka, I nā mea huna i ka lipolipo.* Look until the eyes have seen all they can see of the things hidden in the deep darkness. The line asks us to look beyond what we see in this world, to look into the lipolipo, the darkness we all came from. I've only seen a picture of the portrait, but one thing that struck me right away was the mysterious look that the artist captured in the eyes. *Pali kū makani, o Kalākaua.* Kalākaua is an upright cliff buffeted by the winds. This could refer to the difficulties the king had to face and the honorable way he met his troubles, including death. This is one way of looking at the words. But as you know from hula, Mina, words can have so many meanings in our language, and Hawaiians were so fond of playing with and hiding things in language. Grandma has told you about Kahikina saying that he hid the proof of the king's murder, and that the secret was in these words. Some of us have always believed it was true. Remember the portraits were in Britain, and we didn't know what the words were until someone first wrote about the portraits. Now when I first read these words, I looked at them as if they were a reference to a place. If they are, I think it must be a place by the sea, an out-of-the-way place with cliffs, and perhaps the reference to the eyes is some kind of formation in the rocks or on the cliffs. I've always felt it was somewhere on this island."

"Kahikina did come to the Big Island after he returned from San Francisco," Grandma Hannah said. "I remember the queen mentioning he was away for a short time."

"But," said Mina, "a high dark cliff near the ocean. There must be dozens and dozens of places like that on this island."

"That's right," Hīnano agreed. "And I couldn't go crawling across every cliff on the island, so I asked the old folks. I asked anyone who might have this kind of knowledge, but no one knew. Or if they knew, no one would tell me. After a while, I just gave up." Hīnano paused for a moment. "Now, Grandma tells me these words may be involved in another murder."

"I think they might," said Mina, "although I hope that stays between us for now."

"Of course, my dear," Hinano said. "We must always be careful whom we entrust our secrets to."

The three of them sat there without talking for a few minutes, each lost in their own thoughts. Mina looked out of an open window. A fresh gust blew off the Kona sea and into the parlor, washing over them and leaving them feeling cool and refreshed.

"I'll go over all my notes again for you, and if I find anything, I will let you know," Hinano said.

"Thank you so much, uncle."

"I would so much like to see the real portrait of the king." He sounded almost wistful.

"Oh, I would too," said Grandma Hannah. "I'm going to Honolulu pretty soon. Why don't you come over and stay with us? You can see the portraits, and we can have a good holoholo on O'ahu."

"Yes, uncle, please come," said Mina.

"I'll think about it. I'd have to find someone to take over for me for a few days."

Mina and Grandma Hannah said their good-byes, and as they left, they turned and waved to Hinano one last time from the gate. Mina stood for a moment to take one last look at the palace, and before she left, she was surprised to see an 'ua'u, a beautiful Hawaiian petrel, fly up, perch on the roof, look directly at her with a definite air of curiosity, and then fly away.

23

WATCH WHERE YOU STEP

BACK IN HONOLULU, a week later, Mina unpacked and reflected on the trip to the Big Island. They had all returned the previous afternoon, and she thought everything had gone very well. She'd had time to talk to Ned, enough time with her father and grandmother, and some time alone. Nyla had appointed herself as Ned's official tour guide, and had kept him so busy that Mina saw little of him after her sister's arrival. Hīnano Kahana had offered his help on the verse. Best of all, Grandma Hannah had agreed to come to Honolulu for a visit in a few days. Mina realized it was the first time since Len's death that she'd been to the ranch and enjoyed the visit.

This morning, the brisk wind from the south brought the occasional flurry of sand and salt mist toward the house. She finished unpacking and went to close all the windows that faced the sea. Just as she was closing the last one, there was a knock at the door. It was Ned, looking so fresh and cheerful that it made her smile.

"Good morning," he said. "I won't bother to ask if you're hungry, since you always are. I'll just ask if you would like to go out to breakfast so we can get back on course."

"Yum!" Mina grinned.

"I take it that's American slang for yes. How long will it take you to get ready?"

"I'll meet you at the car in ten minutes," she answered.

They drove to the Green Lantern, a small restaurant in Waikīkī that was across the street from the beach. Because of the windy weather only a few halfhearted bathers strolled along the sand. Mina ordered pancakes, and Ned decided on a Denver omelet.

"I haven't talked to you for longer than five minutes since the day we went riding," she said stirring her coffee. "Nyla kept you so busy."

"I think she wanted to make sure you didn't feel obligated to entertain me. Remember we wanted her to feel like my presence was her idea."

"Did you enjoy it?"

"I did. It's a special place, isn't it?"

"I think so," she said.

The food arrived, and Mina ate with her usual enthusiasm. "I decided to do it tonight," she said in between pancake wedges.

"What's that?"

"You know," she leaned forward and whispered, "the Halperns' house."

"Mina," he began, unable to conceal his disapproval. "I just don't think it's wise."

"I don't care. You just go to the rehearsal and make sure they stay there."

"You're serious, aren't you?" He put down his fork and looked at her.

"Very. Just make sure they stay there until nine thirty. Say you want to meet with them, you know, to discuss the lighting or her character—anything. I know they're both called for tonight."

"I don't like this," he groaned.

"I know. I'm sorry, but like I said, I'm doing it anyway."

"Any news from Cecily?"

"I talked to her last night. She still can't remember what happened. I think it'll just take time."

"I wish we could find out more about that housekeeper," he said.

"It's been a week. She must be back on her feet."

"I think we should get someone to tail her. Do you know anyone?"

"I know a little juvenile delinquent," she laughed. "His name is Alika, and he loves to do stuff like this."

After they finished breakfast, they decided to take a walk down Kalākaua Avenue, the main street of Waikīkī. Just after the streetcar rolled by, with its passengers buffeted by the wind and hanging on to their hats, they crossed the street. Past the Moana Hotel, they saw that the lei stands had their flower garlands covered up with white muslin to protect them from the wind. Mina stopped to talk to one of the lei sellers while Ned wandered into a grass house that was now a curio shop. The entrance of the shop was flanked by two tall koa surfboards. When Ned emerged, they crossed the street again to look at the new Waikīkī movie theater that was under construction, and then continued down the avenue. Soon, they found themselves standing in front of Gump's.

"Shall we go in?" Mina walked through the door without waiting for an answer.

They looked over the exquisite treasures, some in the display cases, and other objects displayed with artistic taste throughout the store. A sculptured bronze lamp had captured Ned's attention, and Mina was looking at a celadon vase when Alfred Gisolfi walked into the showroom from a back office. He greeted them and began to tell them interesting things about individual pieces.

"This antique Japanese tansu here is a recent arrival." Gisolfi pointed to a wooden chest of drawers.

"It's so minimal in design that it looks quite modern," Ned observed as he ran his hand along the top.

"This is a fine example of Japanese country furniture," said Gisolfi. "It's simple and practical, but striking and beautiful, reminiscent, I think, of Shaker furniture in New England."

A clerk from the back office approached Gisolfi and told him there was a delivery. Gisolfi strode over to a rear window, looked out, asked to have the deliveryman place the parcels in the storeroom, and said that he wanted to unpack the objects himself. The clerk went away, and Gisolfi returned to Ned and Mina. Mina was admiring a pearl necklace and matching earrings.

"Here," said Gisolfi, opening the case. "You must try them on."

Mina put on the two earrings and the necklace. The pearls felt cool against her skin, and a wave of pleasure passed over her.

"A very fine set of Mikimoto pearls." Gisolfi smiled at her.

"Where do you find such unique things?" Ned asked.

"Most of it, like this set, comes by way of the San Francisco store, but I have authorization to make private purchases here in the islands. You would be surprised at the treasures that some families have—families with ties to Asia. Sometimes they decide, for different reasons, to dispose of them. We buy them outright."

"They're beautiful," Mina said as she placed the jewelry back on the tray.

"These pearls are some of the finest quality I've seen in a long time. The shape, surface, luster, and orient are nearly perfect," remarked Gisolfi. "And they're very well matched."

"It's a big investment," she said.

"It is," said Gisolfi kindly. "One that deserves careful consideration. But remember, this kind of jewelry will only increase in value over the years. More importantly, if I might say so, they looked like they were made just for you, my dear."

"I think you've talked me into it. Could you hold them for me for a couple of days? I didn't bring my checkbook."

"It would be my pleasure."

They thanked Alfred Gisolfi and left the shop. Ned suggested they cross the street and walk back to the car along the beach. The wide avenue appeared to be quiet as Mina stepped first off the curb and was in the process of moving out into the street. As if from nowhere, a big blue truck came roaring around the corner. Ned grabbed Mina and pulled her out of its path just in time. She let out a small gasp and closed her eyes as she fell back against Ned. He felt her body go cold, and he held her up by both shoulders.

"Mina? Mina? Are you all right?"

"I am," she whispered as if trying to convince herself. "I am."

"Are you sure?"

"Yes, let's just get away from this corner."

After making sure there were no rogue trucks in sight, they crossed the street and walked through the open, sprawling gardens of the Royal Hawaiian Hotel to the beach. She took off her shoes and went straight to the water's edge. Ned followed her. They walked in silence along the shoreline with the waves washing over their feet, and when he thought she had recovered somewhat, he decided to talk.

"That was, what would you call it? A close shave?"

"I'll say. Thanks, Ned." Her brow was furrowed as she looked into the water. "I guess you just saved my life."

"Well, at least I got the morning off to a useful start. You know," he said, "I think that truck was the one that made the delivery to Gump's."

"You think?"

"I saw it outside the gallery window."

"I didn't see who was driving," she confessed.

"It was a man with light brown hair, in his early thirties, I'd say. He had a handsome profile and a birthmark on the left side of his neck."

"It must have been pretty large if you could see it from the sidewalk."

"It was very distinct. It looked like a valentine heart."

"He was a careless driver, whoever he was," she said.

"He may not have been just a carless driver, Mina. The fellow had a smirk on his face."

"Oh, come on, Ned." She crossed her arms and looked away.

"Think about it for a minute. Gump's would be a perfect place for selling some of Halpern's smuggled antiques. It could all be connected."

"I guess it could be." She stopped and dug her foot around in the sand, thinking. "I'll call Alika this morning and ask him to watch the Tsuruda woman for us."

"There's some big pieces of this puzzle that are so close, but we just can't see them yet."

"After tonight," she said as she looked up at Diamond Head, hanging like a huge paper cutout in the distance, "maybe we'll know more."

A BUSY NIGHT

JOHNNY KNIGHT DECIDED to begin a run-through of the play to make sure the actors were clear about their blocking. Rehearsal started at seven, and Ned had to make sure neither Sheila nor Andrew left before nine thirty. Sheila was no problem. She would be occupied until at least ten and maybe longer. Andrew, however, was another story. Before rehearsal began, Ned cornered Andrew and asked if he would sit with him during the run-through so they could review the lighting plot.

"I feel lighting is so important to the texture of a production, much more than anyone realizes." To Ned's relief, Andrew's reply was civil.

"Yeah," said Andrew, "the actors always get all the credit. I have to set some working lights, but I'll meet you in the house, when the first act begins."

Ned went backstage to talk to Johnny Knight. It was the usual hub of activity—the actors talking and gossiping, some of them going over the script. Ned found Johnny in the men's dressing room, and Johnny told him that with luck, they could get through the first and second act tonight, providing the actors had been paying attention and had written down their blocking correctly. Ned was on his way back to meet Andrew when he passed by the doors to the scene shop. He heard a loud voice.

"What did you say?" The man's voice was flustered. "What do

you mean? What are you talking about?" The voice got louder. "Who the hell is this? Hello? Hello?"

A telephone receiver slammed down. Ned stepped back into the shadows and saw Christian Hollister storm out of the scene shop, his face angry and red.

Andrew was waiting for Ned in the house, and the two sat down a fair distance from the stage in order to get a view of the entire playing area. As the run-through progressed, Andrew explained his lighting plan scene by scene. Ned found himself impressed by Andrew's creative ideas and his understanding of the text.

In Nu'uanu Valley, it had started to drizzle as Mina drove past the Halpern residence. All the lights were out except for the one over the front door. Mina passed several more houses, turned on a side street, and parked the car near an old stone bridge that straddled a stream. No house fronts faced this side street, and the lots were so large in this neighborhood that no one could hear her. Over the bridge was a steep hillside, overgrown with plants and vines, and Mina felt secure as she made her way around the bridge rail and down the dirt path that led to the streambed. She walked up the stream on a narrow side trail, hoping that she had correctly calculated where the Halperns' back yard would begin. When she reached her estimated goal, she made her way, with care, through a thick and mucky patch of heliconia. She emerged in an overgrown flowerbed and recognized the Halperns' kitchen window. On the patio, she wasn't surprised to find the sliding doors unlocked. She took off her muddy shoes and entered. It was a few minutes before she found the study. Because the study faced the back side of the house, she felt comfortable about turning on the small desk light. Her watch said seven thirty. The telephone rang and the startling sound made her jump back, and then she laughed at herself as she began her search by opening the center drawer of the oversized desk.

That same evening in an alley in lower Kalihi, a working-class neighborhood close to downtown Honolulu, Alika, a wiry boy almost twelve years old, spun a top on the sidewalk while he watched Kikue Tsuruda's house across the street. He was just beginning to feel sullen and bored when Kikue opened the front door, smoothed her dress, and headed off down the street. She hadn't even noticed him. He walked a cautious distance behind her, fiddling with mailboxes and fences as he went along, blending into the neighborhood scene. The street was a strange mix of homes, small wooden warehouses, and a few deserted buildings. There was a sidewalk, but the street was rough and unpaved.

He followed her all the way to King Street, and near a series of small shops she entered a phone booth. He walked into one of the stores that was still open and bought a bag of cracked seed. That was one thing he liked about working for Mina. She always gave him a little spending money. He liked to do these fun things for her, like spying on this lady. He sat outside the store on a wooden bench, eating the Chinese candy and keeping one eye on the lady. She was making quick phone calls. She didn't even talk very long. It was like she just said a few things and hung up. This was the second time today she'd done this. But now she was doing something different. She was talking to somebody and having a real conversation. She left the phone booth smiling and walked right by the boy who looked into his bag of candy and pretended to be picking around for something. He might as well have been invisible.

After a minute or so, he hopped off the bench and followed her home. It was dark by the time she closed the door to her house. The boy swung himself up into a tree in the yard across the street, high enough so that no one would notice him. It was so easy to hide in trees, he thought. No one ever bothered to look up. He perched in the tree, leaning against the thick trunk, with his skinny legs stretched out along a branch, and put on the jacket that he'd hidden there earlier. Mina had lent him an old watch so he could be sure to get home before curfew. His sister worked until 1:00 a.m. at the bar, but Mina insisted he be at home by ten.

⟶

At the rehearsal, the actors had remembered almost all of their blocking, and it seemed to Ned that the time passed quickly. As they finished the second act, he looked at his watch. It was ten thirty. He complemented Andrew, and he ingratiated himself even more by volunteering to help hang some of the lights when the time came. He enjoyed watching his offer take Andrew by surprise. Most playwrights considered themselves well above technical work. They were still talking when Nyla came toward them. Andrew left as soon as he saw her.

"Well, Ned," Nyla asked, sounding energized, "how did it look?"

"Twice as good as you're feeling," he smiled. "I'm impressed with everyone."

"Johnny has talent, don't you think?"

"I'll be surprised if he stays in Honolulu," he remarked.

"I know, sooner or later all the talented people desert us—the ones that want professional careers in theatre. It's disappointing, but I can't blame them, I guess. Some of us are going out for late-night saimin. Would you like to come?"

"I think I'll pass. I need some sleep, but please, ask me next time."

Ned drove straight home and was relieved to see Mina's car tucked in the garage. He saw the light on in her living room and knocked on the door. A sleepy voice finally responded.

"Ned?"

"It's me," he answered.

"Come in." Mina pulled herself up from a prone position on the couch.

"How did it go?" he asked.

"Piece of cake. Look, why don't you take the stuff? I couldn't read it. I'm too sleepy." She handed him a file folder and marched toward her bedroom. "See you in the morning."

In the tree, Alika had accidentally drifted off to sleep. He woke up with a start and caught himself, just before he fell off his perch. Once steadied, he saw that a big blue truck had pulled up in front of Kikue's house. He was now awake and alert, and he wasn't sure why, but he felt a little scared. After a few minutes he saw the door of the house open, and a man walked someone to the truck, opened the passenger door, and shoved the person in, the way he'd seen someone who was drunk shoved in a car. He couldn't quite see who it was, and his natural instinct for self-protection told him not to get any closer. The man hurried around to the driver's side. He was tall and strong looking. As the truck pulled away, for just a second, the streetlight hit the side of the man's face, and Alika saw a big mark on the left side of his neck. Alika looked at his watch. It was almost one, and if he didn't get home fast, he knew he'd catch it from his sister.

25

NIGHT READING

NED POURED HIMSELF a whiskey and opened the stolen file folder. It contained several items. The first was a notebook that looked like simple records covering about five years. Listed were dates, the names of ships, and individual articles with prices and initials next to them. It was obvious to Ned that these records were about the illegal importing venture that Halpern ran. The next group of papers was more interesting. The pages were torn from another book and clipped together with a note that labeled them as "Blain's journal." They were written with an ink pen in old-fashioned penmanship. He scanned the pages and saw that it was from a diary kept by a young ensign named Blain during King Kalākaua's last visit to San Francisco. Then he remembered what Grandma Hannah had said about the Hollister and Halpern men being there and the ensign being a relative of the Halpern family. He topped off his whiskey, lit a cigar, and began to read:

December 5, 1890

The Hawaiian king arrived as expected. *The Charleston* was in the harbor by 10:30 flying the Hawaiian standard, which looks to me very British. There was a 21-gun salute from *Alcatraz* and another from the *USS Swatara*. The darky king was greeted by the Admiral and followed by official escort to the Palace Hotel. There were other darkies with the king. Some could almost pass for white while others had the look of Negroes. Uncle Eben spoke to me again of the plans. I was happy indeed to finally meet Mr. Hollister who I have heard so much about. He seems a fine gentleman of very good taste.

December 18

We have just returned from accompanying the Hawaiian—King Davy—to the Charity Ball. They had a big chair for him to sit in surrounded by palms and ferns. A good bit of ridiculous if you ask me. He danced with all the ladies like a regular dandy. The food was very delicious and I have seldom seen a finer looking collection of women. I think some of them did admire me in my dress uniform. I wasn't to dance, though. The Admiral asked that I keep an eye on the royal party. Mr. Hollister says we must wait. He says that McNeil, one of the king's lackeys, is suspicious.

December 19

Went to the Mechanics Pavilion so the king could review the local Regiments. The Admiral had me sit with the coach driver. I was able to procure the mountain laurel Uncle Eben wanted.

December 22

Had a long talk with Mr. Hollister. He surely loves this country and realizes how important those islands will be for our safety in the future. He impressed on me the serious nature of our task.

December 23

Had to attend a tea for his majesty with the Admiral. Apparently King Davy's written a book, and he spent the whole time jabbering about it with some egghead professor. I ate some very good pastries, and one of the serving girls, a bit of a flirt and not too bad to look at, took a liking to me and slipped me a bundle to take home.

December 24

Uncle Eben and Mr. Hollister took me out for a fine meal. Uncle Eben gave me a very expensive bottle of brandy and from Mr. Hollister some Cuban cigars. They both wished me a Merry Christmas. The king goes to Grace Cathedral for the Christmas service at midnight. Of course we have to go.

December 27

The king is to make a railway trip down to San Diego on the Southern Pacific. The Admiral informed me today we would be going along.

December 28

We leave in two days. This San Francisco weather is cold and sour. Uncle Eben says the rail journey will be the place to begin.

December 30

Left San Francisco this morning. Our rail cars are mighty fine. Uncle Eben and Mr. Hollister are in great spirits. Uncle Eben is urging me to go to the islands when my commission is over. He says there is lots of opportunity.

January 1, 1891

Santa Barbara is warm and sunny. We all drank champagne to toast the New Year. No change in the king.

January 4

Still no change, but Uncle Eben says we must be patient. I wondered today if somebody went through my things, can't tell. I don't think this Los Angeles will ever amount to very much.

January 7

San Diego is the middle of nowhere, but the ocean makes a very pleasant sight. The king tires easily and had to leave the parade before it was done.

January 9

The king's health is failing, which the doctor believes is due to Bright's disease. Uncle Eben is all concern.

January 10

Back in San Francisco and the king has had a slight stroke. No turning back. They told me to keep an eye on McNeil.

January 14

The king is very ill but insisted on going to the Masonic Temple. Looks like he will not last long.

January 17

The doctors say the king will surely die any day now. I feel a little sorry. Mr. Hollister has promised me a job if ever I should make my mind up to go to Hawai'i.

January 21

The king died yesterday. That Mr. McNeil created a fuss, but personally, I think he is just a crank. Still, Uncle Eben warned me to be on my guard against everyone who was a friend of the king. The Admiral was to deliver certain papers to Mr. Hollister from the State Department, but now they have gone missing.

January 22

Thousands of people came to Grace Cathedral today to see the body of the king. Uncle Eben is very worried about Mr. McNeil. I think he has been watching me and I am going to turn this diary over to my uncle until the whole thing blows over.

A letter followed the journal pages, but it was written in the same hand.

February 1, 1891

Dear Uncle Eben,

Here is a list of the missing correspondence. I hope it will be of some help. The Admiral had a cover letter that was kept in another drawer. I managed to copy these items before it was destroyed. I read it too. It also said these letters were sent by some "prominent persons" of Hawai'i over the years and recommended annexation for military reasons. There were thirteen in all in their original envelopes dated as follows:

July 24, 1851	April 7, 1866
October 11, 1852	June 6, 1875
February 4, 1853	May 12, 1883
July 9, 1859	September 21, 1890
September 14, 1861	October 12, 1890
January 2, 1864	December 2, 1890
February 11, 1865	

Your Nephew, G. Blain

P.S. I guess you might be most worried about these last three.

Ned noticed that beside the dates of each of these letters were small notations that looked like they were penciled in at a later date. The scribbles were abbreviations that made no sense to Ned: m.s., num., v.k., d.k., k-5, and others.

The next letter was from the artist Jonathan Leeds. It had a stamp that identified it as part of the museum manuscript collection. Ned assumed it was something Halpern pinched.

New York, May 1, 1891

Your Royal Highness, Kapi'olani,

I hope you are in good health. My sincere condolences once again for your loss. I am following your request with regards to the portraits. They will be safe with me. At first I was furious when I found McNeil's scrawl on His Majesty's portrait, but when all was explained, I was, as you can imagine, shocked, fearful and pacified all at once. I can only tell you that he said he had taken some evidence and should he die, only the cleverest and most knowledgeable would ever find it.

I pray for your well-being and your comfort. You must take heart and believe that God Sees All. I leave for London tonight, remaining always,

Your Humble Servant,
Jonathan Leeds

The last item looked as if it had been stuck by mistake in the folder. It was an article from a Chicago newspaper dated April 7, 1915. There was a story on one side about a Japanese screen and scroll exhibit at the Field Museum. In a photo, the guest curator, a young Abel Halpern, stood beside a pretty young woman about to cut a ribbon. Ned sipped his drink and read the article about how Halpern had assembled the exhibit by drawing from collections from across the nation. After he finished reading the clipping, he turned it over and looked at the other side. There was an article about a downtown fire, a kidnapping, a court acquittal of a boy—barely in his teens— on a manslaughter charge and his impending custody hearing. The last story had to do with the completion of a men's hospital wing. Ned, a compulsive reader, studied all of the stories and then put the items back in the folder. He felt lightheaded and wasn't sure if it was the alcohol or all the information he'd just digested. He stood up and went to the doorway wanting to breathe in the night air. It was almost midnight, and he could just make out the clean white lines of waves breaking over the dark reef. Such a contrast to the ugliness contained in the folder. Paradise was and wasn't an illusion. All of a sudden he felt old and tired, and he turned out the lights and went to sleep.

26

COLLECTIBLES

THE NEXT MORNING, Mina was over at Ned's house reading the file.

"Holy Jesus," she exclaimed. She'd finished reading the stolen papers and was staring out the window of the bungalow.

"Is that an expression of religious devotion, or have you just figured something out?" Ned was removing scones from the oven.

"I know what he was after." Her voice was calm. She held up the paper with the list of letters. "It's the stamps, Ned. He was after the stamps. These little notations are a big hint: m.s. stands for the missionary stamps; num. is for the numeral stamps because they had big numbers on them, and v.k., d.k., k5—these all refer to Hawaiian royalty stamps. And this statement is another clue: 'in their original envelopes.'"

"Holy Jesus," Ned repeated, as he placed the scones in a bowl. "How valuable are they?"

"These two for 1851 and 1852 are some of the rarest in the world. This list is thousands of dollars worth of stamps, not to mention the prestige of owning them. Some of those aggressive collectors will stop at nothing to get things."

She put the papers away and went to help him with the scones and tea. They sat at the outside table.

"I don't know much about philately," said Ned as he poured the tea.

"I only know because I did an article on Hawaiian stamps for the paper last year." Mina had already buttered two scones for herself. "Those early stamps are called missionaries. They're worth a mint."

"How much?"

"It depends on the value—whether it's a two-cent, a five, or a thirteen. But because the stamps are on, or appear to be on, their original 'covers,' or as it says here 'in their original envelopes' and from an exotic location like the islands, they're worth much more than just the stamps, used or unused." She paused to take several bites of her warm scone and a sip of tea. "At the least, let's say, if there were two thirteen-cent stamps on two letters from the 1850s, I'd guess seven or eight thousand each. But, if it were the two cent, or a combination of the two-cent and the five or thirteen, we could be talking about thirty thousand a letter."

"That's enough to kill for," he said.

"More than enough," she agreed. "And those other stamps are really valuable too."

"I guess that puts your boss, Christian Hollister, back in the picture."

"Why do you say that?" she asked as she helped herself to another scone.

"Mina, he saw Halpern that night. He's an avid collector of stamps, and he fancies you."

"He fancies me?" She laughed. "That doesn't make him a criminal."

"No, but the other things might. And anyway, as we've just learned, he comes from very untrustworthy stock."

"Now we know what they wanted with the portrait." She ignored his last remark. "They just wanted to break up the frame because they thought there might be clues to the stamps hidden in it. That explains why they didn't damage the portrait itself."

"But now we know something no one else does, what your grandmother told us."

"I wrote it in the verse, and they'll never find them." She repeated Kahikina's words. "Ned, it's possible that Halpern could have thought about the verse as a clue."

"We also know that Halpern must have had at least one accomplice," added Ned. "And the nitroglycerin, that was just smoke and mirrors, designed to distract. So what are we left with? We still don't know if Halpern was killed by his associate or associates, or his mistreated children, Sam Takahashi, or . . ." Ned's voice faded.

"Or Todd or Nyla, or both of them?" She finished his thought. "They wouldn't care about the stamps."

They fell quiet and finished their scones and tea.

"Why," Ned began, "would someone want to save those other pages about poisoning the king? They're incriminating and something you think he'd be ashamed of."

"He was arrogant. He was proud of his grandfather's role in bringing down the king." She remembered what Chris Hollister had told her about Halpern's attitude toward the monarchy.

"Was that the end of the line of succession?"

"His sister," she said, "Liliʻuokalani, became the next queen. Then they managed to depose her and take the kingdom for themselves. From there, it was just a short hop to annexation to the United States, their real goal." Mina was quiet for a minute, and then said, "This seems like a big breakthrough, but I don't know what to do next."

"Let's think about it today," he suggested. "Have you heard anything about the verse from your grandmother?"

"No, but she'll be here in a couple of days. She's staying at Nyla's."

"Maybe I'll go up to the museum today and pretend to be researching King Kalākaua. I'll just say the intrigue surrounding the portrait has given me ideas for a play."

After they finished cleaning up, Mina went to get ready for work, and a few minutes later Ned heard her car pull out of the drive. As the sound of the engine faded, he found himself left with a vague uneasiness that gnawed at him and made his stomach a little uncomfortable. Todd called and suggested they meet for lunch. As Ned showered and dressed, he tried to shake off his anxiety. He wondered what would happen if he simply confronted Todd with everything he knew.

THE WHITE GLOVE TREATMENT

MINA HAD JUST arrived at her desk when the phone rang. She recognized Alika's voice right away. "Slow down," she said. "I can't understand a word you're saying."

She listened as he reported everything he'd seen, and then she made him promise to stay at home and not repeat a word of it to anyone. She told him she would be there within the hour. Her pulse quickened as she placed the receiver back in its cradle and stared at the blank pieces of paper on her desk. Then, as if wrenched out of a trance, she grabbed her bag and rushed out to her car.

In about twenty minutes, she pulled up in front of Kikue Tsuruda's house. The street lay empty in a dilapidated silence. She reached into her glove compartment, now thankful for her sister's prissy advice, and took out the pair of white gloves Nyla told her would come in handy for an unscheduled luncheon or dinner date. She laughed, a nervous little laugh, as she pulled the gloves over her slender fingers. She walked right up to the front door and knocked. There was no answer. She tried the door. It was unlocked, and she slipped inside. The interior had been remodeled and bore no resemblance to the shabby exterior. The simple but tasteful decor surprised her, and in one quick glance she could tell that the furniture, the draperies, and the accessories cost much more than anyone on a housekeeper's salary could afford. The rugs and the antique porcelain pieces looked like they belonged in a museum. Then, she realized, they looked like they belonged in a museum because they *did* belong in a museum. This was where Halpern stashed his antiques. She took a quick tour of the whole house and decided to begin in the bedroom. She searched the vanity, the closet, and the dresser drawers, and looked through the boxes under the bed, but couldn't find what she was looking for. Puzzled, but undaunted, she stood for a moment surveying the room as she thought. A light breeze lifted the curtains and rustled the leaves of a Boston fern placed on a carved Chinese plant stand next to the window. Mina caught a glimpse of herself in the vanity mirror. She walked over and sat down at the marble topped beauty station, laid out with powders, creams, perfumes, and a silver-handled hairbrush. With her gloved hands, Mina smoothed out her own hair and sighed to herself. It came to her in a flash. Hadn't she and Nyla always hidden things there when they were teenagers? Her hand slid behind the mirror and removed a small piece of cardboard taped to the back. She copied down the list of phone numbers and was sure of what she'd found when she recognized Todd and Nyla's. She replaced the list behind the mirror and left the house.

She was driving on North King Street toward the boy's house in Kalihi when she started to feel a little panicky. She pulled over, bought a cola from a small neighborhood store, and sat in her car, trying to collect her thoughts. She thought about the justified scolding Ned would give her for pushing the odds and taking such a foolish risk. At the same time, she felt elated at her discovery, knowing that it might take Todd and his crew forever to find this evidence, if they ever found it at all. Evidence, she realized, Todd would most certainly want to see destroyed.

PAST PRESENT TENSE

NED WAS THE only person in the reading room of the museum archives. He sifted through manuscripts and documents about King Kalākaua, and read about his questionable alliance with the notorious Walter Murray Gibson and their Hawaiian nationalist movement. He read a variety of opinions on the king, ranging from intelligent and determined to incompetent and alcoholic, and he realized it would take much longer than one morning to understand this complex monarch. He went through a file of letters to his widow, Queen Kapiʻolani, and noted the place where the Jonathan Leeds letter should have been filed. There were other letters from Leeds after the 1891 communiqué from New York, but they revealed no new information. Ned returned these files to the reference librarian and requested a file from the photography collection. As he waited, he noticed the paintings on the archive walls, wonderful landscapes and a scene of Honolulu harbor during the days of sailing ships. Martha Klein entered the room and seemed surprised to see him there.

"Is there anything in particular I can help you with, Mr. Manusia?" She smiled at him in her very efficient way.

"Thanks," he smiled back, "your excellent librarian is taking very good care of me."

"What is your area of interest today, if you don't mind my asking?" Martha tucked a little wisp of hair into her otherwise perfect French twist.

"All this drama around the portraits," said Ned, "has made me curious about the king. I'm just catching up on what I should already know." Ned affirmed his idea that beyond her aloof personality, Martha Klein was a very attractive woman.

"There was no lack of drama in his life," Martha commented.

"So I've discovered," he replied.

"Well, good luck, Mr. Manusia."

"Please, call me Ned."

"Good luck, Ned. He's a fascinating historical figure, and I'm so looking forward to the opening of your play."

As Martha left the room, the librarian emerged with the photography file.

"I see you know our new director," she said. The librarian had short curly blond hair and a face like a pixie.

"I just met her a few days ago."

"Well, I know who you are. I'm Peggy Kelly, and my daughter's in your play up at Diamond Head."

"Yes, Kīnaʻu, and your son, Kalani, is part of the crew." Ned shook her hand and realized whom Kīnaʻu had inherited her curly locks from.

"Wait until I tell him you remembered his name." Peggy seemed pleased. "You know how the crew always feels forgotten. Here's your folder. I don't want to disturb your research."

"No, please sit down Mrs. Kelly." He stood up and pulled out a chair for her. "Maybe you could help me with some of the photos here."

"Oh, I'd be so happy to be of help," she said with real enthusiasm.

As they went through the file, Peggy Kelly identified, with great expertise, the people, time, and events in the photographs. She appeared to know quite a bit about the relationships between individuals and the general social and political tenor of the times. In one photo, the king and three others sat astride horses. The women wore flowing gowns and the men had hats with flowers twisted around just above the brims. Bedecked in leis, the riders and the horses looked festive. From right to left, Peggy pointed out the king, his young niece the Princess Kaʻiulani, ʻIwalani McNeil, and her brother, Kahikina McNeil. Ned was struck by Kahikina McNeil's handsome face staring out at him from the tattered image. He was looking straight into the camera as if he was challenging the photographer to try to capture his spirit.

"I've heard a little about Mr. McNeil," said Ned. "I believe he was in San Francisco when the king died."

"Yes, he was," Peggy Kelly went on, "He's a relative of ours— not mine by blood, but his sister here, 'Iwalani, was my husband's mother. I was so lucky to have known her before she died."

"Isn't it interesting how everyone in the islands seems to be related?"

"It used to confuse me so much when I came here as a young bride," Peggy confessed, "but after thirty years, I'm quite adapted to it. Kahikina died not long after the king, you know—in a terrible fire. 'Iwalani always insisted that it was deliberately set. There are still rumors, even today, that the king's death was not from Bright's disease, but part of a larger plot. 'Iwalani thought her brother knew who the perpetrators were and that he had evidence."

"And do you think it's true?" Ned asked, interested in her opinion.

"Everyone knows there was a group of men who didn't like the king and thought he stood in their way. And there were people who would have liked to have seen someone as dedicated to the monarchy and the Hawaiian people as Kahikina removed from the political scene. It's a shame he died so young. He could have done so much for his people."

"Have you been with the museum very long?" Ned asked.

"I came here in 1916. The same year as Abel Halpern. He had just returned from Chicago and was hired right away as the assistant curator."

"It's terrible about his death."

"Oh, frightening," Peggy shivered. "Believe me, no one wants to be here alone after dark now." She leaned a little toward him and whispered, "He was not very popular with the staff."

"No?" Ned did his best to act surprised.

"Oh no," she continued. "I don't mean to speak ill of the dead, but I'm sure everyone will be much happier with Martha at the helm.

And he gave her a very hard time. It's so difficult anyway for an exceptional, intelligent woman like Martha, but when your boss is sweet on you too, well, sometimes I wonder how she stuck it out."

"He fancied her?" Ned showed his surprise.

Peggy nodded. "He tried to be secretive about it, but we all could tell."

Ned was almost late for his lunch with Todd at the Harbor Grill, a favorite eatery for Honolulu policemen. The café had wooden booths and a counter with red-topped revolving stools. The clientele seemed to be mostly working-class men. The waitress wore a white uniform with a few stains, and a hairnet.

"I'll have the cheeseburger, potato salad, and a chocolate malt." Todd ordered without looking at the menu.

"I'll have a bowl of saimin," said Ned, "and two of these meat sticks, please."

"Drink?" asked the waitress.

"Coca-Cola, thanks." Ned gave her a wink.

A half smile crept over the waitress's face just before she turned and left.

"Jeez," said Todd, "you almost made Marcia smile."

"Not a cheerful girl, Marcia?"

"A regular sourpuss." Todd made a face.

"Sourpuss," repeated Ned. "I should be writing down all of your quaint expressions."

Todd laughed. "They have the best—I mean the best—apple pie in the world here. Save a little room for it."

The restaurant bustled with customers coming and going. Several uniformed policemen sat at the counter. Todd and Ned made small talk. Their food arrived quickly, and to Ned's surprise it looked very appetizing and tasted even better. He asked Todd about Sam Takahashi, and Todd said the prosecutor thought he had a pretty good case against him.

"It would have been so easy for someone to set him up." Ned tried to say it casually.

"Maybe so," said Todd, "but even if I wanted to let him go, I couldn't. There's no new evidence, so now it's up to the court."

"Any ideas about the portrait theft?"

"Nope. It's not a priority since it's been recovered."

They talked about other things—the play, baseball, and the trip to the Big Island. Todd was telling Ned how great Maui was to visit and suggested they could go there together, "with or without the hen sisters." Todd wiped a bit of ketchup off his chin.

"The hen sisters? I won't mention that to Mina." Ned laughed. "I don't think she'd take it in the same spirit that Nyla would."

"And speaking of Mina," Todd asked, "how are you getting along with your neighbor?"

"Fine," answered Ned, and he looked out the window.

Todd's brow furrowed as he watched Ned's face. "Don't tell me you're—nah—you're not—"

"That's enough, Detective Forrest. No more questions without counsel." Ned tried to make light of things. There was a short embarrassing silence before the waitress appeared.

"Dessert?" she asked, as she cleared the plates.

"Apple pie two times, Marcia." Todd leaned back in his seat. "I'll mind my own business on this one, buddy."

"Thanks," Ned answered.

Marcia rushed back to the table. "There's a call for you, Forrest. They said it's urgent."

Todd went to the phone and returned at the same moment Marcia was delivering the pie.

"We need the tab now and the pie to go." Todd's voice was a little edgy, and he looked pale. "Something down at the dock. Want to tag along?"

"Dead body?" Ned ventured a guess.

Todd just nodded.

After flowing down from the valley interior, through the forest, past the large estates of the wealthy, past the city's oldest cemeteries, and down through busy Chinatown, Nuʻuanu Stream entered Honolulu

Harbor. A fisherman had discovered the corpse just there, floating underneath one of the smaller piers, where the mountain water met the sea. When Todd and Ned arrived, the body had already been hoisted up on the pier and covered with an old tarp, and the police team had started their usual procedure. Ned stood by while the fisherman showed Todd where he found the body and answered questions. The victim was a woman, and the fisherman had never seen her before. He hadn't noticed any strange people or unusual activity in the area. He told Todd he figured that the body floated down the stream during the night and got stuck under the pier, like a lot of the larger objects that get washed down. Ned watched Todd take care of all other business before having a look at the corpse. But finally the time came, and Ned decided to stand by him for moral support as the cover was lifted.

"Oh, shit," Todd blurted out.

There, in her faded flowered house dress with cruel-looking bruises around her neck, lay Kikue Tsuruda.

HUNTING AND GATHERING

ABOUT FIVE MINUTES after Mina got home her phone rang. She answered it and was surprised to hear Sam Takahashi's voice on the other end. He was calling from jail. After an awkward exchange of pleasantries, Sam came to the point.

"There's going to be an announcement in the paper tomorrow. Elizabeth Katsuki is breaking off her engagement to me."

"Oh, I'm sorry," she said.

"Please," he said. "A release from an arranged engagement is something to celebrate. But that's not why I'm calling."

"No?" She tried to sound casual.

"No," he replied. "First of all, I didn't kill that bastard, and secondly, now I don't care who knows about me and Sheila. She said you already knew. She told me how you helped her out. Look, if I change the subject all of a sudden it's because someone else might be listening, okay?"

"I understand."

"You know that Halpern found out about us and beat Sheila up on New Year's Eve, in the afternoon?"

"She told me that too."

"Well, Sheila is going to come forward and say that I was with her all night on New Year's Eve. Do you think they'll believe her, or will it make things look worse for her?"

"Were you? With her all that time?"

"Yes, I was." He sounded a little irritated.

"Did anyone else see you?"

"No, we just stayed in her room the whole time. I left about four thirty or five in the morning. I didn't want anyone else to see me."

"I couldn't say how much weight her testimony would have in court, but if it's the truth, I think she should come forward. It might look funny that she stayed quiet for so long. I don't know if she could be charged with withholding evidence. I think you need to talk to a lawyer."

"I don't have much confidence in my lawyer. He was good with contracts and leases and things like that, but murder is not in his realm of experience."

"Call Louis Goldburn," she said. "He's in the telephone book. He's very good, and he's a nice man too. Tell him I suggested you call him. He's an old family friend."

"Thanks, Mina, I won't forget this."

"Sam, can I ask you something?"

"Sure."

"What time did you get to the house?"

"Around nine thirty, I think. I was sneaking in the back way. I parked by the bridge and walked up the path by the stream."

"I see," she smiled to herself.

"Was Halpern at home?"

"He was at home, and he was having a huge argument with someone."

"About what?"

"I just heard him and some other man yelling at each other. I went straight to the courtyard off Sheila's room. Then I couldn't hear anything. Except a few minutes later, we heard the cars leaving. Sheila told me later it was Hollister. Look, I have to go now."

"Good luck, Sam."

Ned left Todd's office. He wanted to clear his head and decided to walk a bit instead of going straight to his car. It was late afternoon, and the sidewalks were bustling with people leaving work. With his hands in his pockets, Ned walked down Merchant Street and then turned up Fort. He was sure that Todd wasn't involved, at least directly, in Kikue Tsuruda's death. The look on Todd's face when he saw her body was an unrehearsed look of shock and surprise. Ned's shoes made a sharp sound as he trod over a section of metal grating on the sidewalk. He reached Hotel Street and turned east for one block until he came to Bishop. He paused for a minute on the corner and looked around at the fashionable buildings. A slight wind was blowing at his back. Across the street stood the Alexander Young, Honolulu's urban hotel, built in the Italian Renaissance style and famous for its formal and traditional luxury. He remembered staying there with his mother when they left Sāmoa to move to England. It was 1911, and the Alexander Young was the only building on the then single block called Bishop Street. He and his mother had been at sea on the *Sierra* for about seven days. He had never been out of Sāmoa before and was both terrified and delighted by the new things he saw. His mother made him dress up every day in clothes he would have otherwise only worn to church in Sāmoa, and the hotel seemed like a great palace to him, with the biggest attraction being the two elevators that he contrived to ride up and down in at every opportunity. The waiters in the dining room scared and intimidated him with their stern, serious looks, but his mother seemed to know how to handle everyone with ease and authority. At the sound of her voice they became attentive and anxious to please. He couldn't understand where she'd learned these things. Ned paused and looked up at the building. He wondered if he could convince Mina to go dancing with him some night at its new rooftop garden. He'd heard it was quite romantic, with a beautiful view of the city and beyond.

He continued walking at a slow pace toward the harbor and his borrowed Ford sedan. The Bishop Street of 1935 was not the Bishop Street of his childhood. Now it was a street of several blocks lined with architecturally impressive buildings that represented the bastions of island commerce. Honolulu was first a port city built on profits from the Northwest fur trade, the sandalwood trade, whale oil, and now sugar and pineapple. Like these buildings, the companies they represented were planted firmly in the island soil. He passed the Bank of Hawai'i, with its echoes of Spanish architecture, a style popular in California. On the next block to his right was the Castle and Cooke building, and across the street stood the Damon building. Both used the Roman columns that originated in temples and set a grand scale, suggesting a link between the power of the gods and these new princes of capitalism. On the next block on the opposite side of the street stood Theo H. Davies & Company, a solid red terra-cotta structure with its rhythmic arches extending the entire length of the block, and facing it the Alexander and Baldwin building, a true blend of East and West that featured a variety of artistic decorative elements. Ned's car was parked on the next block, just opposite the Dillingham Transportation building. The Dillingham building had an elegant arcade and a façade that incorporated maritime motifs. Ned was standing by his car admiring one of the cast keystones molded into a mariner's face when he heard someone call his name. He turned around and recognized James Russell, from the cast, walking toward him.

"Hi, Ned, I thought it was you." James was one of the younger members, but he was bright and kind. "What are you doing downtown?"

"I just had to make a call on someone who works down here, an old friend." Ned didn't want to mention Todd or another murder. "I was going to look for some kind of dinner to take home for myself and a friend. Any suggestions?"

"Say, why don't you come for a drink with me at the Kamaʻaina Club? I'm on the chef's good list, and I bet I could get him to pack something up for you." James seemed anxious to help.

"Well, thank you, James. I've heard quite a bit about the club, and I'd love to see it."

"Oh, call me Jimmy." He was almost bouncing with delight at the thought of taking the famous playwright to the club. "My car's just over there. You can follow me."

The club turned out to be about five minutes away from busy Merchant Street. It was an intriguing single-level Mediterranean building with whitewashed walls and a red-tiled roof. A Moorish fountain graced the entry, and, beyond, bougainvillea vines had been trained and trimmed to form an archway over the open door. The interior of the club was furnished with rugs, tapestries, large sofas, tasteful artwork, and fresh flower arrangements. Jimmy led Ned toward the back of the building. The weather was clear and the outdoor bar was just opening. It was situated on a raised terrace and overlooked a manicured garden. Ned could see a couple in tennis attire headed down a path, and assumed that somewhere in the distance there must be courts.

"This is a wonderful spot," said Ned. "How long have you belonged?"

"Oh, I just got my membership this year." Jimmy was trying to get the attention of the waitress. "My father gave it to me for my twenty-first birthday. Here comes Candace. What would you like to drink?"

"I'll have a Tom Collins, thanks." Ned noticed that Jimmy seemed to be getting more animated, and when the waitress arrived at the table, he was all smiles.

The waitress seemed to be about Jimmy's age. Her hair was a very light brown with natural blonde sun streaks. She was well tanned and athletic looking, and she returned Jimmy's smile. After exchanging a few pleasantries with her, he ordered the drinks and asked if she could arrange for some food to go.

"That's Candace Furtado. Isn't she a doll?" Jimmy seemed anxious for Ned's approval.

"Adorable," Ned nodded, remembering that she had supplied Hollister's alibi. "Has she worked here long?"

"Since just before Christmas. She's my girl, but we're keeping it a secret. She might lose her job if they found out she was dating a member. She's going to the university here. She wants to be an artist. She's going to come and help paint the set."

Candace returned with their drinks and a bowl of roasted macadamia nuts. Jimmy introduced her to Ned. She was delighted to meet him and gave him recommendations on what to order for his dinner. When she left, Ned said, "Jimmy, could I take you into my confidence about something?"

"Oh, absolutely." Jimmy was flattered and drawn in.

"I was wondering if I could have a word with Candace about something." Ned spoke in a hushed voice. "It's about Christian Hollister, and New Year's Eve."

"Does it have to do with that murder up at the museum?" Jimmy seemed a little alarmed.

"Yes, do you think it would frighten her? Do you think she'd talk to me?" Ned wanted to seem concerned.

"You're not working for the police, are you?"

"Oh, no," Ned shook his head. "Absolutely not. Nothing will get back to the police, and I'll be very careful to protect Candace and her job. I would never do anything to put your pretty young woman in an awkward situation. There's just something I've got to be sure of."

"Okay, I'll ask her now," Jimmy said.

Jimmy left the table and then returned. They finished their drinks, and while they waited for Ned's food to be packed, Jimmy suggested they take a stroll around the grounds. "Candace has a short break now, and she said she'd meet us in the garden."

They walked down a winding path, and Jimmy steered Ned toward the back of the garden. It was getting dark; the path lights had just been turned on. At the end of one of the paths was a small garden room with a stone bench, enclosed by a hedge where they found Candace waiting for them.

Mina kicked off her shoes and went to fill the bathtub. A few minutes later, as she was luxuriating in hot water and bath salts, the phone rang again. Growling, she got out of the tub, wrapped a towel around herself and answered the phone.

"Hello," she said in a grouchy voice.

"Mina, is something wrong?" It was Ned.

"I was just soaking in the tub after an unbelievable day."

"Listen, I just wanted to tell you: Kikue Tsuruda is dead."

"I was afraid she might be," she said.

"Get back in the tub," Ned said. "I've got take-away for dinner, and I've had an unbelievable day, too."

"Hmm, dinner." Mina's tone changed.

"See you in about half an hour."

"Perfect." Mina hung up the phone and climbed back into the warm, soothing water.

"Where did you get this incredible food?" Mina asked as they sat down to eat.

"That fellow, James Russell, the one playing Charles." Ned was busy pouring the wine. "I ran into him downtown. When I told him I was trying to find a take-away dinner, he made me follow him to his club, quite close to downtown, and he arranged it all with the kitchen. We had a drink and voilà! There it was, all packed up."

"Do you think it's terrible that murder doesn't make me lose my appetite?" She asked.

"No," he answered, "because it's never made me lose mine either."

"Thank you, James Russell, and you too, Ned." She raised her wine glass.

She had expected something like hamburgers or Chinese food, but, to her delight and surprise, he had turned up with a stuffed mushroom appetizer, a seafood soup, a salad, and chicken curry crêpes. There were also two small but beautiful strawberry tarts for dessert.

Over dinner, as they exchanged the events of the day, they were amazed and puzzled at the overlapping information they had each gathered. The most immediate and obvious problem was how to let Alika contribute his evidence without revealing his real reason for being there.

"I've figured out a sort of plan," she began. "I'll take Alika and his sister to Todd and say they came to me after they read the news in the paper. I'll say he told me he was playing around that afternoon and left a jacket in the tree. At home, he realized it was missing and couldn't remember where he left it. He was anxious because it belonged to his sister, and he took it without asking. Anyway, he woke up in the middle of the night and remembered that he left it in the tree. He looked at the clock and knew he could get there and back before his sister got home. So, he went back to get the jacket and saw what he saw."

"But can he stick to that story?" Ned asked.

"Like glue, and so will his sister."

"I'm sure Todd will ask why he went to you."

"It's easy. He and his sister, Kaleinani, mistrust the police. I helped them out of a jam once. The sister was arrested, by mistake, as a prostitute, which she is not, and then this social worker tried to remove the boy from her care based on the false arrest. It was an insulting mess, but I helped them straighten it out."

"The sister works in a bar?" Ned looked a little skeptical.

"Ned," she said in a calm but exasperated tone, "there's a depression here, remember? These days, people who have jobs are very grateful. Besides, she works in a very upscale, nice lounge in The Shells Hotel. She and Alika are from Kaua'i. The parents died, and she takes care of her much younger brother. She strings Ni'ihau shells in her spare time for extra money. I've helped her get her jewelry into some of the nicer shops in town."

"Ah, she owes you a favor."

"It's beautiful shell jewelry, and it deserves attention. Have you ever even seen Ni'ihau shells?"

"No," he answered, a little ashamed.

"They're an unconventional, resourceful pair, with great hearts. That's why I like them." She folded her arms and looked at him.

Ned smiled and poured himself another glass of wine.

"It's terrible about Kikue Tsuruda." She ran her finger around the rim of the glass. "What do you think she was doing? I'd put my money on blackmail."

"I'd say the same. She must have known something, but what was it? Did she know about the stamps, or was she trying to guess at and put the touch on Halpern's killer?"

"Either way, it was a foolish venture, and now she's dead."

"You realize how careful we have to be now, don't you?"

"I realize the man in the blue truck who killed her is probably the same man who almost ran me down. And you were right. It wasn't just careless driving." She sat back in her chair. "You know her phone list pretty much matches our suspects—there's Todd, Sheila, Andrew, Christian Hollister, and two phone numbers I can't identify. Of course, she couldn't call Sam."

"She must have called Hollister at the theatre," remarked Ned. "I saw him come away from the phone in a temper."

"You didn't tell me that this morning," she complained.

"I didn't think it meant anything this morning." He wasn't apologizing. "And speaking of your Mr. Hollister, Candace Furtado gave me some very interesting information. He and the sheep woman had a private room. She was instructed to have all their food and drink in the room and then not to disturb them between ten thirty and one. Later on, he told her that if the police asked, she saw him there all evening. She did what he asked because she was afraid of losing her job."

"It still doesn't prove anything. Maybe he wanted to be alone with Lamby."

"That's a frightening prospect."

"We're at some kind of borderline now, aren't we?" She shivered a little.

"Yes," he agreed. "And everything on the other side gets more dangerous. This is where trust and partnership counts."

"So, could I ask you a favor?"

"What's that?"

"Would you sleep on the pūne'e here tonight? I feel a little, I mean, after everything that's happened, I—" She stopped and just looked at him.

"I think that would be a wise idea. I just need to go over and shower and clean up a bit. I'll be right back."

By the time he returned, Mina had taken care of the dishes, made up the pūne'e and gone to bed. He sat up for a while reviewing the contents of the folder she'd filched from Abel Halpern's study. He looked again at the old newspaper clipping, rereading the article about Halpern and the Japanese exhibit. He turned it over and scanned all the articles on the other side before closing the folder. The house sat still and quiet in the night. Unable to help himself, he took another look at the picture on the shelf of Mina's late husband. As he lay back down on the clean sheets, he remembered seeing his mother sorting out his father's things after his death—the way she was sitting on the bed, the way her fingers touched his clothes, the paper-thin look of her skin. The last thing he thought of before he drifted to sleep was the feeling of Mina falling back into his arms as the big blue truck rushed by.

30

MEETINGS

"**G**ET UP, lazybones." Mina's voice jarred Ned awake. "Here's some fresh coffee, and the news about the murder is plastered all over the front page. I'm going for a swim while you wake up, and then I'm going to make us pancakes and bacon."

The sound of the screen door banging behind Mina as she left the house and the delicious aroma of warm coffee were more than enough to wake Ned. He glanced over at the paper she had thrown on the pūneʻe, but decided not to read it. He took one sip of coffee, and then another, and saw that it was going to be a beautiful morning. The air was cool and fresh, and the sky already turning from the pastels of dawn to a brighter shade of blue. Several mynah birds had landed on the veranda and were hopping along the railing, looking for crumbs and things to eat. One of them stared at him through the screen, cocking his head from side to side, and then flew away. He thought about how many people in the world had to live in gloomy climates. He was glad to be in a house on the beach in Honolulu today instead of in London or Chicago. Chicago? Why, he thought, would he think of Chicago? It was such an odd-sounding name. He remembered the folder he'd been looking at just before he fell asleep. He reached for it and opened it again, thumbing through the papers to find the old clipping from the Chicago newspaper. When he found it, he reread both sides again. With his mind racing, he jumped up and went to his own bungalow where he made a person-to-person call to a close friend of his, who also happened to be a very clever private detective living in Chicago.

After pancakes, Ned and Mina went over the phone numbers from Kikue Tsuruda's list. Todd and Nyla's home number was easy to identify, as well as Sheila and Andrew Halpern's numbers. Mina used the phone book to verify Christian Hollister's number, although they suspected Kikue had called him at the theatre. There were two other numbers that were not familiar to either of them.

"Let's just call these numbers and see who answers," she said, already dialing the first one. It rang three times before someone answered. "Oh, Gump's?" She made a face at Ned. "I wasn't sure if anyone would be there this early. This is Mina Beckwith. I'm calling about the necklace and earrings you're holding for me. Listen, my friend is going to pick them up for me today. Ned, his name is Ned Manusia. Mr. Gisolfi knows him. But I need to give him a check for the exact amount to bring along, so could you tell me again what it is?" She put her hand over the receiver and spoke to Ned. "You don't mind, do you? Maybe you can shake something else out of Gisolfi."

"At your service, Miss Beckwith."

"Yes, I'm still here." She was back on the phone. "I've got it. Thanks so much. Bye."

"And Gisolfi seemed like such a nice man."

"Maybe he is a nice man," she said as she dialed the next number. "Remember, Kikue was just shooting in the dark." Mina paused and then dialed the second number. "There's nothing, no ring, no anything." She called the operator and gave the number.

"Well, Ned, that phone number was disconnected, and the party left strict instructions that all information about the account was to be kept private and confidential."

"Clever person," he said. "I don't suppose you have any friends at the phone company."

"I wish I did now," she said. "Rats! I'm running late. I have to get into the office. This afternoon I'm taking Alika and his sister to Todd. I hope it's not going to be an ordeal with him."

"Want me to drop in for a visit around the time you plan to be there?"

"I don't think that would be a good idea. He would suspect something was up between us right away."

"In that case," he shrugged, "I'll just go to the beach and loll around all day until I have to do your errand, and then I'll go to the theatre. Don't forget, you scheduled publicity pictures for tonight."

"Good God! I almost did forget. Thanks for reminding me."

"Better make sure there's a flattering one of Hollister so we'll get a feature article."

After Mina left, Ned changed into his swimming suit and went down to the beach. The ocean was still, and even though the tide was coming in, the waves broke in gentle ripples across the sand. There were few houses along the way and most of the sandy stretch was bordered with green beach naupaka. He walked as far as he could before the coastline turned rocky and the lighthouse and cliffs below Diamond Head Road came into full view. On his way back he began to feel hot. Ned waded into the water up to his waist and then dove under, giving himself up to the sensory shock of the cool water. He swam easily out to the edge of the reef and was halfway back to shore when he spotted something nearby that sparkled and bobbed. As he swam closer, he saw that it was a green glass ball about the size of a grapefruit, floating to shore. He retrieved it and held it up to the sun, turning it around in his hand to admire his good fortune.

As he made his way back to the bungalows, he thought he saw Mina sitting on a towel in the sun under a blue striped beach umbrella, but as he got closer, he realized it was Nyla. She waved to him, and he held up the glass ball, showing off his prize.

"You lucky dog!" Nyla bounced off her towel and ran over to meet him, taking the ball out of his hands and examining it. "These almost never wash up on this side of the island. This is extraordinary."

"I've never found one before," he said, "but I've always envied them in other people's houses. Here for a day at the beach, are you?"

"I'm here to get some sun," she said as they strolled back to her umbrella. "I brought my script because we're supposed to be off book tonight. I thought the beach would be a pleasant place to memorize lines. Maybe you could help by cueing me if you're not busy. And, Ned," she said as she smiled and lowered her dark glasses, "you don't look very busy at all."

Ned sat with Nyla, and they went over her lines several times until she was satisfied that she had them well memorized. Nyla went up to Mina's house to get them something cool to drink, and as the sun was getting very high and hot, they moved their little beach camp under the canopy of a hau tree that grew near the high-water line. Its leaves rustled above them, changing the pattern of light on the sand. The tree had dropped some of its yellow hibiscus-like flowers on the sand, and Ned picked one up, twirling it around with his fingertips and looking at its bloodred center.

"Do you know where Mina is today?" Nyla asked.

"No idea," he lied.

"How are you two doing as neighbors?"

"Fine," he answered.

"I hear you've been doing things together."

"We've eaten a few meals together," he replied. "Your sister has quite an appetite."

"She's a pig," Nyla laughed. "And she never gains a pound. We should find out what she's got and bottle it."

"You didn't tell me she was a widow."

"She told you that?"

"I asked about the picture on her shelf, and then she told me."

"Poor Len," she said. "That was his name, Leonard Austen Bradley. They hadn't even been married a year. He was managing the family ranch on the big island. It was a pretty bad car accident. He was driving in the fog at night and collided head-on with a truck."

"How long ago was this?"

"About three years ago. After the funeral, Mina packed up and moved back here, took back her maiden name, and almost never speaks about him or the marriage."

"Perhaps it's too painful for her," he said.

"To tell you the truth," Nyla said, "and I've never confided this in anyone, so don't you dare repeat it, but she wasn't very happy in the marriage."

"Why is that? Was he cruel to her?"

"Oh no!" Nyla was emphatic. "He was crazy about her. They kind of went together in high school, and after college everyone just expected they would come home and get married, which is what they did. But, you know, college really changed Mina. She loved the intellectual challenges, learning, and the whole package. And she met some real career women there who she admired. Then she found herself married and planted in a rural setting on one of the outer islands, with a husband who adored her but had no clue about this whole other part of her. Well, you can see what she's like now, so you can imagine how restless and unhappy she must have felt. Not that anyone but me, and maybe Grandma Hannah, ever noticed. Len certainly didn't. She made sure of that. Then he died, and I think she felt guilty about not being happy or not loving him enough. I'm not sure, but she just carries on like the whole thing never happened."

"Complicated woman, your sister." Ned stretched out on his back and stared at the sky through the heart-shaped hau leaves.

"She's so good at covering things up," she said. "But I notice everything. We're like that, you know. She can't hide things from me."

"How about you? Can you hide things from her?"

Nyla didn't answer his question. Instead, she got very quiet and stared out at the horizon. "It's terrible about the Tsuruda woman, isn't it?" she said in a faraway voice.

"It was a brutal killing," he said.

"She worked at the theatre, did you know that?"

"I think I may have seen her there."

"I just can't believe all these things are going on." She was near tears.

"Are you all right, Nyla? Do you want to talk?" Ned did his best to be reassuring.

"Oh, I'm all right," she said, recovering her composure. "I just have a lot on my mind with the play, and Grandma Hannah coming tomorrow."

"And these terrible killings so close together," he added.

"Don't you wish the world weren't so ugly sometimes?" She went on, "I mean with all of the things and choices people have in life, why do they always end up going down the most dangerous road and making the worst decisions?"

In the early afternoon, Mina brought Alika and his sister Kaleinani to the police station on the corner of Merchant and Bethel streets. She had called Todd in the morning, and he had seemed cordial and receptive, but as they climbed the tiled stairs to Todd's office, she prepared herself for the worst and prayed that she wasn't exposing Alika and Kaleinani to another traumatic experience with civil authority. Mina figured that any kind of negative reaction to Alika's evidence would indicate the depth of his involvement. That was the big question, she thought, the real depth of Todd's involvement. She knocked on the heavy wooden door of Todd's office, and he welcomed them in.

Alika Nāpili sat between Mina and his sister on the faded green couch in Todd's office. He was a wiry preadolescent with a crew cut and a seriousness about him that often made people think he was holding back a wave of sorrow or a personal tragedy.

His guardian and sister, Kaleinani Nāpili, was eleven years older, beautiful and meticulously groomed. She wore a pretty three-strand necklace of white Niʻihau shells around her neck and matching earrings and bracelets. Mina had never known her to wear any other kind of jewelry except for these beautiful island shells. Her hair was thick and dark, and she wore it swept up in an old-fashioned Edwardian style, giving her the look of a beautiful Hawaiian angel. Kaleinani was graceful and deliberate in her physical movements; it was as if, Mina thought, she had been raised by Grandma Hannah, or someone from her grandmother's generation.

To Mina's relief, Todd began the interview on a calm and reassuring note.

He acknowledged the previous, negative experience that the brother and sister had with the authorities, and thanked them for coming forward with what could be important evidence in a murder case. He listened to Alika's story with nonthreatening attention and then asked him again to describe the man he saw.

"He was tall," Alika began. "And he looked kinda haole but not all haole. Maybe he was hapa. He had muscles in his arms too, like he lifts weights. His hair was kinda long and combed back, and he had that thing on the side of his neck like a stain."

"Which side was that?"

"This side, on the left." Alika pointed to his own neck.

"Have you ever seen this man before?" Todd asked.

"No, I never saw him before."

"And the truck?"

"It was blue. I don't know what kind. I don't know the different kinds of trucks, only cars. I like Mina's car."

"I've seen a man like that before," Kaleinani said, in her soft, gentile voice.

"You have?" Mina asked.

"I'd forgotten about it until now, because it was months ago, and it didn't seem important at the time, but now I remember." Kaleinani seemed surprised at the coincidence.

Todd asked her to continue.

"I work at the Wahine Surf Lounge in The Shells Hotel down in Waikīkī. You know, only women work in the lounge except for the doorman. I'm the bartender." Kaleinani fingered the shells on her necklace.

"My wife and I have been there. It's a great place to watch the sunset," Todd said.

"I just don't know if I should say anything," Kaleinani mused as she looked out of the window. "I don't want to put us in any danger."

"Please," Mina said. "The police need to find this man, and if you're worried, maybe Detective Forrest could get you some protection."

"Of course," Todd said reassuringly. "We would."

"Well," Kaleinani smoothed out her skirt and folded her hands on her lap. "There was a girl who came to work as a waitress at the lounge. Jayling. That was her name, Jayling Preston. She didn't last very long, maybe about three months. She just wasn't the Wahine Surf type. She was nice enough, but a little sloppy in her habits, and you know, we cater to the better class of tourists and local people. She just didn't fit. But I remember one night after work, when I was going home, this man was giving her a very hard time in the parking lot. It was a man who looked like the person Alika saw, a man with a mark on the side of his neck."

"What happened? In the parking lot, I mean?" Todd's voice was eager.

"I ran in and got Sonny, the security guard, and he and some of the boys from maintenance came out. The man caused a scene, but then he left."

"Did you notice his car?"

"I think it was a truck, but I don't remember," Kaleinani said.

"And the girl?" Todd asked.

"I took Jayling home that night, and she told me that the man was her ex-husband, and he was trying to get her to give him money. I think she called him Junior—that's right, Junior Preston, but she didn't say what his real first name was. She said he gambled and was always in debt."

"Where did she live?"

"I dropped her off that night at a rooming house, the one on Punahou Street near Beretania. She quit a couple of weeks later, and I never saw her again."

"Did she have any friends that you know of, anyone else she went around with?"

Kaleinani thought for a minute. "She didn't make friends with the other girls. She kept to herself, but there was a skinny haole man who used to come and pick her up. I saw him waiting for her a few times in the parking lot, toward the end, in the last few days before she quit."

"Did you ever see him again? Did anyone know him?"

"I have no idea who he was," Kaleinani said.

When the interview was over, Mina stayed behind to talk to Todd.

"Thanks for being nice to them. I mean, for not threatening them, and making them feel comfortable." She was trying her best to be sincere.

Disarmed, Todd gave her a hurt look. "I do know how to be nice to people. They came forward, maybe at their own risk, to report something. The boy is probably a witness to a homicide. He needs to feel like he can trust the police and that the world isn't completely bad. I'm not really the jerk you think I am."

"I know how to be nice too," she answered. "That was supposed to be nice, not a criticism. I'm not always trying to criticize you."

Outside the office, Mina wondered if maybe she had just lied. Maybe it was an underhanded compliment, and maybe she was overly critical of him. Maybe in her heart of hearts she thought he wasn't good enough for Nyla. All of this uncertainty and suspicion was beginning to feel like an unwanted weight. Kaleinani and Alika were waiting for her downstairs. She took them all out for ice cream sodas and tried to make Kaleinani accept money for their taxi fare home. Kaleinani refused, saying they had some errands and would take the streetcar, so while his sister wasn't looking, Mina stuffed the money into Alika's pocket.

On her way back to her car, Mina saw Sheila Halpern and the lawyer Louis Goldburn leaving the police station and heading for his Merchant Street office. Sheila was crying, and when Goldburn spotted Mina coming toward them, he motioned for her to join them. He opened the door to his office for Sheila and waited at the door until Mina got there.

"I'm glad to see you." He sounded anxious. "Sheila is about to come unglued. We just had an unpleasant session with your brother-in-law. She's in the Ladies right now. Do you think you could talk to her?"

A few minutes later Mina was sitting with Sheila in a room that Goldburn used for a library. There was a worktable on one end and two comfortable leather chairs with an ottoman at the other. The walls were lined from top to bottom with bookshelves of law books.

Sheila had a handkerchief clenched in her right hand in case she started crying again.

"He said the evidence still made Sam look guilty, and he doubted if a jury would believe my story because I took so long to come forward."

"He doesn't know what a jury will believe." Mina could just hear Todd.

"And even when I explained that Sam didn't want me to tell because of his engagement to that woman, he said it didn't matter what Sam wanted because I had an obligation to report what I knew to the police. He made it sound like it was my fault Sam got arrested." Sheila started crying again.

"Look Sheila, he's a policeman, and he needs to have a suspect in custody. He's just sore because you might blow his case." Mina sat forward in her chair.

Sheila stopped crying. "You think so?"

"Of course. Just ask Louis."

"Ask Louis what?" Louis had just entered with a tray of tea and oatmeal cookies. "Compliments of my excellent secretary, Doris, who always seems to anticipate when tea is just the thing. She's from New Zealand, and she made the cookies herself. Now, what were you going to ask me?"

"I was just telling Sheila she got picked on by Todd because his prime suspect's guilt is now opened up to serious question." Mina reached for a cookie. "He gets defensive."

"Sheila," Louis said as he poured her a cup of tea, "there is no way he could drop the charges based on your testimony, but there is a fighting chance that a jury might acquit Sam now. And look, by tomorrow, he'll be out on bail."

"Someone posted his bail?" Mina asked.

"His friends and business associates in the Japanese community all chipped in and came up with the twenty grand. And they're sending a letter to the editor to both papers accusing the police and the judiciary of giving preferential treatment to white people regarding arrests, bail and sentencing."

"I bet that will send Todd through the roof." Mina sipped her tea.

"Like a bullet," Louis replied.

"The irony is," said Mina, "that Todd's in 100 percent agreement with the letter writers. He's always complaining about, what does he call it? Oh, the HHEC, the Honolulu Haole Elite & Company. I'm sure it just burns him that being part of the police force, he'll be pointed to as part of them."

"I'll have to look at Todd in a little different light." Louis smiled at Mina.

"Sheila, I'm so sorry about Kikue. How stupid of me to forget. You must be frightened out of your wits." Mina was sincerely apologetic.

"I just don't know what's happening anymore. I'm just glad I'll be able to see Sam tomorrow." Sheila had stopped crying but was still shaky.

"Who's Kikue?" Louis looked confused.

"The woman who was murdered, whose body they found yesterday, she was the Halperns' housekeeper."

"Good God!" Louis stood up. "Sheila, why didn't you tell me?"

"All I could think about was Sam. It's terrible about Kikue. Why would anyone want to kill her?" Sheila paused, and then it occurred to her. "I bet it has to do with my father, doesn't it?"

"I'd put money on it." Mina said, reaching for another cookie. "Do you know anything about her outside life? Anything unusual?"

"No, I mean, its funny how you start to think of someone like Kikue in a certain role and you don't stop to think that they might have any other life." Sheila reflected for a moment. "She just kind of stayed in the background, if you know what I mean. She never talked to me unless she had to. Although every once in a while she would comment on an antique my father would buy. There were always different pieces coming in and out of the house. I hate antiques so I never paid much attention, but I do remember Kikue making remarks about different pieces, especially if they were Japanese. She'd know what period they came from and what province, stuff like that. That's right, she said once that her family in Japan either made or fixed furniture—something like that. But then, I guess I must have been blind to a lot of things."

"What do you mean?"

"I know now she lied to me about my father raping her. She was having an affair with him. I guess it had been going on for a long time. I think he even paid for her house and everything."

"How do you know that? Did Sam tell you that?" Mina asked.

"Sam? No! Andrew told me. He told me that night when you brought me home. I think it was another reason he hated my father. He said it was the ultimate hypocrisy—my father going on and on about the Japanese menace and then having a Japanese mistress hidden somewhere in lower Kalihi. Andrew was pretty pissed off."

"I hate to say this," Louis began, "but this second murder, and heaven knows I hope they catch the killer, if it can be connected to your father's killing, it will strengthen Sam's innocence. His alleged motive has nothing to do with your housekeeper, and it's not possible that he was involved with this second killing."

"I have to go." Sheila bolted out of her chair. "Aren't we having publicity pictures tonight?"

"We are," said Mina.

"And now I look like a wreck." Sheila checked her watch. "But there's still time if I go right home."

"Sheila, is someone staying with you?" Louis asked. "I don't think you should be alone in that big house at night."

She was already halfway to the door when she turned around. "Andrew is staying tonight, and when Sam gets out tomorrow, he's moving in, and I don't give a damn what people say." Then she dashed out.

"She's a very strange girl," Louis looked at Mina.

"A little irritating sometimes," she added.

"But thanks for referring me to Sam," Louis said. "He's just the kind of person I'd like to help, and I think there's a really good chance I can get him off."

"Great, because I'm sure he's innocent." Mina was eating her third cookie. "These are the best cookies."

"Doris is a gem." Louis smiled. "Such a gem, that I've gone and asked her to marry me."

"Louis, congratulations! That's wonderful," said Mina. "I'm so happy for you."

"Well thank you, Mina." He looked a little downhearted. "But just to make me feel good, couldn't you at least pretend you were a tiny bit jealous?"

It was ten to four when Ned walked into Gump's. After Nyla left the beach, he had decided to spend some time writing, and as often happened, he had lost track of time. When he saw on the door that the shop closed at four, he considered himself lucky. An Asian woman in a tailored suit greeted him.

"Can I help you?" Her English was as neat as her silk blouse.

"Is Mr. Gisolfi in?" Ned thought he might be in the back.

"I'm sorry, but Mr. Gisolfi has gone for the day."

"No matter," he smiled. "I just thought I'd say hello to him. I came to pick up Miss Beckwith's purchase."

"Oh yes, Mr. Manusia, I believe. I'm Miss Tanaka."

"How do you do?" He was impressed. She had memorized and pronounced his name correctly. He thought maybe they didn't have much business so they could afford to spend time on such niceties, but, considering how things were priced in the store, maybe they didn't need much business. "Oh, sorry, I have her check right here."

"Thank you," she nodded. "I'll write the receipt and wrap up Miss Beckwith's item. Please relax and look around the shop. I'm just going to lock the door, as it's closing time."

"Sorry to have popped in so late."

"It's no problem. I stay at least a half an hour after we close to straighten things up."

He browsed around the store while the clerk placed Mina's jewelry in a case and then boxed and wrapped it. She also made out a receipt and placed everything in an attractive black cloth bag with Gump's scripted in gold letters.

When he picked up the bag, he noticed that the clerk had been cutting stamps off of letters on the desk behind the counter, stamps that looked like they were from foreign countries.

"Do you collect stamps?"

"Oh, no," she smiled. "Those are for Mr. Gisolfi. He asks us to save the stamps for him from all our foreign correspondence."

Ned came down the long drive and parked the car. He saw that Mina was already home, but when he knocked on her door there was no answer, so he took her package over to his bungalow and mixed himself a gin and tonic. He was just sitting down on the veranda with his drink and a bowl of macadamia nuts when Mina came striding up from the beach in a blue terrycloth robe. She had been swimming and her hair was dripping wet.

"Drinking alone is not a good sign, Ned." She laughed, tilting her head to one side and wringing out her hair.

"I suppose that means you want me to make a gin and tonic for you as well." He wished she weren't so appealing.

"I'm only doing it to save you from yourself," she said. "What have you got in that bowl there?"

"Just don't eat all of them before I get back." He went inside and returned as fast as he could with her drink. "Thanks," he said. "I see you left three or four nuts for me."

"I happen to know my sister bought you several pounds of them."

"Speaking of your sister," Ned had moved the bowl of nuts onto his lap so she couldn't get at them. "She came to the beach today. She said to remind you that Grandma Hannah was coming tomorrow."

"How is my sister?"

"Well," he said, "she seemed a little troubled."

"Didn't I tell you?" She squeezed the lime wedge into her drink. "I'm going to take Grandma Hannah to see the portraits while she's here. Maybe she knows more about the verse."

"How did the boy and his sister do with Todd?"

"Fine," she said. "Kaleinani gave him a good lead on the man with the mark on his neck. His name is Preston, Junior Preston. Kaleinani used to work with his ex-wife down at the Wahine Surf Lounge. She even told him where the ex-wife lives—used to live, that is."

"Don't tell me," he laughed. "You checked the place out on the way home?"

"Of course, wouldn't you? Well, at least Todd hasn't found her first. I asked Kaleinani to keep an ear out for any information about her. All we know now is that she may have a haole boyfriend."

"Junior Preston," Ned repeated. "The name sounds so harmless. By the way, Johnny has asked me to be at the theatre for the publicity shots tonight."

"I'm not surprised. He wants to document everything. He's worked out all the scenes he wants photographed in advance. I have to make sure to get everyone's name spelled correctly and to direct the photographer on any extra shots."

"In that case, I think you'd better dry your hair."

"It is getting late. Maybe we shouldn't go together. It may start tongues wagging at the theatre."

"It doesn't matter," Ned replied. "Tongues are always wagging at a theatre."

LITTLE DRAMAS

M INA MADE NED drop her off in the front of the theatre so that she didn't appear to be arriving with him. The cast parked in the rear of the building and used the stage door, but there were several front doors to the lobby, and one of them was always left unlocked for rehearsals. Mina also wanted to use the women's lounge off the lobby to pin up her still damp hair. She knew the dressing rooms and bathrooms for the cast would be a noisy hive of activity, with actors trying on their costumes and putting on makeup for their publicity photos. As she had hoped, the lounge was empty and quiet. She had just enough pins to do up her hair. She looked at herself in the mirror and the thin layer of glass reflected back an image that she knew was her own, but all she could see and think of was her sister. She could sense, almost taste, Nyla's anxiety. She felt it as a kind of restlessness centered in the base of her spine, a discomfort with no direct cause. Her body moved in the chair as if changing positions slightly might erase the unwelcome sensation. She put on lipstick, a shade that resembled soft coral roses and complemented her olive skin, and then moved on to one of the sofas. The photographer wasn't due to arrive for half an hour, so she decided to read over the publicity copy she'd written for the show. The photographer would be documenting the show for the theatre as well as providing photos for the paper, and she wanted to make sure there were some good shots to highlight the story. She had just slipped off her shoes and was stretching her legs out on the sofa when the lounge door opened and Nyla streamed in.

Nyla was dressed in her costume for the first act. It was a Greek-inspired diaphanous gown in shades of blues and greens. Her face was framed by a high deep green collar that resembled flower petals, and her hair was done and covered with a sheer net studded with tiny green glass sparkles. Mina thought she looked exactly like the goddess-muse she was going to play, but she could also see that her sister had been crying.

"Mina!" Nyla was surprised to see her. "I had no idea you were here."

"I came with Ned, but I snuck in so people wouldn't see us arrive together. Plus, I had to do something with my wet hair."

Nyla gathered up her dress and sat down on the other end of the sofa. She stretched out her legs next to Mina's so that they were facing each other. "I'm sure you can see I'm upset," she said.

"Of course," answered Mina, "but I'm sure no one else can."

"That's a small relief," Nyla sighed.

"Are you going to tell me?" Mina asked. "Or do I have to start trying to find out for myself?"

"Please don't say that," Nyla pleaded.

"Then you better start talking. This has been going on long enough. Does it have to do with Todd?"

"Why do you think that?" Nyla looked alarmed.

"Lucky guess," Mina answered.

"It's this Halpern murder," Nyla began. "It's made him a nervous wreck and hard to be with. Now there's the housekeeper's murder, and Sheila saying that Sam was with her on New Year's Eve. He's worried that his case is falling apart."

"Don't you think he should be concerned that he might have the wrong person in custody?" Mina hadn't meant it to sound like an accusation. "I mean, why is he so upset? He's handled other awkward situations before."

"Oh Mina, he's been talking about quitting and moving away from Hawai'i!"

"What?"

"He has, and he's serious. I mean, I always thought this would be our home, and we'd raise our children here. He promised me that before we got married, but now he says that if I love him, I'd be willing to move. I just don't think I could do that, Mina." Nyla was trying to control her emotions, but her eyes filled with tears.

"Hey, Ny, come on. In the first place you don't have to move anywhere you don't want to, and he's probably just saying that because he's bent out of shape. It'll all blow over."

"Maybe you're right," Nyla conceded.

"But," said Mina, "I still don't understand what it is about this case that has him so unhinged."

"Well, I don't either." Nyla stood up and went to wipe her eyes in the mirror.

"You have no idea?" Mina knew her sister wasn't going to talk.

"I have no idea." Nyla was dabbing around her eyes. "My God, look what I've done to my makeup. I'll have to go back to the dressing room and touch it up."

"I've told you this before." Mina's voice was quiet and even. "I'd close ranks for you, Nyla."

"I'm picking up Grandma Hannah early tomorrow morning." Nyla paused on her way out. "I'm sure she'll want to rest, but then I think she's counting on going to the museum to see the portraits with you in the afternoon."

"I'll pick her up for lunch." Mina watched as her sister vanished behind the closing door.

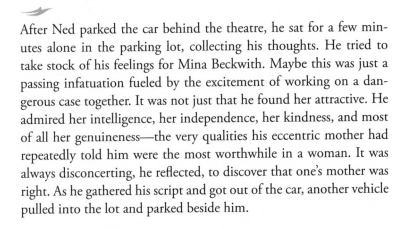

After Ned parked the car behind the theatre, he sat for a few minutes alone in the parking lot, collecting his thoughts. He tried to take stock of his feelings for Mina Beckwith. Maybe this was just a passing infatuation fueled by the excitement of working on a dangerous case together. It was not just that he found her attractive. He admired her intelligence, her independence, her kindness, and most of all her genuineness—the very qualities his eccentric mother had repeatedly told him were the most worthwhile in a woman. It was always disconcerting, he reflected, to discover that one's mother was right. As he gathered his script and got out of the car, another vehicle pulled into the lot and parked beside him.

Ned recognized Martha Klein and went over to open her car door for her.

"Thank you, Ned." She looked at him and extended her perfectly shaped legs one at a time as she got out of the car.

"My pleasure," he replied as he closed the door.

"I have some things in the trunk to carry in," she said. "Would you mind?"

"I'm at your service, Miss Klein."

She opened the trunk and pointed to two cardboard boxes full of odds and ends. "Just some things I've gathered for possible props. I don't even know if they'll be able to use any of this."

"I've stopped by Gump's, since I last saw you," he said. "Your friend Gisolfi runs quite a shop there. He seems to have an eye for antiques and jewelry."

"Yes," she said. "He's quite knowledgeable, and his own collection is something you must see."

"I gather he's also a collector of stamps," Ned added.

"How did you discover that?" she asked.

"Oh, his sales woman," Ned said. "She just happened to be clipping stamps off envelopes for him."

"Alfred has been a determined stamp collector since he was a boy. It's quite a passion with him," she said.

"He's lucky his sales clerk is so willing to help him out," he commented.

"Oh, Miss Tanaka would do anything for him." Martha said it in a simple way that implied a great deal. "She's much more that a sales clerk. She knows a great deal about Asian antiques and has many connections in the Orient. He's very lucky to have her."

They had reached the stage door, and Ned managed to open it for her while holding his box. An aura of subtle but alluring cologne surrounded her.

"Where would you like these?" he asked as she brushed past him and through the door.

"Just follow me," she smiled.

Mina sat in the women's lounge, frustrated at her inability to get her sister to talk. She looked up at the wall clock and realized that she should be meeting with the photographer in just a few minutes, so she gathered up her bag and notes and headed for the stage. As she stepped into the lobby, she saw Sheila and Andrew Halpern near the curtained doorway to the auditorium in a heated discussion. Andrew had his back toward Mina, and both of them were so engaged with each other that they didn't notice her at all. She needed to walk right by them into the auditorium, but she paused for a moment.

"That was a stupid thing to do," Andrew was saying to Sheila, "going to the police."

"I had to get him out of jail. I can't stand it," Sheila whined.

"Yes, but we were off the hook. They didn't suspect us because they thought he did it," he said, exasperated with his sister.

"But he didn't do it, and I'm in love with him," she snapped. "Besides, I don't think they ever really suspected us."

Mina decided to stride toward the door as if she had just entered the lobby.

"Yeah, well how do you know what she told them? She could have told them everything she knew."

"Who cares what she told them?" Sheila replied. "She's dead now and she can't say anything. Oh, Mina," Sheila nearly jumped. "I didn't see you."

"She's probably snooping for her brother-in-law," Andrew sneered.

"Andrew." Mina stopped and looked at him. "I can't help what I hear on my way from the bathroom to the stage. If you want to have a personal conversation, why don't you go somewhere private and lower your voice?"

Mina walked into the auditorium and saw the photographer and Johnny Knight talking on the stage and setting up the actors for pictures. Ned was sitting in the front row watching them pose the actors. Mina put her bag on the seat next to Ned, and while pretending to fuss with her papers, she told him in a quiet excited voice quickly what she had just heard in the lobby. She then joined Johnny and the photographer. Every so often they would confer with her on a photo.

"Oh, Chris, there you are! I was looking all over for you." Lamby Langston strutted on to the stage from the wings. She walked right into the picture just as it was being taken, without noticing a thing. Hollister blushed. Nyla looked at Mina and rolled her eyes.

"Lamby dear," Hollister said as he moved her off the stage and down into the seating area, "they're taking pictures of us now so you have to wait down here."

"Oh! So sorry," she said, smiling and blinking her eyes.

"Sit here next to Ned. He's the playwright. Ned, this is Lamby Langston."

"Hello, Miss Langston," Ned stood up. "It's a pleasure."

"How do you do?"

"You wait for me here, Lamby." Hollister sounded like a father giving instructions. "Say Ned, we're all going out afterwards to a saimin joint. We hope you'll join us this time."

"Oh, I was planning on it," Ned replied.

Lamby sat down next to Ned. She was wearing a dark green sarong dress with a halter tie around the neck. It accentuated her slender waist and startling blonde hair.

"Do you like the theatre, Miss Langston?" Ned tried to make conversation.

"If it's funny or the music is good," she answered. "What kind of play is this anyway?"

"It's a play about a man who can't find his way home." Ned could tell that Todd had made an accurate assessment of her. Although a beauty, she wasn't the sharpest tool in the shop. "I wrote it."

"You have an accent," she observed.

"I guess I could say the same about you," he chuckled.

"No, I'm speaking in a normal way," she insisted. "I'm sure I don't have an accent. Do you know how long this is going to take?"

"It often takes quite a bit of time, I think. Are you bored?"

"Very," she confided, "but I don't want Chris to think I'm impatient."

"I'm a little bored too, and they won't need me for awhile. Why don't we just take a little stroll outside and maybe have a cigarette?" Ned suggested.

"I don't know. I wouldn't want to give Chris the wrong idea." She did look worried about it.

"He won't mind. I'll just ask his permission, and then he'll know it's just a polite gesture." Ned spoke with such confidence that she agreed, and when Ned asked Hollister, he seemed relieved.

"She's always showing up hours earlier than she has to," Hollister told Ned. "She needs an appointment book or something."

Ned and Lamby Langston went out the front door of the theatre. The theatre was situated on a small hill with an expansive view of the city, the mountains, and the side of Diamond Head crater. Ned was sure he could see Todd and Nyla's house up on Maunalani Heights. They walked along the tree-lined streets that surrounded the theatre grounds.

"The military owns the inside of Diamond Head crater," Lamby told Ned. "There's a firing range in there, and I've been to it. Have you ever fired a pistol?"

"As a matter of fact, I have," he said.

"I like guns," she added with real enthusiasm. "They're so exciting."

"Does Chris like them too?" Ned felt the time was right to see if he could get her to talk about Hollister.

"He likes to collect them, and he's one of the best marksman in town. We've gone hunting sometimes. I like that too."

"I guess Chris is quite a collector. I've heard he likes stamps." He tried to sound upbeat and interested.

"Oh, he loves stamps," said Lamby, "the Hawaiian ones in particular. See, he likes to collect Hawaiian things, paintings, stamps, coins, and he likes Hawaiian artifacts too. He just got some stone carvings and things from a burial cave on the big island."

"He's not worried about taking things from a burial cave?"

"No, he's not superstitious at all," she said. "And anyway, they would just rot away in a cave and nobody would ever see them."

"It sounds like more than just a casual hobby to Chris."

"I'll say," Lamby laughed. "Chris is dead serious about collecting. Don't tell anyone this, but once he had the air let out of someone's tires about an hour before an auction started just so he could get the painting he wanted and the bidding wouldn't go up too high. Now, didn't I see you at Nyla's birthday party?"

"That's right. Nyla and Mina's birthday party."

"Oh that's right, Mina." Lamby's voice had a little edge. "She works for Chris. She's kind of different, don't you think?"

"She's very different."

"I don't know why someone like her would want to work. I mean, I can understand someone with no money or no looks going to work."

"Why do you say that?" He thought this was worth entertaining.

"Well, you know, men don't like women who are too smart. If she doesn't change, she'll end up an old maid like that Martha Klein. In fact, people are already starting to say things about Mina."

"Oh?" Ned pretended to be surprised.

"I've heard lots of men ask her out, but she always says no. You know what that could mean." She had lowered her voice to a near whisper.

"No, what do you think?" He whispered too.

"Some people think she could be one of those man-haters."

MISSING PIECES

MINA LAY IN bed dreaming. She had drifted out to sea in a two-person canoe, and she didn't have a paddle. She looked on the bottom of the boat and found a children's sand bucket. It was colored with circus animals and clowns. Inside the bucket was a paper with a wind chant written on it. It was written in an alphabet Mina had never seen before; but she knew if she could decipher it, a breeze would come up and blow her back to shore.

It was morning, but not yet light, when Ned's phone began ringing. He guessed who it was before he answered. After his conversation, he couldn't go back to sleep, so he put on his swimming suit, wrapped his bathrobe around himself and wandered down to the beach to watch the dawn. There was no wind, and the sea stretched out like an inland lake. Light began to come quickly into the sky as the shapes and hues of the clouds were emerging from the night. He spotted a fisherman a little way down the beach with a throw net and watched as the man, graceful as a dancer, cast the net in the morning twilight. It flew out and unfurled like magic into a perfect circle over and into the water. Then, the man deftly gathered the net up, pulling it tighter and closer until the fish were an easy harvest. Ned wondered how Mina would take the news he'd learned from this morning's call. It would make things both clearer and more complicated. He lay back on the sand and closed his eyes.

The next thing he knew was that he heard laughing and felt something tickling his nose. He opened his eyes, and Mina was kneeling next to him with a leaf in her hand. "That was a wicked thing to do, Miss Beckwith," he said as he rubbed his nose.

"I know," she said. "Why are you out here on the beach? You're never out this early."

"Let's go for a swim. I need to wake up a bit, and then I'll tell you."

They sat on Mina's veranda after their swim with big cups of coffee and cinnamon toast.

"Okay," she said, "Tell me why you were sleeping on the beach."

"I got a trunk call this morning, and then I decided to go out and watch the sunrise. I must have dozed off."

"Was the call important?" She knew the answer before she asked.

"It explains what Halpern had on Todd." He was silent and looked at her.

"Well? How bad is it?" she asked with an anxious look. "Just start from the beginning."

"Have you ever heard of La Mano Nera?"

"No, should I?"

"It means the Black Hand. In Chicago, there used to be a number of Black Hand gangs that extorted money from businessmen and other wealthy Italians. These gangs would send extortion demands with drawings of black daggers or the skull and crossbones. The receivers would be threatened with violence if they didn't come up with the money. In 1910, there were quite a few unsolved Black Hand killings in Chicago and things got worse. In 1915, they set off at least fifty-five bombs to make people take their demands seriously. There was a fellow named Colosimo, a wealthy Italian who ran some illicit businesses and had some political influence as well. People say he's the person who started the first real Italian crime syndicate in Chicago. Well then, in 1915, he was being extorted by a Black Hand gang, and he wasn't happy. He sent for one of his relatives from New York for protection, a chap named Johnny Torrio. Torrio hired his own men and started to eliminate the members of the Black Hand gang that had been bothering Colosimo. One night he and his boys went to the home of one of the gang members. These men, on both sides, were crude and rough. They thought nothing of killing an entire family just to make a point. Anyway, they got to the house, and to spare you the details, there was a terrible scene with guns. By the time the police arrived, the family in the house was dead with the exception of a young boy of twelve or thirteen, hiding behind a garden wall, who somehow had managed to escape from the house and with his father's hand gun had killed two of Torrio's men."

"Todd," she whispered.

"He was in a state of shock and was taken into custody by the police. There was some talk of charging him with manslaughter, but when the judge reviewed his school records and talked to his teachers, neighbors, and priest, it appeared that he had been a model student, a fine boy and never involved in his father's business. Then, one of the police officers who had been on the scene stepped up and said that he was willing to take custody of the boy and that he and his wife wanted to adopt him."

"What a childhood memory." Mina was staring out at the ocean.

"What a trauma," Ned said.

"So," she continued, "Halpern found this out, held it over him, and Todd looked the other way when he discovered the illegal antiques. But knowing Todd, he wouldn't put up with it for very long."

"His conscience wouldn't let him. It would be a slap in the face to everything his adopted father had done for him. And somehow, I just don't think he would kill to protect himself either."

"But if he were backed into a corner, or worse, if Nyla were . . ." Her voice and thoughts trailed off. "Poor Todd," she said. "I should try to be a little more patient with him. How in the world did you arrive at all of this?"

He went over to her house and brought back the folder she'd taken from Halpern's study. He showed her the clipping cut from the newspaper with the article about Halpern's exhibit on one side and the small item about the boy's custody hearing on the other. "It pays to be a compulsive reader," he said. "You realize that Nyla must know all of this and has just never told you."

"So where does this leave us?" She stood up and brushed toast crumbs off her beach robe.

"Well, it explains something important."

"Yes, but we still don't know for sure if they were involved in murder." She seemed agitated and looked at her watch. "I have to check in at the paper this morning, and I'm going to pick up Grandma Hannah and take her to lunch and to see the portraits."

He watched her walk over to her own house and disappear through the door. He could see that she was thinking about doing something, and she was not about to tell him what it was.

He tried to work on his new play, but this morning everything distracted him. He gave up and went for a walk on the beach, keeping an eye on the ocean in case another glass ball came floating in. The wind had picked up a little, and the sky was turning gray with clouds. A large 'iwa bird was flying overhead, riding on the currents of air. Ned walked close to the shoreline and let the small waves wash over his feet. The water felt warm and soothing. There was some fact or someone missing in these murders. In the last few days, he had begun to feel something shadowy hanging over both Mina and himself. He wanted to tell her, but he was afraid she would think he was foolish, or superstitious. He'd learned it was dangerous to articulate this sense that had always been a part of his way of navigating the world. Nevertheless, he could feel a certain kind of seething energy getting closer, and he knew that they were getting nearer and nearer to its source. He wondered if the murderer was aware of him in this way too. Perhaps, on some level, that other person could also sense their inevitable meeting. He spotted an offshore rainsquall moving toward the beach and decided it was time to head indoors.

Just as he stepped through the door, his phone rang. It was Mina. She and her grandmother were about to leave the museum and wanted him to join them at the Waiʻoli Tea Room for afternoon tea. Mina said Grandma Hannah wanted to talk to Ned. So a few minutes later, after a brief shower, Ned was on his way.

The tearoom was nestled on the west side of Mānoa Valley, one of the larger valleys behind the city of Honolulu. The valley was known for its refreshing breezes and daily rain that kept everything verdant and green. Near the mouth of the valley were some of Honolulu's nicest residences, and in the back of the valley were flower and vegetable farms. The tearoom itself was set well back from the road and sheltered by a tropical garden with tall trees and hanging vines. A misty rain had just begun to fall when Ned sat down with Mina and Grandma Hannah on the wide veranda that over looked the garden. Red ginger and bright heliconia bloomed in profusion.

"I'm so glad you could join us, my dear," Grandma Hannah said.

"It's lovely to see you again," Ned replied. "Did you enjoy your visit to the museum?"

"Oh yes," Grandma Hannah's eyes sparkled. "There's so much mana stored up in those rooms, you know. I love to visit all those akua, all those carved gods up there. I think they like being in that building. It's so quiet and peaceful, like a church."

"And the portraits?" Ned asked.

"Just as I remember them, wonderful likenesses. It took me right back to the old days." Her voice was filled with emotion. "Mina dear, you order for us, and don't forget some cream puffs. Ned has to try their cream puffs."

Mina ordered their tea, and in no time there was a beautiful assortment of delicacies set down in front of them and three steaming pots of tea. Grandma Hannah insisted they all have cream puffs first. Mina managed to eat two before Ned and Grandma had even finished one.

"I'm sure you've noticed that Mina has a very good appetite." Grandma winked at Ned.

"Very good," he agreed.

"No smirking, Ned," Mina said as she reached for a scone. "Let's see how these measure up to yours. Ned makes scones, Grandma."

"Well?" Ned asked.

Mina took a bite and considered it. She sipped her tea. "Yours are better."

"Well, you'll have to make some for me," Grandma said. "It's so nice when a man can cook."

"He's a great baker," said Mina. "Maybe you could come down to the beach and stay with me, and we'll let Ned make us scones for breakfast every day."

"That would wonderful, dear," Grandma Hannah said. "I would love to stay at the beach for a few days before I go back to the ranch."

"Grandma has something to tell us about the verse on the painting." Mina poured a second cup of tea.

"Something interesting," said Grandma. "Just before I came over to Honolulu, I got a call from Hīnano. He's been like a brother to me, Ned, and so good to the girls."

"He taught Nyla and me to hula," Mina interrupted. "He still teaches us when we want to learn a particular dance."

Grandma Hannah looked very serious. "Anyway, Ned, he sounded a little strange, and he said that he had some new information about the verse. But the odd thing is, he said he would only tell you, Ned, and he would only tell you in person on the Big Island."

"That *is* very strange," said Ned. "I met and spoke with him for just a few minutes when Nyla and I went to Kona. She took me to the palace, but we never talked about the verse at all."

"He must have a reason," Grandma said. "Hīnano is very serious about these kinds of things. Now you two have asked for his help, and if you still want his help, you have to respect the way that he says he's going to give it. And I'm sure he knows something important. He wouldn't waste your time if he didn't."

"I guess," said Ned, "I'll try to go there as soon as possible."

"You could try to go tomorrow." Mina had left off eating the scone and was now sampling a teacake. "I'll see about getting you a charter, and we could call Hīnano tonight."

"Are you sure I could get a plane on such short notice?" Ned was doubtful.

"Those guys at the airline are hurting for business. If there's any way to make another fare, they'll find it," Mina said.

"Mina," said Grandma, "he hasn't even had any time to think it over."

Mina smiled. "Grandma, I bet he'd go right this minute if he could."

SPEAKING CONFIDENTIALLY

"**A**LOHA, MINA my dear. Cecily's so anxious to see you." Mrs. Chang greeted her with a warm embrace. "You go right up. She's waiting for you."

As Mina began to walk toward the back of the antique shop, two large young men stepped out of the office to stop her.

"It's all right, boys," Mrs. Chang called out. "Mina's like family."

The boys dropped their tough demeanor, and they sheepishly wished her good morning.

Upstairs, she found Uncle Wing in the kitchen, placing fresh-baked croissants in a basket. Cecily was seated at the table and wrapped in an aqua blue Chinese robe with beautiful silk embroidery. When she looked up and smiled, Mina saw that her friend was close to a full recovery.

"Hooray! Mina! You're here just in time for the croissant feast with butter and strawberry jam." Cecily waved Mina to sit down at the table.

"You see what happens?" Uncle Wing complained. "I make beautiful croissants for her, and she spoils them by smearing them up with strawberry jam."

"Well, Uncle Wing," smiled Mina, "at least it's not peanut butter."

"Don't give her any ideas," he replied. "I made a nice pot of tea

for you, Mina."

Cecily had already cut open two croissants and was busy spreading them with butter and jam. "I'm so glad to see you, Mina. I'm starting to remember things about that night. Aren't you going to have any jam?"

"No thanks," said Mina, placing two of the warm delicacies on her plate. "I like them plain."

"You see," said Uncle Wing. "She knows how to eat."

"Oh, Pops," Cecily groaned with pleasure after taking a big bite of her gooey croissant, "these are the absolute French heaven."

"The absolute," Mina agreed.

"Where's your handsome shadow with the British accent?" Uncle Wing asked.

"I just dropped him off at the airfield. He's going to Kona this morning," Mina answered. "These are the greatest, Uncle Wing."

"I'm going to take some downstairs to Mama and the boys." Uncle Wing put another croissant on each of their plates and headed for the stairs with the basket. "And don't worry, girls, I have more in the oven."

"Who are those boys with your mother?" Mina poured herself a cup of tea from the blue willow teapot. "They looked like football players."

"Those are my cousins," Cecily said with her mouth full. "They're supposed to be my bodyguards. My father is driving them crazy with his French cooking, and they're always calling their friends and having them drop off regular food—you know, like plate lunches with lots of rice."

"Anyone would think twice before messing around with them."

"You bet." Cecily began to attack her second croissant. "I wanted to tell you that now I remember what happened that night. I remember what he looked like and everything. I wanted to tell you before I tell the police. I haven't even told Pops."

"Only if you want to tell me, Ceci. I don't want you to feel like you have to."

"Are you kidding, Mina?" Cecily laughed. "Geez, don't you know I'm dying to tell you?"

"Okay, tell me." Mina laughed too. "And quick, let me try some butter and jam on this before your father gets back."

"Well," Cecily began, "I was downstairs at the desk, waiting for you. I had talked to Mr. Zane just that afternoon. I can't believe he's dead. Pops is sure that somebody pushed him in the river because he talked to me. Mr. Zane told me that he helped someone get nitroglycerin. He said it was for "that museum gang," and then he wouldn't tell me anything more. Can you believe it? What I don't get is how they knew he talked to me."

"I think someone was listening in at the theatre when you called me." Mina broke a piece off her third croissant.

"Someone at the theatre?" Cecily looked surprised. "That's scary."

"And dangerous," said Mina. "Don't give your cousins any time off."

"Well anyway," Cecily continued, "I was downstairs waiting for you and Ned, and I remember, I'd just lit a cigarette when I heard the alley door open. Of course, I thought it was you, and I called out. I think I said something like 'I'm in here.' Anyway, all of a sudden, this guy rushes in, clamps his hand over my mouth, and drags me into the dark of the shop. The next thing I remember is waking up in the hospital."

"Do you remember what he looked like?"

"It happened so fast. He was tall. He had brown hair, and he had a mark on his neck, on the left side."

"His name is Junior Preston," Mina said, "and I can tell you he's ruthless and horrid."

"It's funny how your mind works when you're in a fix like that," Cecily mused. "I remember thinking that when he was a kid, he must have been teased a lot because of that huge spot on his neck. It just kind of flashed through my mind out of nowhere."

"He tried to run me over with his truck, and I think he killed the Halperns' housekeeper."

"What?!" Cecily put down her croissant.

"And your Mr. Zane too," Mina added. "But I guess that would be very hard to prove."

"I know he wanted to hurt me, but it's almost impossible to think someone came here to kill me."

"I'm so sorry I got you involved in this," Mina said. "I wouldn't have been able to live with myself if—"

"Listen." Cecily reached out and put her hand over Mina's. "I'm all right now, and if it helps catch a murderer, it was worth it. But I'm worried about you. Although I know warning you to be careful won't matter. You'll just keep at it."

"You know how stubborn I can be."

"I have to tell you something else," Cecily whispered. "I haven't told anyone. I'm going to get married!"

"What?" Mina pushed back in her chair.

"To Tom. The guy that picked me up that night from the café, remember? I've been seeing him off and on for over a year—well the last six months it's been completely on—but I didn't want anyone to know, because, well, you know how it is. He's not Chinese, and he's not French, so I expect there's going to be fireworks."

"Where does he come from? What does he do?"

"He's from San Francisco, and he's an art dealer. I met him at an estate sale. You'll love him. He's smart and funny and everything. He's coming over for dinner tonight, and we're going to drop the bomb."

"Are you girls telling each other secrets?" Wing Chang appeared at the top of the stairs.

"We're always telling secrets, Pops," Cecily said.

"Now before you go, Mina," Uncle Wing said as he opened the oven and took out another tray of croissants. "I want you to try one of these. They're almond flavored, and I'll bet you girls a dollar each that you'll eat more than one."

That afternoon, Mina sat at her desk writing the final copy for the feature article on Ned's play. It was slated to appear in the newspaper the following afternoon. It was straightforward, and she was able to finish the job quickly. The photos for the feature had been handpicked by Christian Hollister, and he had even taken it upon himself to write the captions. The feature was to take up the whole front page of the society section and was sure to garner attention and a large audience for the play. She reviewed the photos, which included one of Ned and Johnny Knight looking serious and discussing the script. There was another of Andrew Halpern and Kalani

Kelly hanging lights. Nyla and Sheila were photographed in a dramatic scene, and, of course, one of the larger pictures was a handsome and heroic-looking Christian Hollister. She read her copy over once more, checked to make sure everyone's name was spelled correctly in both the article and the captions, and then walked everything to the copy editor's office.

It was three thirty, and Mina decided to leave. She liked the freedom of being paid by the word and not by the hour. More than once she had been offered a salaried position, but she always declined. She had her own money and didn't want to be tied to regular hours. She knew that not taking the position would provide a full-time job for someone who needed one. Just before she left her desk, Nyla called and asked to borrow one of her evening dresses. They agreed to meet at Mina's in an hour.

Mina arrived home to find Nyla already there and sorting through the closet. "This black dress with the embroidered neckline is a stunner, Mi. Where did you get it, and how come I've never seen you in it?" Nyla was holding the dress up to herself and looking into the full-length mirror.

"I think I bought it on the mainland," said Mina as she kicked off her shoes, flopped into the bedroom easy chair and propped her feet up on an ottoman. "I wore it once to some fundraising event for indigent journalists. Where are you going?"

"It's an engagement dinner for Jennifer Parkes. It's in their home, but it's a fancy affair. This is a great dress."

"Try it on," said Mina. "And speaking of engagements, you can't tell a soul yet, but Cecily is going to get married. Want a beer?"

"Well, that's news! I shouldn't drink before rehearsal," said Nyla, who was half undressed. "But I'll have one anyway. How is Ceci doing?"

"Way better."

By the time Mina returned with two glasses of beer and a bowl full of boiled peanuts, Nyla already had the dress on.

"What do you think?" Nyla asked.

"My God, I wonder if I looked that good in it," Mina said. "If you weren't already married, I'm sure you'd pick up some serious contenders in that."

Nyla slipped out of the dress and was looking at herself in the mirror. "Look at that. I think I gained a little weight in the tummy. So who's the lucky guy marrying our Cecily?"

"I haven't met him yet. He's from San Francisco. I think his name is Tom. I saw him once, though." Mina was shelling peanuts.

"And what? Was he cute, was he handsome?"

"I guess he was handsome. I just saw him for a second. Ask Ned, he saw him too."

Nyla was back looking through the closet. She pulled out another dress that was dark emerald with pale pink roses and a matching solid green velvet jacket. "Have you been hiding all these fabulous things from me? This is great."

"Try it on. I think I only wore that once too. I can't remember where."

"So what about Cecily and her beau? Do her parents like him?"

"Well," said Mina after a sip of beer. "He's going over for dinner tonight and they're going to tell them. Ceci's afraid her father will hit the roof. That looks great on you, Ny. I would wear that."

"I don't know. I like the black too. You have to call me tomorrow and tell me what happened as soon as you talk to Ceci."

Nyla changed into her clothes and hung the two dresses up where they could see them as they drank their beer and ate peanuts. Nyla sat on the bed with her legs stretched out. Mina noticed that she looked a little worn and that there were faint dark circles under her eyes as if she hadn't had enough sleep.

"You look a little tired, Ny. Is everything all right with you?"

"Yes and no," Nyla said in a troubled tone of voice.

"Why don't you just tell me about it?"

"I can't." Nyla looked at her sister. "I want to tell you, but I just can't."

A long silence ensued and then Mina decided to take a risk.

"Look," she said, "you might as well tell me because we've figured out most of it already. Don't act so surprised. Ned and I have looked into things on our own, and we know what Halpern had on Todd. We know that Todd looked the other way when he found out about the antique scam, and we know that you and probably Todd were at the museum on the night Halpern died. What we don't know, and what's eating away at us, is whether either of you had anything to do with Halpern's death or Kikue Tsuruda's."

Nyla looked at her in disbelief. "You and Ned know all of that?"

Mina nodded, not taking her eyes off her sister.

"First of all, I swear to you, Mina, on our mother's grave, we didn't kill Abel Halpern or anybody else. I promise."

Mina got out of her chair and hugged her sister. "You don't know how relieved I am."

"I can't believe you'd think I killed someone," Nyla said.

"Only in self-defense," Mina was quick to say. "That's what I thought. You *might* have done something like that in self-defense. Now I'm having a second beer, and then you damn well better tell me everything. You want another?"

Nyla shook her head. "Nope, one drink before rehearsal is enough."

When Mina returned, she sat on the bed next to Nyla and listened to her story.

"You don't know what a relief it is to talk to you about this," Nyla began, "especially now. I can't remember right when it started. I think it was November. Todd started acting in a way that, well, it just wasn't like him. He was on edge all the time, and then he'd get down and out. I mean depressed. He kept up his public face, but at home he'd just get gloomy and cloudy. Then, in early December, I answered the phone one day, and this weird voice asked for Todd. It sounded like someone was holding a handkerchief or something up to the receiver. I couldn't even tell if it was a male or female. When I asked Todd about it, he just said it was police business, and he couldn't talk about it. He went out a few nights later 'on police business' and didn't come home until one or two in the morning. It happened again in the middle of December, same thing—a weird phone call and few nights later he's gone until all hours. You can imagine what I was thinking. Well, on New Year's Eve, I answered the phone, and it was the muffled voice. Todd made me leave the room when he got the calls, but I listened just outside the door. I heard him say that he was sick of what he was doing and that they had to talk. After I heard that, I was sure he was cheating on me. Then Todd said he had to go somewhere that evening, and he would meet us at the party at ten, remember? So I decided once and for all I would find out what he was up to. He left about eight. I had to be pretty clever about following him, and I think the reason he didn't spot me was because he was so preoccupied. I was surprised when he drove straight to the police station. I waited in my car. Then about an hour later, around nine, he came out, got into his car and drove up to the museum.

"My first thought, and this is so stupid, was that he was meeting Martha Klein. He parked out on the street. I pulled up with the car lights off and saw him walk across the museum lawn and go into the office part of the museum. I drove around the corner, parked my car, and then ran across the lawn and into the building after him. When I let myself in, I could hear him arguing with a man, Halpern it turns out. They were in Halpern's office, and the door of the room next to them was open so I just slipped in and listened. I heard Halpern shouting at Todd, saying that he would ruin him if he didn't cooperate, and Todd yelling back something like 'and if you don't stop what *you're* doing, I'll ruin you too.' Halpern laughed and said, 'I bet that pretty little wife of yours would just love everyone knowing about you.' Then Todd called him a dirty name and left, slamming the door on his way out.

"After a few minutes, I heard Halpern leave his office too, only he headed in the other direction. I guess it was toward the gallery. I thought that would be a good time to get out of there, so I left the room and stupid me, closed the door of the room I was in behind me. I was walking down the hall when I heard someone outside about to come in the entrance, so I ran back. The door to the room I was in was locked, so I ran in Halpern's office and hid in the closet. You can't believe how scared I was. Someone came in the office, and I thought I could hear them rustling through papers and stuff. Then I heard Halpern come into the room and say, 'There you are. I was wondering when you'd get here.' I heard him sit at his desk, pull open and close one of the drawers, and then say, 'What are going to do with that thing?' Then I heard these sounds, like someone smacking a mattress or a pillow, and I heard someone falling over and groaning, and something drop on the floor, and someone walking out of the room toward the gallery.

"I thought I was going to throw up when I opened the door and saw him there. I ran down the hall, outside, and straight into Todd, who had seen my car, realized I was following him, and come back to look for me. I think I blurted out something like 'He's dead, someone just killed him,' and Todd said, 'We have to get out of here.' As we were running in the dark, I remember hearing a kind of small explosion and thinking it was fireworks. Of course, afterwards I realized it wasn't. When we got back to the cars, Todd told me that we were going to the party, and we were going to act like nothing happened."

"I heard you," said Mina. "I was listening in my car when you parked outside of Ginger's party, and he told you what to do."

"Later that night," Nyla continued, "he told me everything, about his past. The thing about it that really got me is that he did it, let Halpern carry on, because he couldn't stand the thought of me or our family being ashamed of him, shamed by his past."

"Oh, Nyla." Mina hugged her sister. "He should know you, know us, better than that. He was a child. Nothing was his fault."

"I know." Nyla laughed and wiped away a few escaped tears. "I don't understand how men think. Sometimes, it's like they don't think at all."

"But does he know any more about Halpern, who he was working with?"

"He knew about Halpern and the antiques," Nyla said, "but he didn't know who was in on it with him. He knows Sam Takahashi probably didn't kill Halpern, but then that evidence turned up and he had to arrest him. And," Nyla paused, "of course it makes him feel safer, for me, for both of us, if he has a suspect in custody."

"We have an idea why Halpern was killed, but can you remember anything more about that night?"

"Sorry," Nyla shook her head. "I was too busy trying not to breathe in the closet."

"I think we're really close to finding out who the killer or killers are."

"There's more than one?"

"I think so," said Mina, "and there's quite a bit of money at stake."

"It's horrible," Nyla said. "Can I tell Todd? I mean, now that you know it's not us?"

"Wait until I've talked to Ned," Mina said. "But I think he'll be all for it."

"Where is Ned?" Nyla looked a little confused.

"He went to Kona this morning. Hīnano Kahana is helping us track something down."

Nyla looked at her watch. "Oh my God! I'm going to be late for rehearsal. I think I'll borrow the black number." She got up, draped the dress carefully over her arm, picked up her bag, and was gone. Mina decided one more beer wouldn't hurt.

34

DARK EYES HIDE SECRETS

HĪNANO PICKED NED up in his Model A truck and took him to his house that was right next to the Hulihe'e Palace grounds. Ned had just enough time to leave his bag in the guest room and meet Hiku, Hīnano's watchful German shepherd, before he was ushered off to the Kona Inn for an early lunch. After lunch, they sat in the shade of the back veranda at the palace. Hiku sat beside Hīnano, and the ocean was like a floating mirror, reflecting the billowing white clouds. Tiny waves fanned over the sand, making a repetitive and mesmerizing sound. The coconut trees that lined the edges of the manicured green lawn rustled in the wind. Ned thought it was so beautiful that it almost seemed unreal.

He and Hīnano had a pleasant conversation over their meal, and Ned had decided not to push or question him. He had learned in his boyhood never to press a subject on a Polynesian elder or to be too inquisitive. Not only was it considered rude, but it was also a sure ticket to never receiving any information. He trusted that his host would unfold the subject in his own time and in his own way.

Hīnano sat in his rocking chair and looked out to the horizon. He had thick white hair that he wore a little longer than was fashionable. His features were finely cut, his skin smooth, dark, and shining. He was tall and well built, but Hīnano's most outstanding feature was his voice. It was low and soft and so soothing that Ned thought he could sit and listen to him forever. Hīnano was quiet now, rocking back and forth gently and looking as peaceful as the afternoon. Ned found himself drifting into a half sleep. He didn't know how long he floated in and out, but at some point he became conscious of hearing Hīnano softly chanting, and the sound of his voice brought Ned out of his sleepy fog and into a kind of comfortable state of awareness and attention.

"I wanted to ask you, Ned," Hīnano began, "if in Sāmoa they have family guardians, the way we do here in Hawai'i. Families here have their 'aumākua who watch over them, and sometimes they take the form of owls or sharks or mo'o, and every family has its own."

"They do, although it would be hard to find anyone who would talk to you about it now. The church is so strong, but my grandmother used to tell me our guardian was the kingfisher bird."

"And what about dreams? Do they talk about dreaming and visits from their ancestors, through dreams, visions, things like that?"

"I remember my grandmother used to talk a little about things like that, but not out in the open, only to my aunt or certain members of the family. She was married to a pālagi, what you would call a haole here, and so she was very circumspect in her behavior. But I know she always used to go to the taulāsea, this woman who was a healer." Ned paused for a moment and collected his thoughts. "It's like this in Sāmoa—everyone goes to church, talks about being a good Christian and in public denies believing in the things of the past, but there's a whole layer of other things right under the surface. A layer full of things that people still believe in, and it's larger and more influential than what comes out of whitewashed churches and black leather bibles. It's something that permeates everything in Sāmoa, only I would be hard pressed to tell you exactly what that something is."

"I'm asking you," Hīnano said, "because I have a little story to tell you that may seem hard for you to believe, but for Hawaiians, I mean old-time Hawaiians, it wouldn't seem impossible. In fact, it would be an important event." Hīnano paused, looked at Ned for a moment, and then continued. "I guess Hannah told you that I had an interest in what was written on the back of the Kalākaua portrait."

"She said you had tried for some time to discover its meaning."

"Yes, I've always had a feeling about it, that Kahikina wanted to tell us something in those words. I remember him very well. Like Hannah, I was young in those days. Kahikina had a great interest in chant and dance, and sometimes when he would come to Kona, he would visit my grandmother and mother, and they would talk and talk for hours. They would exchange knowledge. And whenever I went to Honolulu, he would always take me out somewhere, to meet someone or to eat a nice meal. It was terrible, the way he died. Those were sad times for us. But I want to tell you about something that happened to me, and after I tell you, you can decide what to do, whether you want to go on or not."

"Please," said Ned. "I'm more than interested in anything you might be able to tell me."

"A few days before Hannah was going to leave for Honolulu, she called and reminded me again about the verse. She explained why you and Mina were so interested in it, about the theft and the murder. I told her that I would go and look over my papers one more time and give her a call before she left. So that morning I found the notes I had made about it many years ago. Once, I thought maybe I could figure out what it meant. I talked to several old-timers here about the words and the meaning. Most of them are gone now. It seemed to me the verse was talking about a place, here on this island. It describes dark cliffs, like eyes, that could be any number of places along the coast here. After I read over all my notes, there was nothing definite I could tell Hannah. I went home to eat lunch, and then I came back here to the palace. We don't get many visitors in the afternoon, so I was sitting right here, just where we are now, and I closed my eyes and fell asleep. Then, I thought I heard someone calling me, and I opened my eyes. There was a man right down there on the beach, and he called my name again and waved for me to come. So I got up and walked toward him, but halfway down the lawn, I looked back and saw myself asleep in the chair, and thought 'I'm having a very interesting dream that I must be sure and remember.' The man was sitting on the sand, and I went to sit next to him. It was Kahikina, and he looked so well and healthy. I said something stupid like 'Oh, you're supposed to be dead.' And he laughed and said, 'Not as dead as you think.' He told me to bring the young man who wanted to know about the verse and to go to Kealakekua Bay at sunrise. Near the place where Cook died I would find a rock with ʻilima growing all around it. There we should make our prayers to the gods, and then we would find what we were searching for. He pointed to my right. I turned to look, and all of a sudden, you know the way things happen in dreams, he was gone. Then, an ʻuaʻu, a Hawaiian petrel, came flying toward me and landed on the sand. It walked right up, looked at me, and flew away. I watched it go higher and higher into the sky until I couldn't see it anymore. Then I felt as if I was falling backwards into my body, and I woke up." Hīnano stopped and looked at Ned. "So, what do you think?"

"Could we go there tomorrow morning?"

"We can," Hīnano replied, smiling. "My friend has a house near there on the Nāpōʻopoʻo side of the bay. We should go and spend the night, and in the morning we'll use his canoe to paddle over to the Kealakekua side. You can swim and paddle a canoe, can't you?"

"I can swim quite well, but I'll just have to trust that the canoe paddling will come back to me. I'm afraid I'm a bit rusty."

"We should get our gear together, stop at a store, and leave soon so we arrive before dark. The house doesn't have any electricity."

Ned bundled together a change of clothes and decided to leave his shoes behind in favor of a pair of rubber slippers that seemed to be the standard issue casual footwear of the islands. He helped Hīnano load the truck with some lanterns, dog food, a box of assorted food items, and another box with towels, blankets, and sheets. The afternoon was still early when they set off in Hīnano's pickup, with Hiku riding in the back. They drove along the coast on a dirt road. The dark lava rock lined most of the sea, but every so often it was broken by an expanse of white sand. After a while they drove upland through the coffee belt, past farm after farm of coffee trees. Ned noticed more than one donkey being led along, loaded down with sacks. Hīnano explained that donkeys were used to haul coffee, and he laughed and said that they were nicknamed Kona nightingales on account of their beautiful voices. They stopped along the way at a small stand selling fruit and vegetables, and bought some bananas, Kona oranges, papayas, and a pineapple. The vendors were young Japanese children, shy and polite, and appreciative of the small bag of peppermint candies that Hīnano left for them after his purchase. Just past an old wooden church that Hīnano said was the first Anglican church in the area, they turned down a steep, narrow dirt road toward the coast. In no time, they were once again at sea level, along a wide arching bay.

"This is Kealakekua," Hīnano began. "This side of the bay is called Nāpōʻopoʻo," he said as he pulled the truck up onto a small boat dock. "Across the bay there, where the land flattens out, you can see Kaʻawaloa. That's where we'll paddle to tomorrow. You can get there by hiking down the hillside, but it's a tough walk back up. There used to be a village there, and you can still see some of the house foundations, but everything is overgrown with kiawe and koa haole. These cliffs between here and Kaʻawaloa have many caves that the chiefs used for burials."

The dark, rugged cliffs rose straight out of the ocean, and in the fading afternoon light they looked frightening and alive to Ned, as if they could come crashing down at any second and crush unwelcome intruders to death at the drop of a hat. "That white obelisk, is that the Cook monument?" Ned asked, trying to dispel his uncomfortable thoughts.

Hīnano nodded. "That's it. The house we're staying in is on the beach, right down the road here."

They drove no more than a quarter of a mile from the boat dock and turned into a sandy little driveway toward the shore. Hīnano pulled the truck up next to a plain, boxy one-story house set near the beach with a magnificent view of the bay. Hiku leapt from the car and ran around on the grassy lawn while Ned and Hīnano unloaded the truck. The house consisted of a large room with several pūneʻe for sleeping, and a large kitchen with a big solid dining table. On the seaside, sliding sets of screen and wooden doors opened out onto a huge covered lanai. The showers and toilet were in a separate little house on the side. After opening up the house, they checked the canoe that was kept near the water in a shed, and found the paddles that were set up in the rafters. The canoe was a small one, built for up to four people. Hīnano assured Ned they would have no trouble handling it on their own. By the time they finished unpacking and preparing for their morning venture, the sun was nearing the horizon and Hīnano grabbed a fishing pole and went down to the beach. A few hours later he was cooking fish and rice on the kerosene stove in the kitchen. Ned insisted on helping by making a salad with some of the fruit that they had purchased on the drive. They ate out on the lanai with a lantern for light, and after dinner they wandered onto the beach to admire the clear night sky that was crowded with stars. When it was time for bed, Ned fell right to sleep.

Dawn was just breaking when Hīnano wakened Ned.

"We should start soon, Ned," he said in a soft but serious voice. "I made some coffee and a little breakfast. We should eat before we go."

Ned got up and dressed in his swim trunks and a T-shirt. The air was cool and still. After they ate fruit and toast, they were soon launching the canoe into the water. Hīnano sat in the rear so that he could steer with Hiku in front of him. Ned sat in the second seat from the bow.

They moved through the bay as if they were sliding over ice or the surface of glass. The sun was rising in the sky, and the clouds changed from deeper shades of vermilion and pink into light pastels that finally faded into white. Light spread across the ocean. They paddled by the dock and along the cliffs that loomed up like sentinels, alert and unyielding. Because the sea was so calm, Hīnano steered them close to the rocky base. Ned watched his paddle cut into the still water. He could feel Hīnano paddling in tandem to his own stroke and then stopping to adjust the steering. The ocean floor went gliding by, an underwater forest of seaweed, rocks, coral, and colorful fish. By the time they reached the monument at Kaʻawaloa, there was a slight breeze, and the ocean, while still calm, had lost its mirror-like surface. There was no sandy beach, but they found a safe place to lift the canoe out of the water along the rocky shoreline and placed it on a level patch of eroded stone. Hīnano took a small bag from the canoe and walked to a grassy area that surrounded the monument. When he got to a spot near the cliff, he called Ned over.

"It's right here," he said. "Just they way he described it." And he pointed to a rock with a flat, level top that was surrounded by an ʻilima plant. "This is our hoʻokupu." From his bag, Hīnano took out a ti-leaf bundle and placed it on the rock. He opened the bundle so that what it contained, a beautiful lei of green ferns and budding lehua blossoms, was revealed. He stood facing the bay with the cliffs on his left and began to chant in Hawaiian. The immense power of his voice took Ned by surprise. It was as if every syllable came from another place and another being that was living deep inside Hīnano's body. He could feel the sounds echoing against the cliffs and the whole space contained under the dome of the sky resonating with every phrase. As the chant went on, Ned could sense an energy rising from the soles of his feet and moving into every part of his body. He felt alive and invigorated, and all the petty troubles and anxieties that normally beset him were falling away. With every breath he was becoming more and more in tune with the day and the sky and a purpose, and though Hīnano's chant ended, its essence had penetrated the air around them. From out of the brush, behind the monument, flew a single ʻuaʻu bird. It landed on the stone, ruffled its sooty feathers, looked up at Hīnano, and flew up to the cliff where it landed on a shelf. Behind the shelf was a dark gap in the stone. The bird stood there and gave out a moaning cry as it looked back at Ned and Hīnano.

"That's the ʻuaʻu, the Hawaiian petrel, just like the one in my dream. What you're looking for is up there, Ned." Hīnano said it without turning around. "I think if you walk around behind the monument you can get to the side of the cliff face."

Ned craned his neck, squinting at the rock face high above. "That would put me far above the water, but I'd need to zigzag along those ledges to reach the shelf. It looks like there might be enough footholds to get from one level to another."

"Crumbling rock is what you need to pay attention to. The rock is weathered basalt," Hīnano warned him. "Are you sure you want to do this?"

"Looks like we've been given a special invitation we shouldn't refuse. I'll just have to be careful not to fall. Those rocks below don't look at all friendly."

"There's probably a cave or a tunnel up there. You might need this." Hīnano handed Ned a small flashlight.

"Thanks," said Ned, as he slipped it into his back pocket.

A few minutes later, Ned was easing himself out along the cliff, as Hīnano watched. The first ledge was a little wider than it had looked from the monument, and he moved across it with ease. Climbing up to the next ledge was more difficult. He tested every hand and foothold as best he could before he placed all of his weight in any given spot. Pausing at a secure foothold, he looked above and could make out the bird's head, peering at him from one eye, then the other. With the bird as his guide, he made his way slowly from shelf to shelf, working alternately from left to right and right to left until he finally reached its perch. The bird flew away. There was a narrow gap in the stone. Hīnano was right in guessing there was a cave. Ned bent over and edged in. He waited a moment for his eyes to adjust. When the inky shadows began to dissolve, he turned on the flashlight and moved forward. He moved cautiously around a corner, and all daylight and sound from the outside faded into black silence. The cave was now illuminated only by a narrow shaft of light from his flashlight. He kept on and came to an inner chamber that was wider and tall enough to stand. The air was chilly against his damp skin and had the musty smell of soil, dried grass, and dust. He shone the light straight back into the cave and saw several bundles of decaying kapa cloth. Small, carved wooden objects were placed to the sides of the bundles and along the cave walls. Ned was shining his light along the edges of the cave floor when he noticed something out of place. A metallic gleam came from a narrow crevice in the back wall. Ned went over and pulled out a small metal box. He removed the tight-fitting lid while holding the light between his cheek and shoulder. Feeling a surge of elation, he jammed the lid back on, knowing at a glance that he'd found the letters with the stamps.

A rattle of skittering stone startled him. Grabbing the flashlight with his free hand, he began to turn toward the sound when he was hit by a crushing blow from behind that sent his flashlight flying out of his hand, end over end. Spinning arcs of light against the cave walls blended with an exploding flash in his head. A strong arm locked around his neck, squeezing tighter and tighter. His legs buckled, and he fell onto the rough stone floor with the full weight of his attacker against his back. With his head pinned down, his eyes traced the fallen flashlight beam along the cave floor to where a kapa bundle was illuminated by the glow. A glimpse of bone gleamed through frayed edges where the cloth had crumbled away. In the few seconds before his attacker hit him again and darkness took him again, he regretted that violence and greed were shattering the silence of a sacred place where ancestors had been left in hopes of lasting peace.

He didn't know how much time had passed, but he awoke with a start and sat up. Pain convinced him that he had not joined the ancients. The right side of his head felt warm and sticky. Illumination from the flashlight was gone, but Ned was able to scramble on all fours toward the dim light of the cave entrance. As he neared the bright sunlight of the opening, he could hear Hīnano yelling his name. Standing, he ran to the opening and out into the dazzling light.

The sun blinded him when he emerged. Hīnano was shouting, and Hiku was barking furiously. As his eyes adjusted, he spotted Hīnano far below, who was pointing toward a spot on the cliff. A man was hastily making the treacherous descent back and forth, from one ledge to another, clutching the metal box in one hand. Ned felt a surge of anger when he recognized the mark on the man's neck. It was Junior Preston, the man who'd tried to kill Mina. Without a thought for danger, Ned leapt to the ledge below, scrambled to its far end, and leapt again. He dropped straight into Preston's path, and as he hit the pebbly, uneven surface of the shelf, his ankle bent at an unnatural angle. With a flash of intense pain, he stumbled and slid halfway over the edge of the cliff before he managed to grab and hold on to a solid rock. Preston's mouth twisted into an ominous smile as he approached and stomped on Ned's hand. Ned reached with his free hand and secured a second hold on Preston's leg. Preston kicked, shook his leg violently, and bellowed with rage. From high above, the 'ua'u came swooping down toward Preston, screeching, flapping its wings, and pecking at his face. While Preston flailed an arm to protect himself, Ned managed with all the strength he could summon to swing a leg up, gain purchase on the ledge, and pull Preston down with a crash. The box fell and slid toward the back of the ledge. The bird seized the advantage and furiously attacked Preston's eyes. Preston wrapped his arms around his face. Kicking at Ned and turning away from the sharp beak, he rolled too far and fell into the empty air beyond the ledge. After a scatter of stones, his long scream and the sickening thud of flesh on rock, Preston's body lay draped over a stony outcrop while the ocean swirled around him. Ned closed his eyes and turned his face away. He listened to the sound of his own breathing and gingerly repositioned himself toward the back of the ledge. He lifted up the scratched and dented box and leaned against the cliff. A cool, soothing breeze blew up from the sea. The ʻuaʻu circled three times and then soared out and away over the water, and morning calm was restored to Kealakekua Bay.

"Ned," Hīnano yelled. "You take your time coming down. Take all day if you like. Never mind him—he's gone already. You just come down here in one piece. That's all you have to do."

Ned gave Hīnano a wave. It took slow and careful maneuvering to avoid weight on his ankle, but he made his way down the face of the cliff with the box tucked in the front of his trunks. He traversed the tangle of naupaka and koa haole down the sloping hill to the white monument beside the cliff, where Hīnano was waiting to help him home. Ned rested again and then they got the canoe into the water and paddled toward Preston's body. It was unreachable from their little craft, and so they decided to paddle back and drive to the nearest phone to call the police.

Back at the beach house, Ned took a cold shower while Hīnano drove to make the phone call. Ned drank a large glass of cold water and sat out on the lanai staring at the bay. Hīnano returned in about an hour, with several cold beers.

"I went up to the church hall," he said. "No one was even around, so I went in and phoned the police station. I told them I was out fishing and thought I saw someone fall from the cliff by the monument. I didn't even say who I was, I just told them I didn't want to be involved and hung up the phone. No one will even know we were there."

"Are you sure?"

"I'm sure," said Hīnano, "because that ʻuaʻu bird was standing right on the top of the church hall."

"Preston must have followed me here. He must have somehow gotten a flight."

"He saw us paddle out and then drove up the hill to the trail and came down that way." Hinano opened two beers. "Shall we open the box?"

"Three people, probably four, have died so far for what's inside," answered Ned. "And after this morning, I think we deserve a look."

CROSSING TRACKS

MINA WAS SITTING up in bed, drinking a cup of tea and looking out the window. It was a windy morning. The rain was coming from the south, and tiny droplets of water were hitting against the bedroom window that faced the sea. She got out of bed to check the windows in the living room when the phone rang.

"Hello," she said, trying not to sound annoyed at being called before eight.

"Mina," said an excited voice on the other end. "It's Kaleinani. I thought you'd want to know right way. In the paper today, with your article about the play, there's a picture of the haole man I saw Jayling Preston with. Remember, I told you I saw her with a haole man just before she quit?"

"I remember. What's his name?"

"His name?" Kaleinani sounded perplexed.

"Under the picture," Mina explained. "It should be in the caption."

"Sorry," sighed Kaleinani. "I'm a little fuzzy because I'm almost never up this early. I get to sleep about two or two-thirty, you know. Wait, here, it says his name is Andrew Halpern. Isn't that the son of the man who was murdered?"

"The very same," Mina answered. "Listen Kaleinani, are you going to tell the police?"

"Do you want me to? I can pretend I never saw this."

Mina hesitated. "Maybe you could see it later today, in the evening, and then call Todd, I mean Detective Forrest, tomorrow morning."

"That's right. You see, I don't usually have time to look at the paper until right before I'm leaving for work."

"Thanks, Kaleinani."

Mina hung up the phone and went out into the living room and closed the windows. The wind was picking up, and it looked like the inclement weather would last all day. She made herself some toast and scrambled eggs, and then took a warm shower. As she dressed, she decided to wear her black cardigan sweater with embroidered morning glory vines and flowers. She made herself a cup of tea and called Sheila Halpern.

"Hi, Sheila," she began. "It's Mina, and I need your help."

"I'm at your service," Sheila replied.

An hour later, she met Sheila in Kaka'ako outside Andrew Halpern's studio. The rain beat down on the corrugated tin roof while the wind whipped up fallen mango leaves as they ran from Mina's car to the front door. Mina tried to keep an umbrella held over them as Sheila pounded on the door, hoping someone would hear them above the wind. After what seemed like ages, a sleepy-looking Asian woman opened the door.

"Your brother isn't here," the woman said to Sheila in an uninterested way.

"I know," Sheila retorted. Without waiting to be invited she entered the hallway and motioned Mina to follow. "My friend Mina wants to talk to you, Jayling."

"What about?" Jayling looked at Mina.

"She'll tell you when we're sitting down," Sheila answered in an irritated tone.

Jayling shrugged and walked down the hall into Andrew's studio. In one corner there was a beat up round table and some old chairs. Jayling sat down without a word.

"Check the chair, Mina, to make sure you're not sitting on wet paint or something worse," Sheila warned.

Mina sat down and for the first time got a good look at Jayling. She was pretty in a lazy, sultry way, with her rosebud lips and long dark hair. She reached into the pocket of her wrinkled kimono and pulled out her cigarettes. Her fingernails were long, immaculate, and painted a vivid coral. She lit a cigarette, and threw the match in an ashtray that needed emptying yesterday. Her hair fell forward on one side, covering one of her eyes.

"Well?" Jayling said as she ran her hands through her hair, sweeping it away from her face to show off her manicured nails.

"Were you, or are you, married to a man named Junior Preston?" Mina asked.

"What if I was?" Jayling answered.

"Were you?" Mina persisted.

"I'm getting a divorce," Jayling stated. "I married him right out of high school. He was older, handsome, and sexy in that bad boy kind of way. Lots of women eat that up. Only I found out later how bad he really was."

"I was hoping you'd answer some questions about him, like who he was working with, or if he ever did anything at the museum for Sheila and Andrew's father."

"Why should you care anyway? Are you the police?"

"No, she's not the police, Jay," Sheila said. "She's my friend, and she helped get Sam out of jail. So if you know anything, I wish you would tell her."

"I'm not saying any more about him," Jayling said.

"It's really important that we find out about him. Three people have died, and another one was seriously injured," said Mina.

"Yeah, well, I don't want to be next on the list, so forget it."

"What you know might make a big difference," Mina persisted.

"Listen, Andrew got me away from him before he killed me. I value my life, and I'm not saying a word, get it? Now I'm busy catching up on my sleep, so leave me alone." Jayling got up from the table and walked away, leaving Mina and Sheila looking at each other in silence.

"She's not always a little witch," Sheila said. "She's been through some tough stuff so I guess she's always on her guard."

"He tried to run me over in his truck. I'm not surprised she's afraid to say anything about him."

"I'll try to talk to her later," said Sheila. "Maybe she'll change her mind.

Mina dropped Sheila downtown and went to the newspaper building. There was a message someone had taken from Ned asking her to meet him and Hīnano at the airfield that afternoon. She called and arranged with Nyla to trade cars at lunchtime, as Nyla's car had more room. The day drifted by as she worked on an article about the Mānoa Arboretum and the long-term effects of its reforestation program on the watershed. It was more interesting than a lot of the stories she had to write, but still she felt restless and had to force herself to stay at her desk to finish. She finally finished just before it was time to leave. When she walked to the car, the sky was dark and it seemed much later than three o'clock. It wasn't raining when she headed toward the John Rodgers Airfield, but it looked like it could start pouring buckets at any minute.

At the airfield, Hīnano waited for the bags while Mina, seeing Ned's slight limp and bruised face, insisted on taking him to the car.

"Are you all right? What happened?"

"If you don't mind," Ned said as he eased himself into the front seat of the vehicle, "I'll tell you later."

"Well," she said, "I have something that can't wait. Without going into details, I forced my sister to talk, and she swears they didn't have anything to do with anyone's death."

"That's a relief, isn't it?" He gave her a weak smile and tried not to show how happy he was to see her.

"Are you sure you're okay?" Mina gave him a quizzical look.

"I'll be fine," he assured her.

Mina went to see if Hīnano needed any help with the bags, but he was already storing them very neatly in the trunk. She was standing next to the car, buttoning up her cardigan when a dark blue se-

dan pulled up near them in the parking area and out stepped Martha
Klein. She was dressed in camel-colored trousers and a shell-colored
blouse, and Mina wondered how she always managed to look so neat
and put together.

"Good afternoon, Mina," said Martha. "What an unusual sweater,
beautiful morning glories. Are you off to another island?"

"No," smiled Mina. "I'm collecting Ned and Hīnano Kahana.
They just came from the Big Island. Are you going somewhere?"

"I wish I were, but it's impossible to get away from the museum
just now. I'm here to pick up a friend who's coming in from Maui,
but I think I'm a bit early."

"Is that a diamond ring I see on your finger?" Mina picked up
Martha's left hand.

"It just happened a few days ago, but I swore not to tell until his
family knows."

"Well, congratulations," Mina said. "I'll look forward to discover-
ing who the lucky man is."

"Hello there." Ned waved from the car when he saw Martha.
"Did I hear congratulations for something?"

"Martha's engaged," Mina answered. "But she can't say to whom
until he tells his family, so don't ask."

"I'll give you a hint," Martha said. "You both know him."

"Have you met Hīnano Kahana?" Mina asked.

"Oh, hello," Martha said to Hīnano. "I think I met you long
ago at Hulihe'e Palace. I was there to have a look at some of the
collection."

"Oh yes," Hīnano smiled and shook her hand. "I remember. How
are you, my dear? So nice to see you again."

"If we're all packed, we'd better be off before the weather gets even
worse," said Mina.

Martha said good-bye and walked toward the airfield shelter.
Mina asked Hīnano to take the wheel as she knew he loved the ex-
citement of driving in Honolulu, especially in Nyla's big, fancy car.
She was content to sit in the back.

"I remember the time that wahine came to Kona," Hīnano said
as he started up the engine. "She threw a fit because her room at the

Kona Inn wasn't ready, and they asked her to wait an hour before she checked in."

"She always seems so composed," said Ned. "That's hard to imagine."

"I tell you, she raised hell," said Hīnano.

"Martha has always been a perfectionist." Mina commented.

"What do you suppose?" Ned asked. "She must be marrying Gisolfi."

"My guess too. Who else would we both know? But listen, the most amazing thing happened," Mina said. "Kaleinani recognized Andrew Halpern as the haole man Preston's wife, or ex-wife, was meeting with. She saw Andrew's picture with the article about your play."

"When Todd and I called on Andrew, an Asian woman answered the door," Ned remembered.

"I tried to talk to her today, but she wouldn't say anything. I think she's terrified of Preston."

"With good reason," Ned mumbled.

Ned's remoteness was troubling to Mina, and she could only guess that something bad must have happened to him on the Big Island. She sat back and stared out the car window. It was raining harder now. The windshield wipers clicked back and forth, and when they went through a puddle, there was the sound of splashing water. They drove across the train tracks that led to the cannery. Mina recalled her first train ride. When she and Nyla were about six or seven, their parents had taken them out to stay at the Hale'iwa Hotel for a week. They rode the train all the way around Ka'ena Point, and the train made stops at different places to let people take pictures. They watched the dry carved mountains on the Wai'anae coast drift by, and spotted dolphins just before they reached the point. It was one of the highlights of her childhood. She thought she still had one of the pictures from that holiday, she and Nyla in little white dresses with sun hats standing by the train. Hīnano was slowing the car down to pass over an intersection where the water was ponding. She watched the city go by, washed in the grayness of dark clouds and raindrops. Even though it was a little chilly she could sense the humidity on the back of her neck and under her chin. It was four o'clock, but it looked like evening. She saw people drifting along with their black umbrellas and their heads down, forging on through the weather. The water was running fast in small rivulets along the gutters in the streets, and the mountains were covered with clouds.

As they wound their way up to Maunalani Heights, they drove into a thick fog. Hīnano turned the car lights on and slowed down. The wind had stopped, and everything was still and a little eerie. They drove by the carnation fields, empty now of any fieldworkers. The flowers were muted dots of pink, red, and white on green, their colors subdued by the rain and the atmosphere of gray.

"Well, this seems more like my part of the world than the islands," Ned remarked.

"But this is your part of the world too," Hīnano reminded him.

"The clouds come down and just sit here sometimes," Mina said. They dropped Hīnano off and moved Ned's bags into Mina's coupe. As they headed for the bungalows, Mina recounted Nyla's story about the events of New Year's Eve. "She hasn't told Todd anything. I told her she had to wait until you agreed."

"I'll meet with Todd tomorrow and tell him everything. Do you have anything to eat at your house?" Ned asked as they pulled into their driveway. "I'm starved."

"I have a big pot of lamb stew that Grandma Hannah made for me," she smiled. "I just might be willing to make some rice and share it with you while you tell me what happened on the Big Island, but first I think you should take a hot shower."

"Do I look that tatty?"

She gave him a look that was full of concern. "You look like you've just come home from the war, Ned."

After a shower and the warm lamb stew and rice, he told her what had happened at Kealakekua Bay. She made him tell the part about the struggle on the cliffs and the bird twice, as if she were tracking their moves across the face of the rocks in her own imagination. She asked him question after question, and the more he talked about it, the more she could see a sense of relief enveloping him, as if he were letting go of layer after layer of weight. They sat on the pūneʻe, and she opened the box, examined the stamps, and then started to look at the letters. She was engrossed in reading when she realized that Ned had stretched out and fallen asleep. She covered him up with a blanket and then gathered up the letters and took them into her bedroom. She didn't go to sleep until she'd read every single one.

UNSCHEDULED

"**W**HAT'S ON YOUR schedule for today?" Ned asked Mina. They were eating lunch on her lanai.

"I'm checking in at the paper this afternoon," she answered. "Then later I have to go to the theatre before the rehearsal to review the final press releases and the program notes with Johnny."

"After lunch, I think I'll call on Todd," he said.

"I think he'll be relieved to know he can talk to you about everything."

"There could be some hell to pay," he shook his head.

"Did you read the paper this morning? There was an article about Preston's death on the second page."

"I didn't want to read it. Anything I should know?"

"No." She tried to sound casual. "It just said he fell and died, like it was an accident."

"Now, whoever he was working with will know he's dead. They may suspect that we have the goods as well. Maybe I should take the box to Todd for safekeeping."

"Last night," said Mina, "I read every single letter in there."

"Very interesting, don't you think?"

"Very," Mina said just before she took a bite of her tuna sandwich.

"Well," he said. "The stamps are the things of monetary value, but the other information is quite incriminating."

"You mean plotting against the king, as in killing him?"

"Yes, as in poisoning him." Ned stretched out his leg to rest his ankle.

"And as in the relentless scheming and plotting with certain members of the American government to destroy the monarchy?"

"Kahikina had the evidence after all. No wonder they wanted him out of the way."

"It's incredible," said Mina. "Some of the worst letters, in connection with the king's death, were written by Christian Hollister's grandfather and Abel Halpern's father. There are other prominent family names involved too."

"Let me guess. Are most of them members of the Kamaʻāina Club?"

"Of course." Mina started in on the second half of her sandwich.

"It's something Christian Hollister wouldn't like mentioned in public, I'm sure," Ned said with a smile.

"No," she agreed. "I can't see him asking me to do a feature story."

"I think we should turn all this information over to Todd, including what you took from Halpern's study. It's all important evidence."

"Now that we know he and Nyla didn't do anything, I guess that's the right thing to do. I can't even begin to imagine what will happen when, or if, this stuff is made public. I know there are some Hawaiians who still regret and resent things."

"I can imagine it was a terrible time for your grandmother and her generation," Ned said. "In Western Sāmoa, there's a lot of resentment about the colonial government."

"The old folks don't talk about it that much," she said. "But every once in a while, when my grandmother and her cronies get together, they mention things about that time. There's always this certain feeling in the conversation. It's something both Nyla and I recognized in childhood. It gets quiet and sad and hurt and angry all at once. It's like a huge humiliation they were all a part of. They keep coming back to it, as something they can't fight anymore, but can't forget either."

"I've traveled a bit in the Pacific, you know." Ned looked toward the ocean. "And all of this sounds so familiar. It's the same story with different variations. I keep forgetting that you people in Hawai'i are so out of touch with the other island groups."

"I'd say we're out of touch with ourselves."

"You've been told to work at being good Americans."

"I guess it takes an outsider to see that, doesn't it?"

"We're both outsiders, Mina."

It had started raining when Ned's story came to an end. He stopped talking and looked out the window of Todd's third-floor office. Todd was leaning back in his chair and staring up at the exposed timber beams of the ceiling. There was a long silence in which Ned became aware of the sound of the hanging fan and the raindrops that were hitting the windows.

"Does Nyla know all of this?" Todd asked.

"Some. She doesn't know that Preston is dead or that we have the box."

"Does anyone else know besides you and Mina?" Todd looked ashen and worried. "About me and Nyla, I mean."

"Wing Chang knows that you were aware of Halpern's activities. Maybe other people in Chinatown know too. I couldn't say, but I wouldn't worry about it. I don't think it's anything anyone can prove. I not sure what Kikue Tsuruda might have known, but now she's dead. She knew Halpern had illegal antiques, but I suspect he kept her in the dark about the operation. I'd say she was watching, making guesses, and hoping to blackmail someone for a lot of money. I'm not 100 percent positive, but I don't think she knew anything about the stamps. And Preston, he was just muscle; there's no way he could have figured any of this out on his own. We know there must be someone else. We're just not sure who it is." Ned's last words hung in the air.

"And not knowing who that person is, you have no idea how much they do or don't know." Todd finished the thought. "The smart thing for me to have done would have been to leave town when he first put the touch on me, but I thought about Nyla. It would break her heart to leave."

"And you thought she might not? Even if you did?"

"Yeah, I thought that. Then when she followed me up there that night . . . Jesus Christ, Ned, she could have been killed."

"Whoever he was working with is prepared to murder anyone who gets in the way. And I'm almost certain it's not Sam Takahashi."

"I know how it might look to you, but believe me, I had to make an arrest based on the evidence." Todd swung his chair around and looked out the window. "So what do you think I should do? Should I resign? Confess and take whatever comes? Leave town? I made a bad mistake, and maybe I should pay for it."

"You made a bad mistake in thinking that your past would have made a difference to anyone in this department or in Honolulu. People may have had a field day gossiping about it for a time, but to anyone that matters, things like that don't count."

"So what are you saying?"

"What I'm saying is that you should just ride it out and see what happens. I think you should take the lead from Mina and me, and figure out who's really behind all these brutal murders. That's why you became a cop, remember?"

"Is that what my sister-in-law thinks too?"

"Your sister-in-law is a remarkable person, and I think you should, what do you Americans say, 'eat a little crow'?"

"A remarkable person? So how bad have you got it for her?" Todd looked serious, even sympathetic.

"Let's stick to murder and foul play, detective."

"Okay," Todd began, "let's review the possibilities. At the top of your list I would guess is Christian Hollister, aggressive stamp collector and admirer of Mina. It's a shame he has an alibi."

"Oh, please, do you think Lamby brain wouldn't say whatever he told her? She'd do anything for him. She's counting on being Mrs. Hollister."

"What about the waitress?"

"Without divulging my source, I can tell you the waitress was pressured, and there was a big gap in the time she actually saw Hollister in that private room at the club."

"That's interesting news." Todd seemed surprised.

"Then," Ned continued, "don't forget your favorites—Andrew Halpern, barbarian artist and resentful son, in league with his charming sister, Sheila. They have more than their share of motives to kill their abusive, racially prejudiced father—a wronged mother, big inheritance, bigger still with the stamps."

"They're both clever enough to do it, and connected to Preston through his ex-wife, and they could know all about the stamps. It wouldn't be hard for them to snoop into their father's business."

"And despite Sheila's hysterical personality, she is an excellent actress," Ned added.

"And what about that other guy?" Todd had started doodling on a pad of paper. "Gisolfi. Don't you think it's a coincidence that Mina was almost run over by Preston right outside his shop? He's a more than plausible partner for Halpern, and you said he collects stamps."

"It wouldn't be the first time a kind old man turned out to be the devil incarnate. You know, I'm not sure why, but I feel starved."

"I know why," said Todd. "It's because you're spending too much time with Mina. I'm surprised you haven't gained a thousand pounds. Let's go down to the Harbor Grill and have some apple pie. I need to get out of this office anyway. You can give our friend Marcia a thrill."

Todd stopped at the front desk to tell the officer on duty where he was going. It was well after four o'clock. The sunlight broke through the racing clouds and reflected off the droplets in the misty vale of rain that was blowing down from Nuʻuanu Valley. Ned felt invigorated by the fresh air and the slight wind sweeping toward the harbor. He liked the look of the granite sidewalk when it was wet, and the sound of the car tires rolling over the wet street. He began to talk with good humor to Todd about the play, Johnny Knight's direction, and the first-rate performance that Nyla was turning in. He was so busy rattling on that he didn't even notice how Marcia shyly smiled as she directed them to their booth. They had just finished their pie and coffee when an officer came up to Todd and asked to speak to him. When Todd returned, he called out to Marcia for the check.

"This place is turning out to be our bad luck spot," Todd said.

"Not another murder, I hope."

"Might be. There's been an assault at Gump's. I think we should get there pronto before the ambulance crew wreaks havoc."

"Pronto?" Ned frowned in mock surprise. "I didn't know you spoke Spanish."

"Come on, wiseacre," said Todd. "Let's get the lead out."

As they sped toward Waikīkī they could hear the blaring siren of the ambulance just ahead of them. When they arrived, the ambulance crew was just entering the building. Miss Tanaka was in the shop. She looked at Ned, wide-eyed and frightened, as he and Todd passed into the office.

The emergency team knelt on the polished concrete floor around Gisolfi's body, searching for vital signs. Blood had leaked from his chest on to his shirt from what Ned surmised was a bullet wound. "I think I have a pulse," one of them said, and Gisolfi was transferred to a stretcher as the crew worked as fast as they could to try to stop the bleeding. In no time, he was in the ambulance, and the siren began screaming once again as the vehicle sped off to the hospital. Todd stayed in the office to go over the crime scene, while Ned went into the shop to talk to Miss Tanaka. They sat in two comfortable chairs that Ned suspected were designed for bored husbands whose wives were exploring the store for treasures.

"Do you think he'll live?" Miss Tanaka wiped away tears.

"I'm not sure." Ned said. "He looked pretty bad. Are you the one who found him?"

"Yes," she answered. "I left at four thirty, and Mr. Gisolfi was still here, working. I think he was inventorying a new shipment from San Francisco. I drove home. I live just about fifteen minutes away in Kaimukī, on Third Avenue. I was nearly home when I realized that I had left my thermos and my lunch things at the shop. I decided to go back and get them because I needed them for tomorrow, and because, well, I didn't finish my lunch, and we're not supposed to leave food in the shop. You know, we're expected to keep everything neat and tidy."

"So how long was it between the time you left and the time you returned?"

"It was almost five when I got back here. I know because right after I called the ambulance and the police, I heard that clock chime." She pointed to a beautiful antique grandfather clock inlaid with mother of pearl in a floral design.

"Did you see anyone?"

"No one." She shook her head. "I got here and knew something was wrong right away because the back door, the employee entrance, was unlocked. That door is never unlocked after hours. I came in and thought I would tell Mr. Gisolfi. I went to his office, and that's when I found him. I can't believe this has happened."

Ned got up and looked around. Several of the glass cases were smashed and things were stolen. "Do you remember what was in these cases?"

"Oh yes, that was a case for some of our jewelry. There were three valuable necklaces and several bracelets. There were rings, one with an emerald and several with large pearls. The cash register has also been robbed. There was about seven hundred dollars in it when I left."

She showed Ned the cash drawer, which looked like it had been forced open. He was inspecting the register when he accidentally brushed an envelope off a shelf that let loose a small cascade of stamps onto the floor. "So sorry," he said as he bent to pick them up. "I've spilt all the stamps you've saved for Mr. Gisolfi."

"That's all right," said Miss Tanaka, helping to pick them up. "And, anyway, they aren't for him."

"No?" Ned gave her a puzzled look.

"Oh no, he gives them to that woman, Martha Klein."

"Martha Klein?" Ned felt as if he'd been kicked.

"Yes, she works at the museum. I think they've just become engaged."

"Martha Klein," he repeated.

"Yes, and I think she's a very insincere person." Miss Tanaka pouted.

Todd and Ned drove toward the hospital after leaving two of Todd's officers to finish up at Gump's. It was almost six and beginning to get dark.

"I would say it looks like robbery, with a special emphasis on the 'looks like' part of the statement," Todd said.

"I'd have to agree," said Ned. "And now we have Miss Klein, a new stamp collector on the scene."

"Martha?" Todd wrinkled his nose. "You think she has something to do with this? She's such a mousy librarian type."

"Maybe that's what she wants you to think. Let's pray Gisolfi is able to talk to us at the hospital. He must have seen whoever shot him."

"I hope he lasts long enough for us to talk to him." Todd seemed doubtful. "I think I'll place him under police protection and have the doctors keep their mouths shut about his condition."

"I think you should do that, detective," Ned agreed.

"You do, huh?"

"Yes," said Ned. "I think you should do it pronto."

It had just turned dark when Mina arrived at the theatre. She parked next to the blue sedan she now recognized as Martha Klein's. She was looking around for Johnny Knight when she saw Nyla in the costume shop, focused on sewing up a hem.

"I didn't see your car, Ny. How did you get here?" Mina asked.

"Hinano and Grandma Hannah dropped me off. They wanted to borrow the car so they could go visiting. They're starting at the Greenwoods." Nyla laughed.

"Oh, God," Mina groaned. "The last time they went visiting, they were gone for a week."

"I know," Nyla sighed. "They're practiced rascals, but I don't have the heart to spoil their fun."

"Have you seen Johnny?"

"He's here somewhere," Nyla said, turning her concentration back to her sewing. "You just have to wander around until you find him."

Mina did find Johnny, who took her to the theatre office and handed her the copy for the new press releases and the program. Mina went to the ladies lounge off the lobby to do the proofreading. She settled herself on one of the sofas and began to edit the press release, making several changes in Johnny's somewhat florid style. She was close to being finished when Sheila Halpern burst in with Jayling Preston in tow.

"I thought I'd find you here," Sheila exclaimed. "Jayling has decided to tell all." She pushed Jayling onto the sofa next to Mina. Jayling put a cigarette into an enameled holder, lit it, and melted back into the cushions. She was wearing black velvet pants and an aqua blue silk blouse with a mandarin collar. Her fingernails were painted a pale pink and matched exactly the shade of her lipstick. She looked much more arranged and put together than the person Mina had met at Andrew Halpern's house.

"What do you want to know?" Jayling asked in a polite tone of voice. "It doesn't matter now because the jerk is dead, and he can't hurt me anymore."

"Was Preston involved with Sheila's father in something shady?"

"Yeah, I *think* they were importing stolen antiques from Asia. I don't know how they got rid of them. Junior didn't tell me much. I just kind of figured things out."

"Is that all they were doing?" Mina asked.

The lounge door suddenly opened, and Nyla appeared in the doorway. "Sorry to interrupt, but Mina, I've changed my mind about the dress. I think black would be too serious. I want to borrow the emerald instead."

"Fine," said Mina.

"So can I use your car to go get it now? I have some time before they need me."

Mina reached into her bag and threw her sister the car keys.

"I'll be right back," Nyla said as she left.

"She looks just like you," Jayling commented. "I bet people mix you up all the time."

"All the time," said Mina. "So that's all they were up to? Stolen antiques?"

"At first, that was the main thing, I think, but then Junior started talking about some big plan and how it was going make him rich. And he used to say things like Halpern wasn't the big shot he thought he was, and how he didn't know what he was dealing with. He used to shoot off his mouth when he got drunk."

"And he never said what it was?"

"No," Jayling replied. "Anyway, that was right around the time I got away from him. Jesus, I thought he would never let me go. I thought I'd be stuck with him until he killed me. If it wasn't for that haole slut, I never would have gotten away."

"What?" Mina was a little confused.

"That haole slut, she was in on it with them. She was sleeping with Halpern and Junior and who knows who else. Junior believed she was in love with him. He thought she was just dropping her panties for other men to get what she needed out of them. He's so stupid he never thought she might be doing the same thing to him. He thought he was the king of the world because she had sex with him. He thought she was so high class, but she's just a dressed-up whore if you ask me. I know what you're thinking. How could someone like her go for a guy like him? But, believe me, he was a real eager lover with a body that was built to please. And he used it like a drug to make you forget all the other shitty things he did to you. I guess she was smart, though. He said she was the one with the brains."

"Do you mean Martha Klein?" Mina couldn't believe it.

"Of course. He used to say her name in his sleep, 'Martha, Martha, Martha.' After she started things up with him, I didn't matter anymore. That's the real reason he decided to let me go. I guess I should be grateful to her."

"Could I have one of your cigarettes?" Mina asked Jayling.

"Sure. I hope I didn't shock you."

"I am shocked about Martha," Mina admitted.

"I'm flabbergasted," said Sheila. "I can't believe she would have slept with my father."

"She'd sleep with your grandfather if she thought it would get her something she wanted." Jayling stood up and raised her hand to her chest. Her pink nails were set off to a great advantage by the blue of her blouse. "Anything else you want to know? Andrew and I are going to a party."

"Thanks, Jayling," Mina said. "If I think of anything else, can I call you?"

"I guess so," Jayling answered on her way out. "But don't call before noon."

Mina had a vague recollection of Sheila saying something about rehearsal and leaving the room, but all she could do was sit on the sofa and run through the events that began on New Year's Eve. She saw now how Martha could have fit in at every stage, and how Preston must have been doing her bidding all along, including trying to kill Cecily. She remembered the moment when Ned had pulled her back just before Preston's truck was about to hit her. She thought about how Kikue Tsuruda, who was making phone calls in hopes of blackmail, must have caused Martha to panic. Martha and Halpern must have picked up the trail of the stamps while doing research about the portrait. They must have figured out that Kahikina hid the letters, but not exactly where. Halpern either refused her something or found out she was sleeping with Preston. Or maybe Martha just wanted him out of the way so she and Preston could have the antique business and the stamps for themselves. Maybe she wanted to rule the roost at the museum to boot. And at the airport Martha wasn't waiting for a friend. She was there to see if Preston had come back. Martha's car was parked just outside, and Mina thought maybe she should get up and look for her, see what she was doing.

She stood up to leave, and for an instant caught the image of herself in the dressing room mirror. Except it wasn't her image that she saw. It was her sister's. Her breath seemed to catch in her chest and all her energy melted away. She felt like she'd climbed too long or run too far or been swimming for miles out to sea and back. She could hear the wind whistling through the high windows of the lounge and the rain dripping off the roof. She felt like she couldn't think or worry, and she sat back on the sofa, in a daze.

RECOVERY PLANS

NYLA WAS SAYING her lines out loud in the car as she pulled into Mina's driveway. It was dark, windy, and drizzling, and when she opened her car door, she decided to leave the headlights on and the motor running. She didn't see or hear the car that had turned off its lights and engine and was coasting down the driveway just behind her. To avoid getting wet, she ran to the front door. Once inside, she headed straight for Mina's bedroom and turned on the light. She heard the loud sound of the surf breaking over the reef. The wind was blowing through the house, and the damp and cold made her shiver. She saw Mina's black cardigan sweater with its pretty embroidered morning glories thrown on the bed, and put it on. With her back to the bedroom door, she stood before the closet and began going through the clothes, looking for the emerald green dress with the velvet jacket. She didn't hear the front door opening and the quiet footsteps coming down the hall. Suddenly she felt a hand on her shoulder. She cried out as another hand shoved a damp cloth that smelled terrible in her face, and she had a vague sensation of something being thrown over her head just before she passed out.

Mina jumped when she heard someone knocking on the lounge door. It took her a few seconds to recover herself.

"Mina, are you in there?" It was Ned calling.

"I'll be right out," she called back.

"We'll wait out here in the lobby. Todd's here, and something's happened."

Mina rinsed off her face with cold water. In the lobby, she told them what Jayling had said, and they told her about Gisolfi.

"The doctor let us see him for just a bit," said Ned. "He's in very bad shape, and he might not make it. He said Martha came, told him about the stamps, and wanted his help. She admitted to killing Halpern and told him all about Preston killing Kikue and the old man in Chinatown. The poor old guy was stunned and couldn't believe it at first. He said she was convinced I had found the stamps, and she had some crazy plan to kidnap you and hold you hostage in order to get them. He said she was angry, and she blamed us for Preston's death. When he refused to go along with her and told her he would call the police, she went berserk and shot him."

"She's in the building right now," Mina said. "When I got here, I saw her car."

"It wasn't there when we got here," said Ned.

"I didn't see your car either. How did you get here?" Todd asked.

"Oh my God, Nyla!" Mina jumped up.

"What are you talking about?" Todd was alarmed.

"She borrowed my car! She went to my house!"

In no time, the three of them were headed for the bungalows. When they pulled into the driveway, they saw Mina's car parked just as Nyla had left it, with the engine running and the headlights on. Todd raced into the house, and when Mina and Ned found him, he was sitting on the bed, holding a piece of paper. His face had gone pale. Ned took the letter, read it, and then handed it to Mina.

"Well, Ned," she said after she'd read it, "she wants to punish us for getting in her way. She thinks she has me, and she's going to take this opportunity to get at you. I think Preston actually mattered to her."

"By now, she must know I had something to do with Preston's death," Ned added. "But she's guessing. She can't be sure I have the stamps."

"Of course she knows you had something to do with his death," Mina said. "She sent him after you, and he doesn't come back. He falls off a cliff and dies. Why would he be up on a cliff unless it was to get what she wanted from you? Well, maybe she doesn't know for sure you have them, but she's taking the risk. And we have to play it safe because she has Nyla, and she's crazy enough to kill her."

The note gave specific instructions. Ned was to drive alone with the stamped envelopes and letters to the beginning of Round Top Drive. At midnight he was to leave and drive for exactly 3.3 miles. There, he would see a trail on the driver's side of the road. He was to stop the car, take the parcel, and walk down the trail until he found a white bag. He was to place the letters in the bag and leave, going down the mountain the same way he came. The note stated that the roads were being watched, and any interference or deviation would result in the most serious consequences.

Round Top Drive wove up the side of the mountains behind the city, climbing into the rain forest to an area called Tantalus. It was a deserted, narrow, steep, and winding road that skirted along the lower peaks of the Ko'olau mountain range, then looped back down to the city. Streetlights and electrical service didn't go beyond the first mile, where newer homes were built on the lower part of the road. Once into the forest zone, there were a few secluded houses scattered here and there, many of them weekend shacks. Though not far from the city, it was a wilderness, with a crisscross of rugged trails frequented by hunters going after wild boars. It was a place where hikers often went missing.

Ned went to get three glasses and the bottle of brandy he knew Mina kept in her kitchen cupboard. He poured a decent shot for everyone, and they drank it all at once and in silence. Mina was the first to talk as she paced around the bedroom.

"Let's think now," she said in a very determined voice. "Let's think about this note. Besides her vendetta against us, what does it tell us, Ned?"

"She doesn't know we know it's her. She most likely thinks Gisolfi is dead," Ned answered.

"And," she added, "she implies in the note that she has accomplices. But if she was trying to get Gisolfi to help her just this afternoon, I'm sure that's a lie. Still, we can't be too careful. Let's look at a map."

They went out into the living room, where she pulled a map of the city out of a drawer. She identified Round Top Drive for Ned, and using the legend, figured out how far up the trailhead would be.

"I know where that trail is," she said. "There aren't any houses around there. I'll bet you anything she's marked her own route through the forest so we would never know where she was coming from. I have an idea, but I need to call the theatre."

She called the costume shop, and Peggy Kelly answered. "Peggy," Mina began, "I'm just calling to tell you that Nyla won't be coming back this evening. She's having, ah, you know, it's that time of month, and she's got terrible cramps. She's here curled up with a hot water bottle. Could you tell Johnny she won't be back? . . . Thanks. Oh, and Peggy, you know Martha. Maybe you could settle a little difference between Nyla and me. See, we're both remembering that we went to this birthday party up on Tantalus in the fifth grade, and I'm sure it was Martha Klein's party, but Nyla says it was Carol Parker's. Did Martha's family have a weekend house up there? . . . No? I thought they did. . . . I see. Well, yes, that must have been it, because we both remember going there, but we couldn't remember where it was. . . . Near the Ridge Road? It is? Gee, that's too bad. Oh, that's right, the Parkers' place was in Portlock. Well, thanks Peggy. I'm sure I'll be seeing you during the show."

She hung up the phone. "The Kleins didn't have a place on Tantalus, but they used to stay at the Hughes cottage a lot because Mabel Hughes and Martha's mother were best friends. It's been abandoned for some time."

"That was brilliant," Ned said.

"We're all going to have to be brilliant tonight. Let's look at the map again."

"Here's the Ridge Road." Ned traced it with his finger. "It cuts off Round Top Drive right here. And there's the trail I'm supposed to go on. Look, as you go along the trail, right here it gets close to the Ridge Road. It's about a quarter of a mile away and a good place for her to use as a base."

"If she's smart, which we know she is, she'll leave the house to watch you make the drop. I could move in on the house about the same time to see if Nyla is there. I'd be afraid to move in any earlier. I'm sure she'd be on high alert."

"Maybe you could take Hīnano," Ned added. "I don't think you should go alone. Do you think Johnny Knight might help us?"

"I'll get on the phone. I'm sure Johnny's at the theatre. Let's pray I can find Hīnano, and he's still reasonably sober. I think Nyla said they were going to Emma Greenwood's place first." She was already dialing. "Where's Todd? We need him. We can't let him fade out on us."

Ned went into the bedroom and found Todd sitting with the letter in his hand. Ned sat for a minute and poured Todd another shot of brandy. He let Todd drink it down, and then said, "We're going to get her back. Come on and snap out of it. We need you."

"Johnny said to call him at the theatre if we need him. Hīnano is on his way. He's taking Grandma Hannah home first." Mina was hanging up the phone when Ned and Todd came into the room.

"Can I get you something?" Mina asked Todd.

"No." Todd shook his head. "I'll be okay."

"Look, Todd." Mina raised her voice like a scolding teacher. "I know we've had our differences, but right now we have to forget all of that. We three have to pull ourselves together and use everything we can to get Nyla back. We can all fall apart afterwards, but right now we're going to fight any way we can, okay? Are you with us?"

"Damn it, of course I am," Todd snapped back.

"Okay, that's better." Mina took his hand and drew him close. "It's eight now, so we've got about four hours. Let's get to work."

A CLOSE WILDERNESS

AT 10:00 P.M., Todd sat behind his desk at the station. He loaded a small revolver and handed it to Ned. "I know you don't like guns," he said, "but it would make me feel better if you carried this with you."

"If it makes you feel better." Ned was not about to argue.

"How's your ankle? Are you sure you can do this?"

"I bound it up, and I'm just going to make it work," Ned answered.

"I've arranged for an old truck, and some police dogs. If we're going to pass for pig hunters, we need some dogs. I've picked a place that I think will be pretty dark for the switch. I'm just not sure if all of this is necessary."

"I'm 99 percent sure Martha is on her own," Ned said, "but we can't take any chances."

"Let's go over this again, so you're clear about the meeting place." Todd spread the map over his desk. "This is the trailhead. About half a mile before that, there's a dirt road that leads to an abandoned house. Johnny and I will be parked with the dogs down the road in an old truck. When you drive by, flash your lights, and I'll respond. After you drop the letters, come back there as fast as you can."

"Then I'll give Johnny my coat and hat," Ned continued, "and put on some old clothes. We take off in the truck toward Ridge Road. Anyone spying for her will think we're just pig hunters. Johnny goes down the hill, in my car coat and hat, and if she does have someone watching below, they'll think they're seeing me."

"If you're not at our meeting place in an hour, I'm going after her with a gun." Todd stood up and kicked the desk. "Damn it, I want to just move in there right now!"

"Look." Ned tried his best to sound calm and confident. "She won't do anything to Nyla until she has possession of the stamps. Nyla is her bargaining chip, and by the time I'm on the trail, Mina and Hīnano should be watching the house."

"You're assuming that Nyla is going to be in that house. We don't know that."

"If she's not," Ned answered, "Your men will be waiting at the bottom of the hill to follow Martha. They know her car, and you said there are only these two ways down, right?" Ned pointed to the roads on the map. "Have you squared things away with your chief?"

"I told him we're acting on a tip from Gisolfi, and going after her. I didn't tell him anything about Nyla being kidnapped."

"Well, let's go, old boy. Let's go find her."

Just as they were leaving, the phone rang, and Todd stopped to answer it. His conversation was brief and clipped. He hung up and half whispered to Ned, "Gisolfi didn't make it."

At midnight, Ned started up Round Top Drive. It was raining again, and the big drops fell like little bullets onto the windshield. He rolled down the window on his side about an inch to keep the glass from fogging over. The cool air felt good, but the rain blew in a little, and he had to keep wiping off the left side of his face. There were no other cars on the road at this time of night. After about five minutes of driving up steep and winding curves, there were no houses or streetlights. Soon he reached a peak on the edge of a ridge and the vista opened up. Through the rain, he could see the vague city lights of Waikīkī, and a black space that he guessed was right about where Diamond Head would be. Then the road turned, and for a very short time he saw a dim glow from the neighborhood of Mānoa Valley before he reached another stretch of curves where the overhanging trees and thick jungle blocked out everything. He traveled along the dark road, seeing only what was illuminated by the headlights of the car. When he passed the place he thought was his rendezvous point with Todd, he flashed the lights. As he looked in the rear view mirror, he saw Todd answer as the blackness behind him lit up for a split second.

The rain slackened into a light drizzle, but now he was driving into an eerie mist. White wisps flew by, and the air became colder. He saw the trailhead, but went a little past it and turned around so that he would waste no time when he got back to the car. His watch said twelve fifteen. He got out, put on Todd's old raincoat, and slung a satchel containing the old metal box with the letters over his shoulder. The weight of the revolver in the coat pocket made him feel uneasy. He turned on his flashlight and started along the trail. It was muddy, and his rubber boots made squeaking noises as he walked along. There was almost no wind, but the mist persisted, and when he shined the light in front of him, he couldn't see more than a few feet. There was the strong smell of overripe guavas and damp decaying leaves, and he thought he heard the rustling and grunting of a wild pig in the forest. In the edges of the beam from his flashlight, he could see lush, wet ferns on either side of the trail. He thought about his grandfather's glass greenhouse and how the tropical plants there were tended like colicky children.

The trail went down into a ravine, and he had to cross over a small stream on a precarious little plank bridge. Then the trail went uphill and became a switchback, winding up to the top of a rise. All at once, he found himself in a clearing. He looked up and saw the clouds racing by in the night sky. The trail went straight on into a small field of grass. Just in front of him, a few yards away on the trail, was a white canvas bag. He checked his watch again. It had taken him fifteen minutes at a pretty good clip to get here. His ankle hurt, but he refused to let it slow him down. He shined the light around him, and saw that he was in the middle of a large open space. If Martha were watching him, which he was sure she was, she had the great advantage of being hidden, as well as knowing the lay of the land. He stood there for a moment and looked at the bag. He reached in the satchel for the box, and as he tossed it into the bag, he turned off his flashlight and rolled onto the ground.

He heard the first bullet graze the ground near the bag. A second shot sent him crawling as fast as he could through the grass, and then along the edge of the brush until he found the trail. As he crawled onto the trail, he heard a third shot crack a tree branch a few feet away. He took out the pistol from his pocket and fired in the direction he thought the shots came from. He knew he couldn't hit her, but reasoned that if she knew he was armed, she might not pursue him. He fired again, and then moved into the protected part of the trail. Once under the cover of the jungle, he got to his feet, crouched low, and moved as fast as he could. A sudden shower of rain came down, making the trail more slippery. His ankle was throbbing, but he was able to straighten up and move along. He was sure she wouldn't follow him. When he got to the plank bridge, he risked turning on his flashlight and limped as fast as he could on the muddy trail. He got to the car, jumped in, and raced down the hill to meet Todd, taking the corners as fast as he dared on the slick, wet pavement.

Mina and Hīnano had driven up the mountain ridge from the opposite side in an old borrowed car and were headed for Ridge Road. It was risky, but they turned off the headlights for the last half mile. When they reached the road, they cut the engine and rolled off the road and down the long driveway of a cabin that looked unoccupied. They got out and began walking. Mina had a vague idea of where the house might be. They kept very close to the side of the dirt road in case they had to hide. Even in the rain and fog, they easily found the decayed and half-broken wooden sign that marked the driveway of the old Hughes place. Through the mist, Mina spotted Martha's car parked next to a run-down shingled cottage set about four feet off the ground with a water tank on the right. It was very quiet as they crept down the drive. Mina went up to the car and peered inside for some sign of her sister.

She was about to open the car door when Hīnano tapped her shoulder and pointed behind the house. Mina listened and heard someone coming through the forest toward them. Hīnano grabbed

Mina's arm and led her to the side of the water tank, where they hid in the shadows. The noise from behind the house got louder. Mina and Hīnano crouched down and saw a figure in a raincoat near the car fumbling with something, and then they heard Martha laughing.

"Do you smell something funny?" Hīnano whispered in Mina's ear.

It took Mina a few seconds to realize that she did smell something like kerosene or gasoline. Her attention was drawn back to Martha, who had gotten in the car and turned on the engine. Then Martha got out of the car again, and took out a box of matches. She stood near the house and shouted, "Good-bye, Mina. I hope you stay warm tonight." Then she lit a match and threw it under the house. In an instant, a fire blazed up as Martha calmly got in her car and drove off.

The fire raced in a line under the house and all along the perimeter, where Martha had laid out and doused lines of old rags and newspapers. Mina ran up the stairs to the front door. It was locked. She and Hīnano pushed and kicked, but they couldn't get it open. Mina ran around to the back, where she found another door. She threw her weight against it with all the force she could and found herself sprawled on the floor of the main room. The fire had caught the outer walls of the house, and in some spots small flames were coming through the floorboards. She couldn't see Nyla anywhere in the room. She crawled along the floor, spotted an open door to another room. The heat and smoke were making her sick, and she tried to keep her mouth and nose covered with her jacket. She found Nyla on the floor, semiconscious, with a pillowcase covering her head and her hands tied. Mina grabbed her sister by the shoulders, but the smoke and heat were so overwhelming she could hardly move. All at once, Hīnano was beside her. "Come on, Mina," he shouted. "We both can do it." In a burst of energy and strength, they picked up Nyla by the shoulders, and struggling to see through the smoke, they managed to drag her outside. As soon as they were out the door and down the stairs, the floor of the cabin was engulfed in flames and began to collapse.

Hīnano took out his pocketknife and cut Nyla loose while Mina removed the pillowcase. Then, they rushed her over to the water tank, turned on a faucet and held her head under the cold water.

"Oh my God!" Nyla screamed. "That's enough. It's goddamn cold."

"We have to get out of here," Hīnano said. The whole house was caving in and flaming debris began to fly away in all directions.

The three of them were moving as fast as they could toward the road just as Todd and Ned came barreling around the corner. Todd bolted out of the truck almost before he came to a stop and ran to Nyla. There were quick embraces and urgent words. After Nyla assured Todd that she was safe, he and Ned jumped back in the truck and went after Martha Klein.

Martha was not in any great hurry as she drove along the mountain road. She felt elated, and she kept looking at the little metal box next to her on the seat. She had outwitted all of them. Halpern was dead, and he deserved it. So did that snoopy little Japanese maid and that stupid man in Chinatown. Alfred Gisolfi deserved it too. He said he loved her, and if he did, he should have done what she wanted. But when she needed him, he wouldn't. He didn't really love her, not the way Junior had. Junior was the only one, the only one who loved her enough to do whatever she wanted. And it was Mina's fault he was dead. Mina thought she was so smart, but right now she was burning up to a little crisp. And that Ned Manusia, she wished she could have shot him in the dark, and left him to die by himself in the rain.

Martha was alert, but not alarmed, when she saw the headlights of a vehicle weave in and out of the night along the road behind her. It was getting closer, but not going very fast. It looked like some kind of truck, and she thought it must be hunters. The truck came up behind her, and she slowed down to let it pass, but as the truck pulled beside her she recognized Ned Manusia motioning her to pull over. Two dogs in the back seat snarled and growled at her. She stepped on the gas and swerved toward the truck, hitting them on the right front as she pulled away. Todd and Ned were forced off the road. The dogs were whining and pacing from side to side in the back as Todd started the engine back up and followed her, but the old truck was no match for Martha's roadster.

As she took the downhill corners, the tires of her car screeched in the night. She smiled as she glanced up in her rearview mirror. She knew they could never catch her. She had the stamps, and all she had to do was outrun them, dump her car, and hide for a while. One of the women in her garden club had gone away for a month on a trip, and she had the keys to her house. She could stay there, cut and dye her hair, use a little cleverly applied makeup to change her appearance, and then leave on a freighter to California or Australia or the Far East. She'd already bought several steamer tickets under different names just in case, and she'd already lined up the buyer for the stamps. Collectors were a greedy lot. Some of them didn't care where things came from, and they were willing to pay. Maybe she would go to Europe, and take a long tour that ended on the Riviera. She thought about herself lying in the sun and perhaps meeting someone, a man with lots of money, a cultured man who could appreciate her brains and beauty. As her car navigated another hairpin turn, the metal box slid from the seat and rattled to the floor. She stepped on the brake, but the car didn't slow down. She tried again, pumping the pedal several times before she realized that the box was wedged behind it. She managed the corner but felt the left wheels lift up and land back down making the car bounce from side to side.

All her planning, all this time, it couldn't end like this. She was so close. She knew she could get away with it. Another corner was coming up. She bent down around the wheel and groped for the box while trying to maintain control of the car, but it was too late. The car began to bounce violently from side to side, and then Martha felt the car begin to roll over. She saw the night, the road, and the trees spiraling around and around, as her body became light, like a rag doll—tossing, twirling, smashing, and then falling into a cold, final darkness.

Todd and Ned pulled off the road, got out of the car, and Ned moved toward the twisted wreck while Todd hung back a little and let the two dogs out. The car was upside down. Martha's body was in the back, against the ceiling. Her head was turned up and her blue eyes were opened in a wide unnatural stare. One of her arms extended out of the side window. The metal box lay outside on the ground, a few inches from her pale, limp hand. Ned knelt down on the damp ground, lifted the exposed wrist, and tried to find a pulse, but he knew, from the expression on her face and from the feel of her skin, that he wouldn't find one. He tried several times and then backed away. The dogs moved in, sniffed the exposed arm, lifted their eyes to Ned, and whined a little as if to confirm that she was dead. Ned looked over at Todd, who stood a few feet away. Ned shook his head and said, "She's gone."

"Come on." Todd turned away. "Let's go down the hill, and I'll get the boys to deal with this. We've had enough for one damn night."

DOORS THAT OPEN AND CLOSE

M INA ROLLED over under her quilt and began to wake up. The morning was dark with clouds, and it was still raining. In her half sleep, the events of the night began to surface. She remembered taking Nyla home and helping Grandma Hannah get her into bed. She remembered feeling exhausted and driving in a downpour to her own house. She opened her eyes and saw that she had fallen asleep on the pūne'e in the living room. On the table next to her stood a glass and the brandy bottle. There was still a little brandy in the bottom of the glass. That's right, she had come home, showered off the ashes and the mud, put on some clean clothes, poured herself a drink, and was waiting for Ned to call or come home.

Ned—Mina thought of him and sat up. She realized she had no idea what happened to Ned or Todd after they parted on Tantalus. She threw off the quilt, and in no time was knocking on Ned's door. There was no answer. She could see his car in the drive, so she knew he must be in there. Impatient, Mina opened the door and let herself in.

The house was quiet and dark, just like hers, but as soon as she stepped inside it seemed bigger, and a little bit foreign. She could hear the sound of the rain hitting the roof in sheets, and the faint ticking of the silly owl-shaped clock that hung in the kitchen. Its eyes moved back and forth, and its hands said eight thirty. In this dim light the hallway looked like a long tunnel, and the bedroom Ned was using at the end seemed miles away. She hesitated for a moment before she tiptoed down the hall, and even though she did her best to be very quiet, the floor creaked a little under her every step.

She stood in the doorway and looked in. The space was a mirror image of her own bedroom, but sparse and empty in comparison. The dark wooden floors were bare, and the few pieces of furniture, a chest of drawers and a chair, stood there looking as if they wanted more company. Ned's shoes and socks were beside the chair and his trousers and shirt thrown across the seat. The bed was placed against the middle of the wall, and he was sleeping on his side. The covers had slipped down around his waist. His arms were wrapped around, as if he were embracing himself or trying to keep warm. She smiled to herself, feeling relieved and satisfied to see him lying there. Some of his hair had fallen forward over one of his eyes, and she thought he looked romantic and vulnerable. She knew she should leave, but she found herself wanting to stay, wanting to watch and make sure nothing disturbed him. She wondered what he was like when he was a little boy, what he dreamed about at night, and what he imagined in his daydreams. Unbidden, a wave of embarrassment swept over her. What did she think she was doing? What if he woke up and saw her intruding this way? She turned quietly to go.

"Mina," he said in a soft, sleepy voice, "don't leave."

She froze.

"It's all right," he said, not moving. "Please come back. Don't just walk away."

She turned around, walked back into the room, and sat down on the edge of his bed. "I'm not exactly sure what I'm doing," she said.

"It doesn't matter." Ned looked up at her and touched her cheek. "We don't have to know exactly what we're doing."

"I just wanted to make sure you were all right."

"Ah, Mina." Ned sat up, kissed her, and put his arms around her. "Are you scared, about us? About how you might feel?"

"Yes," she answered. "I don't want to make another mistake."

"I'm not," he said. "I'm not scared, and I'm positive this is not a mistake. And," he added, "I'm sure I know exactly what you need right now."

"Oh, you think so?" she replied in a sassy voice.

"Of course," he said, smiling. "You need some food."

Mina burst into laughter.

As they made breakfast together, Ned told her about Martha's death and how Todd was supposed to talk to the police chief today. He was turning over all the evidence, saying that he found the folder with Blain's journal himself in Halpern's study and that the box with the letters and stamps was sitting in Martha's wrecked car. This morning, Ned would have to go to the station and make an official statement about what Gisolfi said before he died, but it looked like Todd and Nyla could be erased from the picture. It would be obvious now that Martha had framed Sam Takahashi. Todd would say he guessed that Preston died looking for the box in the wrong place and somehow Martha must have found it on her own. Given the standing in the community of those involved, and the definite discovery of the murderers, it was probable that the police chief would want to close the case as soon as possible. While the scones were baking, Ned showered, and Mina made omelets and Portuguese sausage.

"As soon as she killed Gisolfi, she must have written the ransom note," Ned reflected as he sat down. "She must have been in an enraged and disjointed state of mind."

"I'm sorry for him. He was a very nice man." Mina poured the tea. "I still can't believe she was sleeping with all those men."

"I can," Ned said matter-of-factly, as he buttered a scone.

"Why?"

"Because she flirted with me in a brazen way in the theatre parking lot."

"And did you like it?"

"Of course," he answered. "Every man loves it when a deeply disturbed murderess flirts with him. I'm shocked you don't know these things, darling."

"I guess I haven't had your experience with female criminal types." She looked over at him and paused before she took a bite of her omelet. "I'm surprised I don't feel bad or frightened out of my mind. I guess I'm just glad none of us were hurt."

"And it's over."

"When are you leaving for Sāmoa?"

The question took Ned by surprise. "After the play closes, in about three weeks. Why don't you come with me? It's very beautiful, you'd like it."

"I don't think so. I mean how would that look? Besides, I have my job to think about."

"You'd still have your work when you got back. You're a great bargain—you're paid by the story, and I'll bet you're the best writer there. You could take a three-year vacation, and Hollister would still have you back. Maybe you could write a story about Āpia."

"I don't think it's a good idea." Mina frowned. "You'll have to come back here on your way home, right?"

"I'll have to come back here because you're here, Mina."

After they finished eating and cleaned up, Ned went downtown to make his statement. Mina went to her house and called work. She was told by a colleague that there was a big flurry over the events of last night. She was relieved to hear that someone else was covering the story. Next, she phoned Nyla, who sounded like her old self and insisted that she and Ned show up for drinks and dinner before the evening rehearsal. Mina walked around the house and over to her little shelf with the family pictures. She picked up the photograph of Len and sat down to look at it. He looked so bright and handsome on horseback. It was true, she had liked him, even admired him, but she hadn't loved him. And he loved what he thought she was, but couldn't see her, or maybe, like most men, never really thought to look at her beyond being a potential wife and mother. She had changed, and he hadn't. She realized now it wasn't her fault. It wasn't anyone's fault. She thought she'd made a mistake, marrying him, but maybe it wasn't a mistake. His life was cut off while he was young and full of vitality, and during the short time they were married, she had made him happy. Yes, she said to herself, I made him happy.

Now there was Ned, who seemed to see who she was from the very beginning. She could take another chance, but she'd have to be very careful. He lived so far away, and it had the potential to turn into an impossible situation. And she'd only known him for about a month. She dusted off Len's photograph and placed it back on the shelf. For a few minutes, she sat on her pūne'e and watched the rain. Then, she went to her bookshelf and picked out her favorite Jane Austen, and for several peaceful hours lost herself in the fortunes of

Anne Elliot. At three o'clock she decided it was time to get ready to go to her sister's house. She took a bubble bath and put up her hair. She picked out a pair of navy slacks and a deep red sweater, as it was probably going to be a little cold up in the heights. Then, she put on the pin Ned had given her for her birthday. At four, when Ned came to get her, she opened the door and greeted him with a kiss.

"You look stunning, Mina," he said. "Are you ready to go?"

"Ready," she smiled.

Maunalani Heights was covered in mist and rain, and when they got to the house, Hīnano had the fireplace lit, and Nyla was busy making mulled wine. Grandma Hannah was sitting in the living room watching the fire and crocheting. Hīnano brought out some cheese and crackers, and everyone was settling around the fire with their drinks when Todd arrived. Nyla got him a mug of the warm wine, and they all sat looking at him.

"What's the news, governor?" Ned asked.

"It's a little distressing." Todd was staring at the fire.

"Well, tell us for God's sake," Nyla said.

"The good news," Todd began, "is that the chief, after a cursory read of the letters and the folder—minus the newspaper clipping, of course—accepted the story about the box and Preston's death just as I presented it. Gisolfi's evidence, as told to Ned and me, and Alika's statement satisfied him as to Martha's guilt in Halpern and Gisolfi's murders and Preston's guilt in the Tsuruda murder. He was pleased that the three murders were solved and considered the case closed."

"So what's the bad news?" Nyla sighed.

"After I talked to him, he must have looked at the things in the folder and the box more closely because he called me into his office again early this afternoon. Apparently he reread the stuff and took it right over to the governor. The governor read it and then called the FBI. I just came from a special meeting in the governor's office at 'Iolani Palace with the governor, the chief, and the FBI. I was first reminded that in this murder case there would be no trial, as the perpetrators were dead, and therefore no real need for the police department to keep the evidence. Then I was quizzed by the federal investigators about who else might have seen the contents of the box and the folder, to which I lied and said, no one but myself. Next, I got a lecture on the politically volatile and sensitive nature of the material, and was informed that the federal government was taking possession of all of it. I was instructed that I was never to talk about or mention the documents to anyone, and that should I ever, in the course of my lifetime, make reference to them or this meeting, everyone present was sworn to deny their existence. Furthermore, the FBI would be writing a statement for the press that would be the official statement on the case, and the chief was instructing everyone in the department not to talk to the press or anyone else. And, get this. Christian Hollister has already agreed to print only what is in the statement, before he's even seen it, and to tell his reporters to back off."

"I can guess where the stamps will end up," said Ned, looking up at the ceiling.

"In other words, they're covering up all the political plotting and the king's murder," Mina said in a disgusted tone.

"At least now *we* know the truth," Grandma Hannah sighed. "It won't bring the king back. It won't bring Kahikina back, but now we know the truth about what happened."

"And who was in on it," Hīnano added.

"But only the people in this room know," Mina complained. "What good will it do if no else knows the truth about the things they did?"

"Well, now they've fixed it so we could never prove it," said Todd. "People would say we were making it up."

"There must be a reason we're supposed to have this knowledge," Hīnano added. "We had some special help in finding it, didn't we, Ned?"

"We had some extraordinary help," Ned agreed.

"So I think we'll have help again," Hīnano said.

"Some knowledge comes to us like a seed, Mina dear." Grandma Hannah looked at Mina over her glasses. "Then, we have to bury it and leave it alone in the dark. When it's time, it comes up again and grows."

"At least we're all here," Nyla began. "Here's to all of us being safe and together."

"And off the hook," Todd added, "thanks to Ned and Mina."

They raised their glasses in a toast, and all gathered around the table for dinner. The fire cast a beautiful glow over the room, and everyone was grateful to be in each other's company. Grandma Hannah and Hīnano had made a delicious island curry with all the condiments, and Nyla's coconut cake dessert provided a great finish to the meal. Ned and Nyla went off to rehearsal, and Mina stayed behind to visit with her grandmother.

After the rehearsal, Nyla drove Ned back to the bungalow. By the time they left the theatre, the sky was clearing and a few stars were visible. It was a little chilly, but they rolled down the windows and let the night air blow through the car. Johnny had been more than pleased with the cast, and Nyla was feeling elated and looking forward to opening night, which was only four days away.

"Say Nyla, would you like to help me on a new project?" Ned asked. "It might be long term and involve a little travel."

"Oh, tell me," she laughed. "Both Todd and I owe you one, Ned. What's the project about?"

"I was wondering if you would help me to get your sister to marry me."

"Hmm," said Nyla. "That could take some time. But I'll help you do it, Ned, because I want to see that Mina gets just what she deserves!"

40

CURTAIN

THE AUDIENCE ROSE to its feet to give the cast a standing ova-
tion. The house was full. It was a Sunday afternoon and the last
performance of the play. Though the theatre-going crowd in Honolulu was small, Ned's reputation and word of mouth had resulted in
people scrambling for tickets. The cast had done quite well. Ned was
proud of their performance, and he was even more pleased that Mina
was here, standing beside him, applauding his play.

As the cast took its final bow, Mina, looking radiant, turned to him,
smiled, and said, "Ned Manusia, you are a brilliant playwright."

The audience was beginning to disperse, and Mina told Ned she
was going straight home to help get ready for the cast party. She urged
him to stay, as there were bound to be many people who wanted to
meet and congratulate him. He protested, but she insisted, saying
that it would mean a lot to the people who came to be able to meet
the playwright. As they walked out to the lobby, a crowd of people
moved toward him, and she disappeared through a side door.

When the lobby had cleared, he went backstage. There was a confusion of costumes and props being sorted and set pieces being dis-
mantled. Johnny Knight came over to shake Ned's hand.

"I'm hoping," said Johnny, "to talk the theatre into doing another
one of your plays soon. This has been such a great success. And listen," he lowered his voice to a conspiratorial whisper, "if you ever
need any help on another caper, I'm your man. But next time, for

safety's sake, I think I should pack some heat." Johnny winked and walked off, leaving Ned with a bemused smile.

The cast members were starting to stream out of their dressing rooms, bedecked in leis from their friends and family, and everyone was eagerly looking forward to the cast party. Nyla finally came out of the women's dressing room. She was wearing a pretty blue and white holokū with a little ruffle at the hem.

"Sorry, Ned," she said, "that costume was hard to get out of. I hope they're all set at the beach. Looks like we're the last to leave."

"I'm sure everything will be splendid," he said. "You haven't forgotten about our plan, have you?"

"How could I forget?" She laughed. "I'm dying to go along with it!"

"And Todd is as well?" He sounded a little worried.

"Don't be silly. Todd would do anything for you. Now, don't worry. Just leave it to me."

When they arrived at the bungalow driveway, a valet opened their doors and took charge of the car. It was late afternoon, and the day had been still and cloudless. The yard was transformed into an extraordinary setting. White paper lanterns were strung all around. Long lūʻau tables sat low to the ground on lauhala mats, and colorful zabutons were set for each person. The tables were covered in green ti leaves with three long strings of yellow plumerias running down the center of each table. There was a pretty little stage built up at one end with a backdrop of woven coconut fronds and tropical flowers, complete with a piano. A Hawaiian trio was already tuning up and beginning to play. Mina came up the drive to meet them. She was wearing a holokū that was identical to Nyla's, but in dark green and white. They each took one of Ned's arms and walked down to the party.

"Well, look at you, Ned," Todd commented as they approached. "Just arrived and you've already got the two most beautiful women in tow."

"Bad luck for you, old man," Ned quipped.

"Well, Mina," said Nyla, "do you think it's safe to leave these two on their own while we go and see to our guests?"

"I've already paid Alika to keep an eye on them," Mina chuckled. "He's reporting any mischief to me."

"Come on, Ned," Todd grabbed Ned's arm and pulled him away. "Let's go find some *nice* women to spend the evening with."

"Not too nice," Ned shot back, laughing.

The tables were all arranged with place cards. Todd and Ned found their table, reclined on their cushions, lit up cigars, and enjoyed the scene. Kaleinani Nāpili, wearing a stunning choker of delicate pink, yellow, and pale brown Niʻihau shells, appeared to take their drink orders. A crew from the Wahine Surf Lounge, in matching sarong dresses, were moonlighting and doing the serving at the party. Kaleinani returned with their drinks. "There's a special plate of appetizers arriving for you from the kitchen," she said with mysterious smile, "about to be delivered by the chief cook."

A few minutes later, Uncle Wing Chang appeared in chef's attire. "Poisson cru for the playwright," smiled Uncle Wing, "from French Polynesia, raw fish marinated in lime with a little coconut cream and a few additions of my own. In celebration of both of your achievements." He winked. "Mina enlisted me to make this as a first course for everyone, but you two are getting a preview."

Ned tasted a spoonful. "Tres oo-la-la. How is Cecily doing?"

"She couldn't be better. She and her fiancé should be here this evening. Did you know he's lived in Paris, and he speaks French?" Uncle Wing beamed.

"No, I didn't." Ned shook his head. "I met him briefly when they came to the play."

"The wedding is in June. I'm already busy planning the menu. I hope you'll be here."

"He could be," said Todd. "I think he has some new interests in the islands."

"Hmm, I wonder what that might be?" Uncle Wing laughed as he walked back to Mina's kitchen.

"Look," said Todd. "It's our favorite couple, Chris Hollister and Lamby Langston."

Christian Hollister and Lamby Langston were just sitting down at their table. Ned noticed that Hollister had not bothered to wash off his stage makeup and was still full of the excitement of acting in front of hundreds of people. Lamby was wearing a tight fitting halter dress with a plunging neckline, and smoking a cigarette from a long mother-of-pearl holder. When Lamby saw the look Chris gave Mina as she came to greet them, she turned her head with the long holder in her mouth so that Mina was forced to jump away or get burned.

The sun was beginning to set, and the sky was changing colors. Ned watched as Sam Takahashi and Sheila Halpern walked up from the beach. Sheila's red hair was glowing in the evening light, and she looked flushed and happy. Sam had one arm wrapped around her. Ned thought about the trials they would have to go through together as a couple. Even in Honolulu, it was still rare for a Caucasian woman to date or marry a Japanese man, and Sheila was bound to receive the scorn of more than one Honolulu matron. And though Ned knew little about Japanese customs, he guessed that Sam's family would not be pleased with his choice. But perhaps it wouldn't bother either of them. She had inherited quite a bit of money, and because of her father she was immune to disapproval. Andrew, on the other hand, would have a much easier time of it if he stuck with Jayling. White males marrying nonwhite females was a much more acceptable arrangement to the Western world. Ned could never understand why it didn't work the same way in both directions. He saw Peggy Kelly, the librarian and costume assistant, sitting by herself and decided to go over and say hello.

"Oh, Ned. It's so nice to see you." She looked grateful that someone had come over to talk to her. "Your play was such a wonderful success. I hope you're happy with our little production. Not what you're used to in London, I'm sure."

"I was very happy with everything," he smiled. "And the costumes were very well done. I know you helped a lot."

"It's just frightful about Martha, isn't it? Who would have ever suspected she was capable of all those wicked things?" Peggy shook her head. "It's just fortunate her poor parents died before her. What a disgrace! I just don't understand it."

"It's very puzzling, isn't it?" He looked into his half-finished gin and tonic and swirled it around. "She was beautiful and intelligent.

Perhaps she enjoyed the dark side of things. Some people do, you know. They get a thrill from knowing they're doing wrong."

Just then, Peggy's two children, Kalani and Kīna'u, showed up with their dates and descended on the table. Ned excused himself after greeting them and left Peggy surrounded by her family and friends. It was almost dark now and a soft light settled over the garden party. He walked out to the beach. The sand felt warm beneath his feet, and his long shadow streamed out behind him in the last evening light. The tide was low and the waves were small and barely audible as they broke over the reef. He saw the sun glide below the horizon and felt a little twinge of regret, knowing that the play was over and that he would soon be leaving this place. For a few more minutes, he stood watching as the sky faded from one color to the next and the first star shone in the west, and then he made his way back to the party.

The Hawaiian trio stopped playing, and Johnny Knight, who Ned discovered had given up a career as a concert pianist for a wicked life in the theatre, was taking his place at the piano. He began to play a beautiful island song that Ned guessed he had arranged himself. The white paper lanterns now glowed over the colorful scene of flowers, food, and people who were clustered happily around their tables. Nyla, Todd, and Mina were all seated and waiting for him. "Where have you been, Ned?" Nyla shook her finger at him. "You-know-who must be starved."

"I'm not that hungry," Mina laughed. "Uncle Wing's been feeding me in the kitchen."

After a dinner of traditional Hawaiian food, the party progressed and the drinks flowed. There was singing and dancing on stage. Nyla and Mina did a funny hula about sassy girls from different parts of Honolulu. James Russell did some magic tricks with Candace Furtado as his charming assistant. Christian Hollister got up and danced a party hula about a ranch called 'Ulupalakua, and Sheila and Andrew sang a cowboy song in which Andrew actually yodeled, causing a great sensation. Several other members of the cast danced or sang. As the evening progressed, Kīna'u Kelly got drunk and fell into the large tub of ice and water that was keeping the beer cold. Jayling called Lamby Langston a bitch to her face, and Cecily and her fiancé, Tom, climbed a nearby mango tree with a bucket of ice and threw pieces at random onto the stage and into the crowd. By the time everyone was leaving, they all agreed it was one of the best cast parties ever.

It was nearly two in the morning when the last guests had left. Mina, Ned, Nyla, and Todd were all lazing around Mina's living room and drinking big glasses of water. Mina and Nyla were stretched out on the pūneʻe. Ned lay on his back on the lauhala mat with a pillow under his head, and Todd sat in a rattan chair with his feet up on the matching ottoman.

"Well, that was a night," Nyla said. "I wish I had a picture of the look on Lamby's face when Jayling called her a bitch."

"She is a bitch," mumbled Mina. "She tried to burn me with her cigarette."

"That's because her blond boyfriend fancies you," Ned said playfully.

"Anyone care to place a bet about how soon the blond boyfriend gets his hands on the stamps?" Todd asked. "I say six months."

"I'll put twenty dollars on a year," said Mina.

"Okay, I'm in," Nyla clapped her hands. "I'll say nine months, tops."

"And I'm betting he has them already," said Ned, "and he's just keeping it hush-hush."

"I think we just lost all our money to Ned," Todd laughed.

"Oh, Mina, I forgot to tell you," Nyla said. "Ned's invited us all to visit in Sāmoa! Isn't it great?"

"What?" Mina sat up on the pūneʻe, frowning.

"Yes," continued Nyla. "Me and Todd, Dad, Grandma, Hīnano, oh, and you, if you want to go. Ned's family has a big house and a guest cottage."

"And how did this come about?" Mina asked suspiciously.

"We were sitting around," said Todd, "and Ned was talking about Sāmoa, and I said we'd love to see it someday."

"And I invited them." Ned smiled.

"I've always wanted to sail to the South Pacific on the *Monterey*," Nyla added.

"So all of you have already decided to go?" Mina asked.

"Well, Todd and I want to go for sure. Dad and Grandma Hannah are thinking about it, and Hīnano is too. You are interested, aren't you?" Nyla gave her an incredulous look.

Mina lay back on the pūneʻe and pursed her lips. "Well, I'm not letting all of you leave me behind, that's for sure."

Ned closed his eyes and smiled.

ACKNOWLEDGMENTS

My heartfelt thanks to my editor, Masako Ikeda, for all her kind support and enthusiasm for this project. I am especially grateful that providence saw fit to send both of us to the grocery store at the same time. I thank the University of Hawai'i Press for choosing to publish this book. Thanks also to Ginny Daniel at BW&A Books, Paul Betz, and David denBoer for their attention to the manuscript. I would also like to extend my gratitude to Craig Howes at the Center for Biographical Research for his valued advice and to his assistant Stan Schab for being so helpful. Mahalo to Rick Barboza for his mana'o on native birds and to Gaye Chan for a wonderful cover. Mahalo also to Hina Kneubuhl and Lalepa Koga for their poetic contributions to the Hawaiian verse. I would also like to acknowledge my father, Ben Kneubuhl, whose sharp memories of a Honolulu I have never seen enriched this story. To my friend Molly Giles (who happens to be one of the best writers on the planet), my special aloha for her thoughtful review of the manuscript and her practical suggestions. I am entirely and forever indebted to my husband, Philip D. Haisley Jr., for all his help, love, and constant faith in my writing.

ABOUT THE AUTHOR

Victoria Nalani Kneubuhl is a well-known Honolulu playwright and author. She holds a master's degree in drama and theatre from the University of Hawai'i. Her plays have been performed in Hawai'i and the continental United States and have toured to Britain, Asia, and the Pacific. An anthology of her work, *Hawai'i Nei: Island Plays*, is available from the University of Hawai'i Press. Ms. Kneubuhl worked for over twelve years in the field of museum education and has developed many public humanities programs that address historical issues and events in her island community. She is currently the writer and coproducer for the television series *Biography Hawaii*. In 1994, she was the recipient of the prestigious Hawai'i Award for Literature.